ALSO BY SEJAL BADANI

The Days Before Us: A Short Story

Trail of Broken Wings: A Novel

The Storyteller's Secret: A Novel

THE
SUN'S
SHADOW

THE
SUN'S
SHADOW

A Novel

SEJAL BADANI

LAKE UNION
PUBLISHING

Text copyright © 2025 by Sejal Badani
All rights reserved.

Published by Lake Union Publishing, Seattle

www.apub.com

Amazon, the Amazon logo, and Lake Union Publishing are trademarks of Amazon.com, Inc., or its affiliates.

ISBN-13: 9781662509742 (hardcover)
ISBN-13: 9781662509735 (paperback)
ISBN-13: 9781662509728 (digital)

Cover design by Shasti O'Leary Soudant
Cover image: © Stephen Mulcahey / Arcangel; © detchana wangkheeree, © anmark / Shutterstock

Printed in the United States of America
First edition

Hema, Keith, Prashant, and Mom: You believed in me when I couldn't see my way, stood by me when I was sure I was alone, loved me when I was empty, and carried me on your shoulders when I fell. I am so fortunate and forever grateful for you and for your unconditional support. I love you more than you will ever know.

Kiran, Akash, Sienna, and Serena: You are my everything. My darlings, thank you for being the joy I never imagined I could have, for allowing me to be a part of your lives and for being the best part of mine. Your laughter, your light brightens every moment of every day. You are my heart, my happiness, my inspiration. I love you with all that I am.

CHAPTER ONE

CELINE

I lean over the saddle, my body aligning perfectly with the horse as I prod him to go faster. The cool Boston wind whips loose strands of hair into my face, temporarily blinding me. But having ridden this path hundreds of times, I guide the new horse, Recluse, on instinct. I shift two inches lower, forcing my spine to stretch impossibly longer as he jumps over a series of log fences.

"Good boy." I fight against the urge to push the colt faster. Though born from two winning thoroughbreds, the horse has refused to train as his pedigree would demand. "Keep pace."

Though Kaitlyn, a childhood friend who helps me manage my farm, and I have created a standard training schedule for all the new horses we have acquired, I allow Recluse to set his own pace. I have learned over time that a horse's personal speed is only determined by its innate desire to win.

As I guide Recluse past scattered trees that provide shade from the sun's occasional appearances, I promise myself a few more minutes as I admire the farm I grew up on. I arrived at nine years old, clutching my mother Elena's hand while holding a suitcase filled with

Goodwill-bought clothes, staring at my uncle Greg, who had offered us refuge in exchange for my mother's servitude.

My watch beeps, reminding me of Brian's game. My mind immediately relaxes, pulling me from the gnawing past and back into the present. My twelve-year-old son is the joy I never believed would be mine to have. Once he was placed into my arms after I had endured nearly twenty-four hours of labor, I understood the unconditional love parents always speak about. The love my father had failed to have for me.

"Was getting ready to send out a search party," Kaitlyn murmurs on my return, leaning her athletic frame against the fence, her hands stuffed into her figure-shaping wear. She readjusts the ponytail that secures her purple-and-pink hair, showcasing the four piercings in one ear and the three in the other, then pushes her black-rimmed glasses up with the tip of her finger. A passing jockey shoots her an admiring glance, which Kaitlyn promptly ignores. "We need to talk."

Inside the oversize paddock, a trainer tosses a ball to a thoroughbred with Triple Crown potential. Like a child gifted with a new toy, the horse uses its nose to hit it back. I smile in response, always in admiration of their intelligence, innocence, and playfulness.

After handing Recluse over to a farm employee, I dust my hands off on my tan jodhpurs, grimacing at the streaks of dirt left in their wake. Recluse, refusing to be led, neighs loudly as he kicks his hind legs. The employee jumps back, barely missing being struck in the face, as another trainer jumps forward to help. I'm jumping the fence to assist when Recluse finally settles down. The employee shakes his head and murmurs something under his breath as he leads Recluse back toward the stable.

"That was fun," Kaitlyn says quietly, the concern in her voice matching mine.

"You and I have different concepts of 'fun.'" Making a mental note to speak to one of our trainers about the horse, I shift gears. "What's going on?"

Kaitlyn motions me toward the renovated house that serves as a combination of entertainment rooms, offices, and bedrooms for overnight guests. Though money remains tight, the expenditure proved worth it when horse owners, breeders, and trainers, impressed with our organization, began to give us their business. Pride fills me at the years of hard work and late nights that have finally yielded our small training facility the admiration and respect of the industry.

"Your uncle Greg called." Kaitlyn takes a seat on the sofa in the main room. Sunlight filters in from the bay windows, basking the room in a warm glow. "Wants to meet. He said it was urgent."

I drop down into the chair alongside her. "We're paid up?"

Kaitlyn and I met during high school, when she took a job on the farm. Her father worked as an assistant trainer for another local farm, so she had grown up riding horses. With her being at the local public school, I was relieved she wasn't part of my elite private school's crowd, which continued to ostracize me. We immediately became good friends and have remained so over the years.

"Of course. Ahead of schedule."

As if anticipating my question, she hands me a folder of all our business receipts from the last few months. This past year, when for the first time we were in the black, Kaitlyn, my mom, Brian, and I finally celebrated with a dinner after trying multiple times to schedule around my husband Eric's calendar.

"Meet when?" I ask, fearing what my uncle wants.

A promise I made to myself as a child to shift from servant to owner of the farm later drove me to approach him when he put the farm up for sale over a decade ago. Unable to afford the market value price he cited, I feared my dream would be lost. I countered with a rent-to-own offer that would allow me to invest the earnings back into the farm. He reluctantly agreed, stating he was doing me a favor—a harsh reminder that I was still the housekeeper's daughter, and he the benevolent relative.

"Tomorrow morning."

"I have Eric's party tomorrow night." The majority of planning my husband's annual work party at our home usually falls on me. I don't mind, happy to commit to the months of preparation and planning required to make it the success Eric expects. "I'll make sure everything is set up, then meet you here?"

"We'll handle whatever it is Greg wants," Kaitlyn says, seeing the concern on my face.

"How do you know?" I ask, trying to push away my concern in favor of her confidence.

"Belief," Kaitlyn replies. "The key to success."

Kaitlyn's success is a postcollege career that has included stints as a yoga instructor and flight attendant before she considered going to law school. Only after she realized that her love of training and riding horses was keeping her from fully committing to the other ventures did she jump on board to help me run the business.

"I'm going to hold you to that." I glance at my watch. "If I leave now, I'm barely going to make Brian's game on time."

"Tell Brian I said good luck," Kaitlyn yells after me as I rush out.

I jump onto I-95 toward our leafy suburb and the neighborhood soccer field. A slow crawl of Boston traffic traps me next to the exit for the apartment I lived in prior to the farm. Memories envelop me of a building covered in graffiti, me being six years old and riding alone on the T, girls on the streets in their stilettos and short skirts, sleeping to the sound of sirens and cars backfiring, my father there to read to me, play with me, be a father to me . . .

I shake off the memories as I dial Eric's number, then listen to the voicemail. With the car still at a standstill, I send a quick text to him.

Headed to Brian's game. He would love it if you could be there.
Since you're in town.

For all the years we have been married, Eric has spent more time on the road for work than at home. I have always hated that it's meant he has missed most if not all of Brian's games and school events. But I told myself the sacrifice was worth it when he quickly moved up the ranks of his company. Though I missed him terribly, the times he was home were filled with warmth and love.

But now, suddenly, his travel has become nearly nonexistent. Thrilled, I was initially sure it would mean more time for Brian, but it has been the opposite. He works longer hours, and whenever he is home, he's preoccupied and distant. On the few occasions when I have brought it up, he's explained that his mind's been on work and has immediately apologized.

I wait for the ping indicating a response, but the phone remains silent. Curious, I confirm the text was delivered before calling him again, to no answer. A car honk forces me forward, pushing the text to the back of my mind as I navigate the road to make Brian's game on time.

An empty spot in the soccer field's parking lot gives me a direct view of the benches full of parents and spectators ready to cheer on their team. I check my hair and makeup in the mirror. Pale-green eyes stare back at me. Sweat and the wind have scrubbed my face clean of the foundation and lip gloss I barely remembered to dab on before leaving this morning. I grab a handful of shoulder-length brown hair and change the part. Nothing seems to help. Sighing, I forgo the fight and instead grab the granola bar from the back seat that Brian took a bite out of and then discarded. When my stomach grumbles in gratitude, I realize it's my first meal of the day. As I savor the bites, I continue to watch from the security of my car as the parents talk with one another. My mother laughs animatedly at something someone has said. I envy her gregarious personality, having wished fruitlessly over the years to outgrow my own shyness.

Once there's only wrapper left, I step out of the car, trying one last time to wipe the dirt off my pants. I give up and straighten my shirt, clinging to me from sweat. Wishing for a shower, I plaster a smile on my face and approach.

"Celine." The other moms greet me warmly, their smiles genuine and welcoming. "Nice to see you."

I return their hellos before falling silent, finding comfort in listening rather than participating in conversations. Though they are neighbors and parents of Brian's classmates whom I have known for years, I still find myself feeling like an outsider.

Years ago, after acquiring the farm, I was excited to live there full time, but Eric refused, insisting it was too far from Boston proper and not ideal for raising children. Instead, he found us a four-bedroom home in Newton, an upscale, leafy town I never would have dreamed as a child that I would someday live in. The town is filled with the types of people I used to help my mother serve at Greg's parties. In hopes of belonging, I have shifted and reshaped myself in accordance with the life I have now—one unrecognizable to the six-year-old girl my father abandoned in the apartment building.

At the sound of the whistle, the game begins. I search and find Brian among the group of kids charging up and down the field in the hope of scoring a goal. Athletic and sure, Brian watches carefully as his teammate heads the ball. He reaches and tries to strike it, but an opposing team member kicks it first, knocking it into Brian's abdomen. My breath catches as Brian tumbles, then falls to the ground, where he remains.

My mom clasps her fingers around mine. Brian's coach jogs out to the field as his teammates gather around, crouching down to talk to him. The parents around me fall silent, waiting in concerned camaraderie. As the seconds turn into minutes, I hold my breath in uncertainty. Suddenly the stands erupt into applause as the group parts and Brian begins to hobble back toward his team's benches, his coach walking alongside him. I start to exhale when I catch Brian's eyes. Confusion and pain crisscross his face. He says something to his coach, then heads toward me. Fear roars inside me like a petulant child as I rush down to meet him, my mom on my heels.

"Mom, can we go?" His face downcast, he rubs the back of his neck in a move similar to one Eric often makes. "I don't feel so good."

My mother and I keep pace with his slow steps toward the car. Midway, he hands me his bag. My pulse begins to patter. Brian is always the first one at a gathering and the last one to leave. From a young age, he has always insisted on carrying his own bag.

"What happened on the field?" Inside the car, I lay a hand on his forehead, finding it cool to the touch.

"Just couldn't breathe for a minute. Then my body really hurt."

My mom and I exchange a look. Normally tough and stoic, Brian has taken plenty of hits over the years during athletic events. He usually brushes them off, anxious to rejoin the game.

"Let's get home, and I'll call the doctor to make an appointment." The game plan helps to soothe my nerves in response to his unexpected behavior. "We can order your favorite pizza." After Brian agrees, my mom kisses him, then tells me to keep her updated.

We ride home in silence. Once home, Brian heads to his room while I order the pizza, then call the pediatrician's office. The nurse reassures me that there's a virus going around that may explain his symptoms but offers me an appointment first thing Monday morning. Feeling better, I quickly head upstairs with slices of the delivered pizza. I open the door to find the lights off and Brian soundly asleep.

My eyes barely stay open as I review files at the kitchen table. I considered texting Eric but then didn't want to worry him uselessly. Besides, he never responded to my earlier text, nor did he show up to the game. In the past, whenever he was traveling, Brian and I would wait for his calls so that we wouldn't catch him in a meeting. Now, with him in town more often, I have tried to find a new normal. But his actions seem to indicate that his mindset has remained the same—he will call when he's available and only then. I must accept it, regardless of what I want.

In hopes of getting my mind off Brian, I spend the next few hours studying videos and pictures of the horses we have in training, comparing past to present to track changes and improvements. Recluse's speed puts him ahead of the other horses in his class, but his consistency and stability put him further back than I hoped, making me wonder if there's a way to get him to train and race at the level his owner expects. We cannot afford to admit defeat. Our reputation in the industry would take a hit that would hurt us financially in the long term.

I run a tired hand over my eyes. Though I had successfully pushed away concern about the meeting with Greg to the back of my mind, it creeps back slowly in the quiet of the night. I drop my head when the sound of footsteps startles me.

"Working late?" Eric asks from the doorway.

My eyes run appreciatively over him as his tailored suit jacket hangs over one shoulder with a loose finger while his engraved leather computer bag dangles off the other. His sleeves are rolled up to reveal golden hair scattered on his toned arms. His wedding ring and a priceless watch inherited from his father adorn his hands. Born into success, Eric has risen to his inheritance. When we met, I was struggling to pay for community college classes, while he was already finishing up at the Sloan business school. When he asked me out, I was shocked and flattered. He was the Prince Charming I never imagined I would meet, let alone marry.

"Catching up." I glance at the crystal clock on the counter as I stand to greet him. Nearly midnight. "I texted you about Brian's game. Never heard back," I admonish lightly, expecting an immediate apology.

"Work," he says dismissively, moving past me without our standard kiss hello or hug.

I stare at him, taken aback by his response. Seemingly unaware of or indifferent to my reaction, he heads for the pizza box. "Brian missed you. He was hoping you would be there."

"I'll talk to him in the morning," Eric says, as if his solution is enough. He heats up a slice, then offers me one. I shake my head no, still unsure about the interaction. "How was the game?"

"Took a ball in the stomach." When he stops midbite to look up in worry, I see a glimpse of the man I married, the father my son adores. "He left the game, then went right to bed. I was going to call you, but since I hadn't heard from you . . ."

"I told you, I was working," he snaps. I widen my eyes in shock at his unexpected tone. He shuts his eyes, exhales, before opening them. Regret fills his face. "Celine."

"Do not speak to me like that."

"I'm sorry." Eric runs a hand over the back of his neck, then grips the back of a chair.

"What's going on?" I finally ask after waiting for him to say more but only receiving silence in return. "You've been distant and moody for months now."

"Things have been busy."

He reaches for my hand. I consider stepping back but then remind myself of all the ways he has been there for me during our marriage. To be petty would hurt us both. As his hand closes around mine, I welcome his warmth infusing into me.

"How? Tell me, so I can help or at least empathize." I smile to soften my words, but it falters when he stares at me—his eyes unblinking, searching mine as if for the answer only he has. I try to make sense of it, even as my stomach begins to knot in worry. "Eric?"

He drops my hand as suddenly as he took it, then turns away. He picks up the pizza as if the last few minutes didn't happen. "I just have a lot on my plate. Nothing I can't handle." He washes down a bite, then asks, "Sure Brian's all right?"

"The nurse said it may be a virus. No fever, but just to be safe I made an appointment for Monday."

Eric's shoulder drops, as if the answer relaxes him. "I had a lot of viruses at his age."

"Sure it wasn't back-to-school blues?" I tease, trying to get us back on normal footing. "Your mom told me so many stories."

With Eric's previous travel schedule, our limited time together always felt precious and valuable, both of us going out of our way to be fun and loving toward one another and he with Brian. Compromises were easy and egos had no place. A honeymoon that never seemed to end. Now, I think about his reaction, and I wonder how much of him I never saw.

He laughs, and I feel my tension ease at his response. "I remember those well. Drove my mom crazy at the beginning of every school year."

"I think you drove your mom crazy regardless of the time of year." Anxious to reconnect with him, I lay a hand on his chest. He grabs it and holds it close, our fingers entangling with one another, our wedding bands overlapping. "Brian would have loved your parents." Older when they had Eric, both of his parents passed away when Brian was too young to remember them.

"They adored him," Eric murmurs, stepping closer.

His other hand sneaks into my hair as he brings me in. I have started to nestle my head into his chest when his phone buzzes with a message. He releases me as he reads it, his face clouding over with an emotion I do not recognize.

"Everything good?" I ask quietly, the chill from the loss of him feeling like a blanket of snow.

"Yes, of course."

I watch as he immediately types a response, then waits for another text before putting his phone away. The unanswered text from Brian's game slips between us like a lingering virus, threatening to damage the fragile reconnection. There is no reason to bring it up again, I tell myself. It would serve no purpose. He has always been a thoughtful, attentive husband and father. Making a case out of one text feels churlish and childish.

"Everything set for the party tomorrow?"

I review the details in my head. After years of planning and throwing parties at our house, I have an established network to make the event a success for Eric's employees. As Brian grew older and the farm began to take up more of my time, I sometimes yearned to skip the event. But it was the least I could do, I remind myself now. Eric's salary paid our bills while I pursued my dream of the horse farm.

"The caterers and party setup crew will be here at nine a.m. Once they're up and running, I'll drop Brian off at practice if he's feeling better, then head to the farm for a bit." My mom is going to pick him up straight from practice and take him home with her for the night.

I'm getting ready to explain the meeting with my uncle Greg when Eric wraps an arm around me and pulls me in close. Taken aback by the ping-pong of affection, I hesitate. As if he senses my confusion, he kisses my ear softly. Shivers dance across my neck and down my spine.

"Thanks for taking care of the party." He leans his head back so his eyes meet mine as his arms tighten around my waist. I reluctantly wrap mine around him. He glances down at my arms and adds, "That only took a few seconds of thought processing."

"Long day."

Given our limited time together, work conversations are rare, our focus always primarily on Brian. Work has often felt like a separate part of my life—one that is an extension of growing up on the farm. The person I was before my marriage, before this life.

"The horses still running?" Eric asks, surprising me.

Warmed by his interest, I share, "A few are slacking off. There's a mare we thought was ready to stop racing. But her time has improved substantially." My mind drifts back to Recluse and his refusal to take direction. "But some young ones are falling behind their expected schedule. So we gave them a ball to play with."

"That's showing them," Eric says, laughing.

As he starts to move away, I tug at his hand. His fingers tighten in mine as he glances at me in question. Guilt at my earlier coldness grips me. It feels unfair to blame him for his commitment to his career when he has never questioned mine to the farm.

"Thank you for being interested in the farm and the horses."

"You're my wife. I'm interested in you."

I'm squeezing his hand in response when I hear the buzz of his cell phone again. Hoping he will ignore it, I reluctantly release him when he pulls away from me to respond. His eyes narrow as he focuses on the text before heading toward the study.

"Eric?"

He looks up, as if having forgotten about me. "I need to respond to some messages. For work." His face hardens as his phone demands him, again.

"Must be some emergency at this time of night." I try to keep the frustration out of my voice, valuing the time together to talk and reconnect.

"Unfortunately." As he nears the threshold of the kitchen, he pauses to say, "I forgot to mention—can you add one more person to the seating list for tomorrow?"

"Of course." I draft a quick note to the party planner on my phone. "Name?" I ask, ready to solidify the details. At his hesitation, I glance up, curious. "Is it a secret?"

"Felicity," he says immediately. "Seat her with Finance."

I have never heard the name before. Assuming she's a new employee, I briefly wonder why Eric doesn't follow previous years and seat Felicity at his table to make her feel welcome. Too exhausted from the day to focus on it, I quickly add a note to the party planner to do as Eric asked, then head upstairs, where I check on Brian before going to bed.

CHAPTER TWO

FELICITY

I reread Eric's text with details about the party. I tap the screen, ready to reply, then hesitate. Our new house settles around me as I replay options I have already considered. Attending the party makes logical and business sense. Though we are at different companies, our departments work together regularly. It will be an opportunity to socialize with his team, create a more intimate bond that could prove beneficial in our day-to-day dealings. I will learn more about his life, meet his wife, see their home. I quickly type my response, then put the phone away.

Looking forward to it.

Honed from practice, I shut thoughts of work out of my mind as I glance at my watch. Twenty minutes past midnight. Justin is past curfew. I imagine all the ways I will scream at my son, vacillating between whether it should be before or after I hug him.

Though he's only had his car for a short while, he's self-assured and confident in a way that I am deeply grateful for. He approaches the world with an attitude of *do* rather than debating the decision. A trait that he inherited from his father rather than me. Though I know it will serve him in his future, right now I'm not too happy with the results.

When Justin's father gifted him a car for this birthday, I took a mental picture of Justin's joy. His father is good that way, doing things for Justin, showing up for his games and even regular dinners, making sure that our son has what he needs, even if he's not a full-time dad. But he and Justin are close—I am grateful for that. We are a quasi family without ever having been an official one.

As Justin's car pulls into the driveway, I release the breath I was holding. I fight the instinct to throw open the door, instead taking a seat on the sofa and grabbing a magazine when I hear the knob turn. Justin's face shows his surprise when he sees me.

"Mom." I grimace when he tosses his keys toward the bowl, but they instead land with a thump onto the thin glass table. "You're up late."

"Catching up on some reading." I gesture to the magazine.

"Tough read," Justin says. When I raise an eyebrow in question, he replies, "It's upside down."

I roll my eyes, then fling it down next to me. "Fun night?" Though I try to keep the fury and relief out of my voice, his smirk tells me I have failed.

"Sorry about missing curfew." He glances at his phone, then grimaces. "By an hour."

"The phone?" I point to his while softening my words with a smile. "Is for phone calls home."

"But that would've just delayed me further, and then I would've been even more past curfew." He shudders, as if the thought frightens him. My son, the comedian. "Not acceptable."

I bite back a smile. When Justin was young, I struggled between my role as both disciplinarian and his confidante. But he's growing up into a responsible young man who I am so proud of.

"How was the date?" I ask. "Fourth one, right?"

Justin mentioned Lily a few months ago, when he first started at his new school. I had been nervous about uprooting him from his high school in Chicago to move to Boston his junior year but was relieved when he seemed to immediately make new friends and easily fit in.

"Yeah. Date was good."

"When do I get to meet her?" The blush that rises from his neck toward his cheeks tells me how much he likes her. Both surprised and taken aback by the suddenness of their connection, I am anxious to know the girl who has made my son so happy.

"Sunday?" he asks, surprising me. "I thought maybe we could do a barbecue, or I could cook?"

With it just being the two of us, Justin taught himself to cook at a young age, for when my hours ran late. His meals have easily surpassed mine in taste and innovation. Alongside cooking, he also started to help around the house, becoming a man long before his age required him to.

"Making her dinner and meeting the mother in one night? Is it love?" I tease, then fall silent when he fails to respond. "Justin?"

"I like her," he says slowly, seeming to wait for my reaction.

"Tell me about her," I ask, hoping he will share.

"We met at swim. She's captain of the school team." He pauses, then adds almost embarrassingly, "She's great. We like a lot of the same things. She plays soccer too."

I grew up rowing and swimming, so I would often take him on a boat for hours on Lake Michigan near our house. His father is also an athlete, so it felt natural to sign Justin up to participate in as many athletic endeavors as possible. As he got older and was forced to commit, he chose soccer and swimming. His commitment to his sports proved critical when we moved, and he was able to quickly make new friends via his teammates.

"I can't wait to meet her." When he bites back a yawn, then rubs the back of his neck, I say kindly, "You're tired, honey. Get to bed." I remind him, "I have a work party tomorrow night—well, technically tonight. I'll check in before I leave."

After we have said our good nights, I watch him stride down the hall, my thoughts staying with him long after he's disappeared into his room. He's in love. I imagine what Lily looks like, how they interact. My mind flits from one thought to the next, every one of them focused on Justin and his well-being.

I reach for a digital framed picture of Justin throughout the years. The first shows him at ten, after winning his first sailing event; in it, he holds his prize with pride. Dozens of other shots commemorate his life. I run my fingers gently over the images, my throat clogging. Time has proven to be a foe rather than a friend. He has grown up fast. My time with him feels as though it is being counted in months rather than years. Soon he will move onto his own journey. His full life guarantees his happiness.

The moon filters through the curtains, bathing the space with light. I take a seat on the sofa, leaning my head back. As my eyes drift closed, I think about my decisions—relocating to Boston, transferring within my company, moving Justin here before he leaves for college—every decision made with careful consideration. With the stakes high, the secrets and sacrifices over the years have been worth it. But now, I am ready for more. I am ready for my life to begin. And that requires my plans to proceed as expected.

CHAPTER THREE

CELINE

I wake up to an empty bed. Eric left for work before the sun even rose. Disappointed, I drop my head back onto the pillow and cover my eyes with my arm, hoping for a few more minutes of rest. I woke up in the middle of the night to check on Brian but again found him fever-free and sleeping peacefully. If it was a virus, then it seems to have passed through his system quickly. Relieved, I fell back to sleep, only to awake with a start now, the party and meeting with my uncle at the forefront of my thoughts. Happy in his retirement, Greg rarely wants to meet. That he does now makes me worry what it's about. To relieve the anxiety, I let my mind wander, a habit from when I was a child.

After my father left, whenever I could hear Mom crying in her room, I would try to drown it out by imagining myself playing with my friends. Or I would pretend I was a bird, flying far away. Sometimes, when her crying didn't stop, I would imagine myself in the park with my dad the day before he left us. I dreamed about asking him not to disappear. Or at least to say goodbye before he did.

I try the same trick now, but it fails to help. When I hear Brian moving around, I immediately find him in his room, getting ready. I reach out to feel his head. "No fever. So you want to make practice today?"

I smile at his look, admonishing me for asking. "I'm hungry."

"Pancakes?" On his nod, I tell him to meet me downstairs when he's ready. As I reach the foyer, the caterers and party crew arrive. Familiar with the setup, they immediately head to the backyard. I send a quick text to Eric, letting him know Brian is feeling better and headed to practice. Unlike yesterday, he responds immediately.

Great. Tell him I love him.

I think about responding back but decide against it. If he wanted to have a conversation, he would have called me. His text was quick and to the point. I don't want to chance a repeat of yesterday.

Once breakfast is ready, I call Brian down to eat. He glances at the stack of pancakes, then shakes his head no. "I'm not hungry." Shocked at the sudden change of appetite, I ask him if he wants something else instead. His glance lands on the pizza box from last night. "A slice?"

I heat it up while he gathers his things for practice. After checking on the party setup, I get Brian settled into the car and head out. "You sure you're good for practice today? Grandma's picking you up, so you can stay with her tonight." Via the rearview mirror, I see that his eyes are closed and the pizza is untouched. "If you don't feel well, Grandma can bring you home anytime you want."

"Mom, I can't miss practice," Brian insists. "How will I get drafted out of high school if I skip practices?"

"Is that still the plan?" I tease, keeping the concern out of my voice. He's missed two meals now: dinner last night and breakfast this morning. I worry about his energy level for practice. "How about college?"

"I can take classes online or during the offseason." He inspects his soccer cleats for any dirt. Meticulous. He reminds me of the way I am with the horses. "If I wait too long, I'll be aged out."

"Aged out, hmm? We don't want that." Loving these conversations when he opens up, I ask, "Are you still planning to play for the LA Galaxy?"

"Yeah." I grin at his tone, implying I should already know this. His voice lowers, and I see him stare out his window. "But that may be too far. I know you and Grandma would miss me."

My breath catches at his unequivocal statement. He is my unconditional love—the future I was desperate for as a child; I am determined to be the parent to Brian that my own dad chose not to be for me. But never have I intended to become his burden.

"Honey," I start slowly, "Grandma and I just want you to be happy. Wherever that may be."

His gaze grabs and holds mine. "I know. But I know how much you need me."

At the field, Brian jumps out of the car. I watch him until he's disappeared into the throng of kids. On the drive to the farm, his words repeat in my head, worrying me, stopping only when I arrive.

I immediately search for Kaitlyn and soon find her in the office, reading through files. I barely register when she says that my uncle's joining us here for the meeting instead.

"And I thought we could raise giraffes in addition to horses," she adds. "Give the horses a complex."

"Wait, what?" I ask.

"What's wrong? You're more preoccupied than usual." I tell her what Brian said. "Smart kid." When I start to argue, Kaitlyn explains, "Celine, you love that kid more than any other mother I know. That's not a bad thing." She shrugs. "Kid is lucky."

The front door opens, and seconds later, Uncle Greg is visible in the hallway as he heads toward the office. He leans on his cane, but it does little to diminish his stature or power. Though age has decreased his height, leaving him only a foot taller than me, I still see him as the towering figure of my childhood. The man whose rules and regulations kept me in a place of his making.

Kaitlyn stands, and we both meet him halfway. "Good to see you."

"I have a buyer," he says without preamble. "He has the cash ready."

I take a step back, as if in doing so, his words will fall to the ground without a place to land.

"We have a year left on the lease," Kaitlyn says.

"With a buyout clause eleven months into the year." With narrowed eyes, he shifts from me to Kaitlyn and then back. "If I have a buyer, I can sell eleven months in."

"We've made every payment on time." I fight to keep my voice steady, to be the woman I am instead of the child he remembers. "Created a business that's gained a reputation for excellence."

"Contract terms stand."

My mother used to have to wake up at four a.m. to begin breakfast and then serve it to them in bed every day. I would feel the bed shift as she rolled slowly away from me in the two-bedroom servants' quarters on the other side of the farm, away from the main house. She'd quietly dress in the starched black dress and stockings required and then walk in the cold. After seeing tons of uneaten food thrown away daily, she asked my uncle if she could take some back home with her after her day ended at nine p.m. He simply nodded, then turned away as Mom whispered a quiet *Thank you.* That food became my breakfast and dinner every day for years. Grateful then for the scraps, I try now to remember I am worth more. That I am no longer the child he remembers.

"If she has the money before the eleventh month, she has first rights," Kaitlyn reminds him.

"*If* she gets the money." He sighs, offering me hope for a softening, a change of mind, until he speaks. "I really hoped you would. I know how hard you've worked to make this what it is. It's just time for me to move on from this place."

I watch as he walks out, his words reverberating in my head. Kaitlyn turns toward me as soon as the door's closed. "Well, this is unfortunate."

I raise an eyebrow before my shoulders and head slump. I have put everything into the farm—my hopes, my dreams. The thought of losing it . . .

"No matter which way I crunch the numbers, you can't make the purchase." She leans against the wall. "You get close, though . . ." I wait, afraid of what she's going to say. "Race again. Enough wins, and maybe . . ."

I love racing. You never know what a horse can accomplish until it's on a track. A combination of strength and success, mixed with intelligence, together make them willing to fight hard and push past their own limits to achieve. But a horse that's unwilling to take direction, whose power is unchecked, means that any interaction with another horse or rider could lead to death.

"I haven't raced in years," I remind her. All my time has been spent on the business.

After I moved to the farm as a child, my childhood best friend, Austin, would teach me to ride after I finished my chores of cleaning the stalls and feeding the horses. I immediately took to the sport, racing against my own best times. My heart broke when Austin moved away. Memories of us drove me to continue riding. At sixteen, I entered my first equestrian race, coming in third. I was suddenly no longer just the servant's daughter but accomplished in my own right. But even with my past years of expertise in riding, I'm not prepared to reenter the racing arena.

When my phone pings with a message from the catering crew, I reluctantly table the discussion for later. "We'll figure something out." I pause, almost trying to convince myself. "We have to. I can't lose the farm."

CHAPTER FOUR

CELINE

Boston weather delivers a clear sky. The DJ plays a slow song to set the mood while attendees mingle with one another. The lights around the tent twinkle in the evening sky, the backyard transformed into a stunning garden oasis. I smooth a hand down the simple black dress that clings to my toned body. Earlier, I let my dark-brown hair fall in waves, adding diamond studs in each ear; a simple gold bangle adorns my wrist. Not a fan of overdoing my face, I dabbed on lip gloss and eyeliner.

Thoughts of the farm and my uncle force my fingers together, the knot created at his announcement tying every part of me together. My years of hard work and effort for nothing.

Ask Eric for the money.

The thought tugs at me, a possible only option. I have always refused because it's important to me to do this on my own. But before, I was sure I had time. Now, I could lose everything, and he might be my only hope.

Last night and the previous few months play out in my head. The distance, the late nights at work, the disconnect. It feels as if we have stepped apart from each other, with no explanation or reason. I rack my brain, trying to understand if I've done something. I run a critical eye over the room. Eric has always admired a well-done room. I straighten a chair in front of me, righting the silverware so it aligns perfectly with the others. Like a trained animal, I act so as to win the affections of the one whose benevolence I rely on. *Like my mother for so long*, I think. *Now, like me.*

"Thank you," Eric whispers into my ear, startling me. "Everything looks amazing."

I turn, relief flooding me at his words. "Team effort," I say graciously. I haven't seen him since I returned from the farm. He's changed into dress pants and a blue cashmere sweater that matches his eyes. "Everyone seems to be having fun."

"Thanks to you." He runs a gentle hand down my arm, eliciting goose bumps in its wake. I place my hand over his, welcoming his touch after the interaction from last night. "Everything all right?"

"I need to talk to you about something." Though I know now is not the time, I want to broach the subject while my nerves are steady. "It's important."

Eric's gaze focuses on someone over my head, following them closely. "I should see to the guests."

"Our talk?"

"Later," he says, assuming the time works.

He leaves, welcoming his employees with a smile and warm greetings. As he continues to mingle, I know he will make every guest feel welcome and valued. It was the rare charm that enticed me when we first met. Unlike me, he's able to connect with anyone, no matter who they are.

I check in with the bartender, then scan the familiar crowd. I've just waved to the wife of one of Eric's employees when I spot him speaking with a woman I don't recognize. Tall and beautiful, she could easily grace magazine covers. I pause at Eric's unusual reaction—his face scrunched in worry and his head dropped low, as if listening intently.

A light breeze ruffles my dress, stealing through the side slit to wash over my legs. The wine burns down my throat as I continue to surreptitiously watch them, his unexpected demeanor forcing my attention. My husband's head is cocked to the side, his gaze locked on the ground. Similar to how he is with Brian or me when we speak with him about something serious: attentive, concerned, and familiar. A question I have never considered before in our marriage now slips through, like water through a small crack that eventually breaks the levee open: Is there someone else?

On automatic pilot, I'm moving one foot in front of the other toward them when I feel a hand on my arm. Marianne, a longtime employee of Eric's. Arms outstretched, I share a warm hug with her. "I didn't see you walk in."

"Lucy," Marianne says, referencing her daughter, "had to be somewhere at the exact same moment I was supposed to be here." She rolls her eyes in fake frustration. "I used to dread her driving. Now, I can't wait. I'll get my life back."

"I'm not ready for those years." When Brian was little, I yearned for him to grow up so that I would have more time. Now, I yearn to slow time down so I can revel in every minute. Especially when he's already talking about moving away to start his own life and career. "I think I'll follow Brian around, just to make sure he's going the speed limit, staying in his lane. He'll hate me forever, I'm sure." My eyes drift back toward Eric. He's still in deep conversation with the woman, both speaking animatedly with one another. I force my focus back to Marianne. "How is everything otherwise?"

Marianne's eyes follow mine. "Have you met Felicity?" Her voice lowers. "She's president of finance at one of our partner companies. Recently moved to Boston."

Felicity—the plus-one Eric mentioned. "You work with her?"

"Her team overlaps with us on multiple deals." Marianne's eyes linger on Felicity. "She's smart. And tough. Good move by Eric to invite her to a company event. Provide her a sense of familiarity with our people."

"Yes." When relief floods through me, I admonish myself for having questioned anything. Blaming my fraught nerves on the situation with my uncle, I turn fully toward Marianne, my attention no longer divided. "How is Lucy?"

"She just discovered boys," Marianne shares. "And not the sweet kind, because that means they're not chill. Instead, the ones who barely glance at her, which apparently makes them perfect." She shakes her head in disgust. "If she only knew that the good ones are one in a million. If you find one, hold on tight. You and I got lucky."

My gaze shifts once again to Eric. The recent distance between us has hurt more than I have realized. I have missed my husband and our time together. Recently, Brian has felt like the glue securing our relationship. Marianne's words are the reminder I need about how fortunate I am.

"We got lucky," I confirm. Others slowly join our conversation. These are people I have known for years, and I relish hearing about everyone's children, their lives and updates.

"Can I steal my wife for a dance?" Eric joins us, placing a light hand on my lower back. Surprised, I try to catch his eyes, but his focus remains on the group. Everyone voices their approval as he holds out his hand for mine, leading us to the dance floor.

"Everything all right?" My hand slips into his while the other one wraps around his waist. His eyes finally meet mine, blank and screened. My step falters; I have never seen him so cold, detached. His arm tightens around me, helping me to silently regain my footing. He blinks, and the moment passes.

"I'm dancing with my wife. Everything is perfect."

We sway to the music. Cognizant of my hostess duties, I'm gazing over the crowd when I see Felicity, looking straight at us. Our eyes lock, hers unblinking. Like a hill of biting fire ants, anxiety crawls over me, covering my skin. I lower my head, dropping it onto Eric's shoulder, breaking the contact. He pulls me in closer in response to my action, his hand on my lower back, warm and familiar.

"The new guest, Felicity?" Beneath my arms, Eric's back muscles bunch and then tense. I search for a reason but fail to yield a result. "Is she enjoying the party?"

Eric immediately glances toward Felicity's table. He's been keeping track of her whereabouts. "I think so."

My hand moves from his shoulder upward, an instinct to cover his mouth with my fingers. I wrap them instead around the back of his neck, lingering.

"You seemed in serious conversation earlier. I was going to go over to say hello but didn't want to interrupt," I prompt, waiting for the explanation that tells me I'm ridiculous, that my imagination is running rampant.

"Business stuff," Eric says easily. "She heads up a department that's working with us on a number of high-profile accounts." His explanation matches Marianne's. Eric drops his hand from my waist to run through his hair. With a subdued, quieter voice, he adds, "You should've said hello. I'll introduce you later."

Like a seesaw, my emotions shift from relieved to anxious. "You only invited her? Not the rest of her team?"

"Business decision. The party is for my team, not hers," Eric says, his voice tightening in a manner similar to last night. "Why all the questions?"

"Making conversation?" I say, trying to lighten the mood, unsure if I am creating or reacting to a problem.

"How about we do conversation later?" Though the words are smooth, I still feel his annoyance. He clasps my hand and brings me in closer.

"Company," I remind him. Normally, he's the one at these parties who refuses to connect, always expecting me to understand that PDA is not appropriate at work functions. Of a similar mindset, I have more than understood and even agree. "Everywhere."

"Then it's obviously time to end this party." He pauses, then, "You know how much I love you, right?"

The words drift over me, but instead of eliciting warmth, they again cause me to feel uneasy. "What's going on? This"—I motion toward our clasped hands—"isn't like you."

"Telling and showing my wife I love her? Then I clearly haven't been doing it right." He kisses the top of my head, then releases me before readying to walk away. "My mistake."

Still in place, I watch warily as he easily shifts into his gregarious persona, and he has a group of colleagues laughing in seconds. Having always admired his ability to compartmentalize, I wonder now what he's locking down in one part of his brain to move to another.

While he's finishing speaking to one group, he glances toward Felicity's table. As if she's waiting for him, she gazes at him in return. They hold the look before Eric turns away.

They work together, I remind myself. She's the only one from her company here. He's being Eric, welcoming and attentive. I take the few steps to reach her table. The air drops in temperature, sending a shiver down my open back. She watches me approach, standing slowly as I near.

Athletically lean, she towers over me. Wavy, salon-cut blond hair courses past her shoulders, highlighting ocean-blue eyes. She is beautiful in a way that catches both men's and women's attention. A beauty I would have envied as a child. Fine lines around her mouth and eyes add to her intrigue.

"Hello." I hold out my hand in greeting. "We haven't met. I'm Celine."

She assesses me before slowly sliding hers into mine. The handshake is brief but firm, her fingers encircling mine until they're swallowed. "Felicity." Strong and commanding, her voice offers little insight into her thoughts. "Lovely party."

"I understand you recently moved to Boston." I don't share that Marianne, not my husband, told me this. That my husband has left me with more questions than answers.

"I've always loved the city." Felicity takes a seat and crosses one slim leg over the other. Her tailored jumpsuit glides easily with her movement.

"You've lived here before?"

Felicity pauses in her answer, slowly running a manicured finger around the rim of her glass. Growing up, I would help my mom serve at my uncle's parties. One of my uncle's business partners was always in attendance. Smart and successful, he was admired and revered by everyone. Kind in a way I wasn't used to, he'd always ask me how I was and about school. One day, when I was around fifteen, he told me his life story. He was raised poor and by a single mother. Like me, he acknowledged. The secret to his success, he shared, was to believe, no matter what your current circumstances, that you are the most success-ful person in the room. But to act like the poorest. *Then you know a true person's character.* Now, it feels like Felicity is acting out something similar—showing me one thing while being another. But why?

"I grew up in Maine," she finally says. "We used to visit Boston growing up." When the music changes, Felicity motions toward the DJ. "He's really good." She takes a small sip, watching me over the rim of the glass. As if I am a specimen under a microscope to analyze. "Do you use him every year?"

"Every year?" This is her first time attending.

"Eric mentioned it was an annual gathering on the invite," she says smoothly, her tone questioning me. I shake myself mentally out of my mood, cautioning myself that I will look like a fool for making something out of nothing. "Did I misunderstand?"

"No," I assure her, smiling to ease the moment. "He likes to hold these annually. It was nice of you to make it."

"His team works closely with mine, so it's nice to get to know everyone on a more informal basis."

Right. Embarrassed by my own mental misgivings, I recalibrate. "First year, actually," I say, returning to the conversation about the DJ. "A friend recommended him."

"I'm having a belated surprise seventeenth birthday party for my son. My long list of to-dos includes finding a DJ."

"I'll give you his contact information." Thrilled that we have common ground, I settle into the chair across from her. "Seventeen? Mine is twelve."

"It goes fast," Felicity says. "Everything is new, an adventure. Enjoy every minute." She pauses, then adds, "Took me too long to figure out I should worry less, enjoy more."

"I'll have to remember that," I say, wishing I had the luxury as my thoughts veer toward the farm. I imagine being happy instead of worrying and simply trusting that things will work out. It's an emotion I have rarely allowed myself the luxury of indulging in. Growing up as a servant's daughter on a fancy estate, I often felt that not much seemed to work out for my mom and me. Not until I met Eric and he gave me this life . . .

"How is your son adjusting to changing schools?"

"Better than I expected. He has a girlfriend already," Felicity says with a self-conscious sigh. "I meet her tomorrow. I think I may be more nervous than she is. I want to make a good impression." Felicity smiles. "Wish me luck."

All my earlier anxiety melts away, leaving me feeling like a fool. Felicity's down-to-earth attitude draws me in, two mothers connecting over their sons. "Teenagers. I'm not sure I'm ready for that."

"Can I be honest?" Felicity asks. "I'm still not sure I am, and I'm in the throes of it."

I laugh with her; then, noticing the lack of a food plate, I ask, "Did you get a chance to get dinner?"

"I had a heavy lunch. Large events like these take me out of my comfort zone, so appetite gone," she admits.

"Then you've found your mirror image," I admit as well, both surprised at and appreciative of her honesty. "I often spend all day mustering the courage for social events."

When I was young and feeling nervous about attending events at the new private school my uncle had secured a scholarship into, my mom would encourage me to forge ahead. But admission did not mean acceptance, and I continued to struggle.

"Maybe at the end of the night, it's worth it to have met old friends and made new ones," Felicity says, gesturing toward me.

"That's a wonderful way to think about it," I say, really liking her. I hesitate, then venture onto a limb to offer, "If you ever want to grab lunch or a coffee, since you're new in town . . ."

Felicity tilts her head to the side, as if considering my offer. Her face softens and she smiles, almost sadly. "That sounds lovely. Thank you."

As couples start toward the exit, I reluctantly say my goodbyes. "I should see the guests out. It was very nice meeting you."

"I look forward to seeing you again soon," Felicity says. "I'll update you on how the girlfriend meet goes," she says conspiratorially. I've started to walk away when Felicity asks, "Your son? What is he like?"

A sudden coldness masks her features, a calculation that was not previously there. I dismiss it as my imagination and stress from the situation with the farm, instead crediting her question to politeness. "He's wonderful," I answer, thinking of Brian. "Warm, loving. He's everything."

Felicity nods. "He sounds like my son. Would do anything for them, right?"

"Right," I reply, wondering at the direction of the conversation.

"Do you have a picture?"

I hesitate, then chide myself for doing so. Phone in hand, I pull up one of a countless number of pictures of him and show it to her. She smiles, but it fails to reach her eyes. "He looks like you."

I glance at the picture, surprised by her assessment, always believing him to be a perfect combination of Eric and me. "I guess so."

Felicity shifts her gaze off the picture to point behind me. "Your husband wants you."

I turn to see Eric watching us. I give him a small wave to let him know I will be right there. "I look forward to that coffee."

As I head toward Eric, an odd tingling causes me to glance back over my shoulder. Felicity stares at me. Instead of flinching or appearing embarrassed at having been caught, she simply raises her hand in a small wave before picking up her purse and exiting through the side gate.

◆ ◆ ◆

Party over, I slip off my three-inch heels and rub my soles. When I reach for the zipper at the back of my dress, Eric's hands gently push them away to lower the fastener. I have started to turn when he stops me with kisses on the back of my neck. I moan as he slides his hands over my breasts. He separates the two sides until they fall off my shoulders and pool at my waist.

"We need to talk," I say, anxious to have the conversation with him.

"Later. I promise." He continues to kiss me, his hands wandering over my stomach and down to my thighs.

"I'm surprised you have energy after the night."

I search my memory for the last time we have been intimate—months, I realize with a start. When did intimacy become an afterthought in our relationship? Before, we would make love multiple times when he was in town. It was as if the brief time apart heightened our yearning, our mutual desire for one another.

I yelp in surprise when he slips an arm under my knees and lifts me up in a flash. Before I have a chance to react, Eric tosses me onto the bed and crawls over me. "You said something about energy?"

"That was unexpected." Enjoying the rare playfulness, I tug on his sweater. "But unfortunately, feeling only slightly more refreshed. I may need more."

"I love you." When I don't immediately respond, he moves a strand of hair off my face before cupping my cheek. "Everything okay?"

I nod, forcing myself to enjoy the moment and worry about the farm later. Remembering Felicity's advice, I say, "'Worry less, enjoy more'? It might need to become my new motto."

"Where did you hear that?" Eric asks, straightening.

"Felicity." I make a mental note to ask him later for her number so we can have the planned coffee. "She was nice. We swapped stories about our boys."

Eric tenses before lowering his head to kiss my shoulder. "Sounds like good advice." His hands move quickly down my body, as if he's trying to memorize every inch of me. "Given all the years I've known you, I can bet to win that's not going to happen." He kisses me lightly. "But I highly support the endeavor. I like it when you smile."

Eric deepens the kiss as my eyes drift closed. Behind the darkness, I imagine the open air of the farm and the rustling of the trees. As his hands run over my body, I envision my freedom, racing atop a horse through an open field. As Eric moves over me, I arch into him. When we come together, I allow myself a moment to let go.

Afterward, my body covered in sweat, I move toward him when he turns to his side. I stare at his back before pulling the sheet over us and lying on my back. As I stare at the ceiling, my thoughts drift to the sound of his quiet snores until sleep finally rescues me from my worry.

CHAPTER FIVE

CELINE

I wake slowly, similar to when coming out of a dream and unsure which one is reality. The ringing of the phone slips through my mental awareness, forcing my eyes open. Nearly noon. I cannot remember the last time I slept in so late. Eric picks up his phone with a quick "Hello." I have dropped my legs to the floor when Eric touches my arm.

"It's your mom. Brian's on his way to the ER in an ambulance. He had a seizure."

The words fail to penetrate the haze of sleep. Only when he jumps out of bed do the words breach the fog. "Brian?"

Adrenaline rushes through me as I race to get dressed. Brian in the hospital. Seizure. My mind turns on itself, the words getting louder until, like a child, I yearn to cover my ears. Fear fills every part of me. I fight to stay calm, but it only gets worse with every breath, like when on a roller coaster, on the way up the rails before the downturn. Jeans, a shirt, and a jacket. I search for my bag and keys, finding them on the table I have looked at three times already. My cell reveals multiple missed calls from my mom.

"Do you have everything you need?"

Laughter bubbles to the surface, losing steam when it meets the bile in my mouth. The only thing I need is for my son to be all right. For whatever's happening to him to stop. I need him to be healthy and safe. Frozen in place, I don't answer him.

"Celine?" Eric's demand breaks through my reverie.

"I'm ready."

In the passenger seat, I stare blankly out the window as Eric nears almost a hundred miles per hour. I imagine Brian in the back of the ambulance, alone and scared. He would ask for me. Wonder where I was. I didn't call him last night to say "I love you" or to have a good night.

"He knows," Eric says.

"What?" I ask, confused.

"That you love him."

I'd spoken aloud. Unable to form any other words, I return to staring out the window. Blinders can help a horse keep focused, away from any distractions. Now, I shut everything out as I focus on Brian.

On arrival, the red neon **ER** sign guides us into the parking lot. I rush into the building, Eric fast on my heels. A nurse points us toward his room. Inside, my mom hovers over a sleeping Brian. Her relief palpable, she hugs us both, her arms holding me for a second longer. I grip my son's limp hand as she relays the events of the morning—he felt ill after breakfast, then started vomiting and seizing.

"The doctor saw him. He woke up briefly after the seizure but then fell asleep," my mother concludes.

IV drips fluids into a needle in his left hand. Electrodes attached to his body read his vitals. Less than twenty-four hours ago, he was rushing out of my car to practice. Talking about his team. Telling me he was fine. Now, he lies silent in the oversize hospital bed, small and helpless, his face pale and lifeless. I ache, needing him to wake up, to tell me he's fine. To ask for his favorite food and bargain for more television time. *I love you,* I say silently, needing him to hear me.

The door opens, a doctor in a white coat with a stethoscope around her neck entering. "Dr. Johnson." She begins to review his chart after introducing herself. "Given that this is his first seizure, we hope that it's a simple explanation. A virus, high temperature, something innocuous and easily treatable." She checks his vitals. "We will, of course, run additional tests to rule out possibilities."

"Possibilities?" Eric asks.

Dr. Johnson gently lifts Brian's pediatric hospital gown, revealing a large bruise that covers an area below his ribs. I swallow my gasp, staring at it, then at Eric. We mirror one another in our confusion, both silently asking the other if they were aware. The doctor's eyes on us, she silently replaces the gown. Brian stirs at the movement but remains asleep.

"The EMT noticed it during initial assessment."

"He plays soccer." I search for a plausible explanation. "Every day."

Her face devoid of emotion, she adds, "There's one on the back and another one on the leg. Smaller."

"He never mentioned them to me," I whisper, trying to explain what I do not understand.

"Boys this age . . . ," my mom says, laying a hand on my back in much-appreciated support. "They're going to forget about it before remembering to mention it."

The doctor considers us. "I see. We need to run blood work, x-rays, and an EEG of the brain." She glances at Brian. "It's going to be a long day."

Tired and worried, I barely notice when a man joins us. Tattoos cover both his forearms, and he has a black stud in one ear. Streaks of gray run through his blond hair.

"William," he says, introducing himself. "Could I have a few minutes of your time? While they run the tests." He glances at my mother. "Would Grandma mind going with Brian?"

"What is this about?" Eric demands as I watch her follow my son to get x-rays done.

"I'm from social services. We need to try and find the cause of the bruises."

A year after my father left, a teacher contacted Child Protective Services when I came to school too many days without lunch because my mom had forgotten to make it. After she'd worked all night at a gas station, sleeping in the morning was a necessity. They accused her of child neglect, all because she was trying to provide for me.

"Are you accusing us of abuse?" I try to keep my voice steady, even as my throat tightens.

Eric lays a gentle hand on my arm as William says calmly, "Our due diligence saves countless children from terrible situations. We don't pick and choose who we need to follow through on." William maintains eye contact. "The x-rays are going to take about thirty minutes. The trip there and back another fifteen. So, I figure you can spend that time worrying about your son. Or I can piss you off so completely with my very personal and intrusive questions that the time will fly by." He adds quietly, "Eighty percent of the time we read the situation wrong. It's the twenty percent that makes this important."

"What are the x-rays looking for?" Eric asks the questions I cannot string together.

"Old fractures. Anything that speaks to repeat abuse." William points to his form. "This is only preliminary."

"Then we should get started," Eric replies.

William asks a series of questions about our lives at home. Impatient, I try to answer questions about what Brian has for dinner on an average night, his sleep schedule, his friends and their families, and numerous others that dissect our life. The few times I pause, my anger brewing, Eric steps in and answers them as best he can.

"Macaroni and cheese," I correct when Eric says pizza is Brian's favorite food.

"What?" Eric shifts his entire body toward me, his eyes narrowed.

I should have left the answer alone, but my need to lash out found Eric's answer as the easy target. "His favorite food is now macaroni and cheese." I feel William assessing us, watching, studying to see whether, within our interactions, he can find the clues to prove that we beat our son. "Not pizza." I shrug, trying to explain. "In case you're going to corroborate our answers with Brian, I wanted to make sure and get the right one."

"Look," William says, seeming to soften at my statement, "you seem like good parents." He runs a hand over the clipboard that only minutes ago he was frantically scribbling our answers onto. "But I've seen more cases than I care to admit where a parent has looked me right in the eye and lied." He shrugs. "You wonder if people just start to believe their own stories."

"What happens when everything comes back clear?" His apology and explanation are irrelevant to me. I should be with Brian in case he wakes up during the x-rays, not here.

"Then I just wasted your time. Which I am counting on." He opens the door, then turns back toward us. "I was eight years old when my parents brought me into the ER after I fell down the stairs. From the fall, I had bruises on my stomach, thighs, and back. From previous falls, I had two broken bones and multiple fractures."

"I'm assuming you never fell," Eric says quietly.

"Not once, unless you count being pushed. I do this"—he points to his clipboard—"because too many kids, like me, don't have a voice. If everything comes back clear, no one will be happier than me."

I watch him leave. He promised that the time would pass faster, but he was wrong. Every second, every minute, that I haven't been with my son, I have worried about him and yearned to be with him.

CHAPTER SIX

FELICITY

I wake up in the morning with thoughts of Celine and the party. She was not who I expected her to be. In my mind, I'd created a persona of a woman who relied wholly on Eric for her sense of self. A woman who was weak to my strength, who was dependent to my independent. Instead, I found her to be warm, smart, and aware. I saw her curiosity when she found Eric and me talking. Questioned the unmistakable familiarity between us. Celine reacted the exact opposite of what I had expected. Instead of watching me from a distance, assessing whatever threat I might represent, Celine approached me head on to make her own determination. For some time, I have hated her without knowing her. Now I can't help but also admire her.

Forcing myself out of my reverie to focus on my son, I spend the morning cleaning the house, knowing how important Lily is to him. I shop for food and add citronella candles and bouquets of flowers to the cart. Back at home, I ready everything in preparation. Though everything I have done was for him, I nonetheless took him away from everything he knew. I am grateful to this girl for making him smile again, for being good to my son.

"Mom?" Justin enters the kitchen and stares at the table setting. "Is this a wedding celebration or maybe a funeral? What's with all the flowers?" He gapes at the dinnerware, then at me, in horror. "Are these fancy plates? When did we get fancy plates?"

I smack him lightly with the dish towel. "We've always had them, and I just want things to be nice for you."

"She may expect a proposal after this," Justin warns me before pulling me in for a hug. Already inches taller, he sets his chin atop my head. "This is really great. Thanks."

"I want her to feel welcome."

"Not too welcome, though, because I was going to break up with her tonight," he mutters. "Hopefully this doesn't give her the wrong idea."

Shocked, I pull back to see him laughing. "Not okay," I lecture.

"Just trying to match your crazy." He stares into one of the dishes. "I can see my reflection. Did you *shine* them?"

"One more comment and *you* may be uninvited to dinner," I warn.

"Just you and her, huh?" He shudders. "Not sure she's brave enough for that."

Horrified, I stop and stare at him. "I am not difficult."

"No," he laughs. "But scary, yes. Have you met yourself?"

"What does that mean?" I pride myself on being easygoing and calm. Since it's primarily been only the two of us, I've always known I have to walk a fine line between being Justin's confidante and his primary parental figure, even when he caused havoc as a young boy.

"It means you're on the verge of insane, but I love you." He stops and adds, "I mean, I have to but . . ." He laughs when I growl. "You are going to love her and she's going to love you, and I'm going to sit back and watch the two of you suck up to each other. Fun."

"What does she know about us?" I ask, unsure how personal they've gotten.

He pauses as the humor falls away. This is the topic of conversation that always forces him to face what I have desperately tried to shield him from. "She knows that my mom is my best friend. That my mom has done everything, always, to give me the best life possible. That I love my mom."

"And your dad?" I whisper.

He swallows and looks away before shrugging. "That my parents tried to make it work, but it didn't. What they did instead is give me a modern family: he has his apartment, where I have my own room, and that I"—Justin pauses before continuing—"love him because he's a really good dad." Justin heads toward the refrigerator and opens it. "I should marinate the steaks."

I know how much Justin loves his dad. He's never complained about our unique situation, always just grateful for both his parents' unconditional love.

I jump in to help. Working in tandem, I prepare the potatoes for roasting while he chops vegetables. Justin turns on music, choosing a compromised playlist of both our favorite music. I hold out my hand. Justin rolls his eyes but good-naturedly takes it and twirls me before we take additional dance steps. Similar to scenes we've played out hundreds of times over the years. With music as our companion, we spend the next few hours focused on ensuring a perfect evening.

"Hi, I'm Lily."

She is beautiful, I think. A mixture of exotic and earthy beauty. Black hair falls in waves down her back, her olive skin set against green eyes. I sidestep Lily's outstretched hand and offer her a hug instead. Lily returns the embrace immediately. "Welcome."

"For you." Lily holds out a bouquet of flowers. "Thank you for having me over."

I inhale their beautiful fragrance. "You shouldn't have, though I'm guessing Justin told you I love flowers."

"I told her you *live* for flowers," Justin corrects. "You should have been a florist or a bee buzzing from flower to flower."

"Lovely. What every mother wants to hear." I usher Lily in. "Come in, honey. And ignore him. I do."

As Lily follows us in, I smile inwardly at the questioning look she darts toward Justin—clearly asking if she's doing and saying the right things. Justin gives her a thumbs-up.

Justin and Lily help to set the table. Justin teasingly bumps Lily with his shoulder, causing her to nearly drop the plate of vegetables. Lily growls quietly before jerking her chin toward me in warning. I continue to slice the bread as if I haven't noticed.

"Justin tells me you're the captain of the swim team," I say, making conversation.

"I love swimming. Probably the only thing I'm good at." Lily grimaces. "Academics aren't my strong point. Unlike Justin."

"I'm okay," he says, deflecting, always humble. Though Justin has always been proficient with numbers, I'm filled with pride at his innate mastery of them.

"Have you been swimming long?" Though I try to be careful with asking too many questions, I am fascinated by this girl my son cares for and yearn to know more. Though I know he's still young, he's already establishing his own future. A life that will one day include someone of his own, instead of just being the two of us. And as he creates his life, I wonder at what I need to do to create mine.

"My mom is a swim coach for a club team, so I'd often be with her for practices. Between club and school team, I pretty much swim all day." She laughs self-consciously. "It's my favorite thing to do, so I'm good with it."

"I thought hanging with me was your favorite?" Justin laughs when she elbows him. "No, it's cool. You and me is my fourth-favorite activity. Right after walking the dog."

"You don't have a dog," Lily murmurs.

"Exactly."

Hearing Lily laugh, I find myself relieved. She's tough and good natured about Justin's teasing. "Did you grow up around here?"

"My parents brought me home from the hospital to the house I still live in."

I glance at Justin, wondering if he envies her stability and normal family life. After he remains relaxed and smiling, I exhale. Lily shares stories about her life, asking me about growing up in Maine, then going to college in Chicago. She and Justin exchange stories about water sports, and he promises to take her diving one day.

"When did you get certified?" she asks, clearly impressed.

"Unofficially? Five or six." He laughs when I roll my eyes. "Officially, when I was twelve."

"Justin didn't appreciate the word 'no.' He convinced one of the locals to teach him, insisting it was for the safety of everyone involved." I reach over and pat his hand. "If I wasn't so furious, I may have been impressed."

"You just needed time," Justin says. "Now you're fine with it."

"Only because you're not dead. Otherwise, it would have been a problem."

"It's your fault I love the water," Justin says good-naturedly. "Mom was a champion rower at the University of Chicago, then later sailed in Chicago. First thing she did was join a yacht club in Boston when we moved." He sighs, as if carrying the weight of the world. "'Do as I do, not as I say.'"

"Believe that's supposed to be turned around," I tease.

Lily asks questions about my rowing before we move to both general and personal topics. As the sun starts to set, I realize we've been talking for hours. "Justin, have you tried the new ice cream parlor they opened down the street?" Wanting to give them time alone, I start to clear the dishes. "While I clean up, how about you kids run out for some pints?"

"I can help." Lily insists on doing the dishes. Between the three of us, the kitchen is cleaned in record time.

"You need to come over for dinner more often," I say, wiping my hands on a towel. "Justin has never worked this hard before."

They leave right after for the ice cream. From the living room window, I see Justin poke Lily in the stomach before wrapping his arm around her shoulders. She punches him in response, then cups his cheek when he bends down for a kiss. Wanting to respect their privacy, I step back and let the curtain drop.

Young love. I smile at their relationship, so happy for Justin. I consider my own life, and my thoughts once again drift to Celine. Whenever we spend time together, Eric speaks in detail about their life but rarely shares his feelings or thoughts. Sometimes I question if it's purposeful or subconscious.

I send a quick text message to Eric, thanking him for the party. When I don't hear back immediately, I put the phone away. My thoughts wandering, I replay the party and wonder if Celine believed me to simply be Eric's colleague, or did she suspect the truth and understand what it meant for her marriage?

CHAPTER SEVEN

CELINE

I pace the hospital room as day turns to night. Though I feel Eric's gaze intermittently on me, I remain silent, my inner focus completely on Brian. Mom told me he slept through the x-rays, allowing me to exhale that he hadn't woken up during the procedure and asked for me. He then continued to sleep and has only stirred now, when a new doctor walks in. Young, she offers us a smile before focusing on Brian. The meeting with the social worker still in the forefront of my mind, I instinctively position myself on one side of his bed, while Eric takes the other.

"Hey, sweetheart. How are you feeling?" I keep my voice light in hopes of keeping him calm.

"I'm still in the hospital?" Brian's fear fills the room.

I take Brian's hand, gently warming it with mine. My fear percolates, but I push it down so I can carry his.

"Just to check you out, ace." I melt at the nickname Eric started using for him at birth. "The doctors are going to tell us what's wrong." Eric glances at the doctor. "Right?"

"We hope so." The doctor shakes our hands. "I'm Dr. Mendoza." She focuses on Brian. "Can I tell you a secret? I hate hospitals."

"But you're a doctor," Brian says, his voice weak.

"I know." Dr. Mendoza sighs loudly, as if she herself cannot make sense of it. "Silly of me, huh? Brian, can I be rude and ask to see your bruise?" Brian's eyes widen, telling me he's known about them.

"It's fine, sweetheart," I reassure him, masking my own anxiety and curiosity about why he hasn't said anything.

Dr. Mendoza gently raises his gown, her face neutral as the discoloration comes into view. "Do you remember getting this one?"

"I think it was when I ran into my desk."

"And the one on the thigh?"

"Messing around with my friends." He shrugs, obviously unsure under the repeated questioning.

"Have you had bruises before, Brian?" she asks.

Brian looks guiltily at me, then Eric. My heart speeds up, then races at the thought that he's hiding something that I have failed to discover—abuse, bullying. "Honey?"

"A couple. I didn't think they were a big deal."

"That's all right," the doctor says reassuringly. "How about your energy level?" She glances at her notes. "I understand you're a pretty serious athlete."

"Soccer." Brian beams, the smile warming me. "I'm going to be a pro one day."

"I should get your autograph now so I don't have to wait in line." I feel a surge of gratitude toward her for not trivializing his dreams. "So do you get tired often?"

Again, he looks to me as I struggle to find my voice. "Tell her however you feel, sweetheart."

"I've been tired a lot lately," he answers. "Everything hurts."

"Honey . . ." I start to ask him why he hasn't said something when Eric says my name, his tone cautioning me that we should wait and see. Knowing he's right, I fall silent.

"Do you mind if I chat with your mom and dad for a few minutes?" Her facial expression remains the same, making it impossible to read her thoughts. "Boring stuff like what vitamins you take, your daily meals, stuff like that?"

"Yeah, sure." He glances at his grandmother. "But Grandma will stay with me, right?"

"I'm right here, angel," she promises.

I run a gentle hand over Brian's head, then follow Eric and the doctor out. Eric's hand brushes against mine before settling on my back, offering me comfort and support. I smile at him gratefully as we enter the consultation room.

Once inside, the doctor immediately says, "The x-rays are negative. No sign of previous trauma."

I temper my anger at having gone through the process, trying to understand that they must follow their procedures. The muscle in Eric's jaw tics, but he doesn't respond.

"Would you like to take a seat?"

"What's going on?" Eric and I both refuse the offer of the worn sofa. "Please tell us." I barely sense Eric's hand slip into my limp one. Every nerve in my body feels on fire, aching and unsure.

The doctor's face shifts from the warmth she exhibited toward Brian to the grimness she now displays. "We see a skewed white blood count and low red blood count."

"He has an infection?" I try to remember pieces of information from the vet classes I took in college in preparation for work on the farm. After having spent my whole life working and living with the animals, it was fascinating to learn the biology and physiology that created the horses I loved. "The body is fighting off something?"

"The symptoms—bruising, fatigue, vomiting, and seizures—point to something more serious." I tense, unsure of where she's going as she continues, as if she's reading from a well-rehearsed script: "Of course, we'll need to run further tests, and we'd want you to see a specialist outside the hospital. We can recommend someone . . ."

"What are you saying?" Eric demands, his voice low and stern.

"All of Brian's symptoms indicate childhood leukemia."

My hand falls out of Eric's, while my legs, suddenly made of jelly, refuse me the ability to stand. The sofa I previously dismissed now offers necessary refuge. I stare at the light-brown color, matched seamlessly with the rug and tan walls. The perfect decor to offer a haven of false security. Ghosts of families past sitting in the same place we are, their lives quietly and viciously torn apart, swirl around me.

"How long have you been practicing?" She's young, could have misread the symptoms . . .

"I'm a second-year intern in hematology-oncology." A blank face, as if she's answered this question countless times before. Or I may have asked the wrong question. Instead, maybe there's one that would have led to a different diagnosis for my son. In the absence of social norms, is there a protocol to follow? "They called me once all the results were in."

"William was sure we'd abused him," I say accusingly. "He was wrong, and now, so are you."

"Honey," Eric says quietly, his own face ashen. He lays his hand on mine again.

"Our son is not sick." His hand, a burden I can no longer carry, falls off when I move mine away. "He can't be."

"I understand your feelings—" Dr. Mendoza begins, but I cut her off.

"Do you have a child you've been told has cancer?" The first time I rode a horse alone, it refused to move or follow any of my directions. Austin advised me to try another one, but I was sure I'd find the answer to get the horse to comply. Now, similar to then, I refuse to believe what she's saying, sure I can find another explanation for Brian's symptoms. "Then please don't tell me you understand."

The room is not large enough for all the emotions racing through me. Like a trapeze acrobat, I swing from one thought to the next. After my father left, a school counselor explained the five stages of grief. In detail, she told me how I should feel and process each one. I stared at her, refusing to respond. Now, I jump through every stage, not finding a handle on any of them.

"He's not ill." I shake my head as if to dispel the very notion of it. "I'd know if he were."

"Celine." I bite back a scream at Eric's acquiescence, for having taken the pieces they've given us and put them together to lead to the same conclusion as Dr. Mendoza. "Let's take the needed next steps."

"I want a second opinion."

"Of course. We'll give you the name of specialists in the area. Let us know who you decide on, and we'll fast-track the appointment." Dr. Mendoza softens, extending sympathy that I refuse for fear of accepting her version of the truth. "Further tests will give you the answers you need." She doesn't make any promises for his health or his survival. Just that we'll be better informed.

"Could you be wrong?" I demand when she starts to leave.

"The symptoms . . ."

"Could you be wrong?" My voice loses its edge, dropping to a pleading whisper.

"Yes," the doctor acknowledges. "I could be wrong."

Like the reins of a horse, I grip the words as an anchor to hope. Without hope, I chance falling without a net to catch me. I watch wordlessly as the doctor walks out. As the silence looms between Eric and me, I try to remember what we used to talk about, the conversations between two married people that once felt so relevant but now seem so inconsequential.

"I need to get back to Brian," I murmur, the only thing that makes sense to me.

"What are we going to tell him?"

"We say nothing." One hand on the doorknob, I yearn to lean against the door. For it to offer me the strength I no longer have. "Until we know more."

"Lie to him." He shakes his head, his action voicing his disagreement.

"Protect him." I refuse to speak the diagnosis aloud. "From something that may not even be real." In his face I see my resoluteness matched against his. In a battle against the unknown, I wonder at the first step of turning on one another. "What if we told him they were investigating us for abuse?"

"That was a couple of x-rays. We don't know what it's going to entail here to get the answer."

I refuse to tell our son a disease that's taken countless lives is now on our doorstep. A disease that will instantly change life as we know it, as he knows it. Bringing pain and suffering and horrible fear. I refuse to burden him with that until we are sure.

"No." The fight suddenly drains from me. As if from a scene in a movie, the walls begin to close in. "I can't. Please." The pressure on my heart creates a small crack, like a pebble on a windshield, until it's spread through my whole being.

I see the moment he relents. It reminds me of his reaction the first time I took him home to the servants' quarters my mom and I lived in. Then I was sure it was empathy. Now, I wonder if it was pity in disguise.

"Then let's get the tests done immediately."

I can barely sleep. The clock reads past midnight. After we returned from the hospital, Brian immediately went to bed. Eric and I silently followed, neither of us speaking to one another. The silence that normally would have left me anxious and unsure was instead a welcome relief. I have lain in bed since, my thoughts unwanted company.

Now, I crawl out from beneath the covers. Next to me, Eric snores. I envy him his ability—no matter the situation, he's always able to fall asleep, anywhere and anytime. For me, ever since childhood, sleep has often come only fitfully.

I move quietly out of the room and head into the living room. The oversize bay windows allow the moon's light to stream in, bathing the room in its glow. I stand against the pane of glass, staring at everything and nothing at the same time. I imagine the rest of the world sleeping peacefully, regenerating to start a new day with hope and excitement. I am jealous of their happiness, their surety of how their lives will go. I have lost that confidence, and now I stand, afraid and helpless. Familiarity with the feeling causes me to grip the wall for support. I glance at the moon and send a silent prayer out to the world—*Let my son be safe. Let all of this be a mistake, a nightmare that I awake from.* A plea and then anger as I bargain: *If given this gift, never again will I ask for anything.*

Memories of similar childhood wishes remaining unanswered blanket me as I pad on bare feet to Brian's room. My father returning, friends at the prep school, my childhood friend Austin not moving away, being happy . . . I open the door to find Brian in his bed, safe and sound. My heart catches at the sight of his small face, wiped out from the day's events. I slip into the room, leaving the door open in case Eric awakes and searches for me. I gently lift the covers and slip into the bed with my child. Going on instinct, he snuggles into me like he used to when he was little, sleeping with us when he was scared. I wrap an arm around him and hold him close.

Brian stirs. Barely conscious, he murmurs, "Mom?"

"I'm here, sweetheart."

In response, he shifts closer to me. I enclose his hand in mine and listen silently as he drifts back off to sleep. I watch through the window as night turns to day and the sun chases the moon, offering light where there were only shadows at play.

CHAPTER EIGHT

FELICITY

I lean back against the boat's edge as the Boston skyline keeps watch over the bay. Immediately after joining the yacht club, I started to go out on the boat whenever time allowed. Boating offered a reprieve from the stress of work and the daily grind. Plus, with Justin busy with his own life, it gave me something to do.

The ocean's choppy waters rock the boat from side to side. I adjust the sails before retaking my seat. Though Justin and I sailed regularly when he was young, those occasions are rarer now because of commitments and his age. I consider the irony that the thing I have fought for the hardest—for him to have a happy and fulfilling life—is the very thing that's luring him away.

The wind pulls strands of hair out of the clip and against my face. I take a healthy swallow from my water bottle to stay hydrated in a battle against the beating sun. I cross one long leg over the other, then lean back against the boat's edge. In the near distance, other boats settle into their positions. I often drop anchor for hours of relaxation. Sometimes, however, feeling an urge from childhood, I'll challenge myself and race against my best time. It guarantees the win each race.

A boating race as a ten-year-old against a crowd of older, more experienced teenagers cemented my instinct to win. My father, serving as my co-captain, had entered me into the race at his yacht club. Laser focused on me, he watched silently as I desperately tried to manage the sails, overcome the waves, and keep on track in hopes of even finishing.

The CEO of a company, he traveled regularly and rarely had time for me. I was the daughter he'd never wanted. So I spent my childhood excelling in all areas to validate my existence, while he offered an impossible standard to attain.

"It's your decision," he said, the first time he'd spoken since the race began. "Whether to win or not." He pointed to the boats ahead of us. "You're not competing against them. You're competing against yourself." My young self, struggling to compute his words into actions, stared at him. "It's your decision."

I'd repeated the words to myself as I turned back toward the wheel. With this mantra in my head, I felt renewed energy and a sense of purpose. Suddenly, everything seemed to fall into place, and I passed the other boats effortlessly. In disbelief, I was questioning the possibility of my win when a wave knocked me back. I quickly tried to course correct, but the moment pushed me to third. Instead of celebrating the impossible placement, I imprinted the lesson in my mind, refusing to ever fail again. *It was my decision to win, and self-doubt led to my failure.*

After the fateful race as a child, I learned how to play the game, first for my father's affection and later for accolades from the external world. I focused on the end goal and committed to whatever it took to reach it. I rarely allowed emotions to play into my decision-making. I considered and reevaluated each step of my career ladder before closing the deal. I never left anything on the table or to chance. My mindset afforded me few friends and even fewer relationships. The emptiness, I was sure, was worth it. Until Justin.

The night of Justin's conception, I had already endured a few relationship-free years eased by one-night stands. Relationships felt impossible to either find or navigate. Shocked when I learned I was pregnant, I vacillated among fear, sadness, and uncertainty. It felt like a failure on my part—one I'd never believed myself capable of.

I met with Justin's father soon after to tell him the news. Unsure of his reaction, I was stunned when he, a friend and business acquaintance, told me that he would be a part of our child's life. He made as many Lamaze classes as possible, and the day of the birth, he cut the cord, and together we held our son, crying tears of joy.

He remained a hands-on father, attending appointments, making school decisions, and participating in all parts of Justin's life. Justin was raised with the knowledge that he had two parents who loved him deeply and were committed to his well-being. Justin's father had an apartment where Justin had his own bedroom, though we mostly stayed at my place, where he slept in the guest room. For all intents and purposes, we were a family.

As the years progressed, Justin's father and I shifted from co-parents into a deep friendship. Over dinner we would talk about work and future ambitions, life and dreams. My feelings grew until I fell in love. I began to wonder what it would be like to have more—for us to be a real family. I would watch him when he wasn't looking and imagine us holding one another. On one particular night, I decided to tell him about my feelings. To chance it in the hopes he felt the same.

"Everything okay?" he'd asked when I fell silent in preparation.

"I . . ." I struggled with the right words. But when a two-year-old Justin came running into the room, I suddenly realized a truth I'd never faced before—if I admitted my feelings and he didn't reciprocate them, I'd risk pushing him away. Justin would lose his father because of me. Unwilling to take the chance, I refused to say the words. I began to date other men; some became serious, while others were just to pass the time. But my main focus remained on Justin.

But now real love feels like it's mine to have. For me to finally be allowed to have happiness and a relationship I deserve. It was the impetus for the move to Boston. To attend the party and meet Celine. I start to type on my phone to Eric:

Need to talk. Spending the afternoon planning Justin's party.
Let me know when is good for us to connect.

I send the text, then wait for the "Delivered" sign. On the ping, I quickly trim the sails and head for shore. I'm scheduled to meet Lily later in the afternoon during a time when Justin is busy. I'd reached out to her to ask if she'd be interested in helping to plan Justin's surprise (and belated) seventeenth birthday party. Though I have an MBA and am successful in my career, the planning of a party for a teenager stupefies me.

My parents had passed on before Justin was born. I've often thought of my father, imagining how he would have reacted to finally having the boy he had been so desperate for. But life didn't allow him the one thing he had yearned for more than anything. I wonder if it will offer me a different path or if I will also be left yearning, waiting for the love that I have desperately been seeking.

"Thank you for inviting me." Lily takes a seat at the dining room table. "I think Justin will really love the surprise party."

"Thanks so much for helping me," I return. "I have no idea what a surprise seventeen-year-old birthday should look like." I yearn for the days when games, a cake, and a pizza made Justin happy.

We spend the next few hours talking and going over ideas. Lily warms to the idea of a swim party at the house.

"I'll ask around for DJs," I say, making a note to ask Eric for the name from Celine.

"I'll send out a group invite for the party," Lily promises. "And make sure everyone knows it's a surprise."

"Perfect." I offer Lily a warm smile, recognizing why Justin likes her so much. "You're a lifesaver."

As Lily's leaving, she pauses, her hand on the doorknob. "I'm really glad you moved here," she says softly. "Justin is . . ." As if suddenly shy, Lily glances down before meeting my eyes. "He's a great guy."

"Thank you," I say. "He can't stop talking about you . . ."

Lily shakes her head and pauses. "No, I mean, he's a really decent guy. He respects me, you know? Respects who I am. All the girls notice it." She shrugs self-consciously. "When I told him it was one of the things about him that's cool, he said . . ." She hesitates, making me wonder what she's going to say. "He said you taught him that."

I stare at her, moved. Never have I imagined that I would have a child like Justin. If asked to do it again, I wouldn't change a single thing. No matter what it has cost me.

CHAPTER NINE

CELINE

I depart Brian's bed before the sun has risen. In his sleep, Brian pulls the blanket over himself like a protective shield. I long for it to have the power I no longer wield—to protect my son from harm. I yearn to comfort him and offer him strength as his falls away.

I leave a note for Eric that I will be back in an hour or so. Unsure of my destination, I navigate the empty streets in the dark. I stare at the stars in the open sky, wondering if what lies past them holds the solution to what is happening to my son.

I arrive at the farm without even realizing. I park my car in my designated spot next to Kaitlyn's empty one. She usually arrives later in the day and stays late. A few farm employees, having arrived early to prepare for the day, wave hello. I return their greeting, but unlike before, I don't discuss the day with them. Instead, needing something I can't explain, I saddle up Recluse, then ride him out to the open field. He struggles against my commands. I pull on the reins, anger coursing through me. In a battle of wills, I fight to win. He rears up, then drops back onto all four legs.

"Go," I whisper, allowing his fury to fuel mine.

He starts to ride, gaining speed with his every step. I allow him the freedom, needing my own. We ride the open fields, without direction or a set path. The wind whips my hair into my face. I welcome the cold as my body shivers without a coat. Finally exhausted, he slows to a trot. The sun begins to rise over the horizon, but the light refuses me enlightenment from the darkness. I am lost. Without a map to lead me back.

I dismount and drop my head, my hand on my thighs. I fight to catch my breath, to find my footing.

"You're lucky he didn't throw you off."

I turn at the unexpected intrusion. A man I have never seen before dismounts from one of our older horses. He pushes strands of dark hair off his forehead, revealing hazel eyes. In worn jeans and a shirt, he takes a few steps closer but stops when I instinctively take one back. I'm at the edge of the farm all alone. He holds up both hands in a sign of surrender when he notices my reaction.

"Sorry, Greg said I could tour the farm. One of the employees said it was all right to take this horse." The potential buyer. On my silence, he holds out a hand. "Nice to meet you." When I stare at it but do not react, he lets it drop.

"You're touring because . . . ?" I ask, feigning ignorance.

"You're a trainer?"

Answers my question with a question. Two can play this game. "Do you normally tour farms in the dark?"

He smiles, seeming to enjoy my play. "I didn't want to get in the way once the day started."

"How would you have?" Anger from everything driving my words. "Get in the way?"

His grin broadens. He's the one who's trying to steal the farm from me. To take away my dream. The situation with the farm had slipped my mind with everything going on with Brian, but now it comes back in full force.

"I'm sorry, I shouldn't have bothered you. I'll leave you to your ride."

He's moving to mount the horse when I ask, "What are your plans for the farm?"

He takes me in—my jeans, top, and windblown hair. I look a mess.

"To make it a success," he answers, both of us seeming to leave the games behind.

"It already is," I reply, angry at him for suggesting otherwise.

"I didn't catch your name," he says smoothly. "I'm Austin Teller."

"Austin Teller?" It can't be. My best friend from childhood. The one whose family owned the farm next door until they sold it to Greg and moved to Seattle. Austin taught me to ride. Became my friend when I had no one else. He was my constant for years until he moved and we lost touch.

"And you are?" Unaware of my thoughts, he watches me, waiting for a name.

"It's been a long time," I say quietly.

His eyes widen, then soften, as his gaze takes me in. "Celine." His entire body relaxes, and suddenly I see the boy he once was, the friend he used to be. "It's been a long time."

In any other circumstances, I would have hugged him, thrilled at his return. Now, I stand still, dumbfounded by the turn of events. "You're the one buying my farm?"

He sighs. "I head up a conglomerate of investors," he explains, but he seems to understand that it's not good enough. "They're buying the farm."

"Right."

"I was made to believe that it was for sale," he says.

"You were told wrong," I return. The sun rises fully behind him. We stare at one another, memories overwhelming my brain. "I need to go." Brian's appointment is soon. I need to be there when he wakes up.

"Can we speak later?" he asks.

"Did you know *I* was leasing the farm?" Unsure of why I want the answer, I still wait for it.

He pauses before answering. "I didn't know who you were right now, but yes, I learned you were running the farm during our due diligence. It's impressive what you've done with it."

With his answer, I have mine. "Unless you're backing off the sale, I'm not sure we have anything to speak about."

He watches as I mount Recluse and then take off, refusing to look back. In the car, memories of the two of us fill my mind.

I was nine years old. My mother and I had been at the farm for over a week. Inside the barn, I stared at a horse, first one I'd ever seen. Greg had assigned me the chore of cleaning out the stalls. Though I knew the stallion was locked inside the stall, I didn't trust him. His eyes followed me as his huge head hung over the stall door. On his neigh, I'd jumped back three feet. I turned in shock at laughter behind me. Austin, also nine, stood by the barn door, his hand on his stomach as he tried to stop laughing. Round and pudgy, he straightened his oversize glasses with a thick hand. He pushed his nearly black hair off his tan forehead.

"He won't bite you."

"He doesn't know me. I don't want to scare him."

Austin's look told me he saw right through me. "He could crush you with one foot." He stared at me, then asked, "You have seen a horse before, right?" On my slow head shake no, he closed the distance between us, then gently took my hand and laid it on the horse's head, guiding me. "My mom says you have to trust them so they will trust you."

When the horse dropped its head, welcoming my touch, I exclaimed, "It worked." I paused, then added, "Thanks."

Austin smiled. From then on, we hung out together every day, riding horses whenever we could. While attending the same prep school, we were inseparable. For years he was my best friend. When he left, I missed him terribly and wondered if we would ever see each other again. But I never imagined it happening like this.

I push away all the memories and nostalgia. The boy I knew, the one who was my friend, is now a man to whom I have no connection. My thoughts firmly on my son, I finish the drive home.

◆ ◆ ◆

Dr. Garren, the specialist, welcomes the four of us into his office. A sofa stands in the place of chairs, and a small exam table rests against the far corner. Sports decals cover the walls. Brian clutches my hand.

"Want to see something neat?" Dr. Garren hands Brian a baseball signed by one of the local professional stars. Wowed, Brian stares at it.

"He's one of my favorite players," Brian exclaims.

"Really?" Dr. Garren seems shocked. "Mine too." He repeats the players' stats from the last few games. Brian, excited, jumps right in. I gently release Brian's hand as they go back and forth about the season and the team's performance. Having put his patient at ease, Dr. Garren finally says, "So, I hear we haven't been feeling well." He opens a file, then winks at Brian. "These are all your secrets, by the way."

Grateful for his attempts to connect with my son, I like him immediately. The doctor asks Brian for permission to view his bruises. Brian lifts his shirt and the bottom of his shorts.

"We need to figure out what's causing these." Dr. Garren studies them. "There's a test I'd like to run." Dr. Garren speaks directly to Brian, empowering him, treating him like an equal. "We can do it today if you want?"

"What kind of test?" Brian asks.

When he was young, I would encircle Brian in my arms anytime he got hurt, promising that everything was all right. That there was nothing that his father and I could not protect him from. That we were stronger than the dangers of the world, and he could trust us to stand guard. Now, I anxiously watch the exchange between Brian and the doctor, waiting for him to announce that my son is healthy, that all of this has been a mistake.

"We have to stick a really tiny needle into you." The doctor points to the area on Brian's body and says, "We need to get some of the spongy and fluid stuff inside of your bones."

Brian looks to Eric and me before nodding yes. "How long does it take? I have soccer practice today."

"Unfortunately, you may not make the practice today. Your body's going to need a couple of days to heal." He taps the signed ball that Brian's still holding. "How about you keep that ball instead?"

Brian's eyes go wide. "Really?"

"As a thank-you for being such a great sport." The doctor pushes a button on his desk. I have suddenly been cast into the role of bystander as two nurses join us, ready to take my son away. "These two are going to help you get ready while I talk to Grandma, Mom, and Dad."

"We'll be with you in a few minutes, ace," Eric says.

As a group, we watch silently as Brian leaves with strangers. I sit on my hands, fighting the urge to reach out and pull him back. To take him home and then to soccer practice. To keep my son safe from all of this and return him to the life he knows and loves.

"Once I get the sample, we'll put a rush on it," Dr. Garren says as soon as the door has closed behind us. He repositions the legal pad on his desk so it's even. "As soon as I know, you will too."

The rush because of the severity of his symptoms. "How many signed baseballs do you have?" A part of me correlates the uniqueness of the ball with Brian's situation. He will be the exception—the child who defies the odds.

The doctor opens a drawer filled with them. "The local sports players sign all sorts of things, and then they get distributed to the various pediatric doctors." He heads toward the door. "Let's go get the answer we're hoping for."

◆ ◆ ◆

Eric and I pace, passing silently within the confines of the private waiting room. We share occasional glances, but, my nerves tight, I do not speak. There are no reassurances to offer. We are in the same situation—the unknown without an answer. His tension matches my own. I am reminded of thoroughbreds when they haven't been exercised—the initial release angry and potentially dangerous for the rider. It is a volcano that erupts all at once.

I turn inside my self-made circle, approaching my mom, seated quietly in the chair. With almost absent fascination, I watch as she picks up a magazine, opens it, then drops it back onto the table. She's done this over a dozen times, her grip wearing the worn pages. As if she can feel my stare, she looks up, and our gazes clash. I flinch at the sadness, the helplessness on her face. Unable to bear witness, I turn suddenly, away from her and her fear. I grasp for hope, but it's elusive, hidden, nowhere to be found.

The sound of footsteps freezes all of us in place. Eric has taken a step toward the door, readying to fling it open, when they continue past. Like a scolded child who has dared to ask for something that's not allowed, I retreat into a corner. Eric resumes his pacing, and my mom picks up another magazine, our patterns locked into place. It's barely taken an hour for us to acclimatize ourselves to this room that has become our cell.

"We can take him to the zoo afterward," I announce, my mind searching for an escape from the moment. "Or the aquarium."

"The doctor said he'd be tired," Eric replies. There's surprise and a hint of reproach in his response to my recommendation. "He may need a day or two of rest."

"Right, of course." Shame courses up and down my back for the attempt at normalcy when our lives no longer are. I question how other families move forward—do they pretend that everything is fine in hopes that it will be and go on with their lives, or does every second become a desperate wait for something better?

My phone buzzes with a calendar reminder. Inside the silence, I start at the sound. Eric and my mother watch me as I fumble to pull the phone out of my pocket. "The caterers are coming to pick up the rest of the trays." The party on Saturday night. Time has slowed down since, each second drawing into the next one until it now feels like years, even lifetimes ago.

"What?" Eric demands, still angry from my suggestion moments before.

"No one is there." As if in a trance, I try to meld the life before into the one I'm living right now. On a mission, I call and text the caterers, but there's no answer. With this situation now taking center stage, I welcome the reprieve from Brian. "Someone has to meet them at the house."

"Are you serious?" Eric demands. He's started to say more when my mom jumps up.

"I'll go." She smiles reassuringly at both of us, offering a compromise to calm the waters. "Give me a chance to make his favorite dessert and clean up."

"You don't have to do that." I force my voice lower when both stare at me. Irrational fear fights against reality, insisting we're still in the past, where my mom is a servant and cook while I'm still a victim to life's happenings.

"I know, honey," she says softly, as if I am a child instead of a grown woman. "I want to." She hugs me, whispering in my ear that she loves me, then hugs Eric before leaving us alone. I watch her, wishing I could go with her and make all of this disappear.

Eric runs two hands through his hair, then checks his watch before glancing at the clock on the wall. He drops his head, and I see his anguish. No matter what the test results, he's in pain because Brian has to endure the process.

"I'm sorry."

"We don't have a playbook." Eric stares at the door, making me wonder if he's waiting for an answer or seeking an escape. "Right now, I wish I were at work."

Early in our relationship, Eric would talk about business school and his dreams of his future career in detail, while I would share my hope to one day own a training center. He always supported me unconditionally, telling me how much he believed in me. There were nights I'd lie in bed, pinching myself at having found my knight in shining armor. With him, everything felt possible.

Then his travels and the farm began to take up our time. When he was home, the honeymoon never ended. Reality was pushed away in favor of reverie. He carried the weight of his career in private, while I left the farm and its workings behind when I returned home, feeling it unfair to burden Brian and Eric with everything. Soon enough, we'd become strangers who were intimately connected with a shared life.

"What are you working on?" I ask now, trying to find common ground beyond Brian's illness. Guilt plays with me as I try to recall the last time we have discussed his job or that I asked.

On his silence, I bridge the distance between us until our arms nearly touch. The space I needed only minutes ago now feels lonely and isolated. I ache for him to accept my offered comfort, fearing that he will perceive it instead as false reassurance. When he fails to react, I wonder at the reason why.

"Eric . . ."

His phone buzzes. As if in instant replay of the other night, he checks it, then steps back. A mask falls over his features. As he gives it his entire focus, I want to remind him that only moments before, he had been upset over my concern with the caterers.

"What's the DJ's number that we used at the party?"

"What?" I'm sure I have misheard. The question, out of context in the room and in our situation, takes me a moment to process. "The DJ?"

"A colleague is asking for the number of the DJ we used at the party." Fingers hovering over his phone, he waits for my answer.

A conversation tickles the back of my brain, but I can't remember from where. "You're answering that right now?"

"Do you have the number?" His tone, similar to the night before, tells me he expects an answer and little more.

Smarting at the interaction, I take a deep breath, wondering what we're doing. "For the birthday party," I suddenly remember. "For Felicity?"

He masks his surprise but not before I catch it. "Yes—Felicity. She's asking."

"I don't know," I say, irate. "I have it written down at home."

He nods, then types something quickly back. The sound of the text draws me in further. A text, not an email. "She texted you?"

"What?" Wary and angry, he glances at me.

The small room shrinks even more as we stare at one another. Like an animal cornered, I fail to find a good reason for his reaction.

"Your texts make a different sound than emails." Furious at him, at where we are, at everything, I lash out at him. "You told me once you prefer to email work responses."

He drops his gaze to his phone as if seeing it in a different light. "You know the sound of my texts versus email?"

He's answered my question with a question. My interaction with Austin replays in my head. He was trying to hide who he was. I struggle to understand what Eric is doing. Felicity is the exception to his claim that work doesn't matter right now. Confused, I push, "I didn't realize you two were so close."

He slips the phone back into his pocket. He takes one step toward me, and then, seeming to reconsider, he pivots toward a chair in the waiting room. "Everyone has my number. Text and IMs are easier and preferred by most everyone, so I adjusted. No government secrets here, Celine."

His reprimand makes me feel foolish. "I'm sorry." I run a hand over my ponytail. "I'm on edge."

He doesn't move to comfort me; nor do I seek it out, understanding his annoyance. Searching for a distraction, I glance at the clock on the wall. Over an hour since we entered. Time suddenly becomes critical. Every minute I'm not with my son feels symbolic—as if to give me enough time to prepare for the worst. In combat against myself, I push away the negative thoughts, fighting to bring in better ones.

We both turn as the door opens and Dr. Garren enters. In methodical order, he pulls off his mask and removes his surgical hat. Everything else forgotten, Eric and I approach together.

"He did great with the process." On his pause, I glance at the time again, marking it. "We have the initial test results."

I close my eyes, wishing like a child I could transport myself to someplace far away. It's the same thing I tried the first morning after my father left. It did not work then, nor does it now.

"He's sick." I have spent years replaying the conversation my father and I had before he left. He asked me to remember happiness when sadness became overwhelming. If only I had seen then what I refused to believe—that he was saying goodbye. Years afterward, guilt and fury drove me nearly mad wondering if I could have changed his mind. If I could have begged him to stay. To love me. Now, like then, I want to beg the doctor for a different story. One that ends with my son's happiness. "My son is sick."

"Yes."

The floor becomes a puddle, lacking the foundation to hold the weight of my grief. Next to me Eric stiffens, takes a step back away from the doctor. Away from me. I drop my head, remind myself to breathe as oxygen suddenly feels like a luxury.

"It'll take us a few days to learn how far it's progressed."

The stages of cancer. Like the stages of grief, a diagram to describe the body's trajectory of going from healthy to broken. From found to lost. From hopeful to desperate. Every emotion I have known and lived. And now, like a boomerang, they have returned, as if they never left.

My brain shuts down little by little with every following word. Next appointments, treatment, support groups. Though I am consciously aware of the doctor, I cannot see him, nor can I be sure if he is leaving or arriving. Only the finality of the door shutting behind him shocks me back to the present.

"We need to talk about how to tell Brian he has cancer," Eric says.

My husband stares at the floor, one hand rubbing the back of his neck. I see him swallow, then sigh. The last time I've seen him like this was when he learned about his parents' deaths. Brian was still young at the time. He'd insisted on going alone, not wanting Brian to make the trip. He was defeated then, and now, now he's acting as if we should be prepared for . . .

"No," I insist. "Not yet."

"Celine"—his voice is firm, leaving no room for argument—"this is not your decision to make. He needs to know."

A blinding, silent roar erupts from deep inside me. An animalistic need to protect my young. I fist my fingers as the need travels from my solar plexus upward until it shifts into words.

"What's his favorite color?" I demand, out of character.

I am the quiet one, the one who acquiesces to others' demands. After my father left, I knew not to add to my mother's burden. Then to behave with my uncle. Then stay in my place at school. Used to being second best, I accepted the role fate had deemed for me, never rocking the boat or trying to change the dynamic. Only on a horse was I in control, free to ride as fast as I could in hopes of outrunning the memories that refused to release me.

"What?" Eric demands. "What does that have anything to do with this?"

Retreat, my instincts insist. *Keep things steady and safe.* I learned early from my mother's mistakes of demanding more from my father. In the silence of the empty apartment, I remembered the fights that I had barely paid attention to before but in the aftermath suddenly seemed critical. She'd pushed him away by demanding he make more money for his family, be a better father, and grow up.

Now, I seem hell bent on repeating the patterns of the past. I am relentless in my desire to break Eric's belief that his decision to tell Brian has any weight. I am right, I'm sure. And I will do whatever it takes to show him he is wrong. Just as my mother did to my father.

"His favorite movie? His ritual before every game?" I scoff at his silence, sure I'm making my point. "That he wants to play for the LA Galaxy when he gets older? *I* know what my son needs."

"Why do you want to wait?" Eric finally asks, his anger brewing beneath the words.

"He has to remember the good in his life, the small things." *Remember the small things,* my father's voice whispers from the day he left. "Soon the cancer . . ." Acid burns my throat. "The cancer will be the only thing that matters."

In the years after my father left, survival became the cloud that hung over our lives. I considered every action by the reaction it would create. I know now it will be no different. We will learn to dance to the composition the cancer creates.

"Nothing else will matter but the illness," I whisper, almost to myself. "What he wants will become secondary to the disease's power and persuasion. He will lose his sense of self and believe himself powerless to life."

"Celine . . ."

Eric stares at me like he has never seen me. Part of me wonders if I have hidden parts of myself from him—the parts I couldn't share. An elaborate show to become someone he would love and want. To be worthy of the Prince Charming, did I become the damsel in distress?

"We can't, won't let that happen."

I want to smile at his naivete, as if we are having a mild disagreement about the weather. But I know arguing with him or trying to convince him otherwise is a waste of time. Until Eric lost his parents, he had never faced tragedy or loss. It was one of the things that first attracted me to him. He grew up with the happiness and stability I craved. Only someone who has fallen victim to life's random occurrences understands the power of chance.

"The next few days are his." Over the next few days, I want to find a way to lock us in. To keep life far away. In that time, I'll have to find the strength to get my son through this. "After that, we fight."

"You can't run from this, Celine," Eric bites back, the anger finally spilling over. "Taking him to the zoo. Being at the house for the caterers. Going to the farm this morning." Each word is like a razor, meant to cut me, to make me bleed. I stare at him, my mind processing his words but unable to believe them. "There's no escape from this. You can have a day. Then *our son* deserves the truth."

He walks out ahead of me. In preparing for the war we must fight, we've fought our second battle, and both of us have just lost.

CHAPTER TEN

CELINE

I sleep for an hour at the most. When the small hand finally settles on the three, I slip out of bed. Eric snores quietly next to me. I texted Mom from the doctor's office asking if she could come by the house later on this evening. We'll tell her first and then Brian tomorrow, as a family.

After our fight, we came home from the doctor's office and fell asleep without discussing anything further. When he was on the road, he always called in to say good night. And when at home, he and I rarely disagreed about things, especially in relation to Brian. He often deferred to my opinion, and if I was concerned about something, we would discuss it together and come up with a solution.

From room to room, I drift aimlessly. The kitchen, the backyard, and finally Brian's room.

I run a gentle hand over his head while he sleeps. My heart shifts from fear to sadness to disbelief and then back again. When the emotions start to bubble to the surface, I quickly exit so as not to disturb him.

In the kitchen, I sip on my coffee and watch the sun rise. It mocks me with its beauty and promise of a new day. Instead, a darkness hovers over me, drawing me slowly into its vortex. As the sips of coffee continue to lodge in my throat, I finally throw the rest in the drain.

Eric's footsteps shatter the silence. I turn as he enters, both of us appraising the other. I try to remember what I would have said to him only a week ago. After a good morning greeting, we would have planned our day around his work and travel schedule. The only times we wouldn't was when he was already gone, having left for the office before Brian and I awoke.

"You didn't make enough coffee?" Eric asks, reaching for the empty pot.

I glance questioningly at the still-warm glass canister. The bag of ground beans on the counter and my empty coffee cup in the sink belie any attempt to deny his accusation.

"I'm sorry, I drank it all." I find the lie easier than the truth that I forgot to make enough for both of us. With the tension from yesterday still percolating between us, I try to wave the white flag. "I'll make you some."

"It's fine," Eric murmurs. "I got it." He reaches for the ground coffee at the same time I do. "I said I'll make it, Celine."

I step back, my fingers curling into my hand until there are indentations in my skin. "Right."

At the sound of Brian on the stairs, I rush forward, his widening eyes a caution for me to slow down and act normal. Eric, one step behind me, takes his place alongside me. To Brian, we are in sync.

"Honey, how are you feeling?"

"Can I go to the farm?" Brian's eyes dart between Eric and me. Eric visibly tenses, his worry seeping into me as we wait anxiously for Brian to speak. "I don't feel good enough for practice."

Brian has grown up on the farm and has ridden for almost his entire life. To him it's his second home. And neither Eric nor Brian knows it may not be mine for much longer.

"Absolutely." I ignore Eric's body tightening to focus on Brian. "Do you want to eat something first?" On his no, I remind myself to smile, removing all traces of my trepidation. His body is already thinner from the repeated missed meals. "We can leave anytime you want."

"You sure you don't want to rest for a while after yesterday's appointment?" Eric's tone relays his anger at me for making the decision without him. "Maybe you can go tomorrow or another day?"

Brian shrugs his shoulders and falls silent. As if he senses our discord, he stays safely in the middle, afraid to disagree with either one of us. Angry at Eric for putting him in this position, I fight to give Brian the one thing he has asked for.

"We can leave now." I avoid Eric as I gather Brian's things. "There's food at the farm in case you get hungry."

Once Eric has helped Brian into the car, I drive away without a word to my husband. In the back seat, Brian closes his eyes. I check the rearview mirror repeatedly, willing Brian to return to the boy he was only weeks ago. Without cancer. Once at the farm, I park in my designated spot next to Kaitlyn's car, then help Brian out.

As if he's still a toddler, I grip his hand as we walk across the expanse toward the main stables and paddock. Spotting us, Kaitlyn rushes toward us and bends down to engulf Brian in a hug.

"My favorite man," she exclaims with a wide smile. "How are you feeling?" I called her to let her know about Brian's ER visit, but I haven't had a chance to connect with her since.

"Better," he answers. I search Brian's face, anxious for the truth. On his grimace, my heart falters. "I was at the doctor's yesterday." Brian shows her the bandage over his IV bruise. "I had surgery."

"A procedure," I say when Kaitlyn raises an eyebrow in question. Lacking my normal strength, I add, "Tests."

Kaitlyn stands slowly, puzzled. When I blink twice to keep the tears at bay, Kaitlyn takes a deep breath. "Want to ride?" Her question is directed to Brian, who nods enthusiastically, but her glance holds mine. "Felix has been giving me a ton of problems," Kaitlyn adds before I can answer. Felix is one of our oldest horses and barely moves. "Brian, would you mind helping me out with him by us riding together?"

Brian lights up with a smile that immediately makes me glad for my decision to bring him. Before leading Brian toward the barn, she squeezes my hand and quietly whispers that we'll talk later. I watch them walk alongside one another, Kaitlyn seeming to slow her steps to match Brian's.

The sun beats down on me, but my feet, suddenly filled with lead, refuse to move. As if in a trance, I recall the hundreds of times we have been in this same position—me watching as Brian readies to ride. The sudden, unbidden thought comes to mind—how many more times will he be able to do this?

"No," I say aloud, refusing the thought. "No." I repeat it as if in a debate with the universe.

"Something specific or just practicing the word 'no'?" Austin says from behind me. I turn, and all teasing is erased as his eyes narrow at the sight of me. "Celine, are you all right?"

I realize belatedly that tears are coursing down my cheeks. I swipe at them furiously, trying to stem the flow, but, like a dam broken, they refuse to stop. "I'm sorry, I need to . . ." I search frantically for a place to escape. The house would take me past the paddock and the employees.

"There." He gestures toward a set of trees by the cars, away from any prying eyes. He waits for me to take the lead, then falls into step alongside me. Under the canopy of green, I take in a shuddering breath, embarrassed at my reaction in front of him. "Can I get you anything?"

"I'm fine." I hold a hand over my eyes as I fight to stop my reaction. "Thank you, though." He searches in his pocket, then comes out with a handkerchief. I stare at it in disbelief. "You carry a h-handkerchief?" I stutter, a small smile breaking through.

He shrugs and grins in return. "I wear glasses, and I have an obsession about cleaning them, so . . . But this one is unused, I promise." He holds it out to me.

"Thank you." I wipe my face with it, taking deep breaths. We stand in silence, me glancing at the ground while he watches me. "I don't want to keep you . . ."

"You never used to cry," he says softly. My face jerks up in surprise. He seems embarrassed by the comment and tries to explain. "All the years we knew each other, you never cried."

"I didn't realize that." I hold up the handkerchief. "I guess things have changed."

"Yeah." He follows my sight line as Kaitlyn brings Brian out on Felix. Though he's an experienced rider, I'm grateful for her instinct to sit behind him, one arm protectively around him. "Your son?"

I barely hear Austin's question as I watch Brian, clearly weak, try to hold the reins, then hand them to Kaitlyn as he leans back against her. His eyes close as his body struggles. My stomach curls into itself as nausea and bile rise to the surface.

"He has cancer," I whisper. As if they are shards of glass, each word cuts me, seeping away my life force. It's the first time I have said it aloud, the first moment I have acknowledged his new truth. I need to get used to saying it aloud, to telling people when they stare at his bald head or skeletal frame. "My son has cancer."

On Austin's intake of breath, I fall silent, afraid to admit that I don't know how to do this. It's a weakness I cannot afford. I don't know whom to fight or beg or be angry at. I feel like I have already lost, and we haven't even started the battle.

"C," he says, using his nickname for me when we were kids, "I'm so damn sorry."

Is there a proper thing to say in this situation, a handbook for parents on how to navigate this nightmare, to come out intact?

"If there's anything I can do . . . ," he starts, swallowing deeply.

"Why are you here? Another tour?" Tired, I gesture toward the house. "Kaitlyn and I can meet with you at another time—"

Austin interrupts, "We left on a bad note the other day, and I wanted to apologize."

"What happened to you when you left here?" My son's life and my livelihood are both under threat at the same time. For one minute, I want to think about something other than that. "You moved to Seattle?"

74

He seems confused by my question but answers it nonetheless. "My parents bought a farm out there. I helped them run it for years, until they retired. After college, I became part of a group that invests in various endeavors across the country."

"Do you have children?"

"No. Never married."

I take in the information, envying him for the simplicity and success of his life. "Why my farm?"

He looks away, and I wonder what he's thinking. "Your uncle bought my parents' farm when we moved. It's now part of your successful business model. We want to make it even more successful."

My success drew him in. The irony doesn't escape me. "Right. It's nice seeing you again, Austin. I just wish it was under different circumstances."

Inside the stable, I saddle a horse and then lead it outside, to find that Austin and his car are gone. Knowing that Brian's safe with Kaitlyn, I mount the horse and ride toward the far end of the farm, where my father's grave calls to me. After making sure the horse is secure, I approach the headstone, inscribed with the word *Jerk*. Austin and I were already best friends at the time he came up with the idea . . .

Past

"In the shadow of death"—I paused, then shrugged my ten-year-old shoulders—"let him rest in peace."

"He's going to rest in peace in the shadow of death?" Austin demanded.

"This," I said, motioning toward the makeshift grave Austin had made, "was your idea. I've never been to a real funeral. So, deal." I took a step closer, as if my dad were really in the small hole Austin had dug, and whispered, "I'm sorry for your fake death."

Austin had carved a piece of wood with the word *Jerk* to serve as the headstone. When I'd argued that I didn't know if my dad was actually dead, Austin, with all the wisdom of his youth, said that maybe, in my mind, he should be.

"We've never met," Austin said to the grave, surprising me with the unexpected eulogy. He continued solemnly, "But I know Celine. She needs to control everything."

"No, I don't," I argued, but Austin ignored me.

"She's really grumpy in the morning." Not wanting to interrupt the somber moment, I rolled my eyes in response. "She won't eat meat." Austin glanced at me pointedly, which I ignored. "But you lost out." Shocked at his declaration, I stared at him. "And you'll regret it." Before I could thank him, he said, "Your turn."

Rocks outlined the grave in place of a coffin. The wood sat upright at the head of it. Other than divorce papers, we had not heard from my father. Not one word—no matter how many times I'd begged the universe for it.

"What if he really is dead? What if he's watching us?" I glanced around nervously. "What if he can hear me?"

"Then he should know he sucks," Austin said loudly. "That he's a loser. Say goodbye, and that you hope you never see him again."

"I hope I never see you again," I said, wanting to mean it. "You're a jerk."

Austin and I mounted our horses. As I followed him, from my pocket I took out a hidden picture of my dad and me. I ran a thumb over his smiling face. I realized then that I hadn't said goodbye and wondered if I ever could.

CHAPTER ELEVEN

CELINE

Brian and I arrive back at the house to find my mom's car in the driveway. Excited to see her, Brian rushes out of the car. I follow him inside, where Mom is holding Brian tight. As her tear-rimmed eyes meet mine, I know immediately that Eric has told her. She releases one hand to reach for mine. I grip it, laying my other hand on Brian's shoulder, three generations of us connected, our past, our present, and our future intertwined.

Eric comes in from the kitchen, taking in the sight. He waits until my mom releases Brian, then pulls him into a hug. "How was the farm, ace?"

Eric listens intently as Brian relays his adventures with Felix. My mother and I move into the kitchen Eric's vacated, allowing us some privacy. Inside, she immediately takes me into her arms. "Sweetheart." I blink back the tears, wondering if this is how it will be for the foreseeable future, grief always on the brink, ready to overtake everything else. "What can I do?"

"Be here, Mom." Though I know it's already a given, she nods to reassure me. "We need you."

We both head back to the living room, where she takes a seat next to Brian and turns on his favorite show. I search for Eric, finding him in the backyard. When I approach, he watches me warily.

"I'm sorry," I start, anxious to end our fight. "I don't know if I was wrong or right yesterday or if I'll screw up and say something really wrong today, tomorrow, next week." I take a breath, trying to make sense of my jumbled thoughts. "But you and me on opposite sides of this doesn't work." I wait for him to say something, to reassure me that he understands, that we're fine, even if nothing else is. But he simply watches me. Anxious, I say, "Eric, I love you."

He closes his eyes, exhaling. "I love you too." He runs a hand through his hair, and I wonder at the delay in reciprocating my words. "We don't know what tomorrow's going to bring. We have to stick together. Make the decisions that make sense. That's the only way we have a fighting chance." We meet each other halfway. I slip into his arms and lay my head on his chest as he tightens his hold. "We can tell Brian later today," he says. "It's the right time."

I had asked for a few days during our fight. For Brian. For me. Now he's refusing to give me even one. I was sure I had won the battle yesterday and this morning, with taking Brian to the farm. But Eric has simply been lying in wait, readying to make his move.

The fire roars next to me. Sparks fly against the grate as the wood fuels the flames. I watch it burn, once strong, part of a tree, and soon it will be nothing but ashes. Soft music plays from the stereo. We ordered some of Brian's favorite foods for dinner, but he'd only taken a few bites before pushing his plate away.

Next to me on the sofa, Brian stares intently at the chessboard, considering his next move. Eric, across from him on a chair, waits patiently. My mother is on the other side of Brian, seeming to need to be as close to him as possible. Since arriving, she's barely left his side. I assure myself that she's offering him comfort and finding it from him at the same time, rather than acknowledging my worst fear—that she believes her time with him is limited.

Brian moves a pawn, his fingers refusing to release the piece until he once again confirms that it's the right decision. From a young age, Brian has played chess with his dad. It's his favorite game, and I know from discussions past that his strategy includes not only making his own right move but also trying to figure out his dad's moves in advance.

As I watch him now, I yearn to do the same in life—figure out fate's moves ahead of time so I can prepare and counterattack to win.

"Ace . . . ," Eric starts, his gaze focused on our son. "We need to talk to you about the tests you had done yesterday."

"Eric, I don't think . . ." I haven't agreed to tell him. We haven't discussed how we might approach it or what the conversation would entail.

"What's wrong with me?" Brian asks softly. He leans back against the sofa, the chess game forgotten.

"Cancer." Eric moves aside the table with the chessboard and scoots his chair closer. Between the three of us, we encircle Brian in a cocoon. Eric swallows, his jaw tense. "You have cancer, ace."

I slip my hand into Brian's, swallowing repeatedly. I again wish for the day or two to have processed this, to find a way to accept what's happening to Brian. But similar to how I was in childhood, I'm forced to react to others' actions, following their lead rather than charting my own course.

"Cancer?" Brian says slowly, then repeats it as if testing the word on his tongue. "The commercials on TV—it kills people, right?" He looks from Eric to me, then to my mom, and back to Eric.

"Some cancers do," Eric answers when I struggle to respond. Amazed at the steadiness in Eric's voice, I wonder if he's either an extraordinary actor or if he truly believes that our son is going to be fine. "Others just affect a certain part of the body." He takes Brian's other hand while my mom's settles on his back. "Your blood isn't working the way it should, but the doctor is going to tell us how to fix it."

"How long will it take?" Brian asks.

"The doctor will tell us more," Eric replies.

Suddenly I'm grateful for his steadiness and surety. Like a circus performer on a trapeze, I swing from one emotion toward him to the next—anger, appreciation, detachment, and gratitude, among others. He's unexpectedly become both my safe place and my punching bag to process the emotions I cannot show to Brian.

Brian stares at the abandoned chessboard, as if he's considering his next move. "Will I get to play soccer while they fix me? I can't miss practices. That would be the worst."

Yes, I think, *let that be the worst he faces throughout this.*

"I don't know, ace," Eric says slowly, as if avoiding admitting the truth. "The doctor will have all the answers."

Brian makes a sound of disbelief.

"Honey?" I ask, anxious for him to explain.

He shrugs in response. "You and Dad have always had the answer," he says. "Always."

At his unequivocal trust in us, my breath catches, and Eric's jaw tics. I wonder, as his mother, how will I ever have his trust again after failing so completely in shielding him from this?

"I'd like to start chemotherapy immediately," Dr. Garren says to Eric and me. My mom stayed with Brian at home while we met with the doctor. "Unfortunately, as I suspected, Brian is battling advanced acute lymphocytic leukemia."

I hold myself upright in the visitors' chair inside his office in the hospital. My foot taps rhythmically against the pristine white floor, which shines glossy bright like a picture. A crystal clock sits atop the lower shelf, surrounded by a multitude of awards. I wonder if he receives one for every person he saves.

"His cancer is at a stage where we need to hit it aggressively." Eric takes the offered copy of the treatment plan. "He'll need to be admitted to the hospital for the initial rounds."

I jerk when Eric's free hand slips into mine. After telling Brian last night, we went to our room, where Eric pulled me into his arms. I stayed there, both of us silent in the darkened room. That night, for the first time in months, we held one another, both of us seeming to need contact and comfort.

I watch my fingers move evenly apart from muscle memory to make room for his hand. I study Eric's reflection as the doctor continues to speak. Eric's face is handsome in its strength. It's what attracted me when we first met. Whereas I was confused and lost, he seemed to have his life figured out. He offered me a lifeboat in a storm that has never stopped brewing. His concern and love made me believe that, for the first time in my journey, I was not alone. That, for my endurance of the heartaches of the past, the universe had finally gifted me a reward.

"He needs to be home," I suddenly say, the doctor's words just now penetrating my mind, which is split between all the parts of my life.

"The first round of chemotherapy is hard and unknown to the body. We need to monitor him and make sure his body doesn't react negatively." The doctor folds his hands together, as if in prayer, and leans forward. "We'd also like to test every member of your family to see if there's a donor match for stem cells."

"Why?" Eric asks.

"There are usually four stages for categorization of risk. Low, standard, high, and very high. It's determined by age of diagnosis and white blood cell count." As if we are in a college classroom, he reads us Brian's chart, making me wonder if I am being a bad parent for not taking notes. "Brian's initial white blood cell count and age at time of diagnosis place him into the high-risk category."

High risk. My hand slips from Eric's as he demands, "What does that mean? Simple terms."

"He's dying." I lean my head back, staring at the ceiling, my entire being curling into itself. "Our son is dying."

"Celine . . ." I ignore the censure in Eric's words as Dr. Garren speaks.

"We need to hit the cancer hard," he says quietly, not disputing my words. "A donor with a stem cell match would be ideal." He hits a few keys on his computer to bring up a PowerPoint on the far wall. The presentation details what he starts to explain. "All of this information is also in the packet I've given you."

I take the packet from Eric and begin to read. High doses of chemotherapy work better than standard doses to kill cancer cells. But the high doses also kill healthy cells, which results in the bone marrow no longer producing blood cells, which the body needs to live.

"The transplanted cells replace the body's cells," the doctor says.

"The transplant can heal the cancer?" The footnote catches my eyes, becoming a pin of light in a dark tunnel.

The doctor hesitates to affirm my question. "There are some studies that have shown that donated cells may give the patient a fighting chance."

"So a transplant could actually heal our son?" Eric asks.

"We're in a situation where we have to try everything," he says. "We can't afford not to try."

"Eric and I will donate, do whatever we need to." Like a log going over a waterfall, I cling to the elusive hope the game plan offers.

He shakes his head. "We'll of course test you, but unfortunately, parents are rarely a match." He glances at Brian's file again. "A sibling is usually the closest match, but Brian is an only child. Are there any cousins we could test?"

"Eric and I are both only children. No cousins," I whisper, suddenly angry. I had wanted another child, didn't want Brian to be alone like I had been growing up, but Eric repeatedly refused. Said our work and schedules made it impossible. Now, I wonder if that child would have been the savior we now seek.

"What are our options?" Eric's voice remains steady in comparison to my desperation. Suddenly, I have the irrational fear that he doesn't love Brian as much as I do. I'm breaking down, a jackhammer fracturing my mind into pieces. "How do we find a donor that matches?"

"We will search, but it's often difficult to find a match," he says bluntly. "We'll start with the standard chemotherapy regimen and monitor the results." He pauses, then says, "Anyone that's willing, please ask them to be tested. It's our best chance."

CHAPTER TWELVE

FELICITY

I peek out from the window at the gathering in the backyard. Music mixes in with the crowd's laughter to create an ambiance of joy. Two boys toss girls into the pool; they scream as they hit the water. Justin stands with a group of friends, one arm thrown casually over Lily's shoulder. He laughs at something someone says, then pulls Lily in close for a quick kiss. Afterward, she nestles into him, her back to his chest. He wraps his arms around her and locks his fingers above her stomach as they continue to talk to their friends.

Unfiltered happiness flows through me at the sight. No matter how much I yearn to memorialize the event with pictures, I know the age is past. Instead, I imprint the memory in my mind, ripples of joy coursing through me. I send a silent thank-you to Lily for the planning of the successful event. I knew immediately it was a hit when Justin arrived home and his face filled with unbidden happiness when the chorus of "Surprise!" rang out.

"Thank you, Mom," Justin had whispered into my hair as he hugged me tight.

"All Lily," I said graciously. Knowing his friends were waiting, I encouraged him: "Go enjoy your party."

Alone, I check my phone again. No responses from Eric to any of my texts. Has something happened with Celine? Does she suspect? He's always responded immediately whenever I've reached out. Nervous at his lack of response, I fight the instinct to reach out again. The woman I have painstakingly created, the one defined by her accomplishments, would not wait in vain for a text or a call. I am not a reaction to any man's actions.

And yet . . . moving to Boston was meant to give Eric and me a chance. An opening to cement our relationship and move it forward. Though he didn't state a preference when I told him, I assumed it was what he wanted, but now I question if he regrets it. Has everything I have done been in vain?

I was fifteen years old when a distant cousin got married. Family and friends gathered around the night before the wedding.

"Respecting one another is the secret to a long marriage," an older cousin said confidently. "The romance and butterflies you see in the movies and television shows? That goes away when you have to worry about who's doing the dishes or paying the bills." The girl, recently married, continued, "But the respect? Caring about the other person's feelings or about what makes them sad or happy, or being there for them when they just want to talk? Being friends? That's what makes a marriage. It's not perfect, but it's real."

"No," I announced with all the confidence my naivete allowed. "That sounds boring. If I ever get married, it'll be perfect."

"'Perfect' may be an impossible goal," my cousin cautioned. "You may end up all alone."

Now, I wince at my own innocence. The love I daydream about isn't passionate but instead steady, quiet, and unassuming. The friendship my cousin spoke of became the bedrock of my relationship. Everything I scoffed at became my foundation. Eric slipped past my defenses. Quietly and steadily, he took hold of my heart.

I wonder now what Justin's dreams are. Does he hope to find his love early and settle down quickly, or discover the world and himself first? I hope that no matter his choice, he will always be true to himself.

The ring of the doorbell breaks into my thoughts. On opening it, relief floods through me at the sight of Eric. I temper the proof of my fear at the deafening silence of the days past to say nonchalantly, "I wasn't sure if you were going to make it." I push the door back fully to allow him in. His hesitation and drawn face give me pause. "Are you all right?"

Laughter from the backyard draws his attention toward it. "Justin's party? The DJ?" Eric asks.

"What's wrong?" I ask. On his silence, I struggle with what to say. "I'll make some coffee. We can talk in the living room."

"Thank you, but no coffee." As if in a trance, he moves toward the back window. He pushes aside the curtain to watch the kids laughing while playing pool volleyball. "Seventeen years old."

"Eric?" Next to him, I hesitate; then, as if my hand has its own mind, it settles on his back. "What's going on?"

Countless hours, nights, and days spent talking about our lives, dreams, and shared details about Justin and Brian. I'd never imagined such a relationship built on friendship. Now I wait, allowing him the space to speak when ready.

"I need . . ." I can see his anguish.

"Eric?" I fight my own fear at the sight of his. "What's going on?"

Slowly and methodically, Eric details Brian's diagnosis and condition. I listen with shock as he tells me the prognosis—Brian may not survive.

"Eric . . ." I step back, making distance, sensing why he's here but unwilling to hear it. "No."

"Justin could save Brian," Eric says, speaking the words before I can stop him. "He's his brother."

"Half brother," I argue, the fact suddenly feeling crucial. "It may not be enough."

"I, we, have to try." He pauses, then says quietly, "It's for Brian."

Brian—the son of the woman whose fiancé I cheated with. The child who came after Justin. The second son. Brian has the family Justin deserves. Over the years, when Eric and I were alone, we would often talk about Brian. Eric has shared pictures and every milestone of his life. He would comment on the similarities between the two brothers. At times like that, I heard his regret and yearning for the boys to meet.

During those moments and others over the years of sharing our lives, laughter, losses, and everything in between, we eventually crossed the bridge from co-parents to friends and then family. But now everything is gone . . . as he fights for one son, he sacrifices the chance to be a family with his other one. Anger and regret roil through me at the circumstances, to my hopes shattered before they've even had a chance to come to fruition.

"To put Justin through this . . . How do you know it could work?" I fight to build a wall of defense for my son, brick by brick. I cannot choose his son over mine. I have been doing that for seventeen years.

"I have to try." His voice falls low. "I can't lose him."

His pain spreads like a wildfire through the room, devouring every inch. Our years together have created a connection. Through it I feel his pain until I can't breathe or think.

"In asking him this, we tell him . . ." I pause, then add, "The truth." The truth that could tear everything I have built apart. The truth that could make me lose him.

"I know." Eric rubs his forehead in a habit I know is borne from nervousness. "This isn't the way I wanted it." His gaze locks on me. "I never wanted to hurt him or . . ."

I wait for the *you*, but he never finishes the sentence. I glance away so that he won't see my yearning or hope.

"We decided it would be later, when Brian graduates high school." Random ages determined without any proof that the lies will suddenly be understood. But I have recently made my own exception to the decision. "Or earlier, if you and I . . ." I stop when Eric's face contorts into confusion.

"If you and I . . . ?" Eric prompts, curious.

Were together. If we were together, a family, then Justin would understand. It was the rationale that drew me to Boston from Chicago to fight for Eric. Together, we would make Justin see why we'd lied. If together, then all the years would have been worth it for Justin to have the ending he deserves. That I deserve. My family finally together.

When I remain silent, Eric, clearly oblivious to my thoughts, whispers, "Brian may not make it to high school graduation. Felicity, please."

I start at Eric's pleading, recalling all the years I was the one to silently beg for whatever he offered. Grateful when he turned out to be a man of honor, I knew it could easily have been another story. One in which Justin yearned for the father who was never around, viewing the relationships other kids had but assuming one like that was not meant for him.

I have constantly questioned if my decision the night of Justin's conception was sound or selfish, if I robbed him of a family he deserved for my own needs. Guilt ridden and anxious for Justin to have as much of a traditional family as possible, I'd stepped cautiously with Eric, never asking for more, never complaining if there was less, for fear that he'd leave, and Justin would be left alone. In my mind, Eric held all the power, and my son became the unwitting pawn.

Eric's kindness, support, and unconditional love for Justin shifted me from desperation to determination. I gathered the changing pieces of my life's kaleidoscope and created a collage of memories and experiences from which Justin could become a happy and healthy man. And along the way, I fell in love with my son's father.

"Let me speak to him." Before he can offer, as I know he will, I add, "Alone."

"You don't have to do that. It's not fair to you."

"And what's happening to Brian?" I reach for his hand, his fingers curling around mine, holding on for hope. "That's not fair to you."

My desire to claim my stake falls to the back burner. Now, I can only focus on my son. I pause before saying the words to test him, to see how easily he'll push back across the line that's always existed between us. "Or to Celine."

I shut my eyes momentarily against the pain as Eric immediately drops my hand. He runs a weary hand over his face before standing. He glances once more at the party in the backyard. I follow his gaze as it lands on Justin. One son celebrating his birth while the other lies dying. It's an irony I would never wish on anyone—not even the woman who has everything I want.

"I need some time," I say. "I'll let you know as soon as I've spoken to him." Eric nods, then says his goodbyes. After casting the room in darkness, I watch Justin and his friends through the darkened window.

In a moment of clarity, I decide to let him have some time to live the life I have painstakingly carved out for him. *When the time is right for him, and me,* a voice whispers inside my head, *I'll tell him. Then we will face the rest.*

CHAPTER THIRTEEN

CELINE

I shift in the chair next to Brian's hospital bed. Curled onto his side, he's taking labored, erratic breaths as he struggles after his latest treatment. Since his admission, friends have filled the previously bare and sterile room with flowers, balloons, and every stuffed animal imaginable, all brightening his day and promising he will get better soon.

Like passing ships in the night, Eric and I have barely seen one another, him working during the day while I'm in the hospital and then him sleeping here while I go home to take care of emails and sleep for a few hours. I miss him, talking to him, being with him, a disconnection resulting from our situation. My mom fills the gap, being with Brian as much as possible.

I open my computer to do work, but my mind wanders. Though Kaitlyn has assured me she has the farm under control, and I should take as much time as I need, I know it's not fair to her. I wonder how other parents do it when their world stops, but everyone else's keeps going?

Updates on games played around the world blast from the television set. Though Brian barely pays attention, he seems to like the white noise it offers. Or maybe it provides a connection to his life before the cancer, when the status of his favorite teams used to be one of the most important things in his life.

On his cough, I jump up and offer him the juice container, anxious for him to take a sip, as if it's the solution to the disease that's ravaging his body. "Honey, it'll soothe your throat."

He shakes his head, then pulls at the IV tube that feeds him his necessary nutrients. "My stomach hurts."

Gently, I disentangle his fingers from the wiring. The pain in his voice settles inside me, taking root, growing like a weed. "Do you want some crackers?"

My mother, arriving from the cafeteria with coffee, immediately takes her place on the other side of the bed to help soothe him. "The nurse said he may not want to eat for a few hours." She strokes his hair, her hand shaking as it moves gently from his forehead to the top and back in a soothing rhythm. Her other hand grips the bed railing, the veins standing out as her knuckles pale from the exertion.

He tosses and turns, trying to sleep. I have reread the treatment plan until I can recite it verbatim. The hope for the intense chemo treatment is to put him into remission. His fever is a response but is barely responding to medication. Though the doctor has cautioned that it could be a long journey, I know he's hoping for a quick remission. Because if not, Brian's body may not be able to survive the process.

As Brian's eyes finally flutter and then close, I exhale at the same time that Mom clasps her hands together to steady them. For every second he's awake, we force a smile, refusing to let him see us afraid or agitated. I fear burdening him with my emotions as he struggles through his own.

"You'll meet with the doctor soon," she says. "Learn how the chemo is working." She's read through every piece of literature; I often find her researching, trying to learn as much as she can about Brian's illness.

"Mom . . . ," I start, then stop, searching for words. New stress lines surround her eyes and mouth. She's been with us every step of the way, and the toll it's taken is clear. "Mom, thank you." I grip her hand. "For being here."

She smiles sadly. "Where else would I be?"

It was true. Even when things were their hardest, Dad having just left, Mom working too much, she was always there for me when I needed her.

My mom moves to the window, which overlooks a garden. She stares out at it blankly. "He needs to know that you're fighting for him."

"Mom?" I join her, both of us keeping our voices down. "What are you talking about?"

"When your father left, I was so afraid of how we were going to survive. In trying to provide for you, I failed to protect you from the greatest threat of all—my fear. It ate at you, but I didn't know how to shield you from it."

Shocked, I listen. It's the first time she's spoken about how things played out when I was young. Sadness and regret tinge her words but also a hope that history won't repeat itself. "Mom . . ."

"Brian is scared because you are."

"What should I be?" I whisper, unsure. "This is not a game."

"You are my child, and I love you almost as much as I love that boy." She smiles sadly at the running joke between us. "But you're reacting, not fighting. Life has hurt him. He's going to be scared, have PTSD, confusion." She cups my cheek like she did when I was a child and I was afraid, alone. "Somehow, someway, find your strength, if only to give it to him. Let him know he can still trust."

Eric and I walk in tandem to the doctor's office. He's silent, his thoughts seemingly elsewhere. I consider starting a conversation, then decide against it. Any topic would feel inauthentic, betraying Brian in trying to be normal. Our steps are the only sound to break the silence.

Sometimes, when I'm all alone in the hospital room and Brian is sleeping, I imagine the weeks before the party, before Brian's illness, before the farm's potential sale. It all feels like a perfection I couldn't see or was too foolish to appreciate. Now, I would do anything to turn back the hands of the clock and stop time in that moment.

Inside the office, Eric and I take separate seats. I fixate on a spot on the wall before I randomly begin to count my fingers, pinkie to thumb and then back. I did the same thing when Brian was born to confirm he had what he needed to start his life right.

"You'll get to know what the lingo means very quickly." Dr. Garren hands us papers. "Red blood cell count, white blood count. Terms like 'induction,' 'consolidation,' and 'maintenance.' All language to describe the process we're going through."

"The red blood cell count is highlighted," I say, scrutinizing the numbers. "They're dropping?"

"As I feared, yes, they are."

Eric's hands grip the handles of his chair. I want to comfort him, but my hand refuses to move. Paralyzed, I stare at them, confused, my mind in jumbles. My son is not getting better but instead is getting worse. The doctor turns his monitor screen toward us as he continues to speak.

"Thank you both and your mom for getting tested. Unfortunately, none of you are compatible stem cell donors, nor were any of the other candidates."

Everyone we knew had come in to get tested, including Kaitlyn and several farm employees. My hope, a fragile lifeline, starts to slip away, leaving me in the deep water of the ocean without a life vest. "You said there was a donor database?"

"Not large enough. Most donors get tested specifically for family members or friends." He sighs. "Brian's body is rejecting the treatment. It is in distress. We will watch him carefully for any signs of infection, but"—he pauses—"based on initial results, we are going to have to slow down the intensity of the treatments."

"So the cancer will spread faster than you will kill it," Eric says, an odd tenor in his voice. Steady and angry, he uses both to control the conversation as he seeks the answer he wants.

"Yes." Dr. Garren shuts off the computer, the blank screen reflecting our nearly unrecognizable faces—drawn with hollow eyes. "This doesn't mean we aren't going to win this fight. Just that we have to come up with a new battle plan."

◆ ◆ ◆

Eric and I barely speak on the drive back from the hospital. As we near our home, I stare at the five-bedroom brick house. The gardeners have cut the lawn and trimmed the hedges, offering perfection on the surface, while every other part of my life lies in imperfect shambles.

"We bought the house for Brian." Brian would normally be arriving home now. I would focus on dinner, homework, soccer practice, and then catching up on work, only to repeat the pattern the next day. It was the monotony that I relied on, a stability and steadiness that felt luxurious in childhood. "For him to grow up in."

Eric, silent, follows me from the garage into the house. From the kitchen cabinet, I grab a bottle of wine and two glasses, only to find myself alone. I pour myself a glass, then settle into the living room. Curling my legs beneath me, I take a sip, then a mouthful, welcoming the burn as it travels down my throat, punishing me for wanting to forget, to drown my sadness, my fear.

The time between the diagnosis and now blurs together. At every step, I have yearned to take Brian home, for my love to be a shield to deflect, to withstand any harm toward him. But I was wrong. Love is not enough. Our marriage, the happy home I have created, is not enough. I am not enough.

My fingers tighten their already-hard grip on the stem of the glass, nearly spilling wine over the rim. I replay the doctor's words, my hand trembling as my anxiety rises. I jump up, needing air. The glass slips out of my hand. I reach for it but fail. With morbid fascination, I watch as it seeps through the plush carpet, creating a red halo over the design.

"Celine?" I jerk at the sound of my name. Eric stares at me from the doorway, then the fallen glass. "What happened?"

"The wine spilled." I nearly laugh at the absurdity of the situation. Years before, I searched endlessly for the perfect carpet to pair with the room's decor. But now all of that's irrelevant, perfection marred by a stain, an event, by cancer. "From my glass."

Eric stands in front of me, the puddle of wine and the crystal glass between us. His eyes shift to the glass, then the sofa, avoiding me, my eyes. Though he's right in front of me, it's as if we are strangers who are first meeting.

"Can we talk?"

"Brian?" My heart thunders against my chest. It's the only conversation that matters now. Everything else feels at a distance. Though I know life is still happening, I barely find any interest in it. "Did something happen?"

"No, not Brian." Eric takes a step back and turns away. For a second, I wonder if he's leaving; then he motions toward the sofa. "Can we sit?"

"What's going on?" Something in his voice draws my attention, keeping me frozen in place.

Eric retreats, then moves toward me, as if in a game of "Simon says." Confused, I've started to ask him about his behavior when he finally says, "A stem cell donor for Brian."

"They found one?" The heaviness in my heart begins to lighten.

"Maybe. We don't know yet."

I bite back my anger at him for the circles he's speaking in. "What does that mean?"

"Celine." He swallows as his face fills with apology and regret. "Over seventeen years ago, when you were finishing up school, busy planning for our wedding . . ."

We were going to get married while in the middle of establishing our lives. Though I feared we were too young, Eric had already graduated from business school and was working. He'd generously taken over my community college payments and supported me while I continued to help my mom at the farm. With his support and love, I dismissed any reservations and excitedly planned our life together.

"What does it matter?" That time feels irrelevant. Nothing matters except here and now.

"Let me finish, please." Eric reaches for my hand, then steps back before making contact. "You were gone for long hours with everything going on. We barely saw one another . . ."

His eyes lock on mine. I try to hear what he's not saying. My mind, already exhausted and drawn from the day, begins to twirl. As if in a cup on the saucer ride at an amusement park, I'm thrown from one thought to the next, dismissing all of them as ridiculous. There's no reason to bring up that time, I'm sure. Angry, I step back.

"What does that have to do with anything?" I've shifted toward the kitchen, ready to grab towels to clean up the mess, when his words stop me.

"It was one time. We didn't mean anything to each other then."

His words repeat in my head on a loop. With every repetition, I reject their meaning. This is a dark joke that my mind is playing on me. I glance at the wine stain, wondering if it's a hallucination created from an alcohol stupor. That I actually drank it all and will wake up after having blacked out to learn this is all a nightmare.

"You're lying," I insist, angry at him. "Nothing happened."

"Celine . . ." His pain, regret, cut through the haze of my mind, of my insistence that this is not real. "Honey . . ."

"Why are you telling me this?" My mind screams the words, but they come out as a whimper, with barely enough oxygen to speak. "Why are you doing this?"

"I have a son who may be a match. I asked if he would be tested."

"Your son?" He means our son, I'm sure. He misspoke. I want to laugh at his mistake, correct him. He doesn't have another son. "You have a son?"

When my father left, I refused to cry. Every emotion that bubbled to the surface—disbelief, anger, sadness, fear—I pushed it away. When my mother took me on her lap to break the news, I stared at her as if she were a stranger telling me a story. From then on, whenever someone asked me how I was doing, I insisted I was fine, refusing to react or show emotion. Soon enough, they stopped asking.

"Yes. He just had a birthday party." He's rambling and, as if suddenly aware of it, stops. "I spoke to his mother last week, and she agreed to speak with him."

"His mother." The woman Eric slept with as we were planning our wedding and life together. "How long have you known about having another son?"

A week after my father left, I asked my mom dozens of questions—where he went, when did she know he wasn't coming back, why did he leave—details meant to trip her up. I had convinced myself he was playing a game, and if I figured it out, then he would come back. Now, I do the same, sure that what didn't work then will work now.

"Celine," he says, then pauses.

I fell in love with Eric's strength. His sense of self and confidence. In front of me is a man broken. His voice wavers, unshed tears threatening to spill over. A dark veil begins to lift, revealing the truth. With it a hurricane of emotions. I'm in the eye of it, and though our words are stilted, broken in between with silence, I can feel the path of destruction the storm will soon wreak. I know because I have lived through a man's betrayal before.

"How long?" I say, each word a bullet that ricochets back to me.

"Since before his birth."

I take a step, and my foot hits the glass on the ground. Fascinated by the light reflected off the crystal, I tap it and then push down. It shatters, the pieces falling around my foot.

"Jesus, Celine."

Eric bends down to check my foot for a cut, but I step back, away from him. From his concern. The broken glass gives me a sinister sense of satisfaction, a freedom from this conversation. But it's temporary, a momentary reprieve from this never-ending darkness.

"You've known?" He's been living another life while immersed in ours. "This whole time?"

"Yes."

"No." It's the only response I can think of. "You're lying." He must be because otherwise it means our entire marriage has been a lie. "When did you meet him?" On his silence, I scream, "It's not a difficult question. A month ago? A year ago? When?"

"I've always been a part of his life. He knows me as his dad."

I take a step back, and then another until my back hits the wall. A son. Another woman. A family. All of it a lie that he's perpetuated as he lives a double life. "You said she didn't mean anything *then*. 'Then'? Are you . . ."

"No," Eric insists. "It was one time. It's just . . . the time we've spent together over the years." He drops his head before facing me. "He's my family. She's become . . . my family." He slowly comes toward me. I hold up a hand, halting him. Half a foot away, he stops. "I didn't know how to tell you. So many times, over the years, I tried but . . ."

I slap him. My hand stings as my breath comes out in uneven spurts. The sound reverberates through the living room. The same room where we told my son he had cancer. The same room where Eric and I, after purchasing the home, celebrated by making love with the empty walls as our witness.

"I'm sorry," he says. "Please, Celine . . ."

"I need to get out of here." I need to leave. To be anywhere but here. My world, already crumbling, now stands in ruins.

"Justin." He says the name softly. I pause, staring at him, "If he's a match—he could save Brian."

The words penetrate past the grief in my heart, traveling to my brain. Logic defies everything else as what he's saying breaks through— my husband's betrayal could be the difference between Brian's life or death. With one hand he takes, with the other he gives. My rage wars with gratitude. Justin could be a match to potentially save my dying son. With it, the sacrifice of my marriage.

"Justin? That's his name?" An eerie calmness comes over me.

"Yes."

"Did you name him?" The question is irrelevant. But my mind demands an answer. If only because he named Brian, and I idly wonder if that was his second choice. The name for his second son.

"No. She named him."

"She?" *Walk out of the room,* a voice insists in my head. *Get as far away from this as possible.* But like an addict desperate for another hit, no matter the consequence, I forge ahead. "What's her name?"

"Felicity."

The woman at the party. The one who asked me for the DJ's number. The woman I saw Eric talking to and wondered at the familiarity between them. She came to our home, knowing I had no idea of the secret they shared. The son they've created and the life they've lived.

I grab my purse and, under the sound of him calling my name, walk out of the house.

CHAPTER FOURTEEN

CELINE

Past

After my father left, I'd crawl into my mom's bed, tuck myself under her arms, and pray for sleep to drive away the sadness and fear about our future. Sometimes it would come, but mostly my thoughts would shift from one scenario to the next, until I fell into a deep exhaustion.

"Is he coming back? Daddy?"

"I don't think so, baby."

"Are we going to be okay?"

On her silence, I fitfully slept.

Present

I arrive at the hospital after driving around for hours. Inside the car, Eric's admission began like a whisper until escalating into a roar. It repeated, until there were a countless number of him, each one saying the words differently—some with laughter, others with disdain, and a few with regret. But their message was the same—he'd cheated on me; he had another son.

The clock on my dashboard reads midnight. Inside, the halls are quiet with a few staff members mingling about. The elevator speeds me toward Brian. I grip the handrail for false support. When the doors open, I feel a mixture of relief and sadness to lose the few minutes alone when I didn't have to face anyone. From years of perfecting it in childhood, a mask drops over my face to hide the pain. Past the nurses' station, I smile when they say hello.

"He's sleeping peacefully." The nurse, fresh out of nursing school, greets me warmly. "Your mom is with him."

In preparation for the next few months, the doctor told us that the hospital staff and other patients would become as familiar to us as our own family. I want to laugh at the irony. I wonder what he would say if I told him that I have never really known my husband or the other family he has. That I have never met my son's half brother or even known he existed. Between my father and my husband, *family* has become a foreign word.

I walk quietly past the closed doors of the patients' rooms. The silence in the hall offers little solace to the rampaging thoughts in my head. A headache starts to form, beginning at the base of my neck and traveling rapidly toward my mind's eye.

At the threshold of Brian's door, I pause, searching for the words to tell my mom that not only is her grandson broken, but so is her daughter. She will hurt with the knowledge of my hurt. Only when a passing attendant glances at me curiously do I turn the knob until the door creaks slightly open. Inside, the machines watch silently as my sleeping son takes in ragged breaths.

I'm relieved to find my mom fast asleep on the second bed next to him, hands tucked beneath her chin. I shift from her to my son. *It isn't supposed to be like this,* I think. *The pain should have ended years ago.* At some point, I am sure, happiness was meant for me.

Careful to step lightly, I make my way to my child's side and gently move stray strands of hair off his eyes, my hand lingering on his head. From other patients I know the chemo will soon steal his hair and the plumpness from his cheeks and body. He will need everything he has to fight but will be left with very little after the battle.

"Mom?" Brian stirs, then opens his eyes.

"Hi, honey." I fight back the tears that have been threatening ever since I left the house. "How are you feeling?"

"I'm okay." He squints in the darkness and then looks out the window. The moon stares back at us, a single source of light in the expanse of the night sky. "What time is it?"

"Late, honey." I keep my voice low to not wake my mom. "I just wanted to say good night and tell you I love you."

As he strains to smile, I barely bite back a sob. What I once took for granted now feels like a gift. "You say that a hundred times a day. You didn't have to come now." He winces, and his fingers grip the bedsheet.

"Honey?" I struggle to keep the anxiety out of my voice.

"It hurts." He curls into himself. My fear multiplies until I lose all other definition. "I'm going to get better, right?"

My palms go damp. I replay Eric's admission in my head. He has another child. He has lied to me for our entire marriage. *But his deceit,* a small voice whispers, *may be the only answer we have.*

"Yes," I say, forcing my sorrow from Eric's admission deep inside me until it's hidden from my son. "You are."

He accepts my answer with a faith I no longer feel. I tuck him in and watch until his breath evens out with sleep. I drop my head, fighting to find my breath in a room with no oxygen.

After the hospital, I drive for hours before heading to the farm. Once there, I make my way through the dark to the house and head inside, where lush carpeting and luxurious decor welcome me.

I drop my purse onto a table and lean back against the door. I try to remember my life only a few weeks ago, but the images are blurred, as if on a screen filled with static. Everything now feels like a farce, a joke in which I'm the punch line. The fatigue heavy, I slip off my shoes.

I'm headed toward one of the smaller bedrooms near the back when I notice a stack of papers on the coffee table. A quick glance through them reveals that we've been hired to train four new thoroughbreds. Horses that at any other time we would have fought hard to secure for the farm. Ones normally reserved for the larger training centers with a long history of prestigious wins. I review the statistics of the horses—all with numbers that almost guarantee race wins. Which means extra revenue for us.

"I can't think of one good reason why you would be here."

I turn in shock to see Kaitlyn in the doorway of the kitchen. A tumbler in hand, she swirls the amber liquid, slamming the ice cubes against the glass. She takes a sip and waits.

I hold up the papers. "When did this happen?"

She joins me on the sofa. "This week."

"Better question," I say. "How did this happen?"

She hesitates, then, "Austin. He hired us."

I drop the papers back onto the table as if burned. "Why?"

"You're going to have to ask him. He's dropping the horses off tomorrow." Kaitlyn skims the numbers. "We can't say no, Celine. Even if you lose the farm, having our names on their training résumé puts you in a different category."

I know she's right but nonetheless hate the answer. "What's his play?"

"Wish I knew." She gives me a look. "He was your friend. You tell me."

Earlier, Kaitlyn listened carefully to the history of Austin and me but didn't say much else. Since Brian's diagnosis, we haven't had a chance to discuss it further.

"Back to my original question. What are you doing here?"

I lean back against the sofa, glancing longingly at the liquid in her hand. "You have more of that?"

"That bad, huh?" Kaitlyn disappears inside and returns seconds later with another full glass for me, plus the bottle. "Cheers."

Nearly two in the morning. I try to be at the hospital every morning before Brian wakes up. That means I'll get barely a few hours of sleep if I go to bed now. "If only." The initial sip burns, and I cough. "What the hell is this?"

"Can't be sure." Kaitlyn peers at the label. "One of the ranch hands brought it." She takes a sip of her drink. "Take a few more swallows," Kaitlyn encourages. "Practice makes perfect."

"Am I going to regret this?" I ask, but I nonetheless drink as instructed. With the third swallow, the liquid slides down my throat, warming my system as it travels through my body. "I don't want to ask how many drinks you had beforehand to know it would work."

"Probably smart." Kaitlyn refills my glass to the halfway mark. "How much before you're ready to talk about it?"

I stare into the amber liquid, wishing it held the answers to questions I never imagined I'd have to ask. Who is Eric? Where does our marriage stand? Will Brian survive? "There may be a donor."

"Yet we aren't celebrating," Kaitlyn says quietly.

"He's Eric's . . ." The word lodges in my throat. I blink rapidly and glance at the ceiling to keep my emotions at bay. "It's Eric's son. His other son."

Kaitlyn visibly draws a breath and reaches for my hand, her fingers curling around my limp ones until they stop the blood flow. "How old?"

"Seventeen." I know Kaitlyn is doing the calculations in her head. "It happened right before we were married. A one-night thing that led to Eric having another family."

"Wow." Kaitlyn takes a drink, this time straight from the bottle.

"I want to wake up," I say. "All of it be a bad dream."

"I'm happy to pinch you," Kaitlyn offers with a sad smile. "How long has he known about him?"

"His whole life," I answer. The truth feels like a shredder that's running over every organ and cell of my body. "They were, are, a family."

"You have to take a minute. To process this."

"I don't have a minute. He may be the donor we're searching for," I say. "He could save Brian's life. That's all that matters right now."

"I never liked Eric," Kaitlyn announces. When I give her a look, Kaitlyn defends herself. "I didn't. But I couldn't exactly tell you that the guy you were head over heels in love with wasn't my first choice for you."

"Who was?" I demand. "It wasn't like there was a line at my door."

"You know what your biggest problem is?" Kaitlyn demands in return.

Feeling the liquid loosening me up, I answer, "My son having cancer or my husband cheating on me? Him having another family? Or us losing the farm? It's a toss-up."

"You live in your own head," Kaitlyn answers. "You can't see what's right in front of you."

"Again—the cancer, farm, or the betrayal? Not much else to see," I respond.

"The prize horses we get here at the farm?" Kaitlyn starts. "Best pedigree, born to win. I can't stand them."

"Could you have told me that before I hired you?" I ask, surprised by the revelation.

"They aren't real," Kaitlyn explains. "They're trophies before they ever step foot onto a racetrack. My dad worked with horses that were broken. They were vicious, angry, and trusted no one. They couldn't accept love because they'd been trained by pain. My dad used to have to punish them to get them to react." Kaitlyn finishes her glass, sets it down on the table. "He was as kind as possible—putting blinders on their eyes or showing them a whip but never using it on them. It was the necessary catalyst."

"What are you saying? That I need pain to react?"

"Do you? You've always liked the fight."

"I've had to fight." I think about the battle to move from the apartment to the farm, adjust to a school where I was the outcast, find my sense of self when surrounded by the message that I was a nobody. "I didn't have a choice."

"Maybe you still need it," Kaitlyn says quietly.

Anger drives me to my feet. "Are you saying I brought the cancer forward? That I caused Eric to cheat on me?"

"Both of those would be neat party tricks," Kaitlyn says calmly in the face of my fury. "I'm asking you, How much do you want to hold on to the pain? Sometimes the good is hard to see in between the bad." Kaitlyn pauses, then adds, "In darkness, it's hard for our eyes to adjust to the light."

"I can't see any good right now," I argue.

"Fair enough," Kaitlyn agrees. "But maybe that's exactly when you have to." She grabs the bottle. "The reason my dad worked with those horses? Because he said they had real spirit. Strength. They were true warriors. Broken and put back together? That's someone I'm going to trust any day to have my back." She shrugs. "The trophies fall at the first sign of failure." Kaitlyn squeezes my arm before heading toward a room. "All of this is bad, no argument. But past the pain, what is there for you to find?"

CHAPTER FIFTEEN

FELICITY

Have you spoken to him?

I wake to the sound of the text from Eric. Over a week has passed since the party. I glance outside at the rising sun but feel only the shadow of fear and dread. Hating myself for the emotions that I'm sure weaken me, I shore up my resolve and get dressed. I make Justin's favorite breakfast, then sit at the dining room table sipping my coffee as I watch the minutes move past the start of every hour. I recall the story Eric and I had decided upon when Justin was still too young to ask—we tried to make things work, and although they didn't, we were still a family. Justin made us a family.

Justin accepted the story without question. Since Eric spent so much time with us, it never became an issue of Justin needing more or questioning Eric's life outside the one we had together. The times Justin visited Boston, he stayed with Eric in his apartment. But between school and sports, the distance between Chicago and Boston became too far for Justin to travel regularly.

Eric has also been diligent about scrubbing the internet of any personal information. He has no social media pages, his work information limited to title only. A refusal to take pictures has kept his image off other people's sites. I know it's time consuming, but he's always insisted that it's worth it. And since it never would have occurred to Justin that Eric has another life, let alone another son, he's never questioned the situation.

I hear the minute Justin wakes up. From years of knowing his routine, I imagine him sitting up in bed, checking his phone, brushing his teeth, then throwing on a T-shirt and pants before running a hand through his ruffled hair. He would glance in passing at the mirror before padding down the hall to grab some breakfast in the kitchen. He is as disciplined in his routine as he is every other part of his life. It reminds me not only of Eric but also of my father.

"Mom?" Justin pauses at the threshold between the dining room and the hallway to stare at me in surprise. "I thought you were going out on the water."

"I'll go later," I lie. "I just got up." I find a smile to convince him I'm telling the truth. "How are things? We haven't had a chance to catch up since your party." In actuality, I have used late work nights to avoid seeing him, to avoid telling him.

"They're good. By the way, the party was amazing." Having bought my story, he wraps his long arms around me in a tight hug. "Thank you again for it. You're the best."

I will him to remember his words. "Lily was the key," I promise him. "I had a whole 'sit-down dinner, poetry reading' thing planned. She set me straight."

He winces while he laughs, then devours his favorite meal of eggs, avocado, and vegetables. "Lily and I were going to hang out with some friends today."

"That sounds like fun."

His eyes narrow at my tone. He drops his fork and sits back in his chair. His movements, the tilt of his chin and the color of his hair and eyes, all remind me of Eric. In the time he's transitioned from a boy to a man, he's become a reflection of his father.

"What's wrong?" Justin's tone tells me not to make excuses or reassure him. "Mom? What's going on?"

I yearn never to tell him. I'll explain to Eric that I never found the right time. That, as Justin was on the verge of starting his own life, he deserved to hold on to the version of the life we've given him. But that would mean saying no to Eric when, in hostile negotiations, the key is to know the points you absolutely need to win and those you can concede without losing the battle. If I fail to tell Justin, I chance losing Eric. But what happens when I tell Justin . . . ? I push down the fear to focus on my son and the situation at hand.

"There's something I need to speak to you about."

Justin offers me his full attention. With it, he shifts from a young man who's just celebrated his birthday to the man of the house who will help carry whatever burden I may be laden with. I cup his cheek before slipping my hand over his. He turns his palm up and intertwines our hands.

"You're scaring me."

"Dad and I haven't told you the full story of us . . . ," I start, unsure of the right words or order.

"What story?" he asks.

Every year, I've debated how much to tell him, but I always found it wasn't necessary to change our story. With Eric's almost-weekly trips to Chicago, he became infused in our life. Holidays, momentous occasions, birthdays—all the events were worked out carefully to reinforce the lie we had woven so seamlessly.

"Dad is married." Shame washes over me as I start to tell Justin the truth that I've desperately tried to hide. "To someone else."

Justin's face conveys his confusion and then disbelief. "Married? Dad?" He shakes his head as if to refuse the statement. "When? Why hasn't he said something?"

"Because he's been married for a very long time."

Justin's face freezes as he processes the underlying truth in my words. "How long?" His tone tells me he's putting the pieces together. His hand slips out of mine. "Mom?"

"Since before you were born."

On Eric's wedding day, I spent the day on the water. I allowed the boat to drift as my own mind wandered at the future and the choices I had made. Now, Justin lets out a disgusted laugh. He glances at me with disbelief and then away, as if he can't bear the sight of me. My stomach knots and then unravels with every second that passes. His hatred bears down on me as I try to find a way around it.

"Justin," I whisper when he holds up a hand.

"You had an affair with Dad?" he accuses.

"No." My denial is immediate, refusing the term and implication of me as a mistress or the other woman. "It was one night. We'd both been drinking, and . . ." I peter off, unsure how to explain.

"You knew he was with someone else?"

A thousand answers and excuses go through my head, but he's too smart and aware to believe any of them. "Yes," I say, ashamed. "I knew."

I'd known Eric over the years from work circles. We socialized with mutual acquaintances and soon became friends. I began to value our time together and the connection between us. As our evening together began, Eric was open and detailed about his upcoming marriage. There were no pretenses or lies. Only as he continued to drink did he admit his hesitation and concern. I latched on to them as the excuse I needed for one night of companionship and warmth. I never imagined it would lead to Justin. To my falling in love.

I jerk in surprise as Justin pushes his chair back and paces the room. I feel his anger and disappointment, understand it's deserved. I have always told Justin to let character and integrity be his moral authorities. He must be seeing me now for the hypocrite I am.

"Honey."

"I was a mistake." The words are torn from his mouth.

His agony breaks me into small pieces. I jump up and reach for his hands, but he jerks back, away from my touch.

"Never," I insist and plead at the same time. "You're the best thing that's ever happened to me." I think back to the time before him and can't imagine life without him. It gives me pause as I imagine Eric's fear of losing his son. "You are everything. How can you not know that?" I send a silent prayer to the universe to help him see past the circumstance to the truth of the situation.

He glances at a picture of himself, Eric, and me on a table. "Everything he told me was a lie."

"Do you really believe that?" Without logic as a defense, I pivot to whatever words will convince him. "He spends every second he has with you because he loves you. You are his son and mine." I fight without armor against the anxiety that's bubbling. "How you came to be doesn't matter. All that does is how very much we love you." With shaking hands, I pick up the picture he glanced at and hold it out to him. "We are a family. Always."

He drops his head, but not before I see his anguish. Eric asked me if I wanted him here when I told Justin, but I insisted it wasn't necessary. Now, facing my own naivete, I wish more than anything for his partnership and help.

"Why tell me now?" Justin says, finally breaking his silence.

My mother and I were never close; I always kept her at a distance. To my young mind, I felt like I had a choice between my father, who represented strength and success, and my mother, who was taken care of and had no career of her own. The choice was clear. I could do better.

As a result of my surety, I rejected every attempt my mother made to forge a bond. If my mother recommended something, I would pick the exact opposite. I resented her not only for who she was but for who she wasn't. When my mother passed away, I saw my father cry for the first time in my life. In his despair, I realized my own misconceptions. His death less than a year later felt like it was more from heartbreak than any medical condition. I faced the uncomfortable question—had

I failed both to give my mother the benefit of the doubt and value her for the force that she represented?

Now, I hope my son gives me the benefit of the doubt that I failed to offer my mother. In my answer, I can only hope that he sees past my indiscretion to the larger picture.

"Your father"—I pause on my next words—"has another son."

"Another son?" Justin physically slumps while his eyes challenge my statement. "How old is he?"

"Twelve."

Eric speaks often and proudly about Brian. If there's an important occasion or if he's considering a gift for Brian, he'll comment about what Justin liked at the same age. I have always listened and given him my thoughts whenever I believed it was appropriate. Internally, it's proved a challenge to chime in on the child who has Eric full time, leaving my son without his father.

"I have a little brother?" Justin's face briefly brightens. As a child, he often begged for a younger sibling. In moments of weakness, I imagined it to be with Eric. Though now I feel foolish, it never seemed possible to connect Justin with the brother he already had. "What's his name?"

"Brian." The clock in the kitchen chimes, reminding us of each passing minute. "He doesn't . . ." I hesitate before admitting, "He doesn't know about you."

Justin's fingers curl into fists as his body betrays his varied emotions and reactions. As Justin was growing up, I walked a fine line between mothering him and giving him space to find himself. I knew there were times I had to allow him to fall so he could learn how to stand. But right now, I would give anything to take away his pain and his sense of betrayal.

"Why tell *me* about him?" Justin demands, but the vulnerability in his voice and demeanor belies his tone.

"He's dying."

Justin's face jerks up, and I see Eric reflected in my son's fear and anxiety. "What?"

"He has cancer." I try to imagine Justin at Brian's age and how I would have reacted if anything had happened to him. Of Celine's reaction when she learned the news. When she spoke of Brian at the party, I saw her love for her son. Similar to the one I feel for mine. "They're desperate for a donor."

"And hope I'm a match." Justin holds my gaze until I confirm with a small nod of my head, worried about what this means for him. He stares at me until finally choking out, "Who asked you?"

"Your father came by the night of your party. To wish you a happy birthday," I lie, adding to the mountain of ones already told.

"Why didn't he come outside?" Justin asks.

"He saw you with your friends. I told him it was an adult-free zone." I agreed with Eric when he said it was best not for him to see Justin. I knew Justin was too intuitive not to pick up on something being wrong.

"What cancer?" Justin asks softly, sounding years older than his age.

I give him the specifics, repeating what Eric told me verbatim. I answer his questions about when they learned of the diagnosis and Brian's chance of survival. In those few moments, Justin shifts from furious son to objective examiner. As if the intellect in him yearns for concrete facts to help him sift through his emotions. It's a tactic I use often to help me navigate the nuances of life.

"If I say no?" Though he's asked a question, I sense more curiosity than resolve. Part of me wants him to say no, to walk away from the brother who has stolen his chance of having a family. "What happens to him then?"

"I think they continue the chemo, but Eric was . . ." I hesitate, unsure how much to burden him with.

"Dad was what?" Justin demands.

"He was scared," I admit. "I think they've tried every route they had. No one was a match."

He stares at the picture of the three of us. "How did you do it?"

When Justin was small, my senses always felt heightened. I seemed to know when he was in trouble, emotionally or mentally. Even without him saying a word, I sensed his inner thoughts. Now, however, I struggle to read between the lines to the underlying question—how did I maneuver through the maze of lies and half truths?

"I focused on the good. On you." I start to say more, but he interrupts me with the question I have dreaded ever since the conversation began.

"Does she know about me?"

At the party, I wondered if a part of Celine had ever suspected, or if she, like many wives, simply turned away from the truth to keep the marriage safe. But Celine had welcomed me as if I was a complete stranger and, when I asked about Brian, answered me from one mother to another. There was never any indication or suspicion that she and I shared something in common—her husband and our two sons.

"I don't think so, honey."

The pain crisscrosses his face like the web that forms on shattered glass. Justin seems to retreat into himself as he takes a step back. I fight the urge to reach out to him, knowing my comfort will hurt more than help. Instead, I yearn to go back a few hours to when he was oblivious and believed his life to be everything I had told him. When all our secrets were safely hidden, and he was fully encased in the life I had created for him.

"Dad's been lying to me all this time?"

With those few words, I see everything Eric's spent building with Justin scattered into pieces too small to ever put back together. The standard Eric has created as an example will no longer be the compass for Justin's life.

"He loves his wife, honey." I plead with him to understand Eric's love for a woman I have hated for seventeen years. "And he loves us. It's complicated."

"Sounds like an excuse," Justin bites back.

"That's not fair." I fight for my child, the fear of losing him forcing me into a battle I created. "We did the best we could. We love you unconditionally. We thought the rest didn't matter."

"Yeah." My heart aches as Justin rubs a hand over his eyes, wiping away the moisture gathered there. "Except there are two of us who have no idea we're brothers." He falls silent as I struggle to guide him through this, back to me and to our relationship.

"Justin?" I plead for him to speak, preparing myself for what he might say.

"I want to meet him," Justin says quietly. He heads to his room without saying more.

I stare after him, trying to process everything that has happened, but all I feel is emptiness. I quickly send a text to Eric: Justin wants to meet Brian. The bubble comes up a few seconds later. I wait, fighting against the horror that our son, the one we have fought to protect, now might hate us forever. It disappears, only to reappear with a simple Thank you. I drop my phone on the table and walk away.

CHAPTER SIXTEEN

CELINE

Past

Austin and I stood on the porch, waiting for him to leave for Seattle, where his parents had bought a horse farm. Both sixteen years old, we had been best friends since I arrived at the farm. I toed one foot with the other. I was sure if I just kept staring at the ground, then I could keep the tears from falling.

"Here." He handed me a mahogany wood box inscribed with symbols. "For you."

Knowing what was nestled inside, I opened the box slowly to find the feather reputed to have belonged to his ancestor, who had been chief of his tribe. The feather indicated his courage and leadership and was promised to offer luck to the bearer. Austin had shown it to me hundreds of times over the years, so proud of the keepsake that had been handed down through generations.

"Austin," I breathed, overwhelmed with gratitude and love for my friend, "I can't take this."

"It's for you." A typical boy, he dismissed any further emotions by grabbing a stick and tossing it. "Keep it safe, yeah?"

His mom, Sedna, joined us on the porch, to let us know it was time to go. He and I said our goodbyes; then I watched as he stepped into his waiting car.

"Austin is going to miss you," Sedna said softly, always having been very kind to me.

"Me too," I said, wondering what she would say if I begged her to stay.

"You're a good girl." Sedna cupped my face between her two hands. Dark eyes stared at me as the wind ruffled her jet-black hair—both gifts from her Native American mother. "You always have been." She raised her eyes toward the farm they had sold, where Austin had grown up since birth. "My mother's people believe that we always return to our true love. He will be back. Hold on to that." She kissed my cheek before slipping into the passenger seat.

I watched the car until it was only a speck in the distance. Only then did I drop my head and allow the tears to fall.

Present

The sun barely peeks over the horizon as I wake up with one leg on the sofa and the other dangling toward the ground. I barely bite back a moan as a headache hammers through my temples. Crust covers my eyes as I fight to open them.

"I'm going to need you to keep it down," Kaitlyn orders, sprawled on the other sofa.

"I didn't say a word," I argue.

"I could hear you thinking. And it's way too early for that."

"As soon as I have the energy, I'm going to kill you," I promise, regretting taking the first sip. "That was not alcohol we drank last night."

"So much better than," Kaitlyn argues. "Now, I know for sure you need your beauty sleep, but shockingly, today, me too. So either go back to sleep or get out."

I think about rolling my eyes at my oldest friend, then decide the pain is not worth it. Instead, I make and down three cups of coffee before feeling like I can see straight. I brew another pot for Kaitlyn after taking a couple of painkillers.

As I get ready to leave the house, Kaitlyn opens one eye. "You need me today?"

I smile in gratitude. "I'll be okay."

Kaitlyn stares at me, seeming to assess the truth of my statement. "I'll come by the hospital later."

With my marriage in shambles, I'm grateful for her support, her friendship. Inside the barn, I reach for Recluse, who throws his head back, refusing my touch. I saddle another horse, then lead him out to a slow gallop toward the outskirts of the farm. Dew clings to the stems of the evenly cut grass. The crisp, clean Boston air breathes oxygen into my depleted cells.

As I pass my father's makeshift grave, I pause, then stop to disembark. Since the ceremony, I had convinced myself it was best for us if we never heard from him again or even whether I knew if he was still alive. If he had returned, I always wondered what I would say to him. Maybe my fury would erupt like a volcano, or the sadness might simply mask the pain.

"You weren't supposed to leave," I whisper. "You were going to teach me how to roller-skate." Something so small felt so important in the weeks after he left. I watched with envy as other kids mastered the skill, while I struggled with the oversize skates my mother found at a garage sale. In a fit of fury, I threw them away after falling repeatedly. The next day, I searched every trash can on the street in hopes of finding them. A pendulum of emotions that swung erratically by the hand of my father's ghost. "You lied to me."

The sound of morning fills the space around the emptiness. I listen to the noises of the farm that indicate life is continuing. But mine feels frozen, without anyone asking me what I want or need. Everything else in my life has stopped, with the cancer and betrayal taking center stage.

"When I was young, you used to tell me every problem has a solution." It was his way of reassuring me when I struggled with my schoolwork. He promised I would find the answer because it existed. "But you lied again. It doesn't."

The pain of the past and present hover around me, both clouding my senses. Then, startled by the sound of hooves, I turn to see Austin riding toward me. I shake myself as memories from all the years he would ride toward me, or us riding side by side through the fields, fill my mind. The hours of laughter and conversation echo in my ears. From the moment we met, we fell into lockstep, never missing a beat. But that boy has changed, grown into a man I barely recognize. Except his eyes, currently locked on me, are still the same. He easily dismounts, then approaches.

"You and Kaitlyn had quite the party last night." Explaining himself, he says, "I went by to let her know I was here with the horses. She mentioned you needed to speak to me."

"Did she?" I steel myself against the visions from the past as I shake my head at her antics. "The horses you're bringing to us for training?" I gesture toward the thoroughbred he arrived on. The money from training them is generous but still not enough to save the farm. "Is it out of pity?"

"That would be a very expensive pity party," he replies. "My investors would probably fire me." He purses his lips. "It's a sound business decision. Your team's performance speaks for itself. Because you're still a small organization, I'm getting more for my money versus a larger training center. Plus, I get an intimate insight into your business practices without you accusing me of trespassing."

His logic makes sense, but I nonetheless add, "You won't get special treatment. Since you are stealing my farm and all."

His lips twitch. "I'd expect nothing less." His voice softens as he glances at the gravesite behind me. "You still come here?"

I shrug, half-embarrassed by it. "Haven't in a while. It's a special occasion."

On my silence, he asks, almost hesitantly, "Did you ever hear from him again? Did he ever come back?"

I barely shake my head no, the pain still ever present, even after all these years. "Maybe he died after all." Curious, I gesture toward the site. "This was pretty advanced for a ten-year-old. Freud would love you."

Austin laughs self-consciously. "More selfish than advanced, unfortunately. I wanted him to never come back, and if there was any way to make that happen . . ."

Sure I heard him wrong, I say, "What?"

"You were my best friend." Looking guilty, he says, "When you moved to the farm, I suddenly had a friend. I didn't want to lose you."

Shocked by his admission, my head turns. "You grew up here, you had everything." He had the perfect life, I was sure. Two parents who loved him. They owned the farm, were able to pay for the private school. He had everything, and I always felt so lucky he was my friend.

"I was fifty pounds overweight, about a foot and a half shorter than my classmates, and wore bifocals. You remember how cruel those kids could be. I didn't want him coming back and taking you away."

Ashamed, I think back to those years. Though I knew the other boys teased him, I assumed it wasn't a big deal. That he had the upper hand. "I'm sorry," I say, feeling terrible for not having been the friend he was to me. "I never knew that."

"Thanks." He smiles and adds, "I'm sorry he didn't come back. I know how much you were hoping he would." He exhales, then asks, "How is your son?"

I wonder at the right answer. Austin was once the closest friend I had, shared everything together. Tired of the lies, I test the truth on my tongue. "There may be a donor to heal him." I'm both touched and taken aback by the hope that lights up his eyes. "My husband's other son. From an affair I learned about last night."

His eyes widen, then briefly shut. "Jesus. C"—he pauses, seeming to search for the right words—"I'm sorry." He hesitates, then, "You're having a really bad few weeks."

It's unexpected, and yet it so reminds me of the boy he was, funny while kind, that I can't stop the quick laugh. "That's an understatement." I point to his horse. "So, you may want to reconsider your decision. I haven't been able to be as involved as I used to be."

His face softens with understanding. "I trust you."

His words touch me at the same time I think that he has no reason to. "That's brave."

He looks at me intently. "I think you may be taking home the trophy on that one."

The thing is, I don't feel brave. Just broken. I can't admit to him or anyone that I fear never finding the glue to put myself back together.

The ping of my phone interrupts my thoughts. A text from Eric telling me that Justin and Felicity will be at the hospital later this morning. With shaking fingers, I slip the phone back into my pocket.

I wonder if, when I first met Eric, anyone had told me then that each step forward from that day—every interaction, every decision, every moment of connection—would lead us to this moment, would I have walked away? I thought life was going to be perfect. He'd save me from myself, from my past . . . And yet now, here I am, having lost everything, or maybe never having had anything.

"Everything okay?" Austin asks.

"My husband wants me to meet his son and his"—I hesitate, unsure of the word to use—"his son's mother at the hospital." I don't tell Austin that I have already met Felicity. That she lied to me, made a fool of me. That all I feel is hatred and betrayal for a woman who, until recently, I didn't even know existed.

"What do you want to do?"

"I just want my son to get better," I admit, surprised he picked up on my confusion. "Nothing else matters."

"Then focus on that," Austin pushes.

I scoff at the overly simple solution. "So, what? I give her a hug at the hospital, and we chat about our boys?" I try to imagine the scenario, but my mind refuses to create a scene in which I'm meeting my husband's mistress.

"You can scream and yell and hate her for what she did. Or you can look at her son as a possible solution." Austin stuffs his hands into his jean pockets and rocks back on his heels. "Personally, I prefer the catfight."

"Nice," I chide.

"I'll ride you for it," Austin challenges, reminding me of the countless races we had when we were kids as dares, to settle disagreements, or just to pass the time. "We race two laps around the track. If I win, you scream at her and give her a piece of your mind."

"And if I win?" I ask.

"You see her son for who he is."

It sounds so straightforward that I almost yearn for the latter choice. I try to imagine the interaction with Felicity, but fatigue from the sleepless night claws at me, demanding relief. I have no time or energy for human needs or emotions. Now, I must greet the woman who betrayed me as potentially the only answer I have.

"Why do you care?" I wonder.

He points to his horse. "Keeping an eye out on my investments." His smile belies his words.

"Two laps," I agree, happy for the diversion.

We mount our horses and head back toward the track. When Austin and I line up at the starting line, we hear hollers of excitement from a gathered crowd. From inside the house, Kaitlyn emerges. When she sees us lined up, she runs to the fence with a whoop of excitement.

"Who am I rooting for?" Kaitlyn yells.

"The right answer," I yell back.

Kaitlyn purses her lips, then nods. The start signal sounds, and we take off in a fast gallop. I bend low over my horse, my entire focus on the track and pushing him forward. I lean left, taking advantage of the space on the track. In my peripheral, Austin comes up parallel to me. Both horses speed up as the crowd's roar crescendos.

As we approach the second lap finish line, I shift into a crouched position, nearly floating above the horse's back, pushing him faster. With little time left in the race, I cannot afford to fall behind even an inch. I ignore the gathered crowd as Austin's horse nudges ahead. For just these few moments, I forget about Eric, Felicity, and the betrayal. I push the cancer outside of my brain and into the atmosphere. I breathe full breaths instead of broken ones. The air hits my face, soothing my fraught nerves. I fight to win, because suddenly it matters more than anything to have a win, no matter how small. I lay a hand on the horse's back. Using Austin's directive from childhood, I reach for a connection with the animal.

"You can do it," I whisper. "Come on, you can do it."

Austin glances at me as we keep pace side by side. With the finish line in sight, I will the horse faster. Just as I'm sure it will be a tie, my horse finds a source of energy and flies forward. We pass the finish line with Austin coming up a fraction of a second behind. I throw up my hands and laugh for the first time since the night of the party.

"You did it," Austin says, coming up alongside me. Both horses continue to trot in a cooldown. "Congratulations."

"Good race." I shake his hand before reclaiming the reins. We finish the lap before dismounting and handing off the horses. "Thought you had me for a minute."

"You won. Barely." He gives me a nod of respect. "Nice finish, by the way."

"Yeah." I watch him head toward the barn. "Hey, Austin?" He turns back toward me. I hesitate, then admit, "I hated it when you left. I missed you every single day." I wonder now if I have ever stopped. "You needed me as a friend? I was so grateful to have you as mine."

His gaze holds mine. "Good luck at the hospital." Without waiting for more, he walks back into the house.

"You good?" Kaitlyn asks, joining me.

"I have to be." I head to my car. Only when I'm halfway to the hospital do I recall Austin's horse's recent statistics. His time in the race was fifteen seconds slower than he's been running for the last month. Shaking my head, I finish the drive.

As the elevator climbs to each floor, I try to prepare myself to see my husband. The hangover having fully worn off, I'm tired and unsure. Austin proved a nice distraction, the horse race a reprieve. But the sterile smell of the hospital walls, the doctors and nurses rushing about, and the worn, tired faces of patients' families and friends all bring me back to the present.

I twist the gold wedding band still secure on my finger round and round; with each loop, a new memory wraps around me. The nights when Brian was little and wailing through an ear infection—Eric and I would take turns walking him, soothing him with songs and back rubs. His birthday parties where we would stand behind him for pictures, the perfect family. The days Eric would return home from a trip, and we would count the hours until we were alone and could make love, reconnecting after the week apart.

And then one final memory fills my brain, pushing all the others away. The night before our wedding, Eric had found me at my mom's house, where, unable to afford my own place, I was still living. He asked me to meet him in his car, where he had hot chocolate and a single rose waiting.

"I love you." He gripped my hand in his before turning to stare out the window. "Tomorrow is the first day of the rest of our lives."

"Eric, is everything okay?" I asked, worried.

"We say our official vows tomorrow, but tonight, I want to promise you that no matter what happens, I will always be with you. I will always love you."

We kissed; then he watched me until I was safely back inside the house. I lay awake that night, wondering why the conversation reminded me so much of the one I'd had with my father before he left. Now, I wonder if he was trying to tell me then what he couldn't until now.

I grip the handrail in the elevator, hoping for strength, for support. There was a time when Eric would have been the one I turned to. The one whose advice I would seek when faced with a problem. When we first started dating, I would talk things over with him, seek his business acumen on the farm. I trusted him and respected him. I love him. Loved him, I correct, as my heart hammers against my chest. Sweat fills my palms. Yesterday's anger has broken down, until now it's just a bloody wound that feels as though the knife is still deeply plunged in.

As the doors open, I straighten my back and tilt my chin, reminiscent of when I entered my prep school as a child. I frantically search for a memory to sustain me through the interaction with him, but everything now feels like an act, a farce to keep up his lies.

As if he's a magnet, I spot him immediately in the far distance, checking his phone. My step falters, then stops, as I stare at him. I remember the first few months of dating, how mesmerized I was by him. Handsome, strong, successful—everything I didn't believe myself worthy of. I'd fallen completely in love with him, grateful that he loved me.

As if he can feel my stare, he looks up. Sorrow, regret, and uncertainty are all etched into his face. Instinct draws me in, and I yearn to soothe him, support him, before remembering. My mind is creating a defense mechanism against the pain he caused. A cost-benefit analysis—forgetting will be easier than processing. The survival of the fittest.

"You didn't come home last night. I called, but . . ."

"I had my phone off," I lie. Now my phone is always on, always waiting for the good news that never seems to come.

"I was worried about you," he says softly, out of earshot of passersby. "I didn't know where you were."

I want to laugh at the absurdity of our small talk. "It doesn't matter."

A small voice says it does matter. He's my husband. Our son is in a hospital bed, fighting for his life. I want to scream at him, demand how he could have done this to me, to us. But the roar dies before it finds its voice. Like the rest of me, the battle is lost before the fight's even begun.

"Are they . . ." I hesitate, then ask, "Justin and Felicity? Have they agreed?"

"Yes." Before the happiness settles in, Eric quickly adds, "To meet you and Brian."

Pain grips me as his words sink in—Justin hasn't agreed to be tested, only to meet me. "What?"

"Justin asked if he could meet both of you before agreeing to get tested. I said yes." It is the first time I have seen his normal demeanor of strength and assuredness diminished. "Justin deserves at least that."

He loves him. His voice softens the same way it does when he speaks of Brian. I drop my head momentarily, wondering how I'd missed the signs all this time.

"When?"

"They're waiting in a private conference room." He hesitates before adding, "I wanted to check with you first."

I want to ask him where the concern was to check with me all these years. For all the times he lied straight to my face. He saw Brian and me as pieces on the board in his and Felicity's game. The revelation of his affair and Justin's existence, even if just a month ago, would have led to an immediate divorce. But now I'm left vulnerable—I cannot hate or fight him when he offers a potential solution for Brian. I swallow my emotions, accepting that, similarly to when I was a child, I must simply accept the decisions of others and how they affect my life.

"Then we should go," I say quietly, desperation driving my decision.

I stay one step behind him, refusing to walk alongside. He glances over his shoulder at me, his yearning clear to say more, to bridge the physical and emotional gap between us. I look away, the pain tearing me into shreds.

When we reach the conference room, I ask suddenly, "Does he look like you?"

I see his surprise, then understanding. Brian is a perfect mix of the two of us. He has Eric's eyes and height and my hair and bone structure. I can't be sure whether, when the boys meet, I fear more that Brian will recognize Justin immediately as his brother or that he'll be oblivious to their connection.

"Yes," Eric says softly. "With Felicity's eyes."

Bitterness churns in my gut at his easy description and familiarity with the two of them. Hatred spews its lava until my love for him twists around me like a burning ring of fire. He opens the door, then waits for me to go in first. The perfect gentleman. A cheating husband. All the faces of him revealed, forming a full picture. One I've refused to see.

Inside the room, Felicity stands up. Unlike before, she's dressed in jeans and a casual button-down, her hair pulled back, and with barely any makeup. Her beauty has shifted from the cover of a magazine to all natural. A thought pushes past everything else—she looks like she belongs next to Eric. Both of them beautiful, carrying themselves in a way that I've never learned or mastered. We stare at one another, the night of the party replaying like a scratched record. Her watching Eric, speaking to him with the familiarity of a wife. Watching me. Asking about Brian. Bile rises until I'm sure I'm going to be sick.

I swallow, the acid dripping down the back of my throat. Justin—a carbon copy of a younger Eric. If I had seen him on the street, I would have stopped him, wondering if he was my husband's doppelgänger. Laughed at the possibility, never imagining the truth. Felicity watches me, her eyes assessing, aware. She knows what I'm seeing—her son is Eric's exact replica. The picture of Brian she saw showed him to be a combination of the two of us. A score for her that the world would immediately know Justin as Eric's son. Eric watches me, as if seeing the situation through my eyes. Pain spills over from him while he lays a hand on his son's back, introducing him as if I'm the stranger.

"This is my son Justin."

"Hello." I struggle with what to say next. *Where*, I think, *does this situation ever arise?* I search for the instincts to guide me through this labyrinth of human betrayal. "It's nice to meet you." I will my hand to stop shaking as I hold it out for him.

"Celine?" Justin's shake is firm and confident, making me wonder about his childhood. "Should I call you that?" His glance flies first to Eric and then Felicity for confirmation. A son seeking his parents' approval. Exactly what Brian would have done.

"Celine is good." I am the outsider, the one being introduced to this fully functional family. The memories I'd sought earlier for comfort now burn inside me, leaving only ashes in their wake. Searching for footing, I shift from betrayed woman to a mother. "How was your party?"

Felicity straightens, her jaw tense. She couldn't have imagined I'd meet Justin so soon after. Like Brian and Eric's speed chess games, I feel as though we're both keeping score, seeing who can best the other one fastest. This is who I am now, what Eric's betrayal has made me into. Competing against a woman I have already lost to.

"It was good." He glances again at Eric, who watches me carefully. *He doesn't trust me with his son,* I think. *Believes I might say something to hurt him.* "A surprise."

"Seventeen, right?" Angry at Eric's assessment, I question if we've ever really known one another. He's the one at fault, and yet he's looking at me as if I may cause harm. "Happy birthday."

"Thanks." He shows first surprise, then gratitude, making me wonder about this young man, who's not just my husband's firstborn but also Brian's older brother.

"Brian's birthday comes later." The urge to cement his place, to remind everyone that I also have a son, a family, pushes me to continue: "He loves celebrating." He used to insist that we celebrate his half birthday, complete with a cake and birthday song. Though he stopped the ritual around the age of nine, I suddenly find myself wanting to revive the tradition. "Next year he insists on a pool party." Justin, Felicity, and Eric share a quick glance, a secret between the three of them, and just like that, I'm the fourth wheel, the one that doesn't belong. I yearn to grab Brian and leave the hospital, their orbit, Eric, and create a space just for me and my son. Where nothing and no one can hurt us.

"I'm excited about meeting him," Justin says, as if it's a question that only I have the answer to.

"Right." Though we are strangers, we are intimately connected. He and my son are blood related. His father is my husband. His mother is the other woman in my marriage. The young man standing in front of me offers both salvation and devastation. "He doesn't know about you." My words are an accusation, a judgment on him and what he represents. "My son is going to be confused."

"So was Justin," Felicity says, shocking me. She lays a protective hand on Justin's back as we face off, two mothers protecting their own. "He had no idea about any of this until recently."

Pain and embarrassment crisscross Justin's face, a silent acknowledgment of his mother's words. He takes a step forward, toward me, forcing Felicity's hand to drop. Her face hardens as her fingers curl into a fist. Still in disbelief, I look to Eric, who confirms the story with a brief nod. Justin's head drops, ashamed, as if he were the perpetrator rather than a victim.

As a mother, I ache to reach out, to offer him comfort. But it's not my place. Instead, my heart swells with anguish for him and disgust toward Eric. Brian, Justin, and I have all been pawns in Eric and Felicity's game. Two families hurt by his actions. Yet, not one of us will come out the winner. A silent scream inside me questions how many more lies have been hidden in plain view.

"Then you will understand his reaction." I shift fully toward Felicity, my voice hardening. Afraid the anger will spill over uncontrolled, I shift back to Justin. "But, though confused, I know he will be grateful."

Sejal Badani

"And if I don't decide to get tested?" Justin directs his question to Eric, who's been focused on his son the entire time. "Do I still get to meet Brian?"

It's a test. He's angry at his father for having kept his sibling from him. He wants to know the stakes and his value outside of simply being a donor. A small part of me cheers him on.

"Yes," Eric says. "You both deserve to know about one another." He moves toward Justin, creating a circle between himself, Justin, and Felicity, cementing my place on the outside. I'm the wife whose husband belongs to another. "I'm sorry you haven't until now."

When Justin steps away from both his parents, I wonder at his action and how he must be feeling throughout all of it. I glance at Eric, curious about how he is handling it before I quickly remind myself it doesn't matter. Not anymore. *But easier said than done,* my heart mocks.

"Can I meet him now?" Justin asks me.

Brian's reaction drives my hesitation. "I need to talk to him first. He won't understand."

"I won't tell him who I am," Justin pushes. "I just want to say hi."

I imagine the roles reversed and how Brian would react on learning of the situation. "Of course. We'll just say your mom"—I refuse to make eye contact with her—"is a friend of Eric's."

Justin takes a deep breath, and I suddenly see how nervous he is. The mother in me softens at his reaction. He, like Brian, is innocent in all of this.

"Do you like your school?" I suddenly ask. Both Eric and Felicity jerk their heads up, staring. I refuse to react to either of them, keeping my focus on their son instead.

"Yes." Clearly taken aback by my question, he hesitates. "It was hard at first because we just moved . . ." He trails off, conflicted. His eyes dart to Eric, afraid he's said too much.

"From Chicago," Eric says softly. "Justin was born there."

"Chicago." The nearly weekly trips Eric made there supposedly for work. Every single one of them a lie, an excuse to leave one son for

130

another. One family over the other. I refuse to look at Eric but can feel his eyes on me, knowing I'm doing the calculations, realizing the truth. Refusing to show Eric weakness, to let him win, I hide my reaction. "Did you like it?"

"I had a lot of friends, so yeah, I did."

"Justin plays club soccer." There's pride in Eric's voice, a father speaking about his son and his interests. Or maybe he's hoping to create a bridge between one son to the other. "He was always on the field. He's hoping to play for the LA Galaxy."

My face falls at the same time Eric realizes his mistake—he knew the team Justin wanted to play for but had no idea of Brian's dream. As Eric takes a step toward me, I instinctively move back, away from him.

"I . . . ," Eric starts, but I interrupt before he can continue, unwilling to have the discussion here.

"Brian should be finished with breakfast by now." I have no interest in his false explanations or apologies. I force a note of calmness in my voice, refusing to show vulnerability in front of Eric or Felicity. Felicity's eyes narrow, clearly aware that something's occurred but unsure of what. "We can go now."

I walk out first. In the hallway, I breathe in the stale air through my nose, desperate for oxygen. I silently will all the doctors and nurses away, praying no one tries to speak to us. Barely holding on, I can't be sure that I won't break in front of them. As I travel the distance between the conference room and Brian's door, I plead silently for my strength and resolve. For Brian's sake, I must get through this.

On reaching my son's room, I visualize the concentration required in a race to steady my voice. "I'll go in first. Let him know you guys are here."

"I'll come in with you," Eric says.

Anger boils as I struggle to temper it. Consciously, I know that he has the same right to speak to Brian as I do. Part of me wants to demand to know what he plans to say, but I refuse to ask while Felicity is watching.

Brian lights up on our entrance as Mom offers us a small smile. His mornings, after sleep, are always better than the rest of the day. He tries to sit up but finds it hard to maneuver with the wires. Eric and I simultaneously start to help him, our hands brushing. It's the first time we've touched each other since last night. I shiver, then tense as my body naturally reacts to his. Eric, seeming acutely aware of my every response, shuts his eyes briefly before stepping back, allowing me to finish helping Brian.

"The nurse said you had a good breakfast?" I ask, putting extra energy into my question.

"Waffles." Brian grins as if that's explanation enough.

The hospital tray reveals barely a few bites eaten. Already exhausted, I search for a way to get some food in him so he can have the energy to fight the disease that's ravaging him. "Do you want to try some more bites, honey?"

"I'm okay," Brian says, pushing the tray away.

On instinct, my eyes have met Eric's, seeking his support to help our son, when I remember and retreat. If Eric notices, he doesn't give any indication. Instead, he smiles brightly, as if we're welcoming guests into our home rather than our son's hospital room.

"I have some people here to meet you, ace. Felicity and her son, Justin." Eric trips over the word *son*. He's afraid of hurting Brian, I realize. He's walking a fine line between his two boys—afraid of hurting one with the truth while continuing to betray the other with his lies. "Can they come in and say hello?"

Too weak to ask questions, Brian shrugs in response. I see my mom's curiosity. Though Brian has had plenty of visitors since his admission, I know it must seem odd to her to invite someone he doesn't know. I meet her eyes, trying to let her know silently that I'll explain later. I'm kept from saying more when Eric opens the door, and Felicity and Justin enter. I hear my mom's intake of breath at the sight of Justin, and then her eyes meeting mine—the similarities undeniable.

Felicity stays glued to Justin's side as they approach Brian's bed. Justin, locked on his brother, nods a quick hello to my mom before focusing on Brian.

"Hi, I'm Justin." Justin holds his fist out for a bump.

"Hey." Brian lights up at the older-kid greeting and returns it. The moment surreal, I simply watch as the two brothers meet for the first time. "I'm Brian."

"Sorry about this, man," Justin says, gesturing toward the IV and room.

"Nah, I'll be out of here soon," Brian says with a confidence that makes me catch my breath. "Temporary."

"For sure." Justin glances at me almost guiltily before introducing his mother. "My mom."

"Hi." Brian shakes Felicity's hand, his smaller one engulfed by hers, the woman who had an affair with his father.

"It's nice to meet you," Felicity says, her voice and demeanor softening.

In another time and other circumstances, I would have been grateful for her kindness toward my son. Now, I watch her carefully, distrustful and suspicious. She came to my home and lied to my face. I cannot trust anything she says.

"You play soccer?" Justin glances at Brian's cleats and jersey, sitting patiently on the windowsill.

Brian grins. "I'm not that good, but I'm getting better."

"I bet."

Justin shifts the conversation to the local teams and their best players. I watch with amazement as Justin leads Brian from one conversation seamlessly into the next. Having put Brian at ease, Justin interacts with him as if they are old friends who have just reunited. Justin is warm and empathetic. Everything I hope my own son will grow up to be.

"Do you play sports?" Brian's weaker voice betrays the creeping fatigue.

"Soccer," Justin answers. "Like you."

133

Under any other circumstance, I would rejoice at their connection. For just a breath, I pretend they are new friends instead of long-lost brothers.

Brian slowly brings up his frail hand to stifle a yawn. Justin immediately steps back. "You probably need to rest."

Brian quickly says no, similarly to how he's done hundreds of times in the past when he wants a playdate to go for longer or to stay up late to watch television. Though it doesn't make sense, I wish now I had said yes every time. That by giving him whatever he wanted then, I could now give him back his health also.

"I'm good," Brian insists.

"Maybe Justin and you can hang out another time?" Eric shifts from one son to the next, both of whom respond "Yes" immediately.

Justin lowers a closed fist inches from Brian's hand to give him a goodbye bump. With his energy depleted, Brian barely lifts his own fist in response. "See you soon," Justin murmurs.

"You look like my dad," Brian says, stopping him.

The room falls silent. Mom's eyes widen, but I can't meet her expression for fear of breaking down. Eric swallows deeply before shifting to nonchalance, as if Brian hasn't just exposed the very lie Eric has spent the last seventeen years hiding.

"Everyone says that." Before Brian can ask more questions, Eric gently kisses him on the forehead before motioning Felicity and Justin to exit ahead of him. "We can talk outside."

The door's barely closed behind them before I decide to follow. All three turn in surprise. Suddenly hesitant, I struggle with what to say. Finally, I turn to Justin, ignoring Felicity and Eric. "Thank you for making his day brighter." My hands wring together. When I look up, Felicity stares at my action, then raises her gaze to mine, her reaction unreadable. "He hasn't smiled since he's been here." Knowing what's at stake, I say the only thing I can: "Whatever you decide, I appreciate you considering it."

Justin runs a hand through his hair, reminding me of the thousands of times I have seen Eric do the same thing. "I wish I'd known about him . . . ," he starts, then pauses. "In any way but this."

A sob clogs my throat, forcing my silence in the face of his admission.

"We should go," Eric says when the quiet lingers. "I'll walk you out."

The three of them head down the hall, with Justin between them. I think of the countless times it was the same situation, except with Brian between Eric and me. I barely hear the door open and then my mom joining me.

"Honey?"

I think about all the ways to break the news to her, knowing she will hurt for me and try to find a way to protect me.

"He's Eric's son. From a one-night stand he had before we were married." Her hand slips into mine, her pain radiating like a nerve wounded, from her to me. Tears slip from her eyes over her cheeks in anguish that has no words. "How did you do it? When Dad left?" Though selfish, I seek any strength my mother has for me to draw on.

"What I wanted didn't matter. The pain, the agony, was irrelevant in the face of caring for you."

I must do the same for my child, regardless of the fact that my well is empty. Though my marriage to Eric cannot matter, my heart still loves him, aches for what was. It feels impossible to process that, in loving him unconditionally, trusting him completely, it has left me vulnerable to him hurting me. But through the pain, I hear my mother's teaching—Eric must be irrelevant. Nothing can come before Brian. Not even my marriage.

"Eric is hoping Justin may be a match. If he agrees to be tested."

A question has gripped me from the moment I learned of Justin's existence. Earlier, I watched Justin carefully for any clue to his thoughts, anxious for the interaction to have created enough of a connection for Justin to decide to fight for him. My son, in a twist of fate similar to

Sejal Badani

my own childhood, is dependent on another for his well-being. I would give anything to take on the battle for him, but my place is on the sidelines, watching and waiting.

"Justin didn't know about Brian." For a brief second, I imagine them having grown up together. Brothers from the beginning. Does Justin want that? Or . . . I finally give voice to the fear that has played in the darkest recesses of my mind. "Now that he does, what if he sees Brian as a threat to his family life? What if he can't care about Brian because it takes away from him?" I barely feel my mom's hand tightening around my limp fingers. "What if he refuses to be tested so he won't have to compete for Eric?"

CHAPTER SEVENTEEN

FELICITY

The echoes of our footsteps in unison thunder in my ears. The hallways are eerily silent, as if there is not enough room for anyone else in addition to the three of us and the betrayal that has replaced our former connection. My thoughts drift to Celine and Brian. Over the years, I had imagined multiple scenarios of meeting Brian—never did any one of them include him dying in a hospital room. Or seeing Eric's love and concern for his son emanating from his every word, every action. The child he has chosen every day over ours for the last seventeen years. And the wife who has always come first.

Justin leads us through the doors and into the outside toward the parking lot. On the drive over, Justin remained quiet, refusing to speak even when I tried mundane topics such as the weather. I finally stopped trying, scared that in asking for more, I was pushing him away.

"Would you have ever told me?" Justin suddenly stops and turns toward Eric. "About Brian?"

Eric focuses fully on Justin, refusing to flinch or avoid the question. "Yes. But not for a while."

Justin shudders in a deep breath. His gaze locks on a car that enters the parking lot. "Because you're ashamed of me?"

I gasp at the same time Eric reaches for Justin, who steps back, out of reach. "No. Never." Eric drops his hands and head. "Justin, how could you think that?"

"Then why?" Justin begs.

I yearn to stand between them as a shield, guaranteeing that no harm will come to Justin. For all the years of love and affection we have given him, all of it could be lost in just a few days. But I know it's not my place. Though Justin and I have always been together, Eric has been a present father. He has earned his place to work through this with his son.

"I didn't want either you or Brian to suffer for the situation I created," Eric says after a moment of hesitation. "You are my son, and I love you. As I do Brian." He shakes his head as if disappointed in himself. "It was the only way I knew how to protect both of you."

Justin glances again at the car as he blinks rapidly. I bite back the desire to intervene and tell Justin that he knows his father is a good man who loves him unconditionally. I know I chance Justin recognizing it as me taking Eric's side and trying to justify what he has done. What we have done.

"You lied to me," Justin says, his words tearing at me, bringing me to my knees. "My whole life."

"I know."

I have known Eric for over twenty years as a lover, friend, colleague, and co-parent. In all that time, he has always been strong, confident, and sure of himself in a way that demands others to follow his lead. For the first time, I see him vulnerable and unsure of saying or doing the wrong thing and losing Justin as a result. Unbidden affection grips me as I see him desperately try to do right by our son.

"If I had to do it all over again . . ." Eric pauses, and I wait, wondering what he is about to say and what his words will mean for me, for us. "I would do it the same."

He would choose Celine over me, Brian over Justin. I drop my head, his words revealing to me what I have refused to believe—that we are still second.

"What?" Justin breathes out, his words filled with agony. "Why?"

"Because I never wanted you to think you were second best. That you weren't my family," Eric whispers. "That I loved you any less." He takes a step toward Justin, trying to bridge the distance between them. "You are *my* son. It didn't matter to me how or why. All I know is that I love you."

I shut my eyes to hold back the tears that pool. Moved, my mind dismisses my earlier thoughts as I silently thank Eric for the words that will make Justin whole. That tell both of us that he doesn't regret that night or all the years since then.

"Dad?" Justin pauses, and I hear him struggling to hold back his emotions. He goes silent, then says, "I want to get tested."

My eyes fly open, expecting to see Eric holding Justin in gratitude. Instead, he stands in place, staring at our son, man to man. "That's not why I gave you the answer I did."

"I know. But it's why I need to do it." Justin glances briefly at me but looks away before I can say anything. "Because Brian deserves a chance." Shocked by his words, by his immediate acceptance of Brian, I can only stare at him as he continues, "What you and Mom did . . . I don't understand it. I don't deserve it. Brian doesn't deserve it." On his next words, my breath catches. "Celine doesn't deserve it."

"Justin . . . ," I start, when Justin stops me.

"Lily's parents said I could stay in their guesthouse for a while." He motions toward the car that's entered the lot.

"Justin." My gut tightens, then free-falls. "Please don't do this."

"I need time."

Lily exits her car, offers a small wave, then drops her head, clearly stepping back from the situation.

"I have my phone, so let me know when I need to come in."

As he starts to walk away, I reach for him. My hand grips his as I search for the words that will change the course and bring him back to me. But as if hidden in the shadows, they refuse to show themselves. Desperate, I say the only thing that truly matters. "I'm so sorry."

Justin closes his eyes briefly before exhaling. With his every move, I see his pain and confusion from the truth I have failed to shield him from. The lies, once started, have stacked up, creating a mountain too large to overcome. Each subsequent action was determined by the first one—a story to keep the truth hidden from Celine and Justin and then Brian.

"I know."

Justin slips his hand out of mine. Without a goodbye, he heads toward Lily. There, they hug briefly before he slips into the passenger side. I watch as they pull out of the parking lot and exit onto the freeway. I try to swallow past the lump in my throat, but the grief proves too overwhelming.

"I . . . ," Eric starts, but I just shake my head. There's nothing he can say to make this better.

"It was what we knew could always happen," I whisper. "It was why we kept up the lie, so that Celine and Justin would never get hurt." In his gaze I see his apology, but right now I cannot accept it. "It worked for so long, we began to believe ourselves invincible." I scoff at our naivete. "We were fools."

I head to my car. Inside, I drop my head before mustering the strength to turn it on. Aware of Eric's eyes on me, I exit the parking lot. On the drive home, only one thought pervades my mind—that I am alone, just as my cousin said I would be.

CHAPTER EIGHTEEN

FELICITY

I arrive at the office before the sun rises. Two days have passed since the trip to the hospital. Regret, guilt, and grief have replaced the sounds of my son in the home. Though I have reached out to Justin, as has Eric, neither of us have heard back. Every day since the hospital has been difficult. The house is empty, though I hear echoes of Justin's voice in every room. My solution has been to work late and arrive early, my office a shelter from the sadness.

Nearly eight in the morning. Though I know I shouldn't, I dial his number. It goes straight to voicemail. I hesitate, then leave a message, asking if he needs me during the test. After leaving the voicemail, I follow up with a text, repeating my request. I wait for the bubbles telling me he's responding, but the screen remains blank. I grip the phone, anxious to connect to my son. But the fear that my attempts will only push him further away demands I give him the space he has asked for.

At my desk, I turn my chair and stare out at the Boston skyline, lost in my thoughts. A door shutting down the hall shakes me out of my trance. A glance at the clock tells me hours have passed since I arrived. The building begins to come to life. I smooth my palms on my pants, then straighten my back. I force thoughts of Justin out of my mind as I pull up my email to start the day.

I run through updates from my team, replying quickly to those who need follow-up. I'm ready to move on to voice messages when a new email pops up. An executive recruiter with the subject line "Immediate attention required." Due to my level, I'm on the radar of multiple executive recruitment agencies in the country. Though I've been courted over the years, I've always resisted the call for Justin's sake. As his primary caregiver, I couldn't afford to split my time or attention in two directions. My position in Chicago allowed me the flexibility to be there for Justin when he needed me while also doing my job. With my professional career solidified, my transferring here was supposed to give me my family. For Eric to finally choose us . . .

Curious, I click on the job description. A CFO position for a start-up in Silicon Valley. Across the country. I read through the details. The position would give me a large stake in the company. I would lead it through its IPO. It would require extensive time on the ground. I would run a team larger than any I have had before. They are anxious to meet with me if I'm interested.

I read through the email twice more. Excitement runs through me at the thought of interviewing and learning more about the company and its vision. My feelings are immediately tempered by thoughts of Justin. His school, Brian, and the situation refuse me the option of even considering the position. Between my son and my career, there was never a choice. With a resigned sigh, I close the email and move on to the day's work.

I finish my last meeting before dinner, leaving a stack of reports with my assistant that needs to be filed before heading back to my office. The crystal clock on my desk tells me Justin should be done with practice and heading back to Lily's. I hesitate, then send him a quick text telling him I hope he's had a good day. On receiving the read notification but without a response, I suppress my sadness, then reach out to Eric to ask if he has heard anything further from Justin. He responds immediately, letting me know that he has no more information than I do. Justin is simultaneously pushing both of us out of his life.

Anxiety at my son's reaction drives me to my feet. Needing a distraction, I change into athletic wear in my en suite bathroom, then head to the yacht club. Though the sun is readying to set, I am anxious to get on the water in hopes of easing my mind. Inside the locker room, I've put away my things and am starting to head out when another member stops me.

After introducing herself, the woman mentions she's part of the club's rowing team. "I heard a rumor you rowed in college," Jennifer says. "One of our team members had to quit because of personal reasons. We are looking for someone to replace her, if you were interested?"

My immediate instinct is to say no, explaining that between work and life commitments, I don't have the time. My mind wanders to the empty house and Justin's refusal to come home. I imagine pacing the kitchen, then the darkened rooms, as I go to bed early.

"Happy to try out, see if things work," I say.

"Excellent." Jennifer grins. "I must warn you, we're training for the Head of the Charles. Our team has a record of placing, so our workouts are intense."

I remember the grueling hours I committed to the sport in college and high school while fighting to succeed academically. I miss those days when things felt lighter, and I had a sense of tomorrow while living today. The escape from today into the memories of yesterday is too tempting to ignore.

"Sounds perfect."

The water is choppy as the wind picks up. Grateful for my extra layer of warmth, I blow out my breath, creating a halo. I take the middle of an eight-person racing boat, a shell, with the coxswain steering the boat. The other teammates are seated in front and back of me. We push away from the dock into the open water. Focused on my technique, I move in tandem with my teammates. The memory of hours and years of training in college comes back as I effortlessly help to propel the boat with my oar.

We warm up for the first thousand meters, then begin at twenty-six strokes per minute for the next thousand meters. Steady and sure, I push my body to stay in sync with the crew. The open ocean draws us forward. My mind drifts with the water. As the boat moves forward in a steady rhythm, I imagine my own life as easily aligned with fate and its happenings. The simplicity of the movement makes me yearn for the time in my life when answers came easily and control felt like a choice.

"Next three pieces," Jennifer advises us, "three thousand meters three times at twenty-eight strokes per minute."

I nod and mentally prepare myself. From years past, I know after the initial three pieces we will take the final six thousand meters, or two pieces, at a race rate of thirty to thirty-three strokes per minute to perfect our technique.

The intensity of the workout refuses me the luxury of focusing on anything but keeping pace with my teammates. We maintain our speed after finishing our first three thousand meters, a hypnotic dance of perfectly aligned oars. As we glide through the water, I push thoughts of the past and future to the back of my head. We slow our strokes per minute to twenty-four for the final thousand meters before heading back to the boathouse. The darkening sky welcomes us back.

I help to get everything back into place. Jennifer joins me, and together we take the steps back to the clubhouse.

"What do you think?"

I feel the ache of my shoulders and the weariness in my body from keeping position. Fatigue forces me to finish my water bottle in successive swallows. I run the back of my sleeve over my forehead to wipe away the sweat. From the time I sat on the boat until now, everything else was pushed to the back of my mind.

"If the offer is still open, I'd love to join the team."

Jennifer beams before announcing to the rest of the team that they have found their person.

CHAPTER NINETEEN

CELINE

I haven't seen Eric since I met Justin and Felicity two days ago. He texted me that Justin had agreed to be tested, but he was unsure of the time or date. I asked him to let me know details, but beyond that, I need space. He seems to understand and has been silent since. Though a part of me wants the battle, the fight, I know it won't serve either of us. There's no resolution to his betrayal, to my heart being broken.

Since the revelation, I have stayed at the farm and plan to do so for as long as Brian is in the hospital. My mind, unable to comprehend all the different issues, has prioritized Brian. Now, he must be the only thing that matters.

I stop by the barn before going to the hospital. I walk through the stalls, the horses quiet in the early morning. They watch me with vague disinterest as I rub their heads, speaking to them softly. Austin's four horses are housed in the far end of the stalls. Though still young, their power and possibilities are evident. I pull up their training schedule, surprised by the youngest's. It's faster than I would have dictated at his age. I grab a saddle off the hook and lead him out. Hesitant, he considers me. I speak to him softly, rubbing his mane, reassuring him.

In the field, I let him set the initial pace, using the time to learn about him and his disposition. He takes direction well, shifting his strides in response to my guidance. I can tell he wants to take over, to be the alpha in our interaction. It's common with colts this age, anxious to make their mark. It's a fine balance between encouraging their power while teaching them how to grow from training.

With only thirty minutes to spare, I bypass the training course for the open land. "Go," I murmur, encouraging him. He immediately bucks forward and flies. I bend low, my body aligning with his. His breaths come in quick succession, using all his energy to move faster than his body is used to.

When finally worn out, he slows down until he barely moves at a trot. My face burns from the wind whipping against it, the thirty minutes a momentary freedom from my life. I return him to his stall and then send the manager a note that I have updated the colt's training schedule and timing before heading to the hospital.

Today is Brian's half-year birthday. The thought runs through my head while I listen intently as everyone in the support group updates the others on their child's status. There are a few couples, but the rest are on their own—both mothers and fathers. The nurses gave Eric and me information about the various support groups available when Brian was first admitted.

"I received an email from the school about registration for next year." A mother, dressed in sweats and her hair haphazardly thrown into a ponytail, speaks softly. She focuses on the ground, her fingers playing with the sleeve of her sauce-stained sweatshirt. Her exhaustion and demeanor remind me of myself when Brian was first born: exhausted, mind scattered, with only one focus—keeping your child alive. "It's been six months since my daughter's diagnosis. Since she's left school." She shakes her head in anger. "A standard email sent to all families. I called them up and yelled at them for twenty minutes, and then I hung up and sobbed for hours." The woman takes a deep breath. "I hate everyone who is living a normal life. Parents who get to worry about what teacher their child is getting or birthday party they're being invited to."

"We stopped talking to our school friends two months after our son's diagnosis." A father, older than most of the other parents, shrugs in defeat. "What were we supposed to talk about? We had nothing left in common."

The therapist reassures us that these reactions are normal and similar to those of most other families in the same situation. She encourages us to continue sharing as parents wipe away their tears. As the stories continue of heartaches, confusion, and life changes, with parents sharing their fears of losing their child and fears of being unable to stop it or accept what's happening, I think about Brian in his hospital bed, his body weak and broken.

"Celine, we haven't heard from you." Every head turns toward me as the therapist welcomes me into the group. "Is there anything you'd like to share?"

When I first arrived at the prep school, I would watch the other kids with envy, anxious to be part of a group, any group. The cool group, the rich group, the kids with two parents, the kids whose mothers were able to stay home, the group of kids who talked about going away to college, and countless others. When I was rejected by them one after the other, I began to separate myself in self-defense, choosing to reject anyone before they could reject me. Now, I am being welcomed into a group I would never want to be in, and yet I fully belong.

"It's fine," I whisper, all eyes on me. Do they know that I brushed my hair this morning over a hundred times until my scalp burned, just so I could feel some pain other than the one clawing at me? Do they see the fatigue in my eyes, know that I barely eat one meal a day out of guilt because my son cannot eat, or that my mind begs for a reprieve, any escape that would allow me a minute to breathe? "I'm fine," I say again, sure that if I say it enough, like I did when I was a child, maybe this time it will come true. "Maybe later."

She smiles, but I see her disappointment, as if talking about my son's illness will help to heal it. Another woman, one who shares that her son's been fighting his cancer for a year, speaks about her other son's graduation from high school. "I didn't take pictures," she confesses. "Later, I lied to my husband and said my camera must've been broken. I think he knew the truth, but . . ." She pauses, then adds, "It just didn't feel right to celebrate."

"What happens if my child doesn't survive? Do we change support groups or remain here?"

The young mother clasps her hands together and drops them between her legs. Her hair falls in strings around her face, and red blotches cover her cheeks. I push my chair back just as the therapist starts to answer. Unable to hear it, I fumble my way through the circle, nearly tripping over a man's foot. The clock on the wall indicates thirty minutes left in the session.

"I'm sorry." I pull my phone out in support of my lie. "I just got a text. They said they needed me here. I mean there." I glance at the blank screen, as if I am rereading the text. "I have to go."

They all watch me as I pull open the door that felt so light when I entered but now requires all my weight to open. I rush through it, pulling it shut behind me. Safely on the other side, I breathe as if having just finished a marathon. The last question repeats in my head: What happens if my child doesn't survive? *Please,* I whisper silently, *please let Brian be okay. Please let him heal.*

I hear their voices behind me, trying to find their flow after my interruption. I want to go in and apologize, explain myself, but how would anyone understand my explanation? How can anyone make sense of this convoluted set of circumstances that is my life? Instead, I make my way back to Brian's room, where I find Justin waiting right outside the door.

"Justin." Unsure, I glance around, expecting to see either Eric or Felicity with him, but he's all alone. "Hi."

"Hi." Seeming embarrassed, he stumbles through an explanation. "I w-wanted to come by and say hi. To Brian. If that's okay."

I open Brian's door to see both Brian and my mom fast asleep. He clings to the stuffed animal he was attached to as a child in hopes it once again brings him the peace it used to.

Unsure of how to talk to Justin or what to say, I hesitate. "He's asleep. I'm sorry. I know he'd love to see you, but it's so hard for him to fall asleep, and I don't want to wake him . . ."

"No, it's fine," he quickly reassures me. "I'm just here to get tested, and I thought I'd stop by beforehand."

Tested. Though Eric has told me he's agreed, I don't know if I will actually believe it until it happens. But he is here, now. "Thank you so much. For being tested." I reach out, then drop my hands before they contact his arm, unsure what emotional connection is appropriate or allowed with my husband's son. His confusion at my actions seems to mirror my own. "You doing so . . . it means everything."

"Of course." He shrugs, reminding me of Brian. "I would never not do it. He's my . . ." He hesitates, worry as his eyes meet mine, afraid of having said something wrong.

Brother. The word, still so new and unreal, feels too foreign on my tongue. Instead, I say, "He's lucky to have you."

"What I said, about wishing I knew him before, I meant it." He stuffs his hands into his pockets. "It would have been cool to play soccer together."

"Yeah." I laugh at the simplicity of the image that I now would give anything for. "He'd love that." We smile at one another then, both of us bonding over the boy who connects us. "Are your parents here?" I swallow my nausea at the word *parents*, reminding myself that he is as much a victim in this as Brian and me. "For your test?"

"They don't know I'm here," he says, explaining why Eric didn't tell me as he had promised. "I'm staying at my girlfriend's house."

"Justin . . ." Similar to the other day, I see his pain and sorrow at their betrayal. "I'm sorry."

"Yeah." He points behind him. "I'd better go. The nurse said they'd be ready in a few minutes."

"Is your girlfriend here with you?" It's not my place, I remind myself. I know that and yet . . . he is here for Brian. For his brother. My son. "For during the test?"

"She has swim team practice, and I didn't want to bother her."

I start to offer to go with him, then stop, reminding myself that until recently, I was a stranger to him. That if he wanted someone here, he could have had Eric or Felicity. "If you need anything . . . ," I say instead, leaving it unspoken, the ball in his court.

He nods, then walks away, me watching his solo form all the way until he's safely encased in the elevator, a small seed of hope blooming in the dark desert of my mind.

After speaking to Justin, I left the hospital, asking the nurses to let my mom know when she awoke that I would be back later tonight. I stop by the house to pick up clothes, nearly turning around when I see Eric's car. With nothing to say, I am not ready to see Eric or speak to him in person. I don't have the mental or emotional capacity to deal with my marriage or him. The safest and only plausible answer for me right now is avoidance. But he will have seen me on the cameras, knowing that I drove by. Refusing to show vulnerability in the face of his betrayal, I park the car and prepare myself to face him. He meets me at the door, opening it to allow me to enter.

"Hi." Unlike his normal outfit of a suit, he's dressed in jeans and a henley with day-old scruff. "I didn't know you were coming home."

"I'm not," I say quickly.

Like a guest, I enter our home hesitantly, as if waiting for an invitation to proceed further. I stare at the kitchen I have meticulously put together. Next to it the family room, where we played chess the night before admitting Brian to the hospital. I chose all the furniture with Brian in mind—wanting to create a luxurious but comfortable home for him.

Memories of walking on tiptoes at my uncle and aunt's house, my aunt's eyes always watching for a foot on the coffee table or a stain on the sofa. I swore then that if I ever had children, they would know that home is where they are safe. But Brian wasn't safe at home. No matter how perfect the furnishings or the welcoming warmth, his home has failed to protect him from this disease, from his father's betrayal.

"I just came for some clothes." We stand together, the anger and adultery a mountain between us. "It'll only take me a few minutes."

"Celine," he says, his voice raw and empty. "Can we talk?"

"About?" I scoff at the idea. "The last seventeen years? Our son's cancer? What do you want to talk about, Eric?" My choked voice falls low. I still love him. I want him to take me in his arms and for all of this to be a bad dream. But Justin stands as proof of his infidelity and Felicity of his lack of integrity.

"I never wanted to hurt you."

In all our years together, I have never seen him as lost as he seems now. Though it should offer me some level of comfort that he's hurting as much as I am, it only serves to make me angry. That I have meant so little to him, when all I have ever done is love him.

"It wasn't the lie that bothered you." My mind whirls with the realization. "It was me learning that you had lied." I shake my head in disgust.

"I love you. That's why I didn't want to hurt you," he argues.

"Love me?" The word feels like a slap to my face. "When you love someone, Eric, it's painful to hurt them, regardless of whether they learn about it or not." It was how I knew my father didn't love me. And that my mother did. It's that willingness to do whatever it takes for the person, no matter how much it may hurt or the sacrifices required. "I don't know what you felt for me, but it wasn't love."

"That's not fair," he insists.

"Please, please do not talk to me about fair." Though I want to scream, my words barely come out as a whimper. "I don't want to do this. I can't."

I walk past him to our shared bedroom. Inside, the bed is unmade, clothes thrown haphazardly on the chair. It's completely out of character for him, telling me how out of sorts he is. Sympathy from our years together draws me in until I remember my own pain, and then I refuse it an audience.

I quickly throw enough clothes into a suitcase to last me a few weeks, then head back downstairs. Eric waits in the kitchen. When I start to walk out the door, he calls my name. Exhausted, I've started to tell him that I'm tired and have no interest in doing this again when he holds out a bag.

"Your tea."

Shocked, I grab the bag filled with my favorite green tea that I have before bed every night. I fell in love with it after discovering it from a trainer who shared it with me in my early twenties. Now, I special order it, a rare luxury I allow myself.

I close my eyes, blinking away the tears. If asked, I would have bet money he had no idea I enjoyed a cup most nights. It was often before he got home from work or when he was traveling.

As if he can read my thoughts, he explains, "Your cup is usually in the sink when I get home from work."

The intimate details that come from a marriage, from being together for over a decade. The particulars you stop thinking about and instead just take for granted.

"Thanks." I walk out before he can say anything else, before the pieces of my heart shatter even further, leaving nothing for me to put back together.

I jump into my car, ignoring him standing in the doorway, watching me. I peel out of the driveway without looking back and break speed limits to the farm, in hopes of outrunning my memories and the pain.

There, I drop my things off in one of the larger bedrooms before heading to the kitchen with the bag of tea in hand. I've started to boil some water when my stomach starts to churn. I turn off the stove, silencing the kettle, then drop the whole bag filled with loose tea into the garbage.

I lean against the counter, the adrenaline that carries me through each day wearing off, to be replaced with bone-deep fatigue. Anxiety starting to creep up, I search for a distraction. Brian's half-year birthday. A sudden need to celebrate it has me flinging open the cupboards in search of ingredients. Flour, eggs, milk, sugar, oil, vanilla extract, strawberries, and frosting—everything to make his favorite cake. I throw ingredients into a bowl, and then, skipping the electric mixer, whip it with a fork by hand until my arm aches. After pouring the batter into a greased pan, I put it inside the stove and set the timer.

Firing up my computer, I pass the time by catching up on work. There's a return email in response to my training schedule change for Austin's horse. I open it to read that Austin wants to discuss my changes and that I should contact him as soon as possible. I skip the email to answer dozens of others, stopping only when the stove dings. After taking the cake out of the oven, I inhale the warm vanilla fragrance, reminding me of the countless times I have made Brian a similar cake to celebrate.

I frost it and use smashed strawberry puree to spell out his name and the words *Happy Birthday*. Excited to take it to him later tonight, I begin to clean up, throwing the eggshells, empty frosting can, and flour bag into the garbage. As I reach for the sugar canister, I read *Salt* on it. No, it can't be. I open the cupboard to find the sugar canister still on the shelf. Nervous, I cut a piece, then take a bite, immediately spitting it out as the bitter taste melts onto my tongue.

I throw the paper plate with the uneaten piece into the trash can, a remnant of my failed baking day. I don't have enough ingredients to make another. I clutch the countertop, the ruined cake pushing the tears I have fought all day over the brink and onto my cheeks, a waterfall of pain, fear, and failure. I vaguely hear the knock on the back door of the kitchen, just in time to furiously wipe my face free of the tears before the door opens and Austin enters. We stare at one another.

"I got a message you were here." His words are hesitant, unsure, as his eyes mark the redness in my eyes. "I wanted to discuss your new training schedule with you."

"One of my employees told you I was here?" I ask, astounded. When did they report to him?

"I asked him to. The manager," he clarifies.

"My farm manager?"

"We talked," Austin explains. "Great guy."

Yes, he is. In fact, he's one of my most valued and loyal employees. But apparently it only goes so far when faced with Austin. "And he saw me here and just called you up?"

Austin fights a smile. "I gave him my number. In case of an emergency. With the horses."

"Of course you did," I murmur. "And the training schedule constitutes an emergency?"

"Based on your new timing, my horse should be ready to race in about"—he pulls out a sheet of paper from his back pocket—"ten years. When he's ready to be retired."

I hold out my hand for the printout of the training document I revised this morning, ready to refute his statement. A quick glance at it shows my mistake—I put the decimal in the wrong place. At the pace I had written, the horse would never run a race competitively.

"I stand by my assessment," I say, childishly refusing to concede. After the cake, I feel churlish and petty. Especially since he's stealing my farm. "The schedule stands."

"I see." He folds his arms across his chest, both of us in a standoff. "You don't want to reconsider?"

"Are you reconsidering stealing my farm?"

"Buying," he corrects. "Big difference."

"You say 'tomato' . . ."

"Everyone says 'tomato,'" he argues.

"That's debatable."

He sighs, and I get a sick pleasure out of it. "I feel like we're at an impasse."

"I don't agree."

"I see."

"You can always pull the horses." I'm testing him, wanting to see who he is today compared to the boy I knew yesterday. If he removes the horses, I'll have a clear understanding of the man he has become. And if he doesn't . . .

"Let's see how your schedule works out," he says, shocking me, warming me. "Maybe you'll be open to revising it as training progresses."

He has started to walk out when I call out to him. "Want some cake?" I slide a piece onto a paper plate and hold it out to him. "Brian made it in the hospital kitchen today," I lie. "For the employees at the farm. In celebration of his half birthday." I smile innocently at him when he takes the plate. "And since you've become so close to *my* employees, it's only fair you get a slice also. Wait." I turn on my phone video, gesturing him to eat. "I'll take a video to show Brian. Let him know we were friends as kids. It will mean so much to him, you eating it. Say hi."

"Hey, Brian." Austin waves before cutting a large bite with his fork. "Thanks for the cake, buddy." He takes the bite, and immediately his eyes water and he coughs, nearly choking on his piece.

"He'll be so happy you like it." I keep a straight face. "Once you finish your slice, I'll cut you another to take home." I continue to film as Austin finishes his piece, surprising me. He takes large gulps of water to wash it down. When his plate is clean, I offer him another slice.

"Want to save some for the others," he insists. "Wouldn't be fair if I had it all."

I put my phone camera down, barely holding in the laugh that immediately changes to horror when Austin goes to throw his plate away and spies the makings of the cake and my uneaten piece in the trash.

"I thought Brian made it at the hospital?" he asks softly before cutting a piece of cake, then taking a menacing step toward me as I back up, my eyes wide. "For the employees?"

"Is that what I said? Huh." I rush around the table as he dives for me. Holding a chair between us, I plead mercy as I fight back my laughter. "You deserved it."

"Something else we'll have to agree to disagree on." He pushes the chair aside, then backs me into the corner, holding the piece in between us like a hissing snake. "Your turn."

"No, it's disgusting." I hold my hands up in horror. "I'm sorry?"

"Too late."

"Wait." I search my mind for something to appease him but come up empty. Waiting patiently, he raises an eyebrow in question. "I have nothing."

Austin considers me, then says, "Horror movie. My choice."

"No. You used to force me to watch them every weekend." To get through them I closed my eyes, put my fingers in my ears, and rewrote the story in my head.

Austin rolls his eyes. "Once every few months does not constitute every weekend." He holds up the cake as a threat. "Pick your poison, C."

"Fine. But I don't have to watch. I'll just sit there."

"Perfect."

I move to follow him, then stop, feeling the smile on my face, hearing my laughter from moments ago. Guilt claws at me as I envision Brian lying in a hospital bed, fighting for his life.

"I shouldn't." I try to explain as Austin watches me patiently, "The movie. Laughing." I gesture toward the kitchen, where only seconds ago I had allowed myself to forget. "Brian."

Austin considers me, then says softly, "I'd never presume to tell you how to handle everything you're dealing with."

"I hear a 'but,'" I say.

"My mom used to have a painting on the wall. A Native American medicine woman's prayer: 'I will not rescue you, for you are not powerless. I will not fix you, for you are not broken.'"

"'I will not heal you, for I see you in your wholeness,'" I continue, remembering the painting and the powerful words. His face softens as I continue, "'I will walk with you through the darkness, as you remember your light.'"

The words settle inside me, a reminder that to help Brian through his darkness, I have to find a way to hold on to my own light, even if it means just taking one second of breath in between days of suffocating without oxygen.

"Yeah," I say softly, agreeing to the movie.

"Yeah?" He nods, his excitement clear. "Let's do it."

Austin leads us into the darkened living room, where I take the small chair, curling into it. He follows my lead and takes the other small chair, leaving the large sofa in between us unoccupied. Austin turns on a movie from our childhood that I didn't completely hate.

As the movie begins, he asks, "How did the meet and greet go?"

Touched he's remembered, I say, "Justin, my husband's son . . . he's not what I expected." Locked on the screen, I barely watch what's on. "He's kind. Sweet." I pause, then share, "He got tested today. The results should come back soon."

"I see."

I am grateful he doesn't offer false reassurance that they will be positive or that my son will be fine. Instead, he waits, allowing me to speak or remain silent.

"I'll review the training schedule tomorrow, maybe see if there are some changes we can make."

I hear the smile in his voice. "I appreciate it."

We continue to watch the movie until my eyes refuse to remain open. I drop my head against the arm of the sofa chair and fold my arms between my legs, promising myself only a few minutes of sleep. For the first time since all of this began, I feel a moment of calmness in the company of my old friend. When I open them next, I am settled onto the long sofa with a blanket tucked around me and my shoes off. Through a slit in the window shades, rays of sunlight peek through. I had fallen asleep last night, and Austin must have moved me to the sofa. After folding the blanket, I head to the bedroom to shower and dress so I can get back to my son in the hospital.

CHAPTER TWENTY

FELICITY

I arrive at the hospital an hour before everyone else. Eric texted me earlier to say that the results were in, and the doctor wanted to meet with us. Alone, I pace in the waiting room, watching the minutes tick by.

I spent the morning training with the rowing crew. The hours on the water offered me a reprieve from the constant barrage of thoughts on Justin and missing him. Afterward, I showered and pulled my wet hair up in a ponytail. Feeling like a far cry from my normal perfect presentation, I left for the hospital with a wet spot on the back of my shirt from the damp ends.

"I was just getting ready to call you," Eric says, joining me.

Though he's expertly dressed in jeans and a button-down, his face betrays his fatigue. We offer one another a small smile, as if strangers forced together inside this outdated room with the worn sofa and faux paintings. Though we have texted a few times about Justin, neither of us has reached out for further conversation. For all the years we have been together, this situation has us in uncharted territory and my emotions in a place of uncontrolled turmoil.

"Is Justin here?" I yearn to see my son, his smile, and hear him speak. I ache from missing him.

"I texted him about the results being in. He said he'd come straight from soccer practice."

I nod, used to his schedule being based around his athletic commitments. "Have you spoken to him? How is he?"

Eric grimaces, his response telling me nothing has changed. "I've tried." After taking a seat on the sofa, Eric focuses on the floor, his foot tapping an even rhythm. "I've texted him and called, but I only get clipped responses."

"He's still staying at Lily's." To anyone who's watching, we are two parents having a conversation about our son. Concerned about his welfare and well-being. No one would guess the guilt and fear churning inside me. "He hasn't come by the house."

"I . . ." Eric raises his head. In his face, I see my sadness and grief reflected.

"This isn't how it was supposed to go," I finally admit. "We did everything to give him a good life. To protect him."

Eric shakes his head. "We always knew the risks when we told him." He rakes two hands through his hair. "We had no choice."

I shift from my pain to his. "How is Brian?"

Eric raises his eyes toward the ceiling, blinking against the sheen of wetness. "Not good. His fever keeps spiking, so they've had to hold off on the chemo treatments."

"Eric . . ."

"Do you remember when Brian was born?" Eric drops his head and shoulders, a man defeated; his normal strength is depleted.

"You were so excited." Eric texted me a picture of Brian from the hospital with the caption that he was a miniature Justin. In his mind, it was one friend sharing his joy with another. I stared at the picture with mixed feelings, happy for my son's father while grieving what Brian's birth meant—Eric now had his own family outside of ours. "They looked exactly alike."

"I imagined them meeting hundreds of times. How it would go. Whether they would get along or not. Never did I think it would be in this situation."

"Hey." Seated next to him, I wrap his hand in mine. "Brian is going to get through this."

"What if Justin's not a match?" Eric asks, reminding me of Justin's crucial role. "What if Brian doesn't have a chance?"

Unable to promise him his son's health or life, I wrap my other hand around our clasped hands, offering him comfort however I can. It's the scene that greets Celine when she walks in. As if the screen is frozen, she stares at the two of us. A myriad of undecipherable emotions crosses her face in the silence.

Eric jumps up, dropping my hand. My fingers curl into fists, warming them from the sudden cold. I slowly rise to my feet as he takes two steps away from me to create distance. I lift my chin, refusing to react to his actions, to his desperate desire to make distance from me in front of Celine.

"I didn't mean to intrude." Her voice clipped and cold, Celine keeps the door open as if ready to escape. "The nurses said they saw you come in here." Celine speaks to Eric, avoiding my gaze.

"Celine, no." I watch in muted horror as Eric shifts to her side. "We were just talking."

A clear line of alienation drawn between Celine and me. I tell myself it's normal, that Celine is his wife, and I am . . . I am just his son's mother. He has never asked me for more, no matter how much I have wanted him to. But the logical part of my mind refuses the rationalization. Anger at Eric's desperation to soothe Celine while ignoring me starts to simmer.

"The doctor is ready to see us." Celine keeps her gaze focused on Eric.

"Justin . . . ," Eric starts.

"Justin is already in the office," Celine answers.

"Justin's here?" I step toward the door, my anxiousness to see my son bypassing everything else. Celine's eyes glance at me, but there's no surprise in her gaze or question, making me wonder if Eric has told her about Justin leaving home. I fight a sudden sense of betrayal, of him sharing my life with her, refusing to reflect on how much of her life he has shared with me.

"We walked in together from the parking lot." Celine glances between Eric and me. "His girlfriend, Lily? I think she drove him."

Lily was the conversation the night of the party. Things were easier then. The lies were still hidden and the facade felt real. But now I am in the open, an animal hunted for sport. The truth that my son has left circles around me, like a lion preparing for attack. I struggle to maintain my mask but find it impossible when it comes to Justin.

"We should go." I move toward the door.

"You're joining us?" Celine asks suddenly.

"Celine, Felicity wants to be with Justin," Eric says at the same time as I tense.

"He's my son," I say, leaving no room for argument.

"I didn't mean . . ." Celine faces me directly, her eyes devoid of the cold hatred I would have assumed would be there. It takes me aback, given that if the roles were reversed, how would I feel about her? "I'd never consider asking you not to be there for the results."

Surprised, I nod my head, my only response.

"We should go."

Eric's voice betrays his weariness. Forced to walk a tightrope between their changed circumstances, he seems to struggle for the right balance. Eric has not told me about Celine's reaction or the state of their marriage, nor have I asked. Early in our relationship, I learned that Eric only shared when he felt comfortable. For me, it always felt like a fair compromise, as long as my son received what he needed. Over the years, as the trust built, we became close enough to ask questions. But now, I fear knowing if they are going to fight for their marriage or if the truth has eroded any chance of reconciliation. If so, where will that leave us?

Celine takes the lead. Eric follows, and I, against my nature, stay a few steps behind. At the office, Eric opens the door, then holds it open for Celine, who walks in first. My eyes meet Eric's as I follow, but his expression remains blank, refusing to reveal his inner thoughts. I don't push. In front of his wife, I am forced to remain a silent partner whose stake matches theirs, but I have no standing to speak.

Inside the office, I immediately search for Justin, finding him in the far corner of the room with Lily. My gaze drinks him in. At any other time, I would have rushed toward him, but now I approach cautiously, unsure.

"Justin, honey."

Justin and Lily both look up at the same time. Lily offers a warm smile but remains quiet, deferring to Justin to steer the conversation. From his straight back to the tenseness in his jaw, I know his guard is up. I swallow when he takes a step back. He's always moved *toward* me, both of us in alignment.

"Mom." Cold, without emotion, he acknowledges me.

"How are you?" I normally would include Lily in the conversation, be polite, as expected. But now, all I can focus on is my son and the few minutes I have with him. "How is everything?"

"Everything is good."

Via my peripheral vision, I see Eric watching us as Celine watches him. Onstage, we are actors in someone else's show. My life was never meant to be this. I crave the control of my life I once had.

"Did the test go all right?" I reach for his hand, but he pulls it back. Lily, catching the reaction, shuts her eyes as she exhales. Caught between the boy she loves and the mother she hopes to impress, she's in a position I don't envy. "Are you okay?"

"I'm fine." He glances at Eric, then Celine, before returning to me. "How is Brian?"

I wonder at the shift of focus from himself to his brother. "I don't know." Willing to continue the conversation on his terms, I add, "Your dad is pretty worried."

Justin glances again at Eric, who uses the excuse to join us. Celine watches us, a circle of four where she is the outsider.

"Eric, this is Lily. Justin's girlfriend."

Eric shakes her hand as Justin watches quietly. "It's nice to meet you. Thank you for letting Justin stay at your place."

"Yeah, of course." Lily hesitates, then, showing a maturity that feels beyond her years, says, "I'm sorry about Brian. About all of this."

About taking our son away from his parents, I think. *Being Justin's safety net while destroying our family.* Though I know I should be angry or resentful, all I can feel is relief that Justin is with someone who loves him and will watch out for him.

"You didn't tell us when you were coming in to get tested," Eric says, a hint of rebuke in his voice. "Your mom or I would have been here. One of us should have known about it happening."

"Celine did," Justin says. I stare at him, hiding my shock, as I repeat his words in my head saying that he turned to her over me.

"Celine? I don't understand." I look to Eric, who, with a subtle shake of his head, confirms he has no idea of the answer. "How did she know?"

"I came to see Brian," Justin says without apology. "I ran into her then."

Eric turns slowly toward Celine. Angry, he says, "You didn't tell me you knew about Justin's test. You knew we didn't know."

Celine's steady gaze flitters toward Justin and then back to Eric. "We saw one another. He mentioned he was getting it done. *It wasn't my intention to keep any secrets.*"

A rebuke. A callout of what we have done. Any other time I would have asked why Justin didn't call me, but now I struggle with what to say. We have always stood together, him following my direction and questioning me when he disagreed. But no matter, we always knew that we had each other's backs and were always there for one another. But now, he has decided we are on opposite sides. And somewhere along the division, he has decided he can trust Celine. His mother versus the mother I betrayed. Only a week ago, I was his rock, the steadiness he relied on. Now, he told a stranger about something that was my job to know.

Justin offers Celine a genuine smile, the first one I have seen since entering the room. I breathe in and out, the delineation between her and me clear.

The first time he replaced me was in third grade, when, excited about some new friends, he rushed out of the car, forgetting about our ritual goodbye of a high five and hug. I watched him leave, a bittersweet smile on my face. From that day onward, he seemed to have forgotten about our routine, and I never pushed for it again.

"Thank you," I say to Celine before Eric can say anything. If he uses Justin as a reason for battle, he chances alienating our son even further. Justin has chosen a side. No matter Eric's agenda with Celine, I cannot allow a further chasm between Justin and us. "For being here for him."

In negotiations with companies, I learned early on that the key to winning isn't fighting for your stance but offering as many things that the other party wants as possible. It disarms them and gives them the false belief that you are on their side. Once they believed that, I would subtly but surely win my points, all the while making the other side believe they had won the negotiations. It's a skill that has helped to catapult me to the top of the corporate ladder.

I now play on those strengths to navigate this match successfully. If I show my true hand—disappointed, afraid, and betrayed—I'll chance pushing Justin further away and giving Celine ammunition. Instead, I choose to offer the other side a false belief that I am grateful and appreciative.

As expected, Justin's gaze warms, pleased. Everyone turns at the sound of the door opening and the doctor entering. His neutral expression refuses to give anything away. Still reeling from the situation with Celine, I try to refocus my attention.

"We have Justin's results."

The doctor doesn't ask questions about Justin being a half sibling or why the relationship has come to light only recently. He opens a file and reads through it quickly before motioning for everyone to take a seat.

With only three chairs in the room, two people will be left standing. Eric has pulled a chair out, his eyes on Celine, when he suddenly seems to remember me. He puts his other hand on the middle chair, taking both Celine and me in with a sweeping glance. I take the chair at the opposite end, refusing his offer. He purses his lips, recognizing the misstep.

"I'm good," Celine says, waiting for Eric to remove his hand before taking a seat.

"Justin." Eric motions toward the empty middle chair. "Why don't you sit here, son?"

Lily steps toward the wall as Justin takes a seat. Eric stands behind Justin, one hand on the back of his chair.

"What did you find?" Eric asks in the voice I am used to hearing him speak in, confident and in control. "Was Justin a match?"

"Yes and no."

My gut tightens at the noncommittal response. Eric and Celine remain visibly tense and guarded.

"Half siblings are automatically going to have a lower chance of matching because of a different parent such as, in this case, the mother. That's the bad news." The doctor leans forward, his glance taking in Justin, Celine, and Eric. "Though he doesn't have the exact number we would hope for, the good news is he has enough HLA marker matches for us to do the transplant and give Brian a fighting chance."

Eric grips Justin's chair before reaching for our son. "Thank you, Justin."

My nails dig into my palm as I wait for Justin's reaction. Justin shuts his eyes before offering Eric a quick nod, acknowledging him but refusing anything more. Eric's face falls, a sheen of tears held back. Pained, I shift my eyes, my gaze landing on Celine. Her head is dropped, breathing deeply, as if trying to find her sense of self. The sight takes me aback, this woman who only a short while ago at the party was confident and kind, now broken and barely breathing.

"Justin."

I have moved to hug my son when he turns away from me. He pushes away his chair, forcing me back as he reaches for Celine.

"Is it all right . . . ," he asks her, waiting for her response.

"Thank you," Celine murmurs, her arms immediately reaching out for my son. "Thank you so much for agreeing to be tested, for doing this." Her words begin to falter. Taller than her, Justin wraps his arms around her waist. Celine rests her chin on my son's shoulder. "Brian has a chance because of you."

"You don't have to thank me," Justin says into her hair.

I watch with growing horror as Celine continues to hold my son. Like me, Justin normally reserves physical affection for those he is closest to, avoiding it with anyone else. My gut goes into free fall at the sight of him embracing her as if they are old friends.

When they release one another, Eric takes a step toward Celine, but she silently moves back. Justin catches the movement, his face registering Celine's reaction. Similarly to when he was a child calculating an equation, he puts the pieces together. What should have been a moment of celebration and joy between Brian's parents is instead fraught with pain and betrayal. Justin glances at me and then Eric, drawing a direct line between their reaction to us.

"Justin," I try, but he ignores me as he moves toward Lily, who embraces him. I stand still, my heart feeling as if it's going to burst.

Celine shifts her attention to the doctor, asking questions about next steps and Brian's recovery chances. Eric stands a few feet from her, his focus on the answers. No matter what has happened, they stand together as parents, a family to Brian. What I no longer have.

As the conversation continues, Justin and Lily leave without saying goodbye. Eric and Celine continue to discuss what happens next with the doctor. After everything that I have done, I am the one who's easily dismissed.

"He's seventeen," I suddenly say. Eric turns toward me, a frown filling his face. I ignore him and Celine to keep my focus on the doctor. "My son would need his legal guardian's approval, right? Because he's seventeen." Eric has never legally claimed Justin as his, leaving me with complete decision-making authority.

The doctor glances at Eric in question before nodding his head. "Yes, for the procedure, he'd need approval."

"What are the dangers to him?" Understanding dawns on the doctor's face. He pulls out three folders and begins to hand them out. When he reaches Celine, I say, "She's not his mother. She doesn't need it."

"Felicity . . . ," Eric starts, but I again ignore him.

"Can you summarize the risks to my son?" I grip the folder, my knuckles turning white with the effort. "No one's spoken to me about those."

"The risks are multifold," the doctor explains. As if reading from a textbook, he says, "Donor receives injections of medication prior to the donation to increase the number of blood stem cells in the bloodstream. During the donation, blood is taken, then goes through a machine that takes out the stem cells. The blood is then returned to the donor. The outpatient procedure typically takes up to six hours to complete. Some donors go through multiple apheresis sessions, depending on how many blood stem cells are needed."

"And afterward? How long is the recovery?"

"It can take between a few days or weeks," he answers. "Anytime that amount of blood is taken, it's going to be hard on the body."

"He wants to play soccer professionally," I say.

"What?" Eric stares at me with shock and disgust. In all the years we have been together, I have never seen him so angry. "That has nothing to do with this, Felicity."

"It has everything to do with this." I clutch the manila-colored folder. Plain and inconsequential to mask the severity of the situation. "Justin's future matters. It's my job to guarantee it."

Celine flinches, but I refuse to stop. I speak to the critical information in the documents. Emotional trauma, psychological responsibility, uncertainty of success. All of it a burden on Justin when he's just starting his life.

"I need to consider everything before I approve this." I grab a card off the doctor's desk. "I'll be in touch."

I walk out, barely surprised when Eric follows me into the hallway. "What are you doing?"

"Protecting my son," I say, meeting his gaze without flinching.

"He's a match, Felicity. He can save Brian."

"And who saves Justin, hmm?" I lower my voice when two doctors walk by. "He didn't ask for this. He doesn't even know Brian, and we are now telling him he is responsible for saving his life?"

"He's his brother."

"A fact that didn't matter all this time." The scene in the office claws at me until all I can feel is hurt and betrayal. "Now, suddenly it's the foundation for Justin giving up everything I've sacrificed to give him."

"Sacrificed?" Eric reaches out, but I step back. "Felicity, what's going on?"

My son chose her over me. I will no longer be the woman in the background, dismissed, seen as expendable.

"Nothing." A fluorescent light above begins to flicker, a buzzing sound as it struggles to stay on. "I need to go."

"What about Justin?" Eric moves in front of me, halting my escape.

"I need to think."

Without promising anything more, I leave him, feeling his stare the entire way. I have started down the hallway toward the elevator when I spot Elena coming from the other way. I consider ignoring her or pretending I didn't see her when she offers a small wave—surprising, given we have met only once before and have never spoken.

"Felicity, right?" she says softly, approaching me. "Elena."

I wonder at the social norms demanded by the situation, wanting to walk past her and pretend I didn't hear. "How is Brian?"

"I wish I could say he's better, but . . ." Elena pauses, then stops before visibly inhaling. "Any updates from the doctor?"

"We're in the process of getting more information," I say, fudging the truth.

"I've only met him briefly, but Justin seems like a wonderful young man."

"Thank you." I want to leave the conversation, to ignore this woman whose pain and fear for her grandchild fill the space between us. "I should go . . ."

"Celine's father left when she was six," Elena interrupts. Her voice, quiet and unassuming, conceals a steely demeanor. "Packed his bags, and we never saw him again."

Shocked by the information, I wonder why Eric never mentioned it to me.

"As a mother, all I could think of was how to protect my child. To make sure, with everything happening, that she was safe and taken care of."

I don't want to hear about Celine's childhood or her struggles. I don't want to think about the woman I betrayed as anything but a body, a person who has gotten to love and be married to Justin's father.

"I imagine you felt the same with Justin."

"Yes." My spine straightens, bringing me to my full height. "He's always been my main priority."

"A child knows when they're loved," Elena says. "It explains why he is who he is." She leans against the pillar, seeking support. "As a mother, when our back is against the wall, we will do anything to protect our child." Elena looks me right in the eyes. "You did what you had to do. But now, allowing Justin to be tested, you're stepping forward to protect my grandson. I won't forget this."

I stare at her, taken aback. It was the last thing I expected when the conversation began. But it also drives home that these are real people, with real emotions and events in their lives. Elena's pass on the past offers the necessary relief from guilt or responsibility. I nod, accepting her gratitude. But a small voice inside my head balks at the idea. I say my goodbyes, the ghosts of my choices fast on my heels.

Inside the elevator, I grip the railing as it fills up with people. A few men offer me an admiring glance, while women look to me with envy. I have become used to the reactions since college. My height and natural beauty have always demanded attention. But it was my brain that became the obstacle. Every relationship ended up in a contest, a battle of wills of who was stronger, smarter, more successful. I would search for a partner I'd imagined I could find but would repeatedly come up empty.

Eric offered me a safe alternative. A relationship where, because of Justin, he was bound to me by our child. Our secret became the glue that connected us. Eric and me against everyone else. He was mine by circumstance.

Elena's words become a drumbeat in my head as more people fill the already-crowded elevator. Suddenly desperate for air to breathe, I push myself into the corner until no part of my body touches another. I glance at their faces individually, the different shapes, colors, age lines, all of it coming together to create a person. A person with a life, with a history and a personality. When did I stop seeing them individually and instead viewing them as a whole? When did I tire of connecting and instead find comfort in my solitude?

The doors slide open, and I follow the crowd out. As I reach my car, anxiety overwhelms me. I repeat Elena's words in my mind—I have protected Justin; everything has been for Justin; I am the lioness for my son. I grip the steering wheel as the truth rears its ugly head. I haven't protected him. Instead, I am fighting for my son while the man I love is fighting for his.

I pick up the phone and search for the number. I hit dial and wait. When the recruiter answers, I hesitate for a breath, but I must do this for Justin. Take him away from this situation.

"I'm following up on the CFO position in California. I'm interested in pursuing it."

CHAPTER TWENTY-ONE

CELINE

I barely slept at night, tossing and turning until the sun came up. My every thought was on Brian, Justin, and the transplant. I want to scream at Felicity, to demand that after everything she and Eric have done, Justin's donating shouldn't even be a question. She and Eric destroyed my family; saving my son should be the first step in her bid for forgiveness.

But, a small voice says, *if she's not seeking forgiveness, then I don't matter. Brian doesn't matter.*

Karma is irrelevant to someone who believes they are impervious to life's scales of justice. Or, as I know intimately from my father, sometimes the pain caused to another is justified by the gain achieved personally.

I arrive to Brian's room in the morning, earlier than usual. My mom, preferring the night shifts, has already left for the day with a promise to return later. Eric arrives at various times, trying to spend as much time as possible. The three of us rotating, cogs in a wheel critical for it to run smoothly.

With barely any overlap between us, Mom and I haven't had a chance to speak about Eric or Justin since the initial meeting. Though we exchange texts about Brian, she either seems to understand that I'm still trying to process what happened, or she also needs time. She and Eric have always been close. He didn't just lie to Brian and me; he lied to her too.

"Hi, honey." I kiss Brian's forehead. "Did you sleep well?" I already know from the nurses that his night was fitful and restless.

"I want to go home." In a burst of anger, Brian pulls on his IV tube. I gently grasp his fingers, trying to keep them from doing damage. Too weak to fight me, he lets them fall to the side. "Now."

"Brian, honey, have a few bites to eat." Shifting the breakfast tray close, I hope the smell of pancakes and whipped cream will entice him. "It will make you feel better."

"No, it won't." He grabs the open applesauce container and throws it across the room, droplets spraying everywhere. "I hate it here."

Eric walks in just as Brian pushes the food plate off the tray. It clatters to the ground, syrup dripping onto the sheet as strawberry pieces fall in a perfect circle onto the floor.

"I want to go home." Furious, Brian searches for an outlet for his anger. With nothing left to throw, he pulls at his tubes again, succeeding in pulling out his IV. Drops of blood splatter onto my face. "I want to go home," he repeats, my heart breaking as his anger shifts to pleading. "Please."

Eric immediately takes a seat on the other side of him. "Ace, we can't go home yet," he says softly.

"Please, Dad," Brian begs. "I don't like it here."

Brian falls into Eric's chest. He wraps an arm around our son as I stifle my sob, clutching the sheet around Brian like a lifeline. I meet my husband's eyes over our son's head, our pain flowing between us, washing away the past to bind us in the present.

Eric reaches for my hand, gently untangling it from the sheet to cradle it. I hesitate briefly before succumbing to his strength and comfort, gripping his fingers. My other hand drops to the back of Brian's head as he sobs into Eric's chest. Together we hold our son and each other.

I am reminded of a time when I was in Cape Cod with my parents. As they walked hand in hand along the cliffside, I jumped onto the concrete barrier separating the walkway from the ocean below. Balanced on a small sliver of stone, I threw my hands out in a careful dance of danger and adventure. One wrong step, and I would have either toppled down the rocky cliff into the rushing water or fallen back into the safety of my parents' arms. Brian is on a similar barrier. Eric and I—our family—must be the foundation for Brian to safely fall on. Without it, I fear he will plummet down the cliff and be lost forever.

After a nurse comes in to reinsert his IV, Brian finally succumbs to sleep against Eric's chest an hour later. During that time, we keep holding him and each other, becoming one another's lifeboat. Eric gently lays him back down on the pillow as if he were a newborn, the front of his shirt soaked with Brian's tears. We work in tandem as I lower the blinds and Eric cleans the spilled food.

"Have you spoken to her?" I fight to temper my anger at him as it returns full force, his lies and betrayal like fingernails on the vision board of our life.

I stand by the window, staring out at the garden below. The colorful arrays of flowers sway in the light wind, offering false comfort and beauty, a stark contrast to the darkness and despair inside the hospital room.

"She's not answering my calls." Eric joins me, his height towering over me, casting a shadow in the darkened room.

"Justin is our only hope." I barely hear my own words over the anguish. The momentary connection between us slowly dissipates as Justin and Felicity return to be the focus of our conversation, woven into my every thought alongside Brian. I vacillate between gratitude that there's a chance for our son to survive and grief for the reason why. "What do you think she's going to do?"

I read through the folder that Felicity insisted I did not need. It was a trove of information, detailing everything Justin would go through in his attempt to save Brian's life. Every word, every detail, put me on a seesaw of guilt and gratitude. Justin would not go unscathed for his actions. There are risks to him, both emotional and physical. We are asking him to jump into the deepest part of the ocean without a life raft for a boy he had never met before until recently. After reading through it, I was ashamed for not having considered him before. And yet, even now, I cannot compare the risk to him to the reality of losing Brian.

"I don't know," Eric admits.

"How would the two of you talk . . . before, with Justin?" I stumble over asking him how they have co-parented their son. Another time, another circumstance, I would not be speaking with Eric, let alone talking about his parenting with another woman about another son. Now, I delve into his life to save mine. "Make decisions about him?"

With Eric's travel schedule, I was Brian's primary caretaker, his decision-maker. I struggle to recall if Eric ever disagreed with my decisions. Or, more likely, he was simply too involved with caring for one son to have time to be invested in the other.

"We would discuss them beforehand in detail and then move forward," Eric says hesitantly, seemingly aware of the contrast between the interactions he's detailing compared to our life. "Felicity respected that I wanted to be active in Justin's life, so she acted accordingly."

I swallow the disgust at the image his words conjure, wondering where his respect for me fits in. He and Felicity are a married couple without ever having taken their vows. Trying hard to force my mind off the implications of his words and back to the present, I imagine I'm counseling a friend. It's the only way I can save myself from the dark hole of lies and betrayal.

"Talk to her. She's scared. He's her son."

"What would you do?" Eric asks suddenly, surprising me. "If the roles were reversed?"

A decision between my son versus hers . . . If I had not met Justin, if he was just a name without a face, a person without a personality, another boy instead of my son's brother, I don't know if I would choose a stranger over my son.

"I'd weigh the possible danger to Brian against what he was helping to solve."

In the twelve years I have been a mother, I have learned things about myself I never imagined—the need to research every option, every possibility, when it comes to Brian. Schools, sports, friends. A constant need to mitigate any harm to him, to protect him, to love him. Just as Felicity is doing for Justin. Because he is mine, as Justin is Felicity's.

"I'd hope that I'd make the right decision." My voice is softer, less sure, as the realization hits me that Felicity may be more her son's savior than my son's enemy.

"Hope?" Eric pushes.

"I don't know Justin. How do I chance my son for hers?"

Eric stares out at the flowers, his silence telling me what I already know—that the question deserves an answer. That Felicity deserves to be heard.

"But my choice doesn't matter. Yours does. She's going to question which son you're putting ahead of the other."

Eric flinches. "That's not what this is about."

"It's what the last seventeen years have been about." My anger finally spills over. I can no longer play the part of a friend or neutral observer. Brian is my son, and Eric betrayed us both. "You've put Justin ahead of Brian with every action."

"He had me part time," Eric argues.

"Justin had you when it counted," I correct, reminding him of the missed games, school events, weeknights. "Brian never did." The times together I believed so special now feel tainted, blackened by a truth I never would have conceived and still struggle to—that my husband has another family, that our entire life is a farce. "She's going to want that again. When it counts, she wants to know you have her son's back."

Tired of the conversation and scared of what it means for Brian, I'm starting to shut down when Eric says, "If Justin wishes to move forward, then I'm going to talk to a lawyer."

I stare at him, shocked not only by his words but by the implication. He plans to battle Felicity, the woman he calls his family. His son's mother. She might never forgive him, and Justin would be forced to take sides between his parents.

"Justin doesn't deserve that."

He asked me what I would do if the roles were reversed, but his plan of action tells me the only thing that really matters are the boys and their reactions. In a battle between Eric and me, Brian loses. In a battle between Felicity and Eric, Justin cannot win.

"I know." Eric turns around to stare at a sleeping Brian. "But I can't let her decision be the deciding factor for Brian." He sighs, his hands gripping the back of the visitors' chair. "I'll speak to the doctor about preparing Brian for the transplant. We need him to be ready."

"It seems you've already made your decision."

"Brian is my son. I know with everything that's happened, you don't believe me . . ." He hesitates. "I've always loved Brian." His words resolute and without apology: "But I love Justin too."

"Then tell her that." His words reach the mother in me, and I can only plead silently that they reach the mother in Felicity. "Let her know you're not choosing one son over the other. Let her know that if the roles were reversed, you would ask the same of me."

I am at the mercy of the woman who slept with my husband. I have no hand to play, dependent on others' decisions. But this time, unlike with my father, I understand the architect's plans and purpose. My father failed as a parent, whereas Felicity might be fighting to succeed as one.

He nods and is starting to leave when my mother walks in. Eric flinches, then briefly shuts his eyes in regret as he and my mom take one another in. She glances into the room, her eyes automatically softening when they fall on Brian still sleeping, then shift toward me before returning to Eric.

"Elena . . . ," he starts, then pauses. "I know we haven't had a chance to talk since—"

"Your son, Justin, he seems like a good boy," she says.

Eric exhales. "Yes, he is."

"They deserve to have been brothers from the beginning." On Eric's quiet agreement, she says, "Then let's pray they have the chance in the future."

She holds out her arms, waiting patiently as Eric swallows his emotions before stepping into her embrace. Unable to watch, I shift my gaze as my mother offers my husband a forgiveness I cannot. Only when I hear the door open and Eric leave do I face her, the question clear in my eyes. Weary and worn, she smiles at me softly.

"In a choice between you and Eric, I choose Brian." With the wisdom of a woman who has walked this path before, she adds, "In a choice between hating your father for leaving and missing your father desperately enough to want him back, I only had one option—loving you."

Her words settle inside me as she takes a seat next to her grandson and, with his tired hand in her frail one, she holds him tight.

I arrive at the farm, remaining in my idle car until my mind feels calm enough to walk out. I had fully expected Eric to tell me that Felicity had agreed to the transplant, that she understood that Brian's life was at stake. That her refusal was a temporary moment and that she had seen the error of her ways. I was sure that after everything she had done, Felicity would not seek to hurt my family any further.

But instead, she is holding back the very thing that could save Brian. Though I tried to remain calm in front of Eric earlier, refusing to show him my desperation, now, alone, I feel like I am about to break.

Out of the barn, I spy a trainer bringing only one horse out. I quickly make my way toward him. "Where are the other horses?"

I'm embarrassed to not have the main training schedule memorized as I once would have. With Brian's illness, I have dropped the ball on my job and my commitment to the farm. Though Kaitlyn has insisted that she can handle the extra load, I know her plate is already full.

"Already in the field."

On his concerned look, I question, "What's going on?"

"The new trainer took Recluse out. They should have been back by now . . ."

I don't wait for him to finish. I grab the horse he's saddled and mount him, taking the reins. Ignoring his concern, I urge the horse forward, feeling his strength. Beneath it, a trace of violence. Horses are wild animals. I have often wondered at the intelligence in keeping them in captivity, raised and trained to race for man's pleasure. A horse like Recluse, one whose natural instincts battle against his breeding, forces the question of whether he's a spirit broken or one who believes in his right to freedom.

Feeling a sudden need to set him free, and with it, myself, I lean over the horse's back, aligning myself with his body. A quick tap of my legs in the stirrups against his side grants him permission to increase his pace. The horse responds immediately, his strides longer and faster. Soon, we are flying through the field, me gripping the reins as I cede control to the animal. We continue to ride, the horse seeming to get angrier with each step forward. As if he recognizes his limitations in captivity and now demands his freedom.

I shift in my saddle, holding on as my grip tightens. I direct us toward the open field, where I imagine that the young trainer, still learning, may have taken Recluse. I'm careful as I shift the horse while increasing his speed. From all my years riding, I'm confident in my ability to control the horse, yet I know that if I push too hard, I chance him rearing up and potentially throwing me off.

I spot a radio on the ground at the same time I see Recluse in the distance with the new trainer atop him. Via my radio, I send a quick message for assistance, along with my location. As I make my way toward Recluse, Kaitlyn rides up alongside me.

"I'm going to slow down, hope he reacts," Kaitlyn yells, planning to keep pace with Recluse.

Though her plan is dangerous, her maneuver makes sense. When Brian was young, his heart rate used to increase whenever he cried. Our pediatrician recommended that we offer him skin-to-skin contact, his chest against mine, to help lower his rate. The idea is the same—Recluse will calm down at the sight of the other horse doing so.

The trainer, his fear palpable, exhales as we ride alongside them. My breath held, I wait for Recluse to respond after Kaitlyn has slowed her speed. Nothing. Frustrated, Kaitlyn increases her speed to move past him in hopes that Recluse will lose momentum and either turn or slow down so the trainer can regain control. A dangerous maneuver, it could easily backfire. Recluse could rear up and throw the trainer off, or worse, it could ram into Kaitlyn's horse, causing one or both to buckle.

"No," I yell, refusing to allow Kaitlyn to risk her life.

"It's the only chance we have." Ignoring my directive, Kaitlyn moves in the direct path of them. Recluse neighs in protest before shifting away from Kaitlyn but still maintaining his speed. "Let's corner him," Kaitlyn yells, hoping we can box him in.

We both ride hard as we keep pace with one another. Once past Recluse, we shift together to move in front of him. I barely hold on to my reins as Recluse rears up on his hind legs in fury and distress. Kaitlyn jumps off her horse, grabbing Recluse's reins. Sweat pouring down her head, she battles Recluse's natural instincts, refusing to give quarter. Finally, just as I fear the hold may be lost, Recluse returns to all four legs as he breathes heavily through his nose. Kaitlyn, hands on her hips, assesses the horse, then the trainer and me as I dismount to join her.

"Celine, he's not the horses my dad worked with," Kaitlyn says, her voice tight. "He was born with this temperament." Dangerous, his demeanor has defied training. "What just happened? Never should have." Kaitlyn lowers her voice, a warning in her words. "We need to reconsider his place here."

Without the funding from Recluse's training, we have lost even a fighting chance at being able to buy the farm before our lease is up. Even Austin's horses won't make up for it.

Sad and resigned, I accept what cannot be changed. "We need to call the owner."

"I'll do it tomorrow," Kaitlyn promises. "Celine, I'm sorry."

I watch her and the trainer walk Recluse back to the stalls. The last few months mix with the years prior, picking at me like a scab torn open.

My mom's worry when my father left. I had always been a joy to my parents and then, in one day, became a burden for my mother. Willing to do anything, she cleaned toilets, picked up scraps of food off the floor for people too important to do it themselves, worked any job that would allow her to provide for me.

In school, I was treated as less than dirt because we didn't have the money the others did. And now my marriage is in shambles, while the woman who cheated with my husband is refusing to allow her son to save Brian. Brian could die because Felicity decides it. I barely have the energy to consider the farm and Greg's decision to sell it, refusing me the opportunity to get the necessary cash.

My life is in shambles, every corner cast in darkness. I glance toward the sky, at the sun that peeks out from behind the clouds, and wonder if I will ever again see its light or be forever cast in shadows.

CHAPTER
TWENTY-TWO

FELICITY

I open the door to Eric, having expected him after repeatedly ignoring his calls and texts. I have needed a few days to process my thoughts after what happened at the doctor's office.

"We need to talk." Eric moves past me into the foyer. "You can't avoid the conversation, Felicity."

This is the version of him I rarely see, a man who demands what he wants without concern for anyone or anything else. He has always accomplished his goals with steely reserve and makes clear that he won't leave the room without the results he wants.

I shut the door slowly, taking a few seconds to gather my wits. Ever since the pregnancy, we have been on the same side. Few, if any, compromises have been required, given we have both had the same agenda: to raise Justin with as much love as possible without anyone learning the truth.

Now, we are on opposite sides. He wants to save one son, no matter the cost to his other one. I need to protect Justin and will, regardless of Eric. I draw on my own power, taking a deep breath to prepare for the ensuing battle.

"I'm not willing to take the risk to Justin."

One of his eyebrows shoots up in question and disbelief. "The risk is low and temporary."

He takes a seat, forcing me to either join him or stand towering over him. Refusing to do either, I pull forward a chair, keeping us on opposite ends of the room.

"He's seventeen. What if it doesn't work? What if Justin fails to save him? Or, as I mentioned before, how much of a toll will it take on his body? He has scouts looking at him right now." I know that all the arguments pale in comparison to saving Brian, but I cannot choose Brian over Justin. Not when I have been doing that for all of Justin's life. "If it doesn't work, the sacrifice will have been too high."

"And if it does work?" Eric demands. "What are the results then? Brian and Justin have one another. They have a future together."

"A future that you've cared nothing about for all these years," I return. "The future you've purposefully and methodically kept from them."

"That was different," Eric says. "I was trying to protect you and him."

"Protect us from what?" I dismiss his rationalization with a wave of my hand. "From Celine leaving you? From Brian hating you for having cheated on his mother? What were you protecting us from, Eric?"

We stare at one another, the truth we have never spoken before tumbling out. I look away, the fight draining from me. I yearn for the time in Chicago when we were safe, when Justin and I were in our own cocoon, away from the drama and repercussions.

"I was protecting Justin from learning the truth about his parents' mistake." Eric heads to the door. "Either agree to Justin donating or you'll hear from my lawyer."

He walks out, leaving me staring after him.

CHAPTER TWENTY-THREE

CELINE

My nights turn to days, with little sleep in between. From Eric, I know that Felicity still hasn't agreed. That even under the pressure of a legal proceeding, she has refused to break. Helpless to do anything but wait, I wonder how to get through each day. To find hope in the midst of heartbreak.

My phone pings with a text from Justin, asking if he can visit Brian. From Eric, I know that Justin has no idea about Felicity's decision. He's under the impression that things are moving forward, and we are simply waiting to hear from the doctor.

I hesitate, afraid of getting involved between Justin and his parents. But then I remember how much Brian enjoyed seeing Justin. The boys deserve to spend time together. They are the ones who share blood; their rights trump everyone else's. Eric and Felicity kept them apart. I refuse to do so. I text him back, agreeing to meet him at the hospital.

After I arrive, I find Brian fiddling with his phone, his breath ragged. We were warned that the procedure to prepare him for the transplant would be hard on his body. Without it, his body could reject the transplant and attack his cells, which in turn would attack him.

"Hey, sweetheart." I run a hand over his bald head, yearning for the days when his hair fell over his eyes and past his neck, and I would insist he get it cut. Forcing a smile, I push down the despair and agony. "Guess who's coming to visit?"

I have stopped asking him how he's feeling. The answer, always the same, a grimace and "Not good." As hard as it is for me to hear, I know it's harder for him to admit. In moments when he doesn't think I'm watching, I catch him staring longingly at his cleats and jersey, their place on the windowsill unchanged. When I went to remove them one time, to hide them from Brian's view so as not to torture him with what he couldn't have, my mom laid her hand gently over mine, telling me that they didn't cause Brian to despair but instead gave him hope. Without that, she insisted, he would be lost. I'd acquiesced and left them there as a reminder of what Brian once was and hoped he would be again.

"I don't know."

Brian barely summons the strength to respond. I force a smile, a daily act of pretending everything is perfect.

"Justin. You seemed to really enjoy hanging out with him." Brian's face lights up with the largest smile I have seen in a while. Surprised by it, I ask, "You're excited?"

"He was really nice." As Brian struggles to sit up, I immediately raise the bed and hold his back as he scoots up. "Why is he coming back?"

Hesitant to tell him the truth, any part of it—that Justin is his brother, that he's a match, a possible answer to Brian getting better—for fear of giving him false hope, I demur. A legal battle against Felicity could take time, and there's no guarantee Eric will win. After everything, the despair and then the possibility, Justin could be the answer and yet never become the solution.

"He wants to talk soccer with you." I hope the answer is enough, at least for now. There will come a time when we have to decide how much more to tell Brian, but right now, with everything going on between Felicity and the transplant, I don't have the fortitude to say more. "To hang out. Is that okay?"

"Yeah." Brian looks around, as if searching for something. "What can we do?" Brian asks, his gaze landing on the stack of untouched board games and unread books that have failed to hold his interest.

A wave of dizziness, regret, and agony. The things I have taken for granted have shifted to shards of glass stuck inside my skin, drawing a steady stream of blood. It was his ritual anytime someone came over to put together all the activities that they would play. Like his father, he always wanted to entertain his guests, making sure no one ever felt bored in his company. It's a trait I am so thankful Brian inherited, sure it will serve him in the future.

"Justin is coming to spend time with you, honey." His bedsheet falls to the side, his legs with bones protruding coming into view. "He doesn't need to be entertained."

"But I want him to come back."

My son, whom I have fought to give a childhood that's the exact opposite of mine, has fallen instead into the very hole I lived in—at the mercy of someone else, to whomever is willing to take the time to come visit him. Unlike at home, he is without choices or options. His friends and playmates are no longer his preference but instead those who look beyond his illness to remember the boy he once was.

Grateful for a knock and then Justin entering, saving me from having to formulate a response, I welcome him warmly. He offers me a small wave, then a fist bump to Brian. "Hey, man. Great to see you again."

"Thanks for coming." Brian, drawing on adrenaline, speaks quickly: "We can play a game or a video game. I can show you the kids' room down the hall if you want."

A room filled with activities for the children in hopes of taking their minds off their illness, even temporarily. Though Brian has only attended one or two organized events, he now stuns me as he describes in detail all the things they can do together there.

"We can just hang out here for a while, and then, if you're up for it, we can go check it out?" Justin offers softly, seeming to understand that Brian is fighting his fatigue to make the offer.

Brian nods enthusiastically, and I marvel at Justin's empathy and kindness toward the brother he has just met. It's another reminder to me that the husband who betrayed me and the woman who stole my life are the same ones who created this young man I am coming to admire. Justin is Eric's son, as is Brian. The same traits that I am grateful Brian has inherited from his father are evident in Justin. Both kind and caring humans. The parts of Eric I once fell in love with.

"How long have you been playing soccer?" Justin asks.

"Since I was four."

Brian launches into stories about how he hated the game when he was little, but Eric was patient in teaching him. I watch Justin, wondering at his reaction to hearing stories about his father. I hate myself for wanting to know if his stories are the same or if Eric was a different father for his different families.

"How long have you played soccer?" Brian asks.

"Since I was a kid," Justin answers. "My dad taught me."

My eyes meet Justin's, the simple statement drawing me in. He swallows, then looks down before returning his gaze to Brian. As they continue to share stories, I struggle to differentiate them. Eric played with both of them in the backyard, showing them his favorite moves and helping them to master theirs.

Their favorite foods are nearly identical—macaroni and cheese and thick-crust pizza with pepperoni and mushrooms. Justin hates winter storms, and Brian admits to fearing thunderstorms. Each comment a connection that further cements their relationship. If they weren't already brothers, I imagine one day they would have been friends.

I wish Eric and Felicity could see them now. The secret they have worked so hard to keep was for themselves, not the boys. They have lost years together, memories that will never be made. All of it for a marriage that's built on lies, my love for him irrelevant.

"You want to see something funny?" Justin pulls out his phone and shows Brian a picture of himself face down in the mud. "I fell going for the ball." He moves to another picture with his face covered in mud. "The field was wet." Justin joins Brian's laugh, his joy contagious. "Can I see pictures of you playing?"

I immediately hand over my phone, starting the album from when Brian was young. Both brothers touch heads as they look through the pictures, during a time when my son wasn't ill. When, if not for the age difference, he and Justin could be the same person. When a picture comes up of Eric covered in seaweed from a mishap in the ocean, the boys begin to laugh.

"Dad looks like an ocean monster," Justin laughs.

I tense at the same time Justin freezes, realizing his mistake. Justin looks to me, his face ashen, as Brian stares at him confused. "'Dad'? You mean 'my dad'?"

I wait, unable to make the decision for him. In his fear, I see a child, only a few years older than Brian. He could easily be my son, and if so, I would never ask him to lie for someone else. I'm starting to reassure him, tell him this burden is not his to carry, that he has the right to claim Eric as his father, when he makes his own decision.

"Sorry, man," Justin says slowly, his words hesitant, breaking my heart as he starts to forsake his rightful claim on his father to maintain the lie that Felicity and Eric have started. Memories from my own lost relationship with my father bubble up, reminding me of my pain, similar to Justin's. Unsure of what is the right thing to do, I start to stop him, questioning if another wrong will make any of this right. Before I can say anything, he adds softly, "I meant your dad."

Brian nods, accepting Justin's lie as the only thing that makes sense. I long to convey my sorrow and an apology for the position he's in but remain silent. Brian continues to show pictures and share backstories as Justin listens respectfully. As the last picture comes up, the game before the diagnosis, Brian hands back the phone and lays his head on the pillow.

"I wish I wasn't sick."

I shake as I fight the urge to rush toward him, scoop him in my arms, and offer false words of bravado. To beg Justin to convince his mother to save my son. *Please,* I think, the word repeating like a mantra, *please.*

"I'm sorry you are," Justin says.

"Yeah," Brian says, his voice dropping. "Me too."

A nurse knocks on the door, then pops her head in. "There's a video game contest starting in the kids' room if you're interested. It's supposed to be a lot of fun." She winks at me, then smiles encouragingly at Brian, who lights up; then his face falls.

"I'm not sure I can play like . . ." *Before.* Everything is now measured from before and after his illness. Our new scale, one where Lady Justice does not decide what is fair or isn't, but instead remains blind to the crime of cancer.

"Could I be your partner?" Justin asks, acting as if he hadn't understood Brian's implication. My heart melts more for my husband's son, amazed at the young man he is. "That would be really cool."

"Yeah." Brian's excitement renders me relieved and sad simultaneously. It's my new normal, joy at the small steps but sadness for the times I wouldn't have given a second thought to. "That would be great."

After getting Brian settled into his wheelchair, we make our way down the hall. A few of the nurses give Brian a thumbs-up, happy to see him out and about. They have explained how important it is for Brian to stay as active and engaged as possible during the treatments to increase his endorphins and activate his system's natural immune system. But as the days wear on and the treatments take their toll on Brian's body, he has started to lose interest in almost everything.

Inside the game room, Brian introduces Justin around like a trophy, so proud to have a cool older kid as his friend. I watch with the other parents as the children play one another, the video game competition allowing them to forget, just for a while, the disease that's ravaging their bodies. It gives them the freedom to pretend that they are still like every other child. That they are normal—a word that once might have been considered an insult but now feels like a gift.

Brian laughs as he and Justin joke with one another while they play the game. Some of the other kids have teammates also—siblings, friends, family. A village of support. Brian's thrill at having Justin as a friend makes me want to tell him that he's his brother. Though he might feel angry and betrayed, as I did, I imagine the happiness of knowing Justin is his brother, his forever, would overshadow the rest.

"Mom, we came in fifth place!" Brian announces, excited by the accomplishment.

As I congratulate them, I push back the memories of him fighting for a first-place trophy or feeling defeated if he didn't succeed. Since the illness, I haven't thought past to him healing. Now, with him and Justin together, the possibility feels real. Though I know the illness will change him, impossible for him to remain the same, with every part of me I pray he will remain whole.

On the way back to the room, Brian shuts his eyes, the day's events exhausting him. Justin mentions he should head out after thanking Brian for a fun day. After making sure Brian's settled, I follow Justin out.

"Thank you for coming. For spending time with him." I don't tell him it's the first time he's participated in the games or smiled for more than five minutes. "I think you made his week. Again."

"Could I come again? Maybe later this week?" Justin stares at his shoes. "He's sick and I know the transplant could save him, but . . ."

If it doesn't. Our life seems to have become a series of unfinished sentences, of thoughts too frightening to be spoken. I wonder if other families find themselves in similar circumstances, if their new shorthand is refusing to say the worst while pretending to believe in the best.

"You're his brother." As Justin's eyes widen at my acknowledgment, I am ashamed for not saying it more. For not admitting that I'm not the only one betrayed and hurt. Justin has already lost the chance to be a big brother to Brian, and now, at seventeen years old, he's desperately trying to make up for lost time while also trying to save his life. "Anytime. He would love it if you were here every day."

"Yeah?" Justin smiles. "I have practice tomorrow, but maybe I can come by after? If Brian is up for it?"

"That would be wonderful. If I'm not here, then Brian's grandma will be. You met her the first day."

"She was nice." Justin fiddles with his car keys. "Grandpa and Grandma must have loved Brian." Confused, I am about to ask who he means when Justin adds, "Dad used to say they always wanted more grandkids."

Eric's parents. I lean against the door for support. Eric's parents knew about his betrayal. They had met Justin, knew he was their grandson. All the times we had seen one another before their deaths, they had lied to my face, kept their son's betrayal a secret. I clasp my hands together, trying to stay steady in front of Justin.

"They were very lucky to have you." Justin, a child himself, cannot comprehend the extent of his father's damage. "They must have loved you very much."

"I saw them at Dad's apartment when we visited Boston," Justin murmurs, his gaze shifting to the door of Brian's room. "They would play with me for hours, when Dad had to leave for . . ." He pauses, his eyes widening as if he just realizes something. "I thought it was work, but I guess Dad was leaving to see you and Brian." He exhales, then adds, "I think about what it would have been like if Brian and I had hung out then."

An apartment. That's how Eric has kept his life hidden from me. A mountain of lies and betrayals. If not for my entire focus and energy on Brian's illness, I fear I would topple beneath the weight of them.

"Brian . . . he's so lucky to have you." No matter Eric's actions, Justin must know how fortunate Brian is.

Clearly embarrassed, Justin smiles. "I'd better go. I'm supposed to meet Lily."

As he makes his way to the elevator, two teenage girls glance at him admiringly. Justin, focused on the elevator, seems oblivious. When Eric and I first met, I stopped counting the times women would hit on him, and yet he never looked at them. I counted myself fortunate. Now, I want to laugh at the truth—he didn't look at another woman because he already had a life with one. And an apartment to make them a home.

I pull up a number from my contacts and dial. Austin picks up on the first ring. On his hello, I hesitate. "I'm probably bothering you."

"Not at all," Austin promises me, his surprise at my call clear. "Everything okay?"

"Are you free tonight to meet at the farm?"

I tell him what I am thinking and wait for him to tell me that it's silly or won't work. Or that he's busy . . . too busy for the friendship that once meant everything to me. Just as he had once meant everything to me. He says none of those things, instead agreeing to meet me at the farm later. Afterward, I call Kaitlyn, who does the same. Desperate to do something, to find some way of processing every revelation, every duplicity, I wonder if I'm finding false comfort in my plan of action or if I'm finally taking control of my life.

After arriving at the farm, I walk to my father's makeshift grave instead of riding. The time allows me to think about everything, including the apartment and Eric's parents knowing about Justin. This in contrast to Eric's behavior with Brian when he was upset, to us connecting as a family on the hospital bed. I feel like I am on a roller coaster that's become stuck on the upside-down turn.

Kaitlyn and Austin are waiting when I arrive. Memories take me back to the funeral decades ago. To when I couldn't say goodbye.

"Thank you." I look to both of them, my oldest friends. "I know it doesn't make sense . . ."

"I think it's brilliant," Kaitlyn interrupts. "Let's burn the cancer to ashes."

"Burn?" Confused, I notice the stack of firewood large enough for a small fire. Next to it is a headstone, similar to the one Austin carved for my father's funeral. On it are the words *Cancer* and *Not Today, Not Ever.*

"Cremate the cancer," Kaitlyn explains.

"My mom's people cremated their dead to allow the energy to be released back to the earth," Austin explains. "To free the soul of the darkness in the days before passing." He points to a hole in the ground next to my father's grave, then hands me a set of matches, telling me silently that it's my decision.

From inside my pocket, I pull out Brian's first hospital bracelet, placed around his small wrist on the day of admission. It states his name, birth date, and the name of his oncologist. Bright blue, as if the color would brighten the darkness surrounding him, contradict that his body has become his own worst enemy. The intake nurse explained in detail that the bracelet offers more than just a name tag; it's also a source of protection from anyone unknown interacting with Brian in his parents' absence. I listened passively, fighting the instinct to pull off the symbolic handcuff that shackled him to the hospital. Brian ran his small fingers over his name; then, as if sensing my stare, he looked up. In that moment our grief collided, joining us as if it were an umbilical cord.

"The cremation," I decide, wanting to see the bracelet burn. "Brian and the cancer are not one. It doesn't belong to Brian."

I strike the match twice before it lights, then drop it onto the pile of wood. Smoke curls into the air as the flame burns slowly before gathering strength. As Kaitlyn and Austin quietly watch, I throw the band into the fire. The flames, excited to have new meat, dance around it before striking. In minutes, the blue band is charred before it's burned to ashes. I shut my eyes as I send a silent plea to the universe—*Let my son be free of the illness. Return him to who he was.*

"I have no idea why you came into our lives," I say to the cancer as the fire continues to burn. "Into Brian's life. I understand that a space was created for you somehow. But you have no right to be here. If any permission was given through energy, thought, or beliefs, I rescind it now. Death is yours, and with it the power to hurt my son." I must replace that space with love and healing. To make Brian whole again, first I must heal the emptiness that allowed the cancer in. "Brian is mine. Never will he be yours."

As the fire's heat warms my face and hands, the metal of my wedding ring burns against my skin. I start to step back, then stop, allowing the metal to heat up, then burn me. When it becomes intolerable, I slowly slip the ring off. As it slides down my finger, I think of the apartment, Eric's parents, the repetition of lies. My mind begins to burn as my heart, already fractured, shatters.

I need Brian to heal. Every time I foray into the past, into my marriage and connection, I wonder when I became so lost as to not know my own way. The only purpose of my marriage now is to bookend Brian with support and love. Nothing else. I cannot hold on to Eric for Brian's sake.

"Teach us love, compassion, and honor that we may heal the earth and heal each other," I say, repeating the words Austin's mom said to me once when I told her about my father. *So you can heal yourself,* she had said to me.

Now, I say the words for my husband, for our marriage, as the weight of the ring and everything it once meant and now means lies heavy in my palm. With a final goodbye, I toss it into the fire and watch the flames dance around it before enveloping it. Austin's eyes meet mine over the fire, silent and aware. We stand there until there's nothing left but ashes.

◆ ◆ ◆

I watch the headlights of Kaitlyn's car until they disappear into the night. I lean forward on the porch railing. I have checked in with my mom, who told me Brian was watching television before bed.

"Thank you for coming today," I say to Austin as he joins me on the porch. I crave the nighttime, the quiet and peace in contrast to the noise of the hospital and its machines. "You didn't have to—"

"How is Brian doing?" he says, not allowing me to finish.

I try to come up with an answer that won't leave me in tears. "Justin is a match . . ." Before he can say more, I update him with, "Eric is going to take legal action if Felicity continues to refuse to let Justin do the transplant. She's concerned about what it would do to him."

Austin leans over the porch, dropping one foot onto the lower step. "Celine . . ."

"How are your parents?" My mind needs a break from my life and everything that is a puzzle piece of it. When put together, it's a picture I don't want to see. "Will they come to visit?"

"My dad's had a couple of tough illnesses over the years."

"Austin." I reach for him, my hand settling on his arm. "I'm so sorry."

He offers me a small smile. "Thanks." He covers my hand with his. "He's doing much better now." He gestures toward the farm. "Mom's always wanted to come back here. The farm, this area—it was her home. Dad loves Seattle, but she's never gotten over leaving here."

"Your mom is one of the kindest people I've ever known. If there's anything I can do, please tell me."

"I know how full your plate is, so it means a lot you offering." Austin points to the stars in the sky. "When I was little, I had trouble falling asleep at night. This was before you came to the farm. Mom and I would lay down together on a hammock she'd had my dad set up on the porch and count the stars." His face filled with wonder, he adds, "I don't think I ever got past forty before I was sound asleep."

"Smart mom."

"Yeah." He shakes his head. "I knew Dad was in trouble when he temporarily forgot about those nights."

"Austin . . ." My heart aches for him, for all the tragedies that are part of the human journey. "It's why you came back? For them?"

He doesn't look at me, his face still staring at the stars. "A lot of good memories here. Ones whose value I didn't realize until much later."

"Hang on," I tell him.

I rush into the bedroom I've taken over. When packing, I had grabbed my box that I keep my jewelry and other valuables in. I open it, searching the various drawers until I find it. The wooden box in hand, I return to where he's waiting.

"I know this belonged to your mom's family. You should have it back." His eyes widen as he slowly opens it to find the feather encased safely inside. "She should have it back."

"You kept it?" His gaze holds mine. "All these years?"

I shrug, embarrassed. I don't tell him it's been my way of holding on to him and the memories of our time together. That he had entrusted me with it, and even though we weren't in each other's lives, I could not break his trust in me. "I knew how important it was to you. And you gave it to me . . . so it became important to me."

"C . . . thank you." His voice falls low with emotion.

On my nod, he holds out his arms, allowing me the choice. I step into them, our arms encircling one another. The memory of hundreds of hugs as children, sleepovers curled up together to ward off the cold in my room, hours spent in silence just happy being together wash over me as my arms encircle him.

Now I seek and find comfort in his hold, in his touch, which is both familiar and new at the same time. He exhales as his arms tighten around me, and I realize that he's seeking his own comfort, a sense of self that only we can offer one another—born from years of friendship and togetherness. From years of being the most important people in each other's lives. We continue to stand together, under the stars, holding one another, the other person being the only answer to our pain.

"Is it all right for me to hate you for stealing—" I start to say.

"Buying," he corrects.

I ignore him. "For stealing my farm and still be very happy that you're back?"

"As long as it's all right that I am very sorry for *buying* your farm while being very happy to be back."

My life has become a new balance between positive and negative, heartbreak and hope, a trajectory between the two without anything to connect them. In losing my marriage, I have found Justin, who could potentially save my son. In losing my farm, I have Austin back in my life. In losing my father, I found the farm and my love of horses. I pray for a time when happiness will follow happiness instead of heartbreak.

"Maybe," I answer, half teasing, half telling the truth.

He leans back from the hug, meeting my gaze. Inside his eyes I see warmth, concern, and a connection that tugs at the woman in me, that draws me in until I'm forced to look away from fear and confusion.

"Jockey my horse in the next race."

I step out of his arms, trying to make sense of his request. "I don't jockey anymore," I try to explain. "We have some amazing riders we work with . . ."

"I want you." His words have a finality, an expectation, with no negotiation. "Please."

The thought of racing to win, feeling the wind against my face, for just those few moments not feeling like my life is out of control, without me having any choices, draws me in . . .

"Brian . . ."

"Only if it works for him," Austin says quickly. "He comes first."

"Then yes," I say, suddenly having something to look forward to other than the pain I have been living with. "I'd love to."

CHAPTER TWENTY-FOUR

FELICITY

I arrive at Justin's school after his soccer practice. I wait in the car and watch from afar as his teammates chat with one another. From my own years as an athlete, I imagine them replaying details of the practice and discussing the next game's strategy. When Justin was younger, I waited on the field with other parents for the boys to gather their things. His friends' mothers would comment on how laid back he was, how happy and easy. The words always brought a sense of peace to me—Justin was not suffering for my decisions.

Now, things have changed. Even given the distance, I see his mouth tense and shoulders tight. The joy that normally emanates from him is nowhere to be seen. I came to Boston to unite my family. Instead, I have lost it.

I draw a deep breath to settle my anxiety. I consider what to say to him, then chide myself for being afraid to speak to my own son. *But that was before you told him the truth,* a small voice reminds me. *Before you lifted the veil and revealed your true self to him.*

I push away the thought as I gather my courage. I wait for the field to empty of his teammates before I grab the bag of clothes I threw together and step out of my car. I choose the path behind the cars to meet him at his, my heels against the black pavement in perfect rhythm. He checks his phone and palms his keys. I run my free hand down my dress pants. I gather my sense of self, reminiscent of early days as an executive where, in a roomful of men, I had to exert my power and position. Now, I laugh at the fear I felt in those days in comparison to what I face now. Then I was fighting tradition and an old boys' network. Here, I am battling my own decisions.

"Justin. Honey."

He looks up, his features contorting from confusion to warmth, then wariness. In those few seconds, it's as if he has forgotten what happened and that muscle memory has kicked in as a reaction to seeing me.

"I brought you some fresh clothes." I hold up the duffel bag, as if to give him proof of my intentions. "In case you needed them." Even to my own ears, the excuse sounds ridiculous. "To wear."

I stop, waiting for some sign from him of his thoughts. Right now, I would take anything. Even anger at my having invaded his personal space. But his face remains neutral, the silence serving to remind me of our new relationship—one fraught with lies and deception.

"Justin, honey, please." I hear my own desperation. I try to draw on my professional experience and fortitude, but both fail me in the face of my son. Never have I felt so helpless or afraid. "I miss you."

Justin's eyes shut at my admission. When he opens them, I see remnants of the boy I raised. The one who loved and trusted me before the truth tore us apart.

"Guys have girlfriends . . . ," he starts slowly, as if searching for the words that would explain what he's trying to say. "Girls that they date, that they bring home to their moms." He shakes his head slightly, as if remembering what it felt like when he brought Lily home to meet me. "Girls that they fall in love with."

"Justin . . . ," I start, afraid of where he's going. I want desperately to stop him before he says the words, before I must hear his reaction to my behavior. "Honey . . ."

"Then there are the girls they cheat with." He scoffs and looks down at his shoes. His knuckles turn white as he grips his gym bag. I focus on a streak of dirt that lines his leg. I imagine him chasing a ball and the dirt kicking up as he hits it with his cleats. "The ones that you don't date. Because that's not who they are. And everyone knows it."

I take an instinctual step back. Sex. He's taken everything that has happened, the years of raising him, of supporting him and loving him, down to the moment of his conception. Down to sex. And in the interaction, he has cast me in the role he sees me as—the other woman.

"That's how you see me?"

"Dad was with Celine." Justin states the facts as he knows them. In his tone, he begs me to dispute them, to give him a different version of the events. I search my brain for one that will excuse my behavior or cast it in a different light. One that brings my son back to me. "He was engaged."

"We were drunk." My voice falls to a whisper, as if I am trying to convince both of us of my innocence while hiding the truth from the world. "We didn't know what we were doing."

"What about afterward?"

I stagger back, resting a hand on his car for support. Afterward was about protecting him, about offering him everything I knew he deserved.

"Afterward, I protected you. I loved you."

"At Celine's expense. At Brian's expense." Justin drops his gym bag onto the ground. He shakes his head in confusion. "You knew Dad was married, and you still kept up the lie. Why?"

His question tells me that my explanation isn't enough. I want desperately to go back to the days when he knew me only as his mother. When he valued me for the role I played, not the role I hid.

"For you." I want to shout it from the rooftops. It is him, only him. He is the reason for everything. For the lies and half truths. For the deception that has now derailed my life. "It was all for you."

Justin runs his hand through his hair as he shakes his head. "That doesn't make sense, Mom." He pauses as a car passes by. The sound of the engine cuts through our conversation, drowning out all the noises that are serving as a symphony to our struggle. "How was lying to Celine for me?"

It wasn't. I have always been so sure that, when the truth came out, Justin would believe the story I had created. The one that's driven my every action—that the lie is to protect Celine and Brian. That I am the real victim for having kept the secret hidden, and along with it my hopes and dreams for more.

But my son is smarter than me. At seventeen, he's looked past my rationalizations to reveal the truth—the one I have kept hidden even from myself. The one that casts me not as the victim but the villain. I have lied to protect myself. To keep the relationship with Eric rather than chance losing him to the reveal. Justin is the excuse I have needed to keep Eric with me. An alternative to being alone or too afraid to find a real relationship. Because in doing so, I would chance rejection. I would chance being told I wasn't enough. That between me and another woman, I would come in second. At least with Celine, I know the competition. I helped set the rules of the game so I could win. But the gamble has failed. I've lost. And the cost is my son.

"And Dad." Justin's agony reaches deep inside me, tearing at me. "He would always tell me to be a good man, an honest man. But what he did"—Justin pauses—"it was all a lie. He lied to me. To everyone."

"Justin, we were trying—" I don't get to finish, since Justin cuts me off.

"I should go." He reaches for the bag. "Thanks for the clothes." He pauses, and I wait for him to say more, to tell me that he understands. "I'll see you at the hospital."

"You being a donor . . . ," I say. "I don't know if it's a good idea."

He stops and stares at me. "What?"

"You have soccer practice and school. I don't want it affecting your life."

"No," Justin says. "You are not going to do this." I see his anger and frustration, all of it directed at me. "It's my decision, and I am going to donate."

"Justin . . ."

"Is that why the hospital hasn't called?" Justin demands. My silence is the answer. "Mom, what are you doing?"

"Trying to protect you," I say.

"No, you're not." Justin looks away from me, as if he cannot stand the sight of me. "I don't know what this is about, but it's not about protecting me. Maybe it's to protect yourself." He pauses, clearly struggling. "Don't stop me from donating, Mom. This isn't about you anymore. It's about me and Brian."

I watch as he settles into the driver's seat. Over a year ago, I had sat next to him in the passenger seat as he first learned how to navigate the streets. I carefully taught him the intricacies of driving—small things like when to use your turn signals and bigger ones like always checking over your shoulder before changing lanes. He would listen intently, as if he understood my fear for him and wanted to reassure me that he was safe.

In that and everything else we were partners, always making sure to respect the other one's thoughts. When he passed his driver's test on his first try, I both celebrated and felt a moment of unease. It was the first time that he would be on his own, making decisions without my guidance. Like every parent with a newly licensed driver, I watched him leave on his first solo trip with my stomach in knots.

Now, Justin seamlessly backs out of the parking spot. As I taught him, he looks over both shoulders to confirm it's clear. His head down, he leaves without saying goodbye. Though I know he isn't looking at me, I raise my hand in farewell. I then watch as he drives away. When he got his license, I knew it would change our circumstances—he could drive anywhere he wanted. Never did I imagine that I would one day be watching him drive away from me.

I head straight home after meeting with Justin. The empty house greets me with silence—a reminder that I am alone. I slip off my heels. Normally, I would immediately place them in the closet in my room so that Justin and I wouldn't be tripping over each other's stuff. Now, I leave them where they are in the entrance. I unbutton my jacket and the blouse beneath it. Each one of my suits is tailored to fit my body exactly. Designer material to fit the image I have carefully cultivated—a woman in charge of my career and destiny.

In my bedroom, I unzip my pants, allowing them to pool at my feet. I step over them, leaving them in a puddle on the ground. I toss the jacket next to it, a collection of clothes that serves as a shield. Like the emperor in the folktale, I have been stripped of my facade. By my own son. He's forced me to face the truth I have refused to see for all these years. I have woven my story so seamlessly, so tightly, that even I have begun to believe my own tale. A spider caught in my own web that I now know no way of escaping.

I pass my full-length mirror. The image that stares back at me gives me pause. Beautiful blond hair cascades down to my shoulders. I have had a standing appointment first at a top salon in Chicago and now on Charles Street in Boston. Every six weeks I go in for a trim, barely a few centimeters, to keep my hair perfectly coiffed and colored. Never a strand out of place or a gray root exposed. Eyebrows trimmed to highlight my cheekbones and the ocean-blue eyes I inherited from my father. Rowing and running have kept my body in a condition that my younger self would have envied. And no matter the MBA, I have continued to educate myself to guarantee my mind stays sharp. I have created the perfect life to hide my imperfections.

Still in front of the mirror, I slowly slip off my bra and then my underwear. Naked, I stare at myself. Gone is the girl who slept with Eric. That night, I was so sure of myself and my place in the world. I had mapped out each step meticulously and intelligently, with markers of success in place. Eric was a detour but not without consideration. I cannot pinpoint when it became more for me, but our years together solidified my feelings. Justin became the bridge from Eric being a friend to my future.

But like the emperor's clothes, it's all been a lie. Except I am the one who's woven the tale. The one who has created the lies and tried to make everyone around me believe in them. In me. The woman who stares back at me isn't the woman of my childhood dreams but instead a shattered version of who I could have been. Who I should have been.

I take a shaky step forward. With slow, deliberate movement, I touch my fingers to the mirror, joining my reflection with my reality. My gaze falls on my breasts. Once full and pert, they now hang slightly from age and gravity. Stretch lines detail my stomach, creating an artistry of life. My legs, shaped and toned, carry the weight of my deceit. My gaze flies back up to my face, where the eyes I have always relied on to guide my way now stare back at me with disdain and disillusionment. For all the time and attention I have spent on the outer details, I have failed to correct the most critical one—I am the other woman.

Movies cast me as the villain, the one who comes in like a thief in the night and steals the man from the innocent wife. The one who dresses in lingerie that highlights the body my rival has failed to maintain. Whose clothes cling to me in the places that draw a man's attention, holding it out like a bone to a puppy. The woman who needs nothing more than the occasional nights, stolen calls, and empty promises. The one who is considered second best because she views herself as no better than the leftovers of another. The scraps dropped to a waiting dog who patiently awaits another's benevolence.

I step away from the mirror and my own gaze, unable to see any more. But the damage is done. The veil, once lifted, can no longer hide the hidden truth. I reach for the bed, my manicured nails gripping the bedsheet. How many times did I check my makeup before Eric arrived? Straighten the house so he would imagine it a home? Ordered his favorite foods to sit together and enjoy as a family.

When Justin was young, I enrolled him in soccer to remind Eric of his own years playing. Created a common thread that ran between father and son. Like a lioness who offered the cub to the lion, I offered Justin to his father as a vision of his future. In seeing himself in Justin, Eric would come home.

Like a gambler at a poker table, every act, every move, was done not only to play my own hand but also in reaction to the hand Celine was playing. It was to show Eric what he could have. A competition with Celine in which I was playing the long game—where in the end I would prove victorious. The day would come, I was sure, when Eric would admit his feelings and claim Justin and me as his family. I just had to be patient.

But that day never came, though I continued to wait. Justin got older, as did I. Left waiting, wanting. When did the mathematician in me fail to count the days, years that passed? When did my heart determine my direction rather than the mind I have always valued so immensely? As a child, I scoffed at the girls who dreamed of their wedding day. Mocked their desire to be coupled with someone who would sweep them off their feet and take care of them for the rest of their lives. I was better than that, I was sure. I was strong and self-sufficient. I wasn't the other woman. Instead, I was a mother securing my son's existence.

Except I am the other woman. I have always been the other woman. I am not the victim. I am the perpetrator, the accessory to the crime. Now, if asked, I couldn't confirm if I was the one who decided our trajectory, or if it was Eric. Had he murmured words of telling the truth, and I convinced him otherwise? Or did he insist it was the only way, and I acquiesced? My mind struggles with the answer, unsure if it's still playing games with me. A defense mechanism through which to protect myself from the part I have played.

I flatten my palm on the silk coverlet that decorates the bed of my picture-perfect room. How many times in my bedroom have I imagined Eric sharing it with me? A sheet of shame covers my naked body. I shiver in the warm air. My head drops onto the bed, the only source of comfort. In the lies I have told to fool Celine and the world, I have only succeeded in deceiving myself.

Tears track down my cheeks. My hair falls around my face like a woman hiding from a frenzied crowd. But the roars are only from within me. There's no mob swarming at me, pointing fingers, or screaming obscenities. Celine is not crying or blaming me. There is no one. Because in the decision to become the other woman, to be second in line, I have forgone myself, my place, and my power. I no longer serve a value to anyone. The keeper of secrets becomes irrelevant when the truth is revealed. And that decision, more than any punishment or sentence, has driven me to where I am now—completely alone.

I find my phone and send a simple text to Eric:

I won't stand in the way of Justin donating.

CHAPTER TWENTY-FIVE

FELICITY

I arrive at the hospital an hour earlier than the scheduled time for Justin's blood draw for the donation. It has been over a week since my conversation with Justin. Since then he's been silent, and I have not reached out. Now, all I can do is show him that I am the mother he needs me to be. That I am not the other woman, but my own woman. And that my main priority is him, that it has always been him. In keeping him from helping Brian, he would see me as choosing myself over Celine. Choosing myself over his brother. After all this time, after the relationship that I have slowly and methodically built with him, at the end of the day he has chosen his little brother over Eric. He has chosen Celine over me. The castle I was sure I was building for him was made of sand, washed away with the first wave.

Inside the same waiting room from before, I pace. When Eric arrives, we stare at one another, not having seen each other since the confrontation.

"Thank you . . . ," Eric starts, his voice softening his demeanor. "I know this wasn't an easy decision for you to make."

"He's my son," I remind him. "It's my job to protect him."

"My intention is not to put him in danger," Eric says.

Though I know what he's saying is true, I still can't help but feel he's choosing one son over the other. "We'll have to agree to disagree."

"Felicity . . ."

"You came to my home and threatened me with legal action," I remind him. "The irony? You've never legally taken responsibility for Justin." Though Eric has always been a present father, he has never asked nor offered to legally claim Justin as his. Though I understood the reasons—Celine, legal complications, the truth coming out—now the irony stings.

"Felicity . . ." Pained, Eric stares at me. "I never believed that was something you wanted." He sighs. "Coming to you to threaten legal action was a mistake. I'm sorry." He drops down on the sofa, his hands dangling between his spread legs. "I can't lose Brian. I didn't know what else to do."

"You could have found another way," I say, furious at him, at myself. At the circumstances beyond my control.

A nurse comes in and tells us that they are ready for us. I quickly move ahead, anxious to see Justin and be there for him. I hear Eric a few steps behind me, but my focus is completely on the nurse and the room she's leading us to.

Inside what looks like a lab, Justin lies on a hospital bed with an IV in one arm. A machine next to him whirs to life.

"Justin, honey." I pause, waiting for his reaction. He briefly acknowledges me and then Eric, who takes his place next to me. "How are you doing?"

"I'm good." He glances at the IV in his arm, then shrugs. "They said it could be a few hours."

His eyes focus on someone behind me. I turn to see Celine in the doorway, hesitant. My immediate reaction is to tell her to leave, that this is a private family matter, when Justin says, "Celine, hey."

"Hi." She smiles at Justin, and her eyes dart first to Eric and then to me, where they remain. "I don't want to intrude; I just wanted to come by and say hello. I hope that's all right?"

Taken aback by her asking, I slowly nod, moving to the side to make space for her in the room. Justin's eyes follow the movement, his gaze focused on Celine. She says a quiet "Thank you," but I cannot be sure if it's toward me or Justin.

Justin says, "How's Brian?"

"He's good," Celine says, though the waver in her voice betrays her words. "He wanted to come by later and say hello."

"Yeah?" Justin smiles and then nods before he leans back against the bed. "That would be great."

I meet Eric's eyes, and in that moment the fight between us, the abyss that we have created, falls away as we both are cast out to sea. Our son has chosen a side, and it's the one that does not include us. In choosing him, we have lost him.

The blood continues to spiral from him, into the machine and back out, taking from it his cells in the small chance they can save his brother. The minutes turn to an hour. Justin lays his head back against the bed, closing his eyes.

Eric takes a seat on the ledge near the window, his gaze flipping from Justin to the machine and then the monitors, tracking Justin's well-being. I notice he and Celine rarely interact, seeming to be better on separate sides of the same room.

I try to stay as close to Justin as possible, moving the visitors' chair until it's directly next to his bed. If he notices or minds, he doesn't say anything. Celine stands against a wall, tucked into a far corner. At first I tell myself it's her guaranteeing the job is done; then a small voice whispers that she may actually be worried about my son in his attempt to help hers.

The thought uncomfortable, I jump up. The chair clatters back, drawing everyone's eyes on me. "Coffee," I say in explanation. "Justin, I'll get you some M&M's and your salt-and-vinegar chips." I know without asking he will want his go-to when he wants to pass the time or needs a distraction. I keep the pantry always stocked with bags of both. I've started to turn toward the door when his words stop me.

"I'm good," he says, his voice low from the onslaught of the procedure. "I ate before I got here."

My hand shakes. I slip them into my pockets to hide my fear that his refusal is because he doesn't want me to get them. Eric's gaze clashes with mine. I look away before he offers me understanding and sympathy that I have no desire to accept or react to.

"I'll run down and get the coffee." Celine steps forward. As if she can sense the underlying tension, she tries to soothe the surface. "Grab some sandwiches for everyone. And M&M's and chips for Justin, right?"

Her question is directed to me, acknowledging my place as his mother, the one who knows what he needs. I stare at her, gauging whether she's trying to show Justin that she's the better person—a subtle punishment for my refusal to allow the donation or recognizing my role so that he may remember it also.

"Yes. Thank you."

After she leaves, I turn back toward Justin, who has shut his eyes and is leaning his head back. When I retake my seat, I clasp my hands together and drop my head low in a silent, desperate cry for something or someone to right my wrongs and bring me back my son.

The hours pass, only the attending nurses and doctor breaking the silence. Celine, Eric, and I remain in our self-assigned positions, seeming to find comfort in the familiarity, given the unfamiliar circumstances.

Finally finished, Justin is eating the remaining food when there's a quick knock on the door. Elena, pushing Brian in a wheelchair, peeks in. Eric and Celine immediately jump forward to help, working in tandem to open the door and help them in.

Justin's face lights up in a smile at the sight of his brother. Taken aback by his response, I watch the two boys greet one another with a fist bump. Their camaraderie is natural, easy, making me wonder why Justin hasn't mentioned how close they have become. In my keeping Brian from him, Justin may have believed I wanted them to remain strangers and didn't trust me with the truth.

"Thank you," Brian says, pulling me once again from my thoughts. "Grandma said it's really nice what you're doing."

"It's all good." Justin continues to smile at his brother. "Hopefully, this will help make it better, yeah?" Though he keeps his tone light, there's wistfulness and hope in his words.

"Yeah," Brian says, a catch in his voice, a question of whether he can hope to wake up from the nightmare he has been thrust into. "Tomorrow, we can play video games again if you want. I think it's Pizza Day too." He looks to Celine, who quietly lets him know he's right.

They have played video games together. Eaten together. I have always known about the people in Justin's life, the ones who matter to him versus the ones who are passing through. But he has kept his brother from me. As I have kept Brian from him.

"A hundred percent, I'll be here."

They finalize their plans before Brian and Justin exchange another fist bump in goodbye. Eric holds open the door as Elena starts to wheel Brian out. Celine turns to Justin and me. "Thank you." Her voice catches. She quickly turns and walks out without a word to Eric.

Eric's face falls, his hand gripping the door a bit tighter. This is their family now. The connection I have envied, hated, is now in ruins. The realization gives me no satisfaction nor a sense of hope. Instead, I am simply left with a profound sadness for the role I have played in tearing them apart.

"Justin, thank you." Left with only the three of us, Eric speaks to his son as a man. "What you did—"

"Brian would have done the same thing for me," Justin interrupts. "It was a no-brainer."

"How do you know?" I ask, unable to stop the question. "That Brian would have done it for you?"

"He's funny. Kind. A good guy." He pauses, then adds, "Brian would have been the kid brother I messed with, hung out with, played soccer, video games with. The one who would have looked up to me, made me think twice about doing certain things so he wouldn't follow." I swallow repeatedly as he continues. "And as we got older, we'd know we love each other. As brothers and friends. Maybe even best friends. That's how I know."

Justin walks out, leaving me staring after him.

CHAPTER
TWENTY-SIX

CELINE

"You decided to race Austin's horse." Kaitlyn and I walk the field together as early, smaller races finish up. "Good."

Over a week has passed since the transplant. Since then, Eric, my mom, and I have been taking shifts to make sure Brian isn't alone. The doctor explained to us that the first few weeks were critical to see if his body accepted or rejected the donation. It feels as if I began holding my breath the day of the transplant and haven't exhaled since. Today's race is to remind me to fight for better times.

"It's good for the farm. For us." Our financial position has forced us into a position where we must remind the equestrian world that Kaitlyn and I are still in the game. Riding and placing a horse of this caliber will help us keep our reputation even if we lose the farm.

"How are you doing?" Kaitlyn asks, her standard question every day.

"Still waiting." For Brian's body to accept the donation. For him to heal. For him to come home. I have lost sense of what I am waiting for—baby steps or leaps across buildings. I just want my son to be healthy. And maybe then I can find my way to some sense of happiness. "Thanks for being here."

For this premier event, the area is bustling with trainers, horse owners, jockeys, and spectators. Each race is a step on the ladder toward racing in the big three—the Derby, the Preakness Stakes, and the Belmont Stakes. The Triple Crown is the dream of every jockey, trainer, and owner. As a child, I used to daydream about the win as I rode. With enough perseverance and commitment, I was sure I would one day reach that pinnacle of success. Maybe I am still waiting, or time has forced the larger wins into the background as the smaller ones became the building blocks of my life. A perfect life redefined by its imperfections.

Kaitlyn points to a horse that has just finished first in his race. "See that horse? His leg was fractured."

"He's racing?" Though an injured leg no longer means death for a horse, the healing process is still long and arduous. They often never run the same again.

"Someone forgot to tell him he isn't the same as before," Kaitlyn shares. "I was talking to the trainer. Apparently, the horse still thinks he's the fastest on the farm. No matter how many times or ways the trainer has tried to clue him into his reality, he won't budge. Quickest healing time anyone's ever seen, and back on the race circuit." She looks at me. "Didn't care what the outside world said or thought. Just focused on his strength."

My own strength feels tentative, lost in a series of events where I am forced to put myself back together afterward. I had hoped Eric's love and success would somehow make up for my childhood. In his meaning, I had hoped to find mine. But it hasn't. And now I see it never would have.

Kaitlyn squeezes my shoulder. "Good luck out there. You got this."

As she heads toward a group of people, I turn toward the barns. From a distance, I see my mom talking to Austin. He gives her a quick hug, then waves goodbye. Knowing my mother is going to have questions, I take a deep breath and join her as she watches my approach.

"Just ran into Austin. So nice that he's back in town," she says, then asks gently, "Why didn't you tell me?"

"He's buying the farm. I found out the night before Brian ended up in the hospital."

Understanding flits across her face. "With everything else going on, sweetheart, I'm sorry." She shakes her head. "Before they moved, Sedna would always say that Austin would come back. Said people always return to their true love. I stopped believing it after a while, but now he's here."

"He wants the farm for his parents." I explain about his father. "I think to give them a place to come home to."

Mom looks at me, confused. "You think she was talking about the farm?"

"What else?"

She sighs and takes my hand in hers. "She was talking about you, honey. Austin was in love with you, and Sedna knew it. She swore he'd come back for you one day."

I hear the words but dismiss them, sure my mom is wrong. We were friends. He never gave any indication about more. I refuse the thought without considering it.

"Mom, we were friends then, and now . . ." I try to define the time we have spent together and my reaction to him—feeling calmer when he's around, more grounded. I attribute it to the familiarity of childhood, a friendship that saw me through some difficult times.

"And now?" Mom asks, watching me curiously.

"Now, I'm getting ready to race his horse." I squeeze her hand. "Thanks for coming to watch."

"With the transplant . . . I wanted just a minute of something else. And what's more perfect than watching my daughter?"

I hug her, this incredibly strong woman who has been a rock for me my entire life. "Thank you, Mom," I whisper. "For being here. Always."

I sit atop Austin's horse, ready for the race. Jockeying comes naturally to me after the hours spent on horses at the farm as a child. Anxious to escape my reality, I focused entirely on racing, learning both the physical and mental acuity demanded to partner with a horse.

But no two horses are the same. They are like people—different personalities, demeanors, and triggers. Though they can be trained to run at certain speeds, I had to learn how to match a horse's intelligence to navigate them successfully through a race, to keep my strength in proportion to theirs so I was an asset, not a liability.

At the Call to the Post, I get into position for the nearly two-minute race. Control is paramount but connection critical. *Trust them so they will trust you*—a mantra in my head. Every second of the race will demand me to anticipate his moves as he responds to mine. A partnership in which one wrong move can become the difference between winning or losing. Weakness is never an option.

We start at the sound of the signal. On balance, I keep my eyes straight ahead as I push him faster and farther while remaining centered on his back. We move forward, each step analyzed before navigation. I assess the course and my competition, evaluating and reevaluating my decisions. Trust is essential as we react tactically to any shifts in the race.

I tap my stirrups, pushing him faster. He responds immediately, trusting my directive and instinct. We move between two other horses, fighting for the lead. The horse to my left fights to usurp me. Making a quick strategic decision, I move toward him, demanding space that he must cede to me through moving either ahead or behind. A calculated decision that earns dividends when he tries to go faster but ends up two spaces behind. Enough for me to take advantage of and close the gap.

Visions of my past with Austin—the friendship, the laughter, the tears, and the love—drive me to connect to Austin's horse. Suddenly every other horse disappears in my mind's eye. All I can see is Austin and myself as we flew through the fields as children, laughing over

11

everything and nothing. Him encouraging me to go faster, to trust not only my horse but also myself. To believe in the person he saw me as instead of who I believed myself to be.

Drawing on the memories, I will the horse faster. The finish line in sight, and suddenly needing it desperately, I focus on one goal—winning. With a surge of adrenaline, I dig my heels in and increase my speed. The horse to my right fights to keep up but at the last second fails in its attempt. I cross the finish line first, a feeling of wholeness and happiness engulfing me.

"Nice race." Austin meets me on the field after I dismount. I hear the pride in his voice and smile in response. We walk together in silent agreement toward the outfield, which has less crowds. "Congratulations on the win."

"The horse has real potential," I say. "He can go far."

"Even with the revised schedule?" he teases.

"Careful, I may reconsider it."

Austin holds up his hands in mock surrender, then gestures toward the track. "You're very talented on the track. With everything that you have going on, and you race like this, I can't wait to see you on a good day, when everything is going right."

"You think I'm going to have good days again?" I think about Brian and the transplant. The prayers and pleading every minute of every day for him to heal, for him to come home.

Austin holds my gaze, his eyes steady on mine. "Yeah, I do."

"That's a lot of faith in the unknown." The doctor's words are a constant in my head—no guarantees, no promises. An illusive hope with no road map or compass to guide us.

"Sometimes, that's all we have," Austin replies.

We reach a fenced paddock housing a lone horse. I lean against the freshly painted wood. The horse saunters over, allowing me to stroke its smooth jawline. I think about what my mom said about Austin and his feelings for me when we were kids. I start to ask, then dismiss it, afraid of embarrassing myself, with him having to correct the situation.

"You didn't tell your mom I was back?" he asks softly, breaking into my thoughts.

I glance at him from the side. "I didn't want her to hate you for stealing my farm."

"Buying." Looking proud of himself, he says, "She still likes me. She *hugged* me."

I roll my eyes, remembering all the times she would bake him his favorite cookies and cakes when he was over. He would always leave our house with a plateful of his favorites to last him days.

"She hugged Eric the other day, so I'm thinking her judgment is a little skewed."

"You can't take this from me," he insists. "Personally, I think I was her favorite of your friends."

"You were my only friend," I remind him. "She would have jumped over the moon for you in gratitude."

He nudges my shoulder with his. "Things got better over the years, right?"

"Yeah." Surprised to see the pain and worry in his eyes, I try to reassure him. "Things mellowed out after high school."

"Good." He grips the fence with his hands, staring straight ahead. "I wanted to talk to you about something." He takes a breath, making me wonder what he's readying himself to say. "About you and Kaitlyn managing the farm."

After he buys it. "You have got to be kidding me." I shake my head as I take a step away. "Be your employee? Is that what this race was about? You seeing me in action?" I point a finger at him. "I don't do well with pity."

He rolls his eyes. "Like I don't remember? You used to snarl at anyone who dared to say they were sorry about your father, or anything for that matter."

"I didn't snarl," I scoff.

"I stand corrected. 'Hiss' is the better description."

"It's *my* farm."

"Technically, half of it's my farm, my childhood . . . ," he starts, then stops when I glare. "Look, I know it's not ideal."

"Thank you for the offer. But I don't think so." I'm starting to walk away when he stops me in my tracks with his words.

"You weren't always so polite."

I turn around. "What?"

He shrugs. "I get it. The social etiquette. Fitting in. Playing the part. But the girl I knew? She was a volcano that erupted whenever she was faced with disappointment or refusal."

"Volcanos destroy everything in their wake."

"Fair point." He closes the distance between us. "But afterward, the volcano changes, gets stronger. The cooled lava changes the volcano's shape, reinforces its strength." He motions with his hand. "Stepping away from the volcano analogy . . ."

"And its ability to cause mass extinction?" I murmur.

"Yes, that also. The girl I remember fell off the horse hundreds of times but got back on every single time. Made me spend hours of lost sleep teaching her how to ride in the middle of the night so her uncle wouldn't know. That girl took a setback and made it into an opportunity."

He's talking about a girl I barely remember. One who feels like she's from a lifetime ago. "Going from owner to employee of my own farm? I'm not seeing the movement forward in that."

"Then I guess we're at an impasse," he says on a sigh.

"Seems like it." For just a breath of a second, I envision the girl he's speaking about. The one who feels like a foreigner, someone I barely knew and can hardly remember. But I call on her now, anxious to remember her. "In light of recent events, I get fifty percent of the purse for winning today."

His eyebrows shoot up. "The standard is ten. It's in the contract."

"The contract is invalidated when you're stealing the jockey's farm."

He fights a grin. "I see. Good to know."

I take two steps back, ready to head home. "By the way? That was me spewing lava. You might want to get a Band-Aid for the burn."

He laughs out loud. I can't help but join in, the sound of it taking me back to the days when we spent all our time together. When he helped me find a different part of myself. A part that I never appreciated or cherished. A part I let go of easily, not recognizing its worth.

"Are we friends?" I ask suddenly, the conversation with my mom creeping in. He stops laughing to watch me, his eyes unblinking. "You believed in me to race your horse even though I'm never at the farm. You helped me with the cremation ceremony. You literally held me while I cried."

"Sounds like friends to me," he says softly. He pauses, then asks, "Why didn't you write or call? I tried reaching out to you so many times . . ."

When we were together on the farm, the outside world wasn't a part of us. But then the outside world took him away, and I assumed . . . I assumed he would realize who I really was. Not good enough. No matter how much I wanted to be for him. My own insecurities decided how he must feel about me. So, I ignored his calls and letters, and soon enough they stopped. But I never stopped missing him, and now he's here.

"I don't know," I lie, too embarrassed to tell him the truth, regretting my actions from so long ago.

We stare at one another, both of us lost in our own thoughts until he points behind him. "I'd better go collect my winnings."

"Our winnings," I correct. "If you need help with the fifty percent division, I have a calculator you can borrow."

His lips twitch. "I'll keep that in mind."

"Hey, Austin." I wait until he turns back around to face me to tell him the truth. "We are friends. I'm sorry I was too young, too selfish, too caught up to show it back then."

His eyes warm before he says, "You want to make it up to me by letting me keep my money?"

"Hell no."

He smiles. "That's what I thought."

I'm watching him walk away, smiling the entire time, when my phone buzzes. I look down at the text, then take off running.

CHAPTER TWENTY-SEVEN

CELINE

I break speed limits as I play Frogger on the highway. At the hospital, I park in an illegal spot, then run to the elevator. Eric's text mentioned that Brian's fever has spiked and he isn't doing well. When your child has cancer, you already know he isn't doing well. A text with those words takes the severity to another level.

Inside Brian's room, I am greeted by Brian seated on his bed, leaning against Felicity. I stop, taken aback by the visual. My son in the arms of my husband's mistress. The night of the party, when I spoke about Brian, I assumed they would never meet. But since then she has become a part of our lives, and us a part of hers.

Felicity rubs Brian's back, soothing him with words of comfort and support as he clutches a bag to vomit in. She cradles him like a mother would. But she's not my son's mother. Instead, she's the mother of my husband's other son.

On seeing me, Felicity tenses. She physically retreats while still holding on to Brian. "Eric went to talk to the doctor. Brian thought he was going to vomit, so I . . ." She veers off, not finishing the sentence. She moves off the bed, giving me the room to take her place. Even though it seemed we had taken steps forward during Justin's donation, we are both wary, unsure of our place with one another.

I step past her, careful not to make physical contact. I take the seat she's vacated and wrap my arms around my son, as she had. His head is burning up with fever. "Honey, you don't feel good?"

"My stomach hurts."

"How long has Eric been gone?" I ask Felicity, working hard to keep my voice level, without emotion or reaction to the circumstances. I know consciously that she is just trying to help, that her act was born from kindness, not malice. But my subconscious refuses the explanation, insisting that the woman who stole my husband cannot behave in a well-intentioned manner. She cannot have two sets of personalities, two consciences. Her behavior with Eric will dictate my view of her forever.

"Just a few minutes." Her gaze keeps flicking toward Brian, worry and concern clear. Shocked, I am sure she's pretending. "Does he want some seltzer water or a cold compress? I can go get it for him."

"Yes, please." Both offers make sense. If he were home and this were the flu or any other illness, that would be one of the first things I'd offer. But since it's cancer, since it's a disease that cannot be defined or doesn't have a known trajectory, because it's abnormal, I don't think about the normal things.

Felicity rushes into the bathroom, seemingly relieved with the opportunity to do something. Back in seconds, she hands me the folded washcloth. "I'll go get some ice to keep it cool and find some seltzer water."

With the compress on his head, I gently pull him against my chest, his head over my heart, as she rushes out of the room. My throat constricts on his ragged breaths as I rub a hand soothingly down his back.

I have lost the ability to form thoughts or words in reaction to my son's illness. My brain shuts down, and like a dark mist over a hidden forest, everything turns gray and invisible. The horse race, only a few hours back, already feels like a lifetime ago. Each second with Brian, with his illness, fills the space, crowding out everything and everyone else.

Felicity returns minutes later with both seltzer and ice, making me wonder who she commanded to get the items in record time. She places the glass gently against Brian's lips. "Here you go, sweetheart," she encourages him. "A few sips will help you feel better."

Brian opens his mouth to take a drop and then another, until half the cup is empty. Like a mother, she's reaching out to wipe the droplet from his chin when she freezes. We stare at one another, both trying to process her actions and our reactions.

"I'm sorry . . . ," she starts, when I interrupt.

"Thank you for helping him." It's becoming a habit to say the words to her, to thank her instead of hating her.

Her gaze drops to him as he shuts his eyes and his body relaxes into a slumber. Felicity closes hers briefly. When she opens them, I see her pain unmasked.

"We were here meeting with the doctor about the transplant," Felicity says, explaining her presence. "I didn't want you to think I was with Brian without your permission." She pauses, then adds, "What he's going through . . . what all of you are facing—I'm so sorry."

I struggle with my response. Only a short while ago, she refused to let Justin donate. Before that, she had come to my house and lied to me about who she was and her connection to Eric. For years prior, she was living a lie with my husband. And now, faced with my dying son, she shows a side of herself I cannot believe coexists with all the other parts of her I know. I'm saved from answering by Eric's arrival. He stares at the two of us.

"I appreciate what you did," I say suddenly, needing to acknowledge in front of Eric what she's done. "For being with Brian, for helping me take care of him."

"Of course." Seemingly startled by my clear intention, she hesitates, then motions toward the door. "I should go." She glances at Eric. "We can talk later about Justin."

In that brief exchange, the sadness and anger that have taken permanent root at the edge of my brain inch forward. They are two parents needing to discuss their son, as Eric and I will soon discuss ours.

As the door shuts behind her, Eric asks, "Everything okay?"

Laughter bubbles to the surface as I search for the correct answer, given the circumstances. Deciding on the truth, I explain, "She took care of Brian until I arrived and then got him seltzer and a cold washcloth."

"Felicity's not a terrible . . ."

I don't want to hear from my husband who betrayed me that his mistress is a good person, that she has a heart. I push aside my anger toward her, the fury that shadows every interaction, because no matter her role, Eric is the only one who owes me the truth. The one who tore apart our life together, day by day, lie by lie.

"What did the doctor say?"

Eric runs a hand over Brian's forehead, his fingers curling against the heat. He shuts the curtains and lights, casting the room in shadows. Seated in the chair, his body hunched over, he speaks in a shaky voice as he cradles Brian's hand.

"His body is in distress," Eric says. "It's having trouble accepting the transplant."

"The doctor . . ." I get ready to beg Eric to tell me the doctor has a solution.

"We wait. That's all we can do."

To see if Brian's body accepts or rejects it. His survival depends on the distinction. "I have to go. Are you . . ." The fear and anxiety creep around me, forcing me to my feet. "Please, can you stay here?"

"Yes, of course." Eric stands, staring at me. "Are you all right?"

"I'll be back later," I say, not answering him.

◆ ◆ ◆

I drive without direction or destination, the passing trees swaying as if beckoning me forward. My mind wanders; a car horn jostles me back to the present. I take stock of my surroundings, startled to realize I am only two streets away from the apartment building I lived in with my parents before my father left.

In a few turns I reach the nondescript brick building situated among dozens of others similar in shape and size. The neighborhood has barely changed since my mom and I left it.

A knock on the car window shocks me out of my reverie. A woman in a tight tank top and short skirt with bright-red lipstick asks me if I'm looking to buy something, her thick Boston accent accentuating her words. "I can get you whatever you need."

"I'm good."

"'K, sweetie." The woman saunters off, her hips swaying with each step.

Even as a child, the girls were commonplace to the neighborhood. From their meager earnings, they would sometimes buy me a lollipop or a piece of candy. Some were single moms or ones without families trying to keep food on their table or a roof over their heads.

I watch her until she's lost in a crowd of her friends and coworkers. Each one watching the passing cars like hawks in anticipation of a sale.

Outside the car, I capture their attention when I set the car alarm. I jaywalk across the street toward the graffiti-covered bricks of my childhood home. A worn outdoor playset has replaced the one that I spent hours playing on, gripping the rusted chains as I pushed myself to reach the sky.

A cracked sidewalk leads me to the inside of the building. The smells of cigarette smoke and stale urine waft toward me as I take the steps toward my old apartment. Standing right outside the door, I remember the hundreds of times I went in and out of it. I came home to it as a newborn from the hospital. It was where I assumed I'd live until I became an adult. It was my home, and I was happy in it.

"You here to see the apartment?" A young man with tattoos covering both arms stares at me from the bottom of the stairs. "I'm showing another one in ten minutes but can let you in if you want to take a look."

"It's empty?" I ask.

"That's why it's for rent." He narrows his eyes at me. "You want to see it or not?"

"Yes." I step back to allow him to open it for me.

"Take as long as you want. When done, just pull the door shut—it locks automatically."

Inside, the memory of breakfasts and dinners pulls me into the past. Around the small table we would sit and laugh or watch the Red Sox play from the secondhand sofa in the living room. The hallway beckons me toward my parents' bedroom, where my father dances with my mother as she laughs through the scolding that they have work to do. He always wanted to play, while she fought to be the adult for both of them.

Inside my bedroom, a curtainless window with peeled paint lining the rim offers a view of the world I grew up in. A single bed situated against the wall next to a used squeaky dresser with drawers filled with clothes from Goodwill that Mom mended to fit my small frame.

The small closet housed my prized possessions—stuffed animals, glittering shoes that remind me of Cinderella, and a dress that my mom once bought new for a party. One that I modeled every day, staring in the mirror at the girl transformed into a princess I barely recognized.

I drop to my knees and, with my phone's light, search for the words I wrote on the wall lifetimes ago. I find them hidden in the bottom corner, written in a child's scrawl:

Celine lives here forever.

I run my fingers over the carefully engraved words. Six years old, I'd carved them in the wall weeks before my father left. At the time it felt critical to announce my ownership of the apartment, to solidify my place.

The words seared into my soul stare back at me. Innocent, I believed my life was perfect, that no harm could come to me. Now tears flow unencumbered down my face, refusing me a release from the pain. I cry for everything I lost when he left and now from the fear of Brian's illness. I mourn the dreams I believed had become a reality when I walked down the aisle to Eric. The life I have painstakingly built on a foundation of shifting sand.

As I continue to cry, my heart aches for the little girl still trapped in the apartment, searching for answers to a life that had suddenly become upended and unpredictable. Like a mother, I yearn to bring her close, to reassure her that everything is going to work out, that she will be safe and protected. But the words are a false bravado. I am as lost as that girl is, facing a future without answers or guarantees. Then I had lost my father; now it's my husband and fears of losing my son. I cannot promise the little girl anything when I have no cards to play.

I seek out a compass to guide me or some semblance of hope to hold on to. But they elude me. I send out a silent apology, hoping it reaches the little girl inside me whom I now fear will forever remain lost and abandoned by the father she yearns for.

"I was so scared when you left," I whisper to him now. "You left me with an inheritance of fear, sadness, and a belief that I wasn't good enough. Because if my own father doesn't love me, then who will?" I have been searching for him ever since. But the emptiness has only yielded more emptiness. Because it's the only thing I believed I deserved after he left me and never looked back.

As the years passed, I convinced myself I would never again be as vulnerable as I was when he left. With the faux funeral, I was sure he was no longer a part of my life.

But I haven't healed, only moved forward. If I want my life to change, I can no longer be the woman I was. I have to find the parts of myself that were never allowed to grow, to nurture—my strength, my sense of self and the belief in myself. That has to begin with seeing the truth about everything, even the parts that hurt me—the truth of my marriage and the betrayal that's served as its foundation, my son's illness, and the parts of me that still yearn for the childhood I have lost. I fear that when I buried him, I only succeeded in burying within me the parts that still need him, that still love him.

I drop my head, my hair falling around me like a shield. My body is spent and exhausted from the last few months. Suddenly wanting to leave, I fear this place where I lost myself, and yet I cannot move, cannot escape. As a child I was too young to understand choices. But now I must find my power. My son's life cannot be gambled.

"I deserve better," I tell the ghost of my father. "My son deserves better." I think of all the memories—the good and the bad. The fear and the sadness. The love. Because I do still love him. I just kept waiting for him to love me back. "Goodbye, Dad." I finally say the words I was unable to all those years ago. "Wherever you are, whatever you're doing, I wish you the best."

I imagine the little girl I once was. In my mind's eye, I pull her close, offering her comfort and an apology. I beg her for forgiveness for leaving her behind. For running from her as I tried to forget my past. In holding her, I search for the strength that continues to elude me.

Outside the window, the sun begins to set, shrouding the room in darkness. The sound of life begins to fade as the streets quiet. I imagine Brian and my younger self meeting, wondering how the two would react. They will bond over the fact that both are struggling, both lost by circumstance.

In the image, I cast them both in a shroud of healing light. Begging for God and anyone who will listen to protect them, my past and present joined. I drop my head again, scared and unsure. Only when my phone pings do I look up to read the text from Eric:

Brian's fever is worse. He's asking for you.

CHAPTER
TWENTY-EIGHT

FELICITY

I finish up the race training tired but feeling better than I have in days. The workouts keep my mind off Justin and our continued estrangement. Though I was sure we had taken steps forward during the donation, I still feel his distance. Nearly a hundred times a day I pick up my phone to call him, only to set it back down without pushing send. Every few days I change my route to work so I pass by Lily's house. His car, parked on the curb, feels symbolic about our life and current circumstances. We both are outside the situation and yet heavily involved.

"How are you enjoying the team?" Jennifer approaches me in the locker room as I towel dry my hair after a shower.

"It's been great. I appreciate you asking me to join," I return.

"It's worked out wonderfully for us," Jennifer says kindly. "We were worried about the empty spot, but you've fit in great." She takes a seat on the bench to tie her shoelaces. "A few of us from different boats are going out for drinks, if you want to join us?"

Normally I would have made my excuses after thanking her for the invitation. But now I realize how much I have missed out on these types of interactions. Though I have always encouraged and supported Justin in having a large group of friends, I have failed to allow myself the same.

"That would be great. Thanks for the invitation."

Jennifer gives me the address of a nearby bar. It's one I am familiar with but haven't been to before. After dressing, I head to the location. Inside, the dark lights and muted music welcome crowds. The mahogany bar is lined with regulars who jest with the bartender about the game playing on the television overhead. A quintessential Bostonian, the bartender looks nearly as old as the establishment. With ruddy cheeks, a bald head, and a full smile, he welcomes newcomers while attending to those already seated. After handing off a half dozen Guinness mugs frothing at the top to a waitress, he focuses on me.

"What can I get you?"

I order a whiskey neat before spotting the crew in the corner. With my tumbler in hand, I join the growing group from the club. I clink glasses with the woman next to me before taking a sip. The smooth liquid slides easily down my throat, warming it along the way. I pull my jacket closer around me, adjusting the scarf wrapped around my neck until it hangs loose. Though the sun has been shining, I know the temperature will soon drop, and there will be a chill in the air when night falls.

"I think we have a chance at winning," Jennifer says, teasing the group with her prediction. "It may be our year."

Every year my father took us to the Head of the Charles. Lost in the shoulder-to-shoulder crowds, I would watch, fascinated, as boaters from the Ivy colleges and participants of all ages raced against one another. When I learned from the group that my new team had raced together for years and had always done well but never won, the challenge was too tempting to ignore.

Some people cheer her prediction, while others partake in some friendly jabbing. As the group continues to discuss the race and each team's individual chances, I sip on my drink, enjoying witnessing the camaraderie rather than participating myself.

"You just moved from Chicago?" the man next to me asks. Though he isn't on our boat, I recognize him from the club as an avid sailor.

"This past year." The time period surprises me. It initially seemed to go fast, but since Justin left, the days have dragged by. "It's good to be in Boston."

"I grew up in Chicago." He introduces himself as Jack. "How long were you there?"

In silent agreement, we step slightly out of the group to continue our conversation without disturbing the others. "There since undergraduate."

We share conversation about Chicago and its pluses and benefits. He reminisces about the Saint Patrick's Day celebrations that bring the town alive with a river turned green and everyone out in merriment. I tell him about Justin and how we spent most of my time in the city outside of work either at an athletic field or getting from one sporting event to the next. We compare the two cities and their similarities. And through our conversation, it's apparent how much the two of us have in common.

As we continue to connect, I assess him more carefully. Tall, he stands a few inches over me. Dark-brown hair is mixed in with streaks of white. Lean, he has an athlete's physique. Blue eyes sit against sun-kissed skin. Having shared that he's divorced, he adds that his two teenage children are the highlight of his life.

"What do you do?" I ask after telling him about my work.

"Don't hate me . . . ," he starts before adding, "I'm a lawyer."

"You guys get a bad rap," I say graciously. "Your group keeps our team out of trouble on the daily."

"Thank you," he says with a laugh. "Finally, someone who appreciates the benefits of our vocation."

I find him fun and easy to talk to. As members of the larger group start to disperse and begin to say their goodbyes, Jack mentions grabbing a bite to eat together. A date. Eric and my feelings for him circle around me, always present. A year has passed since my last date, which I called an audible on after two outings where we struggled to make conversation. But Jack and I have an easy camaraderie, and the thought of dinner with good company over going home to an empty house suddenly feels very tempting.

"That sounds great."

Together we make our way to a restaurant around the corner, where we are seated immediately at a corner table with a candle flickering in welcome. We share a bottle of red wine and appetizers before ordering our main meals. I devour the food, only belatedly realizing how hungry I was after the workout.

The hours pass by quickly. Jack insists on paying the bill. After signing off on it, he turns toward me. "I have a confession to make."

I raise my eyebrows. "That sounds ominous."

"I noticed you when you first joined the club. Took a while to find the nerve to ask you out."

Touched, I tease, "You're going to give your profession a bad name. You're supposed to be sharks."

He lowers his voice. "You have to keep this between us. If it gets out, I could be ruined."

"I'm glad you did," I say sincerely. "This has been really great. And needed."

"Then would I be pushing it if I asked you for a second date?"

"I'd really like that," I realize.

"Good."

We walk alongside one another to the parking lot. Boston's historic black streetlamps light our way in the night. A few people rush about, toward their cars or train, pulling their coats tighter around them. At my car, I lean my back against the door. He steps close, waiting for my approval, before bending down for a kiss. I meet him halfway, allowing the warmth of it to wash over me. Desire starts at my spine and travels throughout my body. I revel in his embrace, clinging to the back of his shirt as he deepens the kiss. I moan, forgetting for just a moment that, though hidden by the dark, we are nonetheless in public.

His arm slips around me as he pulls me in tighter. On his touch, my mind drifts from the kiss to Eric. A whisper of dreams forgotten as I imagine him holding me, kissing me.

"I'm sorry." Regret mirrors in his eyes as I pull back. My mind protests my need for Eric, a man whose current life has made it impossible for him to want me. "I can't do this. There's someone else. We're not together, but . . ."

"You have feelings." Jack strokes my cheek, his disappointment clear, before stepping back and taking a deep breath. "I'm sorry to hear that. If things change, let me know."

As he walks away, disappointment coils inside me. He's someone I could easily imagine myself with. But my feelings for Eric have kept him and countless others at bay, refusing me the opportunity for more when I ache from the loss of someone who has never been mine.

Inside the car, I stare at my reflection in the visor mirror—swollen lips, flushed face, tired eyes. Reality filters back as the evening fades, shadowed by the night sky. Justin, Eric, Brian, Celine, the betrayal, and Brian's fight for survival—a Ferris wheel that never stops with shifting highs and lows. And my feelings for Eric an umbrella over all of them.

The car engine comes to life as I head back to my empty home.

CHAPTER
TWENTY-NINE

FELICITY

Days have passed since my date with Jack. Since then, work has failed to distract me from thoughts of Justin. My phone screen remains blank—no messages or texts from my son. I have reached out multiple times to see how he is. Recently, he has started to respond, albeit with short answers, but contact nonetheless. Thus, the silence is deafening.

Concerned by the lack of communication, I text Eric to see if he's heard from him. The response is immediate—Brian is not doing well, and they are gathered together in the hospital room.

Without a second thought, I immediately head to the hospital. From the gift shop I quickly grab an electric car and video game console, unsure what gift is appropriate for a boy with cancer. Before entering, I wash up and don the protective gear as required to keep Brian safe from germs.

Inside the room, I find Justin and Eric standing together, Elena near the window, while a frail Brian lies against Celine's chest. Justin, his head dropped low, barely acknowledges me. Eric stares past me, seemingly unaware of my presence. Brian's labored breaths shatter the silence. He shifts in the bed, his bones protruding from his thin skin. Veins, like streaks of a crayon, color his body. Sallow eyes stare at nothing, while his throat convulses with every heartbeat. Celine wraps her arms around him, cocooning him, as she pulls him in tighter.

"I don't feel good," Brian says quietly, seeming to struggle with the words. "Please . . ."

My heart hurts at his plea, one without purpose or destination— just begging to be better, to be free of his fate. I instinctively take a step back, creating distance from his pain, escaping to my life, where my only responsibility is what I need, what I want.

"What is death like?" Brian asks into the silence.

Justin's fingers curl into fists as he shakes his head silently, as if refusing Brian's question and the outcome underlying it. Eric takes a step toward his son, then stops, as if in acknowledging the question he would validate it. Celine's head drops back against the wall, enough space to keep the tears coursing down her cheeks from falling atop her dying son. Silence permeates the room, leaving his plea unanswered.

"My friend stopped breathing . . . ," I start slowly. Celine's face jerks toward me as I hear Eric quietly say my name in curiosity rather than recrimination. I wait half a second, willing to yield to their refusal, but on their silent permission I continue. "We were in a kayak that turned over. We were eleven years old."

Brian laser focuses on me. "She died?"

"Yes. For a few minutes, the lifeguards on the beach couldn't get a heartbeat." Though it was traumatic at the time, I have rarely thought about it in the years since. Maybe I believed it a sign of weakness to perseverate over it or allow it to affect me. Now, the story feels critical. "After they brought her back, she said dying felt like going to sleep, where you have the most amazing dreams and happiness." His eyes widen, and relief fills his face. "But it wasn't her time to die," I say gently, acutely aware of every eye on me, every change in breath in reaction to my story. "And I don't think it's yours."

Celine's tears fall faster. Brian stares at me, the relief shifting to distress, as if confused by my conclusion. Without a response, he leans back against Celine, his eyes closing. Soon, his labored breaths become even as he falls into a deep sleep.

"Thank you," Celine whispers. "What you said to him—"

"The folder said there are additional procedures that can be done," I interrupt, suddenly needing to do something, anything, other than stand by and watch him die. "Another transplant or . . ." I try to remember everything I have read. "A white blood cell transfusion?"

"Donor lymphocyte infusion," Eric says. "The doctors said there are risks with both. For a transplant, Justin would have to undergo more treatments, give additional blood . . ."

Justin watches me carefully for my reaction, for the refusal that came before. But there's nothing left in me to refute him or the possibility of saving his brother. No matter how much I yearn to hide from Celine's pain, I can no longer ignore Justin's.

"Justin, what you've done for your brother . . ." I pause before continuing: "You are his hero. If you want to talk about options or discuss the situation, I am here. But the decision is yours. As it always should have been."

I say my goodbyes, then leave their family, one that now includes Justin, to themselves. There's no room for me in their heartbreak. Inside the empty elevator, I lean against the wall, gripping the handrail. For the first time since all of this started, tears flow unencumbered down my cheeks. I don't wipe them away or try to stop them, instead allowing the pain of Brian to envelop me as I find myself begging silently for a solution to save him.

CHAPTER THIRTY

CELINE

A week has passed since Justin's donor lymphocyte infusion—a donation of white blood cells to help Brian fight the cancer and accept the transplant. The doctor warned us that each donation could save Brian or kill him—his body could reject the white blood cells as a foreign entity and in turn could attack itself.

I watch his sleeping form, his breaths in and out as his body struggles against the disease that's taken it over. I hear the door open and quietly shut behind me. No longer caring about anything or anyone, I don't turn to see who it is. When Eric comes to stand next to me, I barely acknowledge his presence.

"Celine . . . ," Eric starts, then stops. The agony in his voice matches the pain coursing through me.

"I don't know how to say goodbye," I whisper. My tears choke my words. I reach toward Brian, but my hand hovers in the air; I'm afraid of being a burden on his already-broken body. "I can't lose him."

Eric grabs my hand, wrapping his fingers around mine. Too weak to pull away, I instead allow myself to surrender, our sorrow binding us.

No matter what has happened between us, we are Brian's parents. The ones who love him, who don't know how to live without him.

"Is this our fault?" My sob breaks through. "Did we do this to him?" Eric uses our joint hands to turn me toward him. I see my fear mirrored in him. "Because of what happened between us? Does he know his family is damaged?"

"Celine, no." Eric fights back, but his words hold no weight. "He has no idea. He would have said something."

"Then why?" I plead with him, though I know he doesn't have the answers. No one does. "What did we do wrong? Why him? Why *our* son?" As soon as I ask the question, I feel shame wash over me as I think of the countless children fighting their own cancer battles . . . not one of them deserving of what is happening. "Brian . . . every one of the kids on this floor, on every floor of every hospital, has the right to live. Have dreams they deserve to make come true."

"Celine . . ."

"He can't die. Please." I beg Eric, Brian, anyone who will hear my cry. "Please, he can't die."

Eric takes me into his arms as I sob over the son who remains the only bond between us, a bridge to a lifetime that now lies in ruins. A past that pulls us apart. But right now I don't have the power to push him away, to stand on feet that have lost all their strength. All I can do is mourn the son who's now a shell of the child I raised, to say goodbye as his will to live cedes to the power of death.

The door opens, casting a shadow of light into the darkened room. I step out of Eric's arms as Dr. Garren glances at us both. His face drawn, his eyes stray to Brian before returning to us. "We have updated blood results."

CHAPTER THIRTY-ONE

FELICITY

Our flight lands at Chicago O'Hare early in the morning. I have booked Justin and myself on an afternoon return flight, knowing he wants to spend as much time with Brian as possible. Though he agreed to the trip, I know he's struggling with the possibility of saying goodbye to the brother he has just found.

Justin remains quiet in the passenger seat en route to downtown Chicago. I yearn to ask him about his days, the white blood cell transfusion, Lily, anything that will reconnect me to his life. To return to the days when I was his most trusted confidante and our bond unbreakable.

"Where are we going?" He remains wary and distant.

"Something I wanted to show you." The idea came to me a few days prior. Hesitant when I mentioned the trip, I waited, my breath held, until he agreed. It was my Hail Mary in hoping that he could see that in my life, he is the best thing that's ever happened.

Sejal Badani

I take the exit for downtown Chicago. The skyscrapers loom over us, casting us into shadows. We park near the water, then head into the Financial District. The smell of garlic and basil wafts over us. Crowds of locals and tourists fill the streets as Justin, hands stuffed deep into his pockets, walks alongside me.

As we stand in front of the building where I first interned, the blue glass reflects our image back to us. On my first day, I was sure that my entire life was set, that the rest would be easy and simple. I scoff now at my naivete, never imagining how complicated my life would become.

"I got an internship here before my second year of business school." I had beaten out countless classmates for the prestigious position. "I was so happy, so sure of myself." I laugh softly at myself. "I was sure I'd made it."

"Mom . . . ," Justin starts, but I cut him off.

"I was working thirty hours a week on top of going to school full time." My father had told me in no uncertain terms that I had to make it on my own after college. Another test, another opportunity to succeed or fail in his eyes. I secured a scholarship, but since it only covered tuition and books, I had to find a way to pay for room and board. "I probably slept three, four hours a night. This job meant I could quit all the other odd jobs I'd been doing to pay the rent. I was finally doing what I loved and getting paid for it."

"What odd jobs?" Justin asks.

Tempering my excitement at his engagement, I answer, "I was a waitress, a nanny, delivery person." I spent those years exhausted from my jobs and classes, only to then work through the night on papers and homework. While most of my other classmates were busy socializing or solidifying their lives with significant others, I was trying to find my footing. "I even did maid service in my apartment building for a few months when I fell short on rent." After a particularly bad week, I had considered calling my mom for help but changed my mind at the last minute, refusing to give my father the knowledge of me failing.

"I didn't know that," Justin says softly. "You never told me any of this."

Making a conscious decision to keep everything hidden, I hoped that by focusing solely on Justin and his future, my past would permanently fade away, never affecting him. "It didn't matter. Only you did."

He exhales slowly before he turns away. Though anxious to bring him in and offer comfort, I know I am the last person he's seeking it from.

"This is where I worked after my internship," I point out at the next building. "They started me out as an associate. That's what I was when I got pregnant with you. Between taking care of you and working, I fought hard to climb the ladder to management." My life had shifted from long hours of work and school to work and caring for Justin. Having skipped the step of finding a partner and creating a life together, I went from being a child straight to being a parent. "When they made me a director, you, your dad, and I celebrated with apple juice for you and one glass of champagne for your dad and me."

"How old was I?"

"Two years old." To keep Eric's secret, I had to limit the number of people in our lives. My life suddenly revolved around Justin, my work, and the time with Eric. Whether it was a sacrifice or an excuse, I closed myself off, my entire focus on my son and my professional career. "You smashed the cake with your toy and then burst out laughing."

Eric popped the cork on the expensive champagne he had bought while I laid out the dinner delivery. Justin played between us as we clinked our glasses to my promotion. That night I went to bed happy and fulfilled, convinced that though my life was not as I had pictured, it was perfect.

At the building that houses one of the premier firms in the industry, I explain that I was recruited six months after my promotion.

"Here was my next job. Vice president, managing a team of thirty."

It was the job I had worked my entire career for. The one that would establish me as a player in the industry. That would not only guarantee my and Justin's financial future, but my career trajectory also.

"I was promoted to president within a few years."

"Mom?" Justin murmurs, confused. "I don't understand. You were never—"

"And that building right there?" I interrupt him to point to a corner building. "That's where I spent the next few years as CFO. Where I finally made it."

"Mom." Justin faces me directly. "You didn't work here."

Sadness fills my smile. "No, I didn't. I brought you here because, when I was eighteen and in college, I stood right where we are right now and mapped out my entire future. I researched every company to find the ones I wanted to work with. I detailed every step of my life to make sure that I would be as happy as I could be. You were never part of any of those plans."

Justin's face falls with sadness and disbelief as he takes a step back in retreat. I reach for his hand, exhaling when it wraps around mine.

"You changed everything. You became the happiness that I was seeking. Your smile was what brought me peace and a sense of self." The tension slowly seeps out of his hand. "This was my dream before you. Honey, don't you see? All of this? None of it would have mattered without you. I had no idea what real happiness was until you."

"You sacrificed your career for me, Mom. How is that happiness?"

"I love my career," I return. "I didn't sacrifice it because of you." I pause, then add, "I have everything because I have you. You're the best thing that will have ever happened to me."

"I don't . . ." Justin turns away, the rejection a wound within me. "Why did you show me this?"

"You hate me for what I did—from the circumstances surrounding your conception to every decision over the last seventeen years." Fear that this is a mistake, that I have miscalculated and made the situation worse than it was before, pushes me to speak faster, nearly rambling.

"This was the life I'd planned for. That I was prepared for." I gesture toward the buildings. "I had no playbook where you were concerned. I messed up." For the first time in seventeen years, I reverse the roles and put myself in Justin's shoes. In Celine's shoes. And both of them make me feel a shame I have never imagined before. "But loving you is the best gift I've ever been given. And I wouldn't change it for anything. Not for the career I imagined. Not for a son that came about under different circumstances. If given the chance to do it again, I'd do it exactly the same way so I can have you."

I inhale as I wait for his response. Around us, the world continues as workers swarm in and out of buildings. Food carts fill the streets with the aromas of their offerings. Street cleaners pick up trash with their sticks. A plane flies overhead as it ascends into the clouds.

"What you've done for your brother, the transplant, the donation . . ." I pause, the pride I feel for him overwhelming me. "I am so proud of you. No matter what happens, you've fought for him. You are his hero. And you are mine."

"Mom." Justin blinks, and I swallow at the sheen of tears in his eyes. "That's the thing that's so frustrating. Ask me to choose any mom from anywhere, and I'd still choose you. That's why I'm so mad at you. Because I love you." His next words stop me with their honesty. "And I know you love me. I just wish my mom hadn't hurt other people because of me. You've taught me better than that."

A ping on his phone has him pulling it out of his pocket. His face lights up as he turns the phone toward me so I can read the text from Eric.

Brian is in remission.

CHAPTER THIRTY-TWO

CELINE

Brian's recovery has been slow and steady as he regains energy every day. The doctor is cautiously optimistic about his health. I watch him, wary but with hope and gratitude blooming inside me. The steps that have led us here still feel safer to push into the deepest recesses of my mind, where they can't hold any power over me. Where I don't have to deal with the pain or the repercussions.

Mom and I play a game of Uno with Brian. He grins as he ends up with the final card, readying himself to beat us. His body has begun to fill out with weight as his appetite returns, and his face is fuller, reminding me of the boy he used to be.

"Uno," he says proudly, laying down his last card. Before we can congratulate him, he adds, "Thanks for playing with me."

My mom and I glance at one another. He's never before thanked us for playing games or spending time with him. Now, he looks at us with earnestness and gratitude.

"Of course, sweetheart," she answers first. "It's my favorite part of the day, spending time with you."

Brian lights up with a smile, another thing we haven't seen in so long. Each action is a reminder that he's coming back to us because of Justin. And Felicity.

"Can I go to the rec room?" he asks.

Mom immediately agrees and joins him on the trip there. I take advantage of the quiet and dial Eric's number. Picking up on the first ring, he has a cautiously optimistic response. "Hey, everything okay?"

"I was calling to see if you had time to get together?" My voice hardens into one used for business—disconnected but firm. With all the recent events and revelations, I have to find a new normal with Eric, both for Brian's sake and mine. "We should talk about Brian's release from the hospital." Next steps in preparation of him coming home.

Immediately agreeing, Eric offers for us to meet at the house, but I counter with the apartment. He falls silent, then asks slowly, "How did you know?"

"Does it matter?"

We agree to meet in an hour at an address in the Back Bay. Mom returns as I hang up.

"He immediately started playing with some of the other kids," she says, her happiness clear.

Though still cautious, I cannot help but react to her optimism. "He looks good." We hug, both of us gravitating toward one another more often, needing to celebrate, even cautiously. "I went to the old apartment a while ago."

Her face falls, and she takes a step back. "Why?"

"Everything that's happened, I think I needed to say goodbye." I shrug my shoulders. "It looks the same."

Mom exhales, then takes a seat on the chair, her hands clasped together. "I haven't been back to the neighborhood since we left. There was nothing left for us there."

Though it was where Dad grew up, I have always assumed it was her home also. "You didn't miss it?"

"No," she says immediately. "After he left, I just didn't see the point. My marriage to your father took things away as well as giving me so much. Maybe I didn't want to remember how much I loved him . . . or why."

"It's the same struggle I face," I admit quietly.

She squeezes my hand. "Why did you fall in love with Eric?"

I think about the question, looking past the obvious. "He was kind and funny and sweet. He treated me well. And he was . . ."

"Stable. Reliable. Steady," she finishes.

In offering me those things, he gave me what I had lost when my father left. "I loved him."

Our courtship began with dates that quickly turned from every weekend into every weeknight. I calmed my nerves by convincing myself it was a sign of his love and commitment. And his support of me while I worked to buy ownership into the farm convinced me I had found my happily ever after.

"He swept me off my feet."

"Do you remember when you came to me the night before the wedding and asked me if I was sure you were doing the right thing?"

"I didn't trust my own decision." After Eric came to me, I feared what he hadn't said. Now, I feel like a fool for not pushing, for my gullibility. I believed what I wanted.

"You didn't have an example to follow," Mom says kindly. "Your main goal was to marry someone who wasn't your father. Someone who wouldn't hurt you."

The irony leaves a lump in my throat. I was desperate to get as far away from the memory of my father as possible, but instead he had remained with me every step of the way.

Unable to stop, I finally ask the question that has been haunting me. "Mom, did I make a mistake in marrying Eric?"

My mom hesitates before answering, "If marrying Eric was a mistake, then that makes Brian a mistake. And I don't believe you think that."

A headache begins at the base of my neck, traveling to my temples. I gambled on who I thought Eric was and lost. "I'd do all of this again to have Brian. But"—I pause and ask the question with no answer—"what if I could have had Brian with someone else?"

Part of me expects my mother to scoff at me or lecture me about the absurdity of the question. Instead, she smiles sadly. "I asked myself the same question after your father left. If I'd chosen someone else, would I have had you but in a better situation? I never got the answer. All I had was you, us, and reality. I had to figure it out. Just as you have to now."

Eric watches me silently as I survey the three-bedroom home created for him, Felicity, and Justin. Though the place is sparsely furnished, the decor is warm and inviting, with an air of sophistication. Instinct says that Felicity had a hand in creating the perfect space for their facade. The sofas are luxurious but comfortable enough for a young Justin to use as a foundation from which to fly. The wood coffee table with rounded edges is designed to prevent a child from accidentally harming himself. Warmth exudes from the silk plant in the corner. Multiple lamps fill the room with bright light to keep spirits uplifted during the dark winters. Framed pictures of Justin and the three of them together declare them a family.

"How did you keep it hidden?" My voice loses its battle to remain steady as I admire a picture of a young Justin in his soccer uniform, smiling widely into the camera. If not for the color of his hair, he could easily be mistaken for Brian at the same age. "From everyone we know in Boston?"

"He only came over a few dozen times, mostly when he was young." Hands in his pockets, Eric looks like a stranger in his own home. "When he did, we would order in, make a night of it." He pauses, then admits, "You thought I was traveling."

"You had everything figured out." I have always admired him for his intellect and ingenuity. He used both to deceive me, betraying our marriage. "The perfect setup."

"Celine—"

"We need to tell Brian," I interrupt. The desire for recrimination or arguments fades in the face of my son and what he needs. My mom's words echo in my head. Brian is the only thing that can matter now. "They're spending so much time together . . ."

"Does he not like him?" There's fear in Eric's question, apprehension on his face. He loves his sons and wants them to get along, like any parent who frets when their children fight. "Has Brian said something?"

"Brian loves him," I say quietly. "As far as he's concerned, Justin is the best thing that's ever happened to him." After every one of their interactions, Brian has regaled my mom and me with details of their time together. Brian has quickly and completely fallen in love with his older brother without realizing their blood bond. "And Justin is . . ." I stare at Justin's second home, imagining my husband, his son, and Felicity spending time together as a family. "He's saved Brian. He's an amazing young man."

"The grave . . . ," Eric starts, then pauses on my confusion. "Your father's grave." I took Eric to it once after we had started dating. He asked a few questions but then moved on from it, as he assumed I had done. "I didn't want Justin having to do the same for me."

Stunned, I question if the admission is a play, then see his sincerity. My childhood has served as a cautionary note to Eric about how not to handle his son.

"I couldn't, wouldn't abandon him as your father did to you. I see what it's done to you, how much it's hurt you."

The irony nearly brings me to tears. My father has been a catalyst for Eric's betrayal over the last seventeen years. He calculated the cost and benefit of the truth versus the lie and found that hurting me was the best solution. Too exhausted to sneer at his audacity, I simply shake my head in disgust.

"Did you ever think about Brian while here with Justin?" Did he miss Brian while spending time with Justin?

"Every minute." Eric runs a hand through his hair. "When with Justin, I thought about Brian. And when with Brian, I thought about Justin." When he takes a step toward me, I move back. He notes the reaction but keeps any thoughts to himself. "I didn't plan what happened, Celine. I just tried to make it work."

"Work?" I remind myself that this is not the time or place but cannot help myself. With Brian in recovery, I have the unexpected luxury of lashing out at the betrayal that we have left simmering. "Work for whom? Me? Our marriage? You lied to me for seventeen years, Eric. You didn't just have an affair. You had another family." I finally ask the question that has haunted me ever since he revealed the truth. "Why did you marry me?" There was no Brian at the time. The stakes were low. A broken engagement feels so much easier than everything he has created since.

Eric shakes his head slightly. When his gaze meets mine, I am taken aback by the sadness. "I loved you."

"You slept with another woman." I refute his declaration, hating him for having made me fall completely in love with him. "You knew she was pregnant when you walked down the aisle. How could you possibly claim you loved me?"

"Do you remember our first date?" Eric doesn't wait for my answer. "You spoke about the farm, your mother, your dad, Kaitlyn . . ." He pauses before adding, "Austin. You never once talked about you."

I bristle at his implication. "Are you trying to blame me for what you did?"

"No," Eric insists. "God, no. While we were dating, I learned something new about you every day. But it was tidbits, small things that didn't matter. Your favorite color, your sleep schedule. It was as if the real you, the whole you, was off limits. But the parts you shared with me? I was in love."

"So, the night you cheated?"

Eric sighs, and I see his struggle to explain. "Felicity laid herself bare. In one night, we talked about everything. Hopes, dreams, fears, phobias. I knew more about her that night than I knew about you after two years."

"Then why not walk away?"

"Because I loved who I knew, and I wanted to know the rest of you." I hear his sincerity but cannot react to it. "I didn't want to lose you."

"We haven't been married for seventeen years." Anger at his betrayal drives my words. The loss of him, our marriage, has left an emptiness I hate him for creating. "You lost me the night you slept with Felicity. And every day since, you burned our foundation and salted the earth."

"Celine . . ."

"I think about all the times I rationalized you missing Brian's games or the weeks and weeks you weren't here, with us. And I know"—I pause to quell my emotions—"I know that Justin deserved his father. That he deserved for you to be there with him and to give him love. I see the results. But I deserved the truth. I deserved to know that the man I was sleeping with, the man I called my husband, was someone I could trust."

"It wasn't about you," Eric says, stopping me. "I know it doesn't make sense, but once Justin was born, it was no longer about you or our marriage. It was about my son."

"And what about our son?" I lash out.

"He was mine. The whole world knew I was his father. That we were a family." Eric drops down onto the sofa. "Justin just had a facade."

The fight goes out of me. I take a seat on the sofa next to him. A marriage in ruins. Lives tangled by lies, deceits, and manipulations. But at the end of it all, none of it matters. It can't.

"Every day I think about what you did. And I hate you so much for all of it." I think about love—often discovered during our happiest moments but defined during our hardest ones. "But if not for that night with Felicity, if not for the love you gave Justin, I'd have no hope for my son. Because both of you raised him to be the young man he is— someone who loves his brother and will do anything for him." I pause, then add, "Just like his father did anything for him." I ask, needing to know, "The night before the wedding, when you came to see me, were you trying to tell me then?"

"Maybe. I don't know." He sighs. "I just knew I needed to see you." He pauses, then asks softly, "If I'd told you, what would you have done?"

I have asked myself the same question dozens of times. Each time it comes back to Brian. "Then I would've walked away," I admit. "But now, with Brian as my son, a part of me is so grateful you didn't."

"Celine . . . ," Eric starts, then stops. "I never meant to hurt you."

In my husband's home, I stare at the pictures of his son and his other family. "Yes, you did." I can feel his gaze but don't meet it. "It doesn't matter now, but one day, when all of this is over, when we can breathe something other than fear and doubt and sadness, you have to figure out why." I grab my keys and cell phone. "Until then, let's stop pretending that we're anything other than what we've always been—two strangers who played house."

CHAPTER THIRTY-THREE

CELINE

"One evening." Kaitlyn holds out her hand for my phone. "Brian comes home tomorrow. Tonight, he's being watched by your mom, Eric, dozens of doctors and nurses, and God knows who else." She softens her voice. "After he's home, you're going to be with him twenty-four seven. Tonight, you get to breathe."

Brian is healing. There have been times I have woken up in disbelief, unable to believe that the nightmare might truly be over. And with it my marriage. That situation, though my reality, still feels distant, as if I am watching a movie in which I am the star.

"He'll survive," Kaitlyn promises me, seeming to read my concern at being away from him for too long. "At least for the night."

"Kaitlyn," I admonish.

"Too soon?" Kaitlyn's eyebrows shoot up when I nod yes. "Huh, wouldn't have guessed that."

"Because of the transplant?" I ask.

"No," Kaitlyn says with sincerity, "because he's going to be fine. He has to be. He's too loved to leave us."

A rare warmth steals over me until it replaces the fear in my heart with love and gratitude. I pull Kaitlyn in and hold my friend close, wondering yet again at the irony of my life—in losing my father, I gained first Austin and then Kaitlyn, along with Brian and a career that I love. With the relief of Brian's health returning, I am finding myself grateful for the things I have always taken for granted.

"I love you," I murmur into Kaitlyn's hair. "So much."

"I know," Kaitlyn returns, tongue in cheek. "Kind of hard not to."

"All right, I'm in. What are we doing?"

"Waiting for him," Kaitlyn says, pointing to Austin, who's just exited his car and is walking toward us.

"You invited Austin?" I ask.

"Is that okay?"

Every interaction since he's returned to town has been about being there for me, reclaiming our friendship. "Yes, of course. I'm just surprised he's made the time."

"Part of this was his idea," Kaitlyn shares, surprising me. "He knew Brian is coming home tomorrow so thought it would be nice to give you a few hours of downtime."

"Hey," he says when he reaches us. "You ready?"

So much has happened since Brian's diagnosis and all the changes with it. I have gone from believing I knew everything about my life to realizing I had been blissfully unaware of it as it was playing out. Trust suddenly feels like a luxury. But I refuse to let Eric take that away from me. Even if it requires small steps, I need to take them.

"Yes, let's do this."

◆　◆　◆

"I absolutely refuse to do this," I yell over the sound of the engine. The pilot has just announced that we have reached jumping altitude. "No."

Austin grins at me as he gestures toward my instructor. "He's the best in the business. He's promised me you're safe."

"I don't believe him." I mouth a silent apology to the instructor, who gestures that he understands and has no hard feelings. "And when did you start doing this for fun?"

"It was a rite of passage in my fraternity." Austin tightens the straps of my parachute, then rechecks my helmet. "Once you do it, you'll be begging me to go again."

"No, I won't." I glance accusingly at Kaitlyn, who lounges in her seat. "You're okay with this?"

Kaitlyn shrugs. "It's not me who's jumping."

The second instructor had called at the last minute, unable to make it, meaning one of us had to forfeit. "You can still go instead of me," I offer.

"Wouldn't dream of it," Kaitlyn says graciously.

"I hate you." I point a finger at Austin. "That includes you."

"Disappointed if you didn't." He gestures toward the door. "Time to go, C."

"Why can't I jump with you?" It might make me calmer about this whole thing.

His eyes warm with my question. "I'm not certified, C."

"That's debatable," I reply, playing with words. "It's just that if this thing goes sideways and I die on the way down, I want to make sure and kill you first."

Austin's lip twitches. "Appreciate that."

On the threshold of the plane, I reach for Austin's hand, relaxing in response to his steadiness and security, then give the necessary thumbs-up to the instructor. Together, the three of us leap off the plane into the abyss.

I force my eyes open as the world rushes toward me at a dizzying pace. The wind whips against my face. Like the first time I rode a horse, I vacillate between fear and excitement before everything fades into the distance. The cancer, Eric, and Felicity. Instead, a feeling of power and humility engulfs me. The world that has become too much now welcomes me, offering a different perspective. One from which I can draw strength rather than weakness.

The instructor pulls the handle, drawing the parachute out. As it balloons open, it drags us momentarily upward before settling us into a relaxed pace of descent. As instructed, I push my legs down and hold on to the parachute rope as miles of open land greet us. In the final few moments, I welcome the chance to focus solely on my landing, forcing all other thoughts to the background. Austin, having already landed, waits below, watching. He offers a thumbs-up in support.

As my feet touch the ground, I let out a laugh of triumph. After disentangling from the parachute and thanking the instructor, I rush toward Austin, who smiles brightly at me. "That was amazing!"

He laughs, then stops, his fingers reaching out. "You're crying?" Surprised, I touch my face. His thumb caresses my cheeks as he wipes away a tear. He looks past me toward the instructor and parachute. "Everything go okay?"

I quickly reassure him that it was wonderful. "I guess I'm just . . ." I struggle with how to describe my emotions. Happiness feels elusive and impossible, given the circumstances. "Free. For just a few minutes I was free." Through a deep breath, I fight to bring my emotions under control. "Thank you."

"So, you're not going to kill me?" Austin teases.

"Not today." Suddenly feeling silly, I step back. Similar to the low after a high, sadness creeps over me. "We should probably find Kaitlyn."

"Hey." Austin reaches for my hand as I start to move away. "Don't do that. Don't shut down." His thumb runs across my skin. "You're allowed to have been free for just a minute, C. It doesn't take away from your love for Brian."

"He's not . . ." I try to give voice to what anchors me to the sadness. "How can I be free when Brian isn't fully?" Guilt and despair war together. Though Brian is coming home, I know we are not out of the woods yet. Freedom feels impossible when my son is still fighting.

Seated on the sofas, the three of us devour our takeout food. Kaitlyn chooses her favorite playlist, filling the room with the soothing sounds of jazz and classics. The hours pass by as we get lost in a comfortable silence and a healthy exhaustion.

"Thank you both for today," I say once we're sated. "It's been a while since I've smiled." In the life before Brian's illness, I can remember moments of happiness. Though my days were complicated, they were nonetheless manageable. My marriage gave me a false confidence that the answers, no matter how difficult, would come to me. That some-how, someway, I would find my path. Eric's betrayal has shown me that if you don't seek the right questions, you'll never get the correct answers. "Between the cremation and today, I may have to start paying you both for your time."

Kaitlyn points a spring roll at Austin. "Well, not him. He should be paying us."

Austin holds up both hands in surrender. "Can I wave the white flag for tonight?"

Kaitlyn shrugs in agreement when I agree. "Only because you paid for dinner. Should have gotten caviar," Kaitlyn murmurs before turning toward me. "Tomorrow, what happens?"

The day I have been waiting for every moment since the diagnosis, but wasn't sure I believed would ever come, is finally here. "My mom, Eric, and I will take him home tomorrow after discharge. Eric"—I pause—"will stay with us as long as Brian needs, then be at his apart-ment." I don't meet their eyes as I add, "He's had it for years. For Justin."

"If there's anything you need," Kaitlyn starts, her tone relaying sympathy and support at my revelation, "say the word."

Austin's gaze stays on me as we clean up, then get ready to say our goodbyes. At the door, Kaitlyn hugs me, both of us holding on longer than usual. Austin has started to follow her out when he realizes that he forgot his phone in the kitchen.

"Let me grab it quick."

As I wait for him by the door, I think about our time together, the friendship that has been rebuilt, reshaped from the past to fit the present. Recall what my mom said about his feelings. When he joins me moments later, phone in hand, the question slips out before I can censor myself. "Why did you come back?"

He raises an eyebrow, considering me. "For the farm. For my parents."

"Why did you stay?" The words seem to have a mind of their own. He watches me carefully, both of us aware of the other. "My mom said that your mom said . . ."

"Are we twelve years old?" His smile softens his words.

I ignore him and continue, "That you had a crush on me back then."

"Hmm, sounds intriguing." With his poker face, he does not flinch nor give much away.

Unsure why I am pushing, I do nonetheless: "Did you?"

"It wouldn't have mattered." His vague answer leaves me with more questions. "You didn't want to know."

"Seems to be the story of my life—not knowing."

"What would you have done if you knew?"

A question with a question. "Back then? Maybe had my first kiss?" I grimace, then admit, "It was a real pain to accomplish that one later on." Still essentially alone at the school, I finally succeeded at what felt like an impossible goal at a horse race with another jockey.

He smirks. "First kiss, huh? I'm honored."

"I wouldn't have felt like an idiot during. Since we were friends," I clarify. "You were safe."

His eyes hold mine. "Of course. Safe."

Uncomfortable, I gesture toward the door. "I should go."

He grins. "You live here." Right. Smiling to ease my discomfort, he adds, "Seems to me we have three options. One, I leave and you go to sleep. Second, we stay here and keep staring at one another, or . . ." He trails off.

"You said three," I encourage, waiting for the option that I want.

"I'm letting you decide on the third," he says gallantly.

"That's presumptuous." I keep talking in hopes of finding my footing. "You shouldn't have said 'three'; should have said 'two.' I'm just saying, in negotiations . . ."

"Is this a negotiation?" Austin interrupts, trying hard not to laugh.

"Are you dating anyone?" I vaguely remember talking about it before, but I'm asking again for confirmation. On his no, I ask, "Married?" No. "That's smart."

"I'll keep that in mind."

"Not for everyone," I clarify. "Just when your husband cheats on you." Testing my new reality, I admit, "I'm getting a divorce."

"Figured that out when you cremated your wedding ring," he says gently.

In the deep end of a pool I have never swum in, I remind him, "You're stealing my farm."

"Buying."

"In my mind, I can't see the difference."

He grabs my hand. "I wish I could change your mind." Sighing, he releases it. "For what it's worth? I'm sorry. That I'm stealing it."

I smile sadly. "I'm a bad bet."

"You sure?" he asks, surprising me. "I'm just seeing it from a different perspective, I guess." On my confusion, he adds, "Seems like you're a fighter. Always have been. That makes you a great bet."

Touched by his words, I admit, "I haven't kissed anyone else in over seventeen years. I don't know how . . ."

"You don't know how to kiss? It's kind of like riding a bike."

"No, I know how to kiss," I correct. "I just don't know what comes with it."

"Well, usually there's not this much talking beforehand," he says, seeming to be holding in his laughter.

"What happens after? I'm not someone who jumps into bed."

"Now who's being presumptuous?" he asks me with a straight face, then smiles to show he's teasing. "What do you want?"

I search for an answer. "I fear I'm broken."

He cups my face, his eyes boring into mine. "I refuse to believe that. Wounded, maybe, but not broken." His thumb rubs back and forth over my cheek. "What do you want?"

To fix me feels impossible. Anxious about my answer, I yearn to turn away, to refuse his demand of honesty and the chance of being hurt.

"I want to think about something other than the pain." The past few months and the turmoil that has come with it have left me and everything I was sure about myself fragmented, with some of the pieces too broken to repair. "I want to forget, just for a minute, about everything. I want to be in control of my life."

"How about this?" He gives me a kiss on the cheek, then steps back. "We call it a night? You go pick up your son tomorrow, bring him home, and enjoy it. And then, one day, when your life doesn't feel like a million different directions pulling at you, you let me take you out for dinner."

"A date?" Moving forward, leaving the pain in the past, feels like a luxury reserved for others, never me. "That sounds good." He will go home, and I will go to bed. It makes sense. Except . . . I don't want him to leave. Not yet. In the months since Brian's diagnosis, my times with Austin have been the rare moments of happiness I have had. "Since it's been a while for me and clearly not for you, is it okay to kiss someone before the date or only after?"

He looks at me, questioning. "Before is fine."

"Yeah?" I bridge the distance between us, then stop. "I don't want to take advantage of you."

"I'll take one for the team." Austin takes a step toward me, gently wrapping a hand around the back of my neck and around my waist, bringing me closer. "Say no and I stop." He waits, giving me time.

When my hands reach for him, he bends down low and brushes his lips over mine.

"Austin . . . ," I gasp, my hands clutching his shirt.

"You said you feel out of control. Right now, you're in control. Whatever you want, take it."

My past and everything I believe about myself are in a war against my present. If I do this, it will be the first time I have chosen for myself since having Brian and working at the farm. The first time I have given to myself without fearing I am not allowed or am not good enough. Austin was my childhood friend, my confidant, and my best friend. He now stands before me, offering me the chance to find myself.

On my tiptoes, I set my lips against his. He waits, allowing me to take the next step. I wrap my arms around him and kiss him again. He pulls me in tight, asking for permission before deepening the kiss. My moan matches his as I lose myself in the sensation, the warmth, and the familiarity. Feelings that I couldn't imagine before roar back to life, engulfing me. We continue to kiss, our past, our renewed friendship, and our feelings for one another bringing us closer. As he surrounds me, the wound that was open, always bleeding, finally starts to heal.

CHAPTER
THIRTY-FOUR

FELICITY

The plane comes in for a landing at the San Francisco airport. The transcontinental flight took over six hours from Boston Logan. We circled over the bay for fifteen minutes as we waited for our turn to land. Similarly to Logan, the runway jutted over the water, with lights illuminating the asphalt. The city of hills is shrouded in a low-lying fog.

In the distance, I admire the iconic Golden Gate Bridge and the artistic haven of Sausalito beyond it. Alcatraz sits in the middle of the water, a tourist attraction I have always had on my list of places to see whenever I am visiting but have never ended up making time for. It occurs to me that if I move here, I'll have all the time to see that and more.

I continue to stare out at the city, lost in thought. During the flight, I reviewed the company's financials and the bios of the other executives I'll meet. I've connected with them over video conferencing, so I look forward to spending the next two days with them. Though I excel at these types of meetings and interviews, having been around high-end players my entire childhood, I still feel the need to prove myself, to show myself and the world that I am my father's daughter.

Once at the gate, I quickly check my email and voicemail. As expected, I have a long list of both. I send quick messages to those who need immediate responses and mark others for later before heading out of the plane toward the waiting car.

I've mentioned the trip to Justin without going into details. I want to take the interview, explore the opportunity, without the distraction of explaining the reason for wanting the job or the possibility of me taking it. The decision to interview came after our trip to Chicago. Justin's reaction, his disdain and disappointment, sat like lead inside my heart. But since then, I have received a text or two from him. An opening that I have been responding to carefully, not wanting to push or ask him for more than he wants to give. The interview will give me the chance to get away from Boston. From the fallout of my decisions. From my son not wanting to be around me . . . just like my father.

"Would you like to make any stops?" the driver asks as he maneuvers us out of airport traffic and toward the city. "Food or essentials?"

"I'm fine, thank you. Straight to the hotel, please."

I'll order a quick salad from room service. The time difference and the jet lag have pushed me past exhaustion. I yearn for a quick shower and bed. Though I avoided business trips as much as possible when Justin was growing up, the few I did take, I would either find a way to bring him with me or Eric would watch him. I always made sure to call him before and after school and before he went to bed. Though he never complained about my trips, I never wanted him to be afraid or feel alone. It was one of the thousands of little things that I hadn't accounted for when I decided to become a single parent.

Now, I glance at my phone but don't make any motion to contact Justin. I let Eric know about the trip, repeating the same story to him— that it's a business meeting rather than telling him the truth about the interview. I'm not ready to talk about it yet or put expectations in anyone's mind. And with everything Eric has going on, I knew it was the last thing he would be concerned about. He can barely think about me or anyone else when he's in the midst of fighting for his son's future.

Once at the hotel and in my room, I glance through the menu, but even the salads don't sound appetizing. I take a quick shower and then climb into bed, my eyes closing of their own volition.

◆ ◆ ◆

"We're so happy you decided to continue the process." The CEO shakes my hand and then motions for me to take a seat.

Founder of the company, he started it straight out of Stanford business school. In the eight years since, the company has grown substantially and is considered a unicorn—a high-value company to watch carefully.

We move past the pleasantries of my trip and the city before he leans back in his chair and speaks bluntly. "I'm looking for someone who can get us through our IPO. I'm hoping that's in the next five years, if our schedule holds." He assesses me, his gaze unwavering. "I'm going to be honest. I'm looking for a grown-up. When we started, we were a young crew. People came to work in flip-flops and hoodies. We took naps by our cubicles and played beer pong when things got too quiet." I listen intently as he continues to describe the company's early years. "As you saw when you came in, we have grown up a little. But not enough." He shrugs. "We've narrowed it down to you and two other people. All three of you have experience and credentials."

"It's a great company, and I like what I've read and heard. Everyone on the team is great," I say diplomatically. "I'm excited to move forward with the process."

"Excellent." He stands. "I'll take you around." He pauses, glancing at me. "One point that I should make clear. I know you're currently located in Boston, but this job would require you to be here at all times." I maintain a poker face as he continues, even as a thread of dread unspools inside me. "You'll have a stake in the company. We need you to be as invested in us as we will be in you. I'm hoping that the options will more than pay you handsomely for any inconvenience in making the transition."

My thoughts on Justin, I nod my head. "Let's get started."

CHAPTER THIRTY-FIVE

CELINE

Three days have passed since Brian returned home, every one of them feeling surreal, a normal I wasn't sure I would ever experience again. Eric pushed the wheelchair as my mom and I carried his things. Watching Eric walk into our home . . . I wondered at our new reality, hoping that my heart, which still felt the pain, could find a way to heal.

Early morning, I'm sitting at the kitchen table when I hear Eric's footsteps on the stairs. Immediately I straighten, both of us staring at one another before he gestures toward the coffee.

"Is there enough, or . . ."

Not making enough coffee for one another, watching each other like strangers—our new normal. "Yes, of course. There's plenty." I gesture toward the pot. "Brian had a good night."

"Good. The doctor said the first few days are critical, so the rest will do him good."

Eric takes a sip of his coffee, seeming to forget his normal sugar and cream. I start to remind him, then realize it's not my place. Not anymore, if ever it was.

"What you said at the apartment . . . ," Eric starts.

"It doesn't matter," I tell him. "All that matters now is Brian and his full recovery."

My kiss with Austin helped to free my mind, even if only slightly. A week ago, I would not have known how to be in the kitchen of our home having a civil conversation with Eric, let alone sharing the house with him. The happiness with Austin is allowing me to step back from the pain of my marriage, to see another door even while one is closing.

Eric is halted from answering when Brian and Mom come down the stairs. She offers us a bright smile as Brian takes the steps on his own. Eric and I immediately approach, offering our son a hug one after the other.

"Can I go to the farm?" Brian asks, his gaze locked on me. "I miss it."

"Yes, honey, of course." I replay the scene from a short while ago, after the test, when Brian asked the same thing. Then, I had no idea of Justin or Felicity. Then, I had no idea if my son was going to live or die. "We can leave after breakfast."

Eric surprises me with his immediate agreement. He makes a quick breakfast for Brian while my mom and I help him to get dressed. Unsure if Eric will want to join us, I'm relieved when he tells Brian to have a good time.

"Can we invite Justin?" Brian looks between Eric and me, waiting.

"Yeah, of course." On my agreement, Eric takes out his phone and texts his son as I keep my face blank, hoping Brian doesn't question why Eric has Justin's number. On a beep, Eric says, "He will meet you guys at the farm."

On the drive there, Brian stares out the window at the passing trees. When I try to engage him in conversation, he offers me quick answers, then returns to his musings. I leave him be, wanting him to have his time. In the parking lot, I help Brian out of the car. As we walk toward the barn, Brian slows his steps.

"Some of the kids with cancer won't get better, right? In the hospital."

My heart slows, nearly stopping. I grip his hand, fighting to keep my tears at bay. "No, sweetheart. They won't."

"Why am I getting better?" Brian asks. "Because of Justin?"

"Yes, honey, because of Justin," I say, treading carefully.

Brian stares out at the farm, lost in his thoughts. Finally, he says, "I wish everyone had a Justin."

I bend down to hug him, holding my son close. "Me too," I whisper into his thin shoulder. "Me too, baby."

Against the fence, I watch as Kaitlyn and Brian ride alongside Justin, who explained he has never ridden before. On arrival, Kaitlyn scooped Brian into a tight hug. Now, her arms wrapped around him, she gives him the freedom to ride the horse, to find parts of himself again. Though Justin is on Felix, our slowest horse, I'm grateful a farm employee is staying close to them.

"I wasn't expecting to see you here today," Austin says, joining me. "How are you?"

Not having seen him since our kiss, I struggle against an uncharacteristic shyness. He texted me the next morning, saying to let him know if he could help in any way with Brian. Busy with Brian, I wasn't able to connect afterward.

"I'm good." Unsure of how to do this, I glance at him from the side of my eyes. "How are you?" Sensing my discomfort, he smirks, teasing me. In response, I smack him lightly on the arm, relishing the playfulness between us. "It's not funny."

"I'm sorry." A step closer, his arm brushes mine. He watches me carefully for my reaction, his eyes warming when I close the distance between us so we are shoulder to shoulder. "We're taking it day by day." He gestures toward the boys. "Brian is your priority. He's who matters." Jerking his chin toward Justin, he asks, "His brother?" On my yes, he says, "They're good together."

Every moment spent with Justin drives home how kind and gentle he is. "He goes out of his way to be good to Brian."

"He's being a good older brother," Austin says quietly.

"I wanted to hate him," I admit. With the gripping fear of losing Brian slowly easing, the reality of the rest of my life is beginning to surface. "For being born. For being Eric's first son. For tearing up my family."

"But you don't," Austin surmises.

"Besides the fact that he's a really great young man?" I shake my head. "He saved Brian's life. What kind of monster would that make me?"

"An understandable one," Austin says quietly. "There are no rules here, C. You're playing in unknown territory."

My shirt clings to me from the humidity. The same one I wore yesterday; I can't remember if I put it back on after showering or if I simply forgot to shower. The last few days have melded together as my focus has fixated on Brian and his healing.

"He's staying at his girlfriend's house." On Austin's unspoken question, I share, "He left home after learning what Eric and Felicity did to him." Austin's familiarity draws me in, offering a safe haven in the uncertainty of my life. "For what they did to me and Brian. How is that possible?"

"It sounds like there's a deeper question," Austin says.

"How can two people who did something so terrible create someone so wonderful?" The incessant question in my head after spending time with Justin, learning who he is, separate from his parents. "Shouldn't he be this terrible, selfish, lying kid who doesn't care about anyone's feelings but his own?"

"Like his parents, you mean?" Austin shrugs. "That's a lot of pressure on the kid."

"I wanted to hate him for what happened." When I learned about him, he was both my savior and my demise. "If not for Justin, Eric would have cheated on me once. Because of Justin, Eric's been lying to me for over seventeen years."

"He's an easy target," Austin appropriately assesses.

"And yet, who he is, everything he is, they created that." Which begs the question: Who did Eric sacrifice so he could be there to raise Justin into the young man he is?

"And you think that's at the expense of you or Brian?"

"Eric's never made one of Brian's games, and yet, he was at every single one of Justin's. He and I have been"—I pause, struggling with the words—"strangers. I see that now." And yet, he could have walked away at any point. He could have canceled the wedding, but he didn't. I loved him. So much. And denying the pain of that feels farcical, as if I am fooling myself in hopes of surviving the fallout.

"Together you two created this amazing little boy who is just as kind and wonderful as Justin is." Austin's gaze holds mine. "I'm guessing Eric loves Brian. You wouldn't have stayed with him if he didn't. He may not have done the same things for Brian as he did for Justin, but he loves your son." Austin places his hand over mine, our fingers intertwining for a heartbeat. "And he loves Justin. Maybe that's all that matters."

As he walks away, I process his words—no matter how betrayed and angry I am, it was Eric and Felicity, not Justin, who made the decision. Justin, like Brian, was innocent in all of it.

"Mom." Brian and Justin head toward the paddock exit. Kaitlyn walks a few steps behind, giving me a quick thumbs-up for Brian's experience. "I taught Justin how to saddle a horse."

"Good job, sweetheart." Fatigue and exhaustion lace his words. "How about you boys take a break?"

My heart melts when Brian looks to Justin for approval. "Maybe I'll lie down in the bedroom inside?"

"I want to call Lily and let her know how cool I looked riding today," Justin says conspiratorially. "I'll catch up with you in a bit?"

Kaitlyn offers to walk Brian to one of the bedrooms. Brian moves slowly, carefully, as if he doesn't trust himself or the world to support him. I swallow the pain that remains right on the edge of my throat, waiting quietly in the shadows. Once he's safely inside, I find a smile before turning toward my husband's son.

"Thank you for being here with him today." I laugh self-consciously. "Thank you for everything."

Justin shrugs before looking away. "He's my little brother." His words are so matter of fact that they stop me for a moment. "It's what I'm supposed to do."

No, I think, *it's not. It's what you're choosing to do.* The knowledge, though apparent this entire time, drives home again who he is, regardless of the circumstances that brought him about.

"Would you take a quick ride with me? To the outskirts of the farm?" I ask suddenly. "I want to show you something."

After he agrees, I mount my horse after making sure Justin is settled on his. I set a slow pace, riding alongside him. Watching him as he surveys the property. Normally, I would let the view settle into my being, bringing some semblance of peace and relaxation. Today, I barely pay attention, my mind focused on Justin.

I stop a few feet from my father's makeshift grave. Justin glances at it curiously as we both dismount. "My father," I say in explanation.

"He's buried here?" Justin asks, the surprise bringing his voice an octave higher.

"No," I answer, then correct, "well, yes. Kind of." I send a silent request out to the universe for guidance. "My father left my mom and me when I was six years old. I never heard from him again."

"I'm sorry," Justin says.

I hear his sincerity and am again taken aback by his compassion and empathy. "Thank you." I run a sweaty palm down the leg of my jeans.

"My mom and I came here as servants. My mom was the housekeeper and cook."

"I thought that . . ." Justin looks away.

"That this was all mine from birth?" I ask kindly, my thoughts straying to Austin and his purchase of the farm. "I wish it was. But no, it wasn't. In fact, it's your dad who supported the family as I was putting the money together to buy it."

"Are you trying to tell me that my dad loves you and Brian?" Justin asks, his voice tightening. "I know that."

"No," I promise quicky. "I'm trying to tell you that your dad loves you."

"What?"

"You're still staying at Lily's house?" I ask, hoping he doesn't think I'm prying.

"It's just easier."

"Because you're still angry at what your dad and mom did?"

"It wasn't right," Justin says.

"No," I agree. "It wasn't. And when I first learned about it, I was so angry . . ."

"You're not anymore?" Justin asks, clearly shocked.

"I am. But then, I've been spending time with you." Justin glances at me, curious. "You're an amazing young man."

"No, I'm—"

"You saved my son," I interrupt. "In my book, you are my hero."

Justin nods. "Thank you."

"And the thing is, I can say thank you a million times, but that's going to lose its value after the first thousand." I grin when he smiles. "So instead of a thank you, I thought I'd give you the truth."

"I'm confused," Justin admits.

"Your dad lied to me and Brian, and that is something I can never forgive." Eric's betrayal, his lies, have left a wound in me that I hope one day will heal, but I understand a scar will always remain. "But he also loves you. And it's taken me time to understand that the two are not interrelated, that his love for you is separate and apart from his relationship with me." I replay Eric's admission, drawing on it to explain. "He did it because you're his son." I point to my father's headstone. "My father was a coward. He wasn't strong enough to be a father or even just a man. He abandoned his family. Your father refused to abandon you because he loved you." I take a breath, then tell him the truth. "There were so many choices Eric could have made differently in our marriage. But that's between me and him. Between you and him? Your father fought for you. I wished my father had done the same for me."

"Why are you telling me this?"

"Because I wanted to hate you." I remember Austin's words. "But you are . . ." An avalanche of emotion threatens my next words. "Brian is so lucky to have you as an older brother. And your dad and Felicity are lucky to have you as a son." I take a deep breath. "I'll never understand what your father did to me. My marriage is over. But he gave you a family because you deserved it. Because you are his son. Because he loves you."

Justin remains quiet on our ride back. In the stables, we run into Austin, who teaches Justin how to get the horses settled into their stalls. Justin offers afterward to pick up the pizzas we ordered for an early dinner. Inside the house, I find Brian fast asleep in the bedroom. After kissing him on the cheek, relieved to find it cool, I head back out to the porch just in time to see Justin driving away.

"Justin told me what you said. About your father and Eric," Austin says, joining me.

"He deserved to know."

"I agree. Doesn't mean you had to tell him," he tells me quietly.

"You got in my head," I admit, tapping his foot with mine. "Like a parasite."

Austin laughs aloud. "Good. It was never safe for you in that head by yourself."

I sigh, knowing he's right. "Thank you for putting Justin first. He hates them for me and Brian. He's seventeen, and he cares more about what they did to us than what they've given him."

"He also just found out he has a little brother and that his dad has lied to him his entire life." Austin leans his head back to glance at the still-light sky. "Like you, I think the kid is just trying to find a place to land." He runs a hand through my hair. "But telling him about your dad, and that what Eric did to you was separate from his role as a father? That was good work."

"And if I'd done the opposite?" Barely a foot apart, I gravitate toward him, to his energy that lights up mine. "Told him they were jerks and deserved for him to hate them? What would you be saying to me now?"

"That you're better than that. That you have always been better than that. It's not the Celine I know."

Touched by his words, I consider the situation. "You know what's interesting? I don't hate her. I just feel sorry for her and what's happening with Justin." My admission shocks me, even as the truth helps me to heal. "She doesn't owe me anything. I am nobody to her. But Eric . . . it feels like a bad dream. Like I've been married to a stranger."

"Do you regret marrying him?"

The question that I have asked myself a million times since learning about the betrayal. "Without Eric, I don't have Brian."

"Brian is worth all of this." A statement, not a question.

"Yes," I agree. "Thank you for being there for me recently. Unexpected but welcomed." I reach for him, then drop my hand, unsure. Because of my marriage, I have lost faith, trust, in creating a connection again. Finding safety in the default, I step back.

"You're allowed to touch me, Celine." His eyes darken as he bridges the distance with one step. "Anytime you want." He slowly pushes loose strands of my hair back over my ear.

Curious, I smooth my hand over his arm and then his chest. When he pulls me closer, I go willingly. His kiss shifts slowly from gentle to demanding when I slide my hands beneath his shirt. Alone, with no one else around, he slips his hand beneath my top, sneaking up my abdomen, to stop at my bra strap. I moan as his thumb brushes over the cup, fighting the urge to move closer. Instead, I step back, and his hand immediately falls away.

"Is it okay to take it slow?" My breath in spurts, I fight to catch it. "With everything going on, I don't want to rush things. I'm sorry . . ."

He kisses me lightly on the lips. "C, no matter what is happening between us this way, I want to be your friend. We can go as slow as you need." Sensing my apprehension, he brings me closer. "Make no mistake, I want you." He pauses, then adds, "I need you to come to me in happiness. When you're ready."

"My baggage is pretty heavy," I warn him. "There are a lot of pieces to put back together."

"Maybe I can stand alongside you as you do?"

Touched, I kiss him. He waits a breath to give me time, then deepens it. We continue to kiss until the sound of footsteps barely registers. We pull back simultaneously, turning to find Felicity watching us from a distance. Startled, I school my face in reaction.

"Justin's mom, Felicity," I explain. "She's probably looking for him."

"Do you need me?" Austin asks quietly.

That he would even offer warms me. "I'm good."

I wait until Austin heads to his car before taking a deep breath for courage, then head toward Felicity, my head held high.

CHAPTER THIRTY-SIX

FELICITY

I took the first flight to Boston in the morning and went to the farm straight from the airport. Justin and I are slowly reconnecting, a fragile coming together of mother and son. I texted him earlier that I would love to see him if he's available. He replied with his destination and the address.

After parking, I'm headed toward the main house when, in the distance, I see Celine in another man's arms. Shocked, I watch as he bends low and kisses her. She returns the embrace, stepping deeper into his arms. Anxious to give them privacy, I'm starting to turn back toward my car when Celine spots me, her face freezing. They exchange a few words before he heads to his car, leaving the two of us alone.

Bags in hand, I inhale a deep breath as I approach. Close up, I sense her wariness and unease. As if they are a peace offering and explanation, I hold up the presents.

"I just got in from San Francisco," I explain. "Justin mentioned he was here and that I should come over." I gesture toward the full bags. "Presents for the boys."

"Boys?" Celine asks, the first words she speaks.

Her suspicion is warranted; I don't blame her. Our relationship has been a roller coaster, a never-ending series of twists and turns. In her shoes, I wouldn't easily forget that until only recently, I had refused to let Justin donate.

"I remember Brian loves soccer. I called in a favor and got some LA Galaxy jerseys signed by the team for Justin and Brian." From the bag I retrieve Brian's shirt, carefully folded. "We can have them framed to keep the signatures safe."

Jersey in hand, Celine stares at it. "You didn't have to do this." Clearly taken aback, she murmurs, "Brian is going to love this. So much. Thank you."

Suddenly very glad that I had thought to do it, I ask, "How is Brian feeling?"

"He's getting stronger every day. The doctor . . ." Her gaze drops to the ground, her fear palpable of accidentally saying something that could hurt her son or jinx his health. She's clearly blindsided by the illness, and I wonder how any parent would ever again trust that their child was safe.

"Eric said the doctor was optimistic." I say the words so Celine doesn't have to.

"Yes," she says, her relief clear at hearing the words rather than speaking them. "Justin left to go pick up some pizzas for dinner, if you wanted to join . . ."

The perfect opportunity for Celine to lord over me the karmic retribution of Justin and our estrangement. But instead of glee, I hear only compassion and empathy. In nearly losing her own son, does she feel empathy for me fighting for mine?

"They rode horses and hung out together," Celine continues on my silence. "He was telling Brian stories about the two of you together in Chicago. Your trips and all the things you did for him."

Sure she's taunting me, I find only sincerity in her eyes. "He did?"

"He said if he doesn't do soccer, then he'll follow in your footsteps."

"I see." Shocked, I steal a moment to gather my emotions. "I should go. It's getting late."

Celine gestures behind her. "Eric doesn't know about what you saw. Me and Austin."

The silence lingers between us, her unspoken words loud. I hold the cards and can do what I want with the information. From our history, she must assume I will go straight to Eric and use it as leverage. Shame courses through me at her expectation.

"I was in your life for seventeen years," I say slowly, fully aware of the truth I am exposing. "I knew every vacation you took. I knew the schools Brian was attending. Your concerns about his friends, his favorite foods, how often your mother took him."

Celine gasps and takes an instinctual step backward. If the roles were reversed, I imagine a silk woven handkerchief covering my mouth while a rope strangles me. Evil hidden behind beauty.

"Stop," Celine whispers, her voice crushed, as she fully comprehends the intimate details Eric has shared about their life together. "I can't hear this. I don't want to know this." A hand, shaking with the knowledge, covers her mouth.

"It never occurred to me that it was a violation of your trust," I share softly, feeling foolish even as I speak the words. "I didn't know you. I didn't want to know you."

"You stole my marriage," Celine says, fury fueling her words. "You stole my life."

"I wish I had." Anger and disgust fill her face, but I refuse to flinch or look away, accepting her reaction as my due. "It was what I wanted." The admission shames me, but I force myself to continue. "I hated you because you had, Brian had, what Justin and I didn't."

"Eric," Celine realizes.

"A family," I correct. "I had Justin first. He was Eric's first child, and yet . . ." I swallow as I pause, then add, "Yet you and Brian came first in his mind."

Celine stares at me—the woman who was a part of her marriage and her life and yet stood in the shadows, unseen and unknown. I am unlike the stories of other women; I am not what one would imagine. If anything, we are mirror reflections of one another, both mothers, businesswomen, friends, and daughters abandoned by their father. And now, in having Justin, I am Brian's savior.

"How did you do it?" Celine asks softly.

The same question my son asked. And I still don't know if I have the answer they are looking for. "At first, all of my time went into raising Justin. The late nights, early mornings for work. I had no idea what I'd signed up for. But then Eric . . ."

"He was gone for weeks, months. It never occurred to me that there could be another reason." Clearly embarrassed at having been fooled, she accuses, "He was with you and Justin."

"Yes, he was. As much as he could be. I went from the fear of being alone to being a . . . a family." If there's an apology to be made, it's not for what he gave us but only for what she has lost because of it.

Celine flinches at the word. "Long before Eric, Brian, and I were a family, you were one."

"Yes." I pick up a small stone, running my thumb over it in precise repetition. "For Justin," I make clear. "I didn't realize how important it was to me, to him, until Eric offered it. And then I would've done anything to keep it."

"Even hurting my family."

"I didn't know you," I explain. "You were not part of my equation. Not in the way it mattered."

"Why come back here?" Celine asks. "You had everything there . . ." She pauses, seeming to put pieces together to create her own picture. "You came back for Eric?"

"Yes." I consider lying for a brief second, but there are already too many of them to add to the list.

Her anger increasing with every new revelation, she bites out, "The party. You came to assess me, my relationship."

"Study the enemy. Find the weaknesses." Even to my own ears, my behavior sounds inexplicable, unexplainable. Nonetheless, I try. "You were nothing to me."

"I was his wife," she bites back.

"He was my son's father," I correct. The difference, though irrelevant to her and the pain she has endured, was essential to me. "Your place in Eric's life couldn't trump Justin's."

In negotiations, learning to hear what your opponent doesn't say is almost as important as what they do. I can hear Celine's fury, her disgust, at my actions and rationalizations. To her, all of it is irrelevant in the face of the demise of her marriage.

"Then why not tell Eric what you just saw?" Celine's voice falls so I can barely hear her. "Why not have what you've always wanted?"

"It doesn't matter." My power weakened by the truth, I'm starting to leave when she calls me out.

"You love him," Celine says quietly, one woman reading another. An avalanche of sympathy and empathy follows her words. "You are in love with Eric."

I purse my lips as I shake my head, not in refusal of Celine's statement but instead a rejection of my own feelings. "It doesn't matter."

"Does he know?" Celine asks softly.

I scoff at the question. "He doesn't want to know." Confusion, anger, and love—the trifecta of emotions that have accompanied every interaction over the last seventeen years. "What would he say?"

"You don't know if he loves you back," Celine says. "If you told him about me and Austin . . ." Celine pauses, then shares, "Our marriage is over, but it would kill any hope he has for a reconciliation."

"Because of what we did . . ."

"It's more than that," Celine says slowly, seeming to search for the words. "What he did was symptomatic of our marriage. What he shared with you about our life?" Celine scoffs at the truth. "It's a betrayal I can't comprehend." Celine circles her ring finger, which lies bare. "Our marriage is over. Everything you said to me . . ." She pauses. "He was my husband. He owed me the truth. He owed me fidelity. He owed me respect."

"Celine . . ."

"He took away my sense of self," she admits. "My self-esteem."

Her words diffuse my righteousness, my belief in my actions. In baring her soul, she's shattering mine. "I didn't think . . ."

"You had to make a choice—you chose your son." She drops her head, exhaling. "You didn't *owe me* anything. Eric did." She rubs her lips, as if remembering the kiss I witnessed. "With this information, he's yours. I don't know if he was ever mine."

No, I think, *not this way.* "For seventeen years, I was in your marriage and in your life. I didn't know you, so it didn't matter." Her words repeat in my head, breaking down my shield, forcing me to see what I have done. "But I have to be better than that. For me." I take a breath. "Your life is none of my business. Your choices cannot be the compass that directs mine. You deserve better than that."

"Felicity . . . ," Celine starts.

"I'm sorry for the part I played in your marriage, in your life." I take a deep breath. "I hope one day you can forgive me. I think the first step toward that path needs to be that I get out of your life and let you find your happiness."

Celine grabs my hand as I start to walk away, surprising me. "A year ago, I would have hated you just because you existed. I would have hated Justin for what he represented."

That first meeting in the hospital, her confusion and loss left little room for any other emotion. Since then, our lives have been turned upside down, shifting and changing with each new day. Now, I sense a peace within her that wasn't there before.

"But because of you, because of what you did and the son you raised"—Celine blinks at the tears that threaten—"I have a chance at the happiness you're talking about. My son has a chance to live the life he deserves."

Celine releases my hand and takes a step back. We stare at one another, mother to mother, woman to woman, and find a common ground that I would have thought was inconceivable.

"Brian and Justin are fortunate to be brothers. To have one another," Celine adds. "Thank you for giving Brian that gift."

I'm starting to walk away when, from behind Celine, Brian says, "Justin and I are brothers?"

CHAPTER THIRTY-SEVEN

FELICITY

As I wait for Justin, I watch the trainer walk the lone horse with Brian atop him in circles inside the fenced-in field. Overhead, the clouds cover the sky, allowing the sun to peek through. Otherwise, the day is cast in shadows.

"Mom?" Justin says, joining me.

"Hi." Hesitant, I force the lilt in my voice in lieu of reaching out to hug him. "How are you, honey?" The formalities have become a necessary bridge between us. The only form of communication that seems acceptable.

"Good." His worried glance lands on Brian as he lowers his voice. "Celine called and asked me to head back. She said Brian overheard her say that we're brothers?"

My son and Celine have each other's phone numbers. They have become close. Both bonded by the betrayal by Eric and me. He talks about her as if they are old friends. As if she could replace me . . . I push the thoughts, the paranoia, out of my head. I cannot become my own worst enemy in a quest to reclaim my son.

"She asked your dad to join us," I explain. "To talk to Brian together."

He doesn't ask me why I am here, nor do I tell him that she asked me to stay. Touched by her request, I immediately agreed. I wanted to be here for Justin, in whatever way he would allow me to be.

From inside the house, Celine and Eric exit together. When Eric's hand accidentally brushes hers, Celine shifts away, her mouth tightening. Eric glances at her, his entire demeanor tense and rigid in response.

As they near us, Justin steps into the fenced-in field as if he has done it a thousand times before. He helps Brian down from the horse; then they walk alongside one another toward us. They bonded before Brian ever knew the truth.

Celine and Eric plaster on smiles, an elaborate show with two cast members. After having been sidelined, a shadow in their life, a hidden spectator, I am no longer interested in the position. I join them at the same time Justin and Brian approach. Celine acknowledges me with a smile. Eric says a quick hello, his voice neutral. Together, we create a circle of five.

"Felicity got you a gift," Celine says to Brian, surprising me. She grabs the gift bags left nearby and hands them out to the boys. "Open it, honey."

Brian removes the jersey, his eyes widening in shock, then joy. "It's signed. Thank you so much!"

Brian reaches out to hug me. I hesitate, then bend low to take him into my arms. He settles his head onto my shoulder, and his arms tighten around my frame. My eyelids drift closed as I envelop him.

"You're welcome, sweetheart." When he releases me, I step back, refusing to meet either Eric's or Celine's eyes. Instead, my focus shifts to Justin, needing to check his reaction to the interaction. When I see his smile, I exhale.

"That was nice," Justin says softly. "You getting him the same jersey."

"Of course." I keep my voice light, nonchalant. "I get the feeling Brian likes soccer nearly as much as you."

"It's cool Justin and I have the same jersey," Brian says when Justin removes his.

"Speaking of . . ." Celine takes Brian's hand while wrapping the other around his shoulder, a mother shielding her son. "Sweetheart, we wanted to talk to you about what you overheard about you and Justin."

Justin, laser focused on his brother, takes a step closer to Brian. Clearly worried about Brian's reaction, he lays a protective hand on his shoulder. Between Justin and Celine, they form a defensive circle around Brian, guarding him from any potential fallout. Eric and I created the problem, but now Celine and Justin are offering the solution. In the next few moments, whatever occurs, they are signaling that they will be the ones Brian can rely on. They are the ones he can trust.

"Brian, honey . . ." Celine visibly takes a deep breath. "You overheard some important information that we need to explain." Celine releases him, purposefully stepping back to create a larger circle, with Eric and me included within it. It's a subtle but powerful signal to both Brian and Justin about where she stands. "Before Dad and I were married . . ." Celine emphasizes the word *before*, and suddenly I am grateful for the detail. Celine is offering us a reprieve with the detail, a basis that excuses our behavior. "Dad and Felicity were together."

"Together?" Brian looks to Justin and then Celine, as if picking up on the energy and responding to it. "Like dating?"

"Kind of," Celine says, smiling as if they are sharing a secret. "And they had Justin together."

"Brian . . . ," Eric starts, but he stops when Brian asks a question.

"So, Dad is Justin's dad?"

"Yes," Justin answers before Eric can say anything.

Eric tenses next to me. Used to being in charge, he wants to be the one leading the discussion, to detail the events. But Celine has chosen to control the conversation. If he forces his way in, it would chance ruining the fragile connection between him and Justin and seeming disrespectful of Celine's place. Unlike the last seventeen years, he's no longer in charge of the situation or how it plays out. Now, he's the bystander, the one who must stand back and accept others' decisions.

"You and I are brothers." Justin gets down on one knee to be on Brian's level. "Is that okay?"

My fingers curl into fists as I hold my breath. The group falls silent as we wait for Brian's answer. Brian's eyes narrow as his eyebrows scrunch together in confusion. He looks to Celine and then Eric before returning to Justin.

"So it's real. We're brothers?" Brian asks. The confusion is slowly replaced by a small grin and then a full smile. I exhale as he asks, "Really?"

"Yes," Justin says with a confidence and sense of leadership inherited from Eric. At seventeen years old, he's taking charge of a situation that he has previously just been a player in. His actions declare to both Eric and me that he's no longer a passive participant. "I'm really happy about it."

Brian takes a hesitant step closer to Justin, reaching for his brother's hand, trying to walk the fine balance between childhood and manhood. It reminds me of all the times at the same age when Justin would struggle to be strong while admitting his vulnerability. The mother in me yearns to reassure Brian, to tell him that he's perfect just as he is. Though I know it isn't my place, I am still taken aback by the desire.

"Can I give you a hug?" Justin asks.

With the question, Justin is offering Brian a reprieve, an opportunity to take what he wants without asking. Brian clasps Justin around the neck and brings his body in. Justin laughs while circling Brian's skeletal frame, holding his brother close. Celine holds a hand over her mouth; Eric's hands are stuffed into his pockets. Both are visibly moved by the interaction.

"Why didn't you tell me before?" Brian asks Celine. "About Justin being my brother. We could have hung out." The truth. It is always with us, in every interaction, silent in every conversation.

His question is the foundation of the last seventeen years. The one that could abolish Eric's relationship with Brian and the family he has fought hard for. Celine's answer could destroy it such that it can never be repaired.

"We wanted to wait until we knew you both were ready . . . ," Celine starts.

Eric closes his eyes in relief. I exhale the breath I didn't realize I was holding. With the use of the word *we*, Celine has solidified the unit. No blame will be placed on any individual. As far as Brian is concerned, it was a decision that was made together, in their best interest.

"To make sure you both knew how loved you are," Celine concludes.

"I wish I'd known," Brian says directly to Justin.

"Me too," Justin returns. My gut tightens at his admission. "Me too."

From the fence, I watch the boys ride. Justin sits behind Brian, using the excuse that he's still learning in order to help keep his brother safe. From the smell of his cologne and the sound of his footsteps—from sharing a home, a life—I sense Eric before he joins me. I can't remember when I began to memorize the small details, how he took his coffee, his favorite winter coat, the cologne he wore and the lotion he used, but in time they became as familiar to me as my own.

"It went well." I keep my gaze on the horses, off of Eric, always aware of Justin and Celine close by, potentially watching. Now that the truth is out, I am unsure of the protocol when all of us are together. Though Celine and Eric have an intimacy that comes from marriage, Eric and I have an innate knowledge of one another that's resulted from all our years together. "Celine did amazing."

"She explained it perfectly." Eric sighs as he drapes his hands over the fence. One leg resting on the bottom rung, he shifts closer to the wooden planks. "All this time . . ."

"You would have told her years ago?" I confirm.

"She hates me," Eric admits quietly. Over the years, Eric would share some details about disagreements, but I never prodded, hesitant to hear about the marriage I envied. "She would have hated me then also. But at least the boys would have had each other all this time."

"He's getting better," I say quietly.

"Yeah, he is." Brian laughs at something Justin says. They have seamlessly fallen into the role of brothers from friends. "How are you and Justin doing?"

"Talking. He answers my texts and calls." The sorrow that felt never ending is slowly waning, replaced by a new relationship—one of understanding and acceptance. "I know he's still at Lily's, but . . ." I pause as I try to explain my feelings. "The truth that created an abyss is now the basis of a bridge between us."

"I'm glad," Eric says sincerely. "He takes my calls, each one longer than the one before." Shocked by the sadness in Eric's voice, I realize that, being so focused on my own hurt, I haven't given much thought to his feelings regarding Justin. Eric's not only fighting for one son's life but also trying to hold on to his other son. "But I don't know if we'll ever be the same."

"Eric . . ." I struggle with how to respond. *Sorry* is inadequate, given the situation. "I keep holding on to the belief that one day, when things have settled, he will forgive us."

"Look at them." Eric gestures toward the two boys as they ride the horse around the field. Though Brian wholly believes he's the one helping Justin, it's clear that Justin is watching protectively over his brother. "How does he forgive us for keeping Brian from him? Especially if something had happened to Brian." Eric chokes on the final few words. "If I were in his shoes, I don't know if I'd forgive us. I don't know how he will."

CHAPTER THIRTY-EIGHT

CELINE

A day has passed since the reveal with Brian. Though he asked multiple questions at the time, he seems to have accepted the situation. Now, my mom and I watch Justin and Brian play a light game of soccer. She smiles when Brian throws up his hands in celebration after a goal.

"I'm not surprised he took the news well." She explains, "He's not you. Eric didn't hurt him the way he hurt you. Brian understands Eric as a father. Eric's love for Brian has never been in question. He's been a good father, Celine. He just wasn't a good husband."

"You're saying there's nothing for Brian to forgive?"

Mom motions toward the boys playing together. "In the future, his only anger may be that he didn't know his brother sooner."

"That's what Justin said," I share. "He's angry at Eric for not telling him about Brian years ago."

"The boys love one another," she says, joy in her voice. "This may be very hard for you to see right now, but what happened between Felicity and Eric? It was the best thing that ever happened to you."

"I've processed that thought every day since this began. Eric's betrayal saved my son. How does that make sense, Mom?"

"I don't know if you can." As she leans back in her chair, I see the lines of fatigue and stress around her eyes. My mother has aged right in front of me, but I have refused to see it. "When your father left, I thought our world was destroyed. I was so scared every single day."

"I remember hearing you cry every night after he left. I'd stand outside your room, and all I wanted was to see you happy again."

"I loved your dad so much." She closes her eyes, as if remembering the past. "He was the boy that charmed all the girls. Everyone wanted him. And he wanted me." She rubs her ring finger where her simple gold band once sat. "I thought I was the luckiest girl in the world."

"What happened? Why did he leave?"

My mother pulls her legs underneath her. "Because he wasn't someone who was meant to stay. He always showed me exactly who he was. I just didn't believe him."

"Mom," I say, struggling with the revelation. "You never said a word to me about this."

"You loved your father so much. And he loved you. When he left, your world was destroyed." She claps when Brian makes another goal. "How could I tell you that maybe he knew leaving was for the best?"

"What are you saying? That everything that's happened is for the best? My marriage? Brian?"

"No, what happened to Brian is not for the best. Never would I ever say that. But everything else—Justin, the truth . . . maybe after the shadows pass, the light that shines is brighter than before?" She takes my hand in hers.

"Austin and I . . ." I wonder how to tell her what happened, afraid she might believe I'm jumping from one situation to another. That I may be using Austin to nurse my wounds. "He and I . . ."

"Care about one another?" She smiles lovingly at me. "Austin's mother and I have known that since you were children."

Images of Austin pervade my mind. His touch. Our recent late-night calls. The friendship that was once my bedrock. The love that has lain hidden deep in the recesses of my heart. I soften, and a smile tugs at my lips. He's been patient, allowing me to set the pace. Every kiss reminds me that I am still a woman. Every whispered word of affection shows me that I still matter. That I am more than a mother fighting for her son and a woman betrayed by her husband.

"Nothing has happened. He says that I have to come to him in happiness. Any other way, neither of us can trust."

"He's always been a smart boy." Mom shares, "I would've given anything for another man to have come in and taken care of us. But how much would both of us have lost if that happened? You counted on me. I couldn't disappoint you. We found our way. And you, my darling girl, became a woman I am so proud of. I wouldn't trade that for anything. Not even a knight in shining armor."

"You were my knight in shining armor," I admit, realizing it.

She smiles gratefully. "And now, what you're doing with Brian, Justin, Eric, and Felicity—bringing both families together for Brian's sake—he has no idea, but you are his." She leans over and hugs me.

"How do I trust any man after what Eric did to me?" I wonder aloud.

"Why are you with Austin?" my mom asks after a moment. "Are you passing the time? Is he helping you to get over your hurt?"

"I care about him. Deeply." I run a hand over my eyes. "I don't know if I'm allowed to. What if he's with me now but . . ." Memories of my childhood, of who I was, rear their head, reminding me of times I yearn to forget.

"Ask him why he's with you." She sighs at my hesitancy. "Are you afraid he'll say something you don't want to hear? Or something you do want to hear?"

Trust them so they will trust you. But I'm not sure how I can ever trust again.

"Take the risk, Celine. You deserve to know. But first, find yourself." She smiles at me sadly. "I couldn't accept your father for who he was. Then I couldn't forgive him for what he'd done. Learn from me. Come full circle. Accept Eric regardless of the actions and forgive him for what he did. Then find the connection with him not as husband and wife, or lovers, but as friends and co-parents."

What he has had with Felicity, I realize.

"As for you and Austin? The thought of it makes me so happy. But I agree with him. You must find yourself before you go to him. Any other way, and it's the same path as you and Eric. And in that scenario, everyone loses. Most of all, you."

The ping of my phone catches my attention. A message from Kaitlyn. Recluse's owner is looking for a jockey. The prize money for the win would be enough to buy the farm.

CHAPTER THIRTY-NINE

FELICITY

The call from the recruiter comes as I am finishing up my day. The company in California wants me and is willing to offer whatever it takes to have me. They need an answer within the next two weeks.

Afterward, I stare into space from my top-floor office, then at the framed picture of Justin and me next to my computer. He was eight when we posed during the holidays. Eric has insisted on taking dozens of pictures of the two of us with my phone over the years.

I text Eric, and he agrees to meet me at his apartment. After letting my assistant know I'm leaving for the day, I drive the twenty minutes to reach him. On the way, I rehearse my conversation multiple times, dismissing some topics while focusing on others. As I pull into a parking spot, I spy Eric's car across the aisle.

I check my hair and makeup in the mirror. The face that stares back at me is older than I remember. In the time that has passed, I wonder when I went from the woman I used to be to who I am now. If given the chance again, would I do the same thing? If this is the only way to have Justin, then yes, without a doubt, I would.

My key fob provides me access to Eric's floor. When he moved in, he made sure I had a parking spot and my own key and fob. He wanted me to feel as home at the apartment as I had made him feel at my home. His decision to get the apartment meant so much to me. We essentially shared custody of my son without Eric having any legal obligation to do so.

Over the years, the visits decreased as Justin became busy with school and sports. It was logistically easier for Eric to visit us. Eric never pushed for extra visits, and I never asked. It was as if the changed circumstances fit both of our purposes.

The elevator carries me to Eric's door, where I ring the doorbell. Clearly surprised that I didn't use my key, Eric opens the door. That he believes I still have the right to do so warms me.

Inside, the windows overlook the Back Bay, with breathtaking views of the harbor, filled with ships. On nights we would stay over, I would make a cup of tea and sit by the window in the dark and stare at the twinkling lights of the city below. Oftentimes Eric would join me, and together we would talk late into the night.

"How's Brian?" The relief of the truth being out, of the brothers having one another, is palpable. "He's doing okay?"

The fear that filled Eric's eyes when he came over the night of Justin's party has dissipated. Instead, a smile and relief fill his face. "He's good. He's really good." Eric motions for me to take a seat. "The doctor is optimistic. Brian's body is responding well to the treatment."

I reach for Eric's hand, tightening my fingers around his. "I'm really glad."

"Felicity . . ." Eric swallows. "I know it was your decision to let Justin move forward—"

"Eric," I say, interrupting him, "what I said, what happened, never should have. It was Justin's decision. Once he made it, I never should have stood in the way of helping Brian."

"You were trying to protect Justin."

No, I want to admit. But unburdening my soul about my fury at seeing Justin choose Celine over me would chance pushing him away. "Eric, all these years, the secrets, the lies . . ."

Eric looks away. "They were a mistake. I see that now. I should have told Celine from the beginning. Maybe if I had, then we would be . . ." He trails off.

"You wouldn't have married her?"

Eric shakes his head, and I feel his confusion. "Along with Justin, Brian is the best thing that's ever happened to me."

"Then?"

"I don't know." Eric drops both hands to his knees, his body hunched over. "If I'd told her then, maybe we wouldn't be where we are right now."

Separated. Unable to be next to him, I stand and head toward the wall-to-wall window. I stare out at the city as the sun begins to set. The lights give a glimpse into a city that starts to come alive even as night settles.

"Where is that, Eric?" I demand. "You here in this apartment? Celine at home?" I don't say a word about Austin. I will keep my promise to stay out of Celine's life. Because I now understand that Celine has nothing to do with Eric and me. She was a false barrier between us. The real obstacle was always my fear of Eric's true feelings.

"What's going on?" Eric joins me at the window. "Did something happen?"

Freshman year of college, I took an English course and learned about the hero's journey and the trials the protagonist faces in their quest. At the end, if successful, they will win the award. They go home a winner, better for their experience. I have been waiting for my reward all these years. My sacrifice was never meant to be in vain. I have waited patiently on the sidelines for my name to be called to take center stage. But now I see that there's no one onstage, nor in the audience. It was all in my head.

"I've been offered a CFO position." I stop him as he begins to congratulate me. "It's in California." I tell him the details, with him listening attentively until I finish.

"You deserve this," Eric says, his excitement evident. "We can do whatever we need for Justin so you can take the position."

My stomach drops. He isn't going to try and stop me or convince me out of it so that we can be together.

"I'm in love with you," I say, my voice sounding foreign to me. In every iteration of the conversation in my head, it ended with Eric taking me into his arms and telling me he loved me. That he has been waiting for me to say it first to assuage his guilt. That I have never been the other woman but instead the only woman. "I have been for so long I can't remember a time when I wasn't."

I dare to meet his eyes and wish immediately I hadn't. Shock, sadness, regret fill them, one after the other, until only sympathy is left.

"I don't know when it happened," I continue, hoping, like a debate, that I can convince him to see it my way, to realize what he hasn't until now. "Maybe when you and I held Justin for the first time or how we took turns walking him all night when he had the ear infection."

"I . . . ," Eric starts, but I continue as if I hadn't heard him.

"The nights we spent talking after putting Justin to bed. We shared everything, Eric. Our dreams, hopes, fears about the boys. I learned every detail about your life, and I trusted you with mine. I know your favorite wine, the toothpaste you insist on using, how you take your coffee."

"Those were just conversations."

"They were us sharing a life." I hear my desperation and hate myself for it but refuse to stop now. With the damage done, I have nothing to lose. "Your concerns about work. When you were sick with the flu, we stayed up watching every Godfather movie. I trusted you with Justin."

"He's my son," Eric reminds me. "He's the bridge that brought us together."

"The night we made him . . ."

"I was drunk," Eric says. The words are an ice bucket. I step back, my eyes shutting. "If I was in my right mind . . ."

"You wouldn't have slept with me," I finish for him.

"No." Eric reaches for my hand, but I pull it away. The touch I have craved for so long now feels cruel and unwanted. "I've never seen you as anything more than Justin's mother and my friend. I'm so sorry if I made you believe otherwise."

As if seeing the apartment for the first time, I look around blindly. Pictures of Justin fill the space. A photo of the three of us sits prominently on a bookshelf in the corner. A family that never was.

"I should go." I grab my keys and phone.

"Felicity, please stay. Let's talk about this."

I scoff at the idea. Here is the last place I want to be. "There's nothing to say."

"I need to know you're all right," Eric says, standing in front of me.

He pleads for me to give him what he needs, but I can't. As if I am a fire scorching the earth, I say the words that will push him back.

"I wasn't drunk that night."

Eric staggers back, his face shocked. "What?"

I imagine myself a kaleidoscope, all the parts of me in pieces. With every twist and turn, I shift, vulnerable to the whim of others.

"Tipsy but not drunk. I knew what was happening." I had been so lonely for so many nights. I had held myself off from the world in pursuit of my end goal. In creating that night, I cared little about who got hurt or why. For one night, I yearned for comfort and affection from a man I had admired and valued for years. "I offered you my sofa. You made the first move but then stepped back. I kept it going."

"Why are you telling me this?" Eric demands.

I see his hatred. "Because you and I are both fools. You believed the last seventeen years was to protect Celine, and I believed the last seventeen years was setting the foundation for our happily ever after." I shake my head at my foolishness. "But we were lying to ourselves. I am the other woman. I have always been, no matter how much I've tried to convince myself otherwise."

I gently shut the door behind me. As I walk toward the elevator, I wonder if Eric will come after me. But he remains inside the apartment, and I take the elevator down to my car. As I drive home, all I can think is that there is no winning. Because my entire game has been based on a lie.

CHAPTER FORTY

CELINE

I watch the horses run alongside one another around the track, each one in competition against itself and the other horses in the race. To beat their own time and know that they alone must win the race.

Felicity admitted that she had been in a competition with me for seventeen years. If she had done things differently—thrown her hat in the ring earlier or even walked away—maybe that would have changed the trajectory of Eric and me. But her decision determined her path and influenced mine.

I continue watching the horses fight to increase their speed without an understanding of purpose or prize. If the same applied to my marriage, would I have won against Felicity if my marriage survived, or was it a house of cards that was always meant to topple? My fear is that I have lost more in the last seventeen years than I have gained, that the cost of my marriage is me.

Racing Recluse is something I need to do for myself. A time not so long ago, I would have refused the opportunity, sure it was too dangerous. Acquiesced to others' thoughts, always allowing other people to dictate the direction of the conversation, my life, my hopes and dreams.

Those days did not serve me, instead creating a woman who became a whim to life's happenings. I can no longer afford to be that woman, nor do I want to.

I tighten my helmet before heading to the stalls where Recluse is housed. As I expected, the owner voiced his surprise when I agreed to ride him, given that we had returned him due to his temperament. I didn't bother with an explanation. Other than my loved ones, I think it's past time in my life that I owe people reasons for my behavior.

I stroke Recluse's head, hoping to calm him as he pushes away. "Still the same." A part of me respects the horse for refusing to surrender to our needs, while another part of me wonders what created the reaction in the first place. "You don't have to win today," I start, surprised by my words. "I know from personal experience, that's not always guaranteed. But I'll ask you to fight. Not for the ribbon or even the money, but for yourself. You think everyone in your life owns you. Make this yours."

The horse stares at me, his eyes blinking in response. I smile to myself, not reading too much into the reaction. With the help of assistants, I lead the horse out and onto the field to the starting line. I focus forward, refusing to let my attention drift past me, the horse, and the end goal.

At the sound of the start signal, Recluse jumps out of the gate. Speed is not our battle but instead maintaining control. My body low over his, I give him the freedom to fly, letting him control his speed while I maintain direction.

We move forward from sixth place to third. The final lap faces us. The wind is calm, the sound of hooves pounding against the track a melody in my ears. It brings me a rare comfort, an escape from life. In the few minutes of racing, it's me and the horse against our own time. Though everyone else in the world believes it's a race against horses, I have always viewed it as a race against themselves.

"Come on," I whisper.

I grip the reins tight, fully aware that he could easily choose to change direction. I direct him left, passing the second-place runner and taking his place. In a battle between us and the lead, I fight to win.

I push my feet against his side. Recluse reacts, his entire form seeming to surge with renewed energy. He flies forward, and with only a few inches left, we grab the lead. I lean lower, encouraging him, and seconds later he passes the finish line, in first place. I keep my hands on the reins as waves of shock run through me. I won.

After the adrenaline wears off, disbelief replaces it. I silently thank Recluse as we slow to a jog off the track. We did it. After everything, I have fulfilled my promise to own the farm. After all the years of allowing others' thoughts to dictate my life and my self-worth, I am finally free.

◆ ◆ ◆

The sound of a car arriving breaks through my thoughts. Through the living room window, I watch as my uncle Greg arrives. After letting him in, I take from him a folder of papers transferring ownership of the farm to me.

"I wouldn't have expected you to do it," Greg says.

"You should have." I refuse to respond to his underlying statement—that I was a servant's child, and he expected me to remain so. I sift through the documents, which secure my place as the owner. "Thank you for giving us a place when I was a child."

"You're welcome." If he's surprised by my gratitude, my uncle doesn't show it, only offering, "Best of luck. With everything."

I watch him leave, my thoughts focused on the past and present, trying to find within them the path to the future. I call Austin and ask him to meet me at the farm. When he arrives, he gently kisses me on the lips.

"Everything okay?"

Still amazed at the progression of our relationship, I run a hand over his cheek before leaning back. Every day he has stood by me. Loved me, held me when I cried, and celebrated the minute-by-minute milestones of Brian's recovery.

"I have some news."

He raises an eyebrow as I hand him the papers. Curious, he reads them, his eyes widening as he understands. I wait, anxious, until he says, "You bought the farm?"

"The purse for racing Recluse."

"Congratulations," he says, everything in him clearly meaning it. "You did it."

"I have something else." I hand him the other paper I had the attorney draw up for me. He reads it, then looks at me in shock.

"This is the title to my parents' farm?"

"Buy it from me," I say. "Then lease half of it back to me so I can continue my training center." This would allow me to continue my work while giving him his childhood farm back for his parents.

He reads through the document again before leaning down and kissing me lightly on the lips. "You don't have to do this."

I think about his mother's words to me about him coming back, about returning to our true love. Brian's illness has reminded me of how fragile life is. Of how much every day matters and should be valued. Austin returned without me realizing how much I needed him. He has reminded me of who I am and who we were and can be.

"Yes, I did."

"Thank you. This is perfect."

He pulls me close. I lay a hand on his chest, feeling his heartbeat. Every touch, every interaction, feels needed, both comforting and an awakening. Similar to our childhood, he has been there for me during some of the hardest times of my life. And during those moments and every other one, the friendship has blossomed, and I have fallen deeply in love.

"You told me to come to you when I was ready." His eyes widen at my admission and the implication. "Brian's illness and recovery . . . Every day is an opportunity to live, to make what matters a priority. To find happiness and hold on to it when you do."

"Celine . . ."

"It's a journey," I admit, "but one that I finally need to be on."

He gently lays a hand behind my head before kissing me. I open my mouth to his, welcoming the warmth of his touch. His other hand skates down my torso until it rests on my hip. He pulls me in tighter until I can feel his need for me. I respond in kind; my fingers grip the front of his shirt, then sneak beneath it to caress his bare chest. My breathing speeds up alongside his.

"Your mom told me you would come back to your first love," I say against his lips. He steps back, releasing me. "It's why I needed to give the farm back to you." I remember my mom's words about his real first love. And Austin's words to me so long ago: *Trust them so they will trust you.* "I love you," I whisper.

He tenses as his eyes search mine. "What?"

"I love you," I repeat. "I'm in love with you."

He pushes away. My heart starts to patter against my ribs, afraid of his reaction.

"When?" he asks.

I cannot pinpoint the exact moment I fell or the exact conversation. Maybe because it was seconds of time pieced together over years, interwoven with a valued friendship, a familiarity of the soul that drew us together and then a deep love of the heart that bonded us forever. A barrage of memories floods my mind.

"The first time you took me on a horse and taught me to ride. My dad's funeral. Hanging out with me after school, even if it wasn't cool or accepted." I shrug. "Being there for me throughout Brian's illness . . . Take your pick."

"C . . ." Austin cups my cheek. "I came back for you. I just wanted to see you."

My heart starts to patter. "Austin?"

"I was in love with you, C. Was too foolish as a kid to realize I always had been."

"Why didn't you tell me any of this when we kissed?"

"I couldn't add my feelings to what you were dealing with. If this, what we're doing, is what you needed to get through Brian's illness and Eric's betrayal, then that's who I was going to be for you."

"Let me use you?"

Austin shrugs. "I wasn't being left empty handed."

If it's possible, I feel a blush creeping over my neck onto my cheeks. "And now?" I ask. "What are your feelings now?"

"I'm not sure," Austin teases, then pulls me in. "I've fallen all over again, C." He pauses, and then says the words that make my heart feel like it's shattering. "But my time here . . . between my dad and my work—I need to go back to Seattle."

"When?" I barely get the words out.

"A few weeks," he says.

I take his hand and lead him to the bedroom. I need him, want him. In choosing to be with him, I am choosing myself. We slowly strip each other bare until there's nothing left between us. When he finally enters me, I keep my eyes open, letting him know every way I can how much I love him and always will.

CHAPTER FORTY-ONE

FELICITY

Our boat finishes the race in third place. Though we didn't win, I am surprised to feel the satisfaction of achievement. It's a far cry from my younger days, when winning meant everything.

Once we get the shell back to shore, I am gathering my things, ready to leave, when I hear Justin's voice yelling "Mom!" over the crowd. A minute later, when he comes into view, I feel my heart miss a beat in surprise and joy. "Justin? You're here."

I melt into the hug he offers, holding my son hard. Seeming to mirror my need for contact, he holds on, releasing me minutes after I expected.

"Everyone is here." Before I can ask what he means, Lily, Brian, and Celine appear a few steps behind. Lily offers a shy wave, which I return with a full smile and words of welcome. "We wanted to see you race."

In disbelief, I murmur, "You guys came?"

"Justin told us about it," Celine answers. "I hope this is all right?"

We look at one another, both recognizing how much has changed between us in the time from the party to today. I imagine another time and different circumstances, one in which I would have valued Celine as a friend. That Celine came to support me and brought Brian means more than I can process.

"Absolutely," I say quietly. "Thank you." I bend down to an exuberant Brian. "Look at you!" I exclaim, in a manner and voice similar to how I would have acknowledged Justin at the same age. "I'm so happy you came." I drop to my haunches to be on eye level. "Did you like the race?"

"You were fast," he says, clearly impressed. I pull out my third-place medal and show it to him. His eyes widen at its size. "This is cool."

"It's yours," I say. Brian looks up, confused. I see the yearning in his face, understanding that since the diagnosis, he hasn't been able to compete in any battle other than the one the fates forced upon him. "Because the real winner here? You." I hear Celine's intake of breath. Unsure, I glance at her. Her quick nod of gratitude answers my question. "Go on, sweetie. You can have it."

Brian slips the medallion around his neck. "Thank you!"

"Thank you for wearing it. It looks so much better on you than me." I stand, melding into the circle of the five of us. "Is anyone hungry? There's a tent somewhere around here for participants and their families." I hesitate at the last word but continue when no one reacts. "They also have a band and some fun things for kids." I can't help the yearning in my voice.

"Do you guys mind going ahead?" Justin asks the group. "I wanted to talk to my mom really quick."

Justin and I watch them leave until they are out of earshot. "Everything okay?" I ask, surprised by his request. Ever since the reveal and fallout, I have learned to temper any expectations. Justin holds the control, and I have turned to hope for answers.

"Dad told me about the job in California." Justin leads us away from the crowds. "Congratulations, Mom."

"Sweetheart, I didn't tell you because I wasn't going to . . ."

"You need to take it," Justin interrupts. "You deserve it."

"You just started high school, and for you to change again . . . ," I say, but Justin shakes his head.

"I'd stay here and finish high school."

The world that felt righted before suddenly tilts on its axis again. He is asking me to take a job across the country from him. To leave him. I drop my head, trying to stem my emotions.

"You gave up everything to raise me," Justin says, oblivious to my inner thoughts. "Your dreams, your career. You are so smart. The smartest person I know."

I raise my head, confused by his words. "You want me to leave you?"

"No," Justin corrects. He takes my hand, and for a second I am transported back to when it was just the two of us, together, tackling life and everything that came with it. "I want you to do something for you." It's such a difference from what he has been saying to me all this time that I am rendered speechless. "After learning the truth, I was so angry at you and Dad. So much so that I forgot all the good things. The mom who left meetings early to be there for my games. The one who helped me with my homework every night and, no matter how I did, told me that it was perfect. Who believed in me so much that I couldn't help but believe in myself." Justin smiles at me. "I forgot how much I admire my mom and how proud of her I am."

"Justin, what changed?"

"Celine told me that she wished her dad had loved her enough to do anything for her, like you and dad did for me."

I feel a grip on my stomach tighten until I can barely breathe.

"And then, Dad told me that the person I am, the one that knew to be there for his brother, the one who everyone is so proud of and admires? I am that person because of you. My mom." Justin drops his head. "I think I forgot that along the way."

I pull my son in and exhale when he comes willingly. I glance at the sky and then toward the tent where Celine is with Lily and Brian and send a silent thank-you to Celine for her words to Justin. His arms come around me, and for just a few moments, among the cheers of the crowd as another race concludes, under the sun hiding behind the clouds, we hold one another, and the world—the past, the lies, and the betrayals—all fades into the distance as we remember the one relationship that has sustained us through everything: being mother and son.

"You'll take the position?" Justin asks, pulling back.

"I'll talk to them about flying back and forth while you're finishing up high school." I pause, afraid to ask, then gather my courage. "Does this mean you're coming home?"

"I miss my room." I laugh at his honesty. "When you're gone, I can stay with Dad."

"You would be okay with that?" I ask, aware that his relationship with Eric has been equally as fraught as his relationship with me. "With staying with your dad?"

"I need to be. For Brian . . . and for me," Justin answers truthfully. "So I'll figure it out."

It's such a seventeen-year-old answer that I smile inwardly. I take his hand and feel the warmth as his fingers clasp around mine. There was a time when my hand engulfed his smaller one. Now, I feel his fingers curl around the top of my hand, nearly cradling it in his palm.

"Let's go join the others?"

Justin nods, and together we walk toward the tent, with a lightness I have not felt in years. For the rest of the afternoon, we crowd around Brian as he plays the games. At the ring toss, he wins a small stuffed bear that he immediately hands to a little girl who failed to win a prize. I marvel at his unconditional kindness. Not having known him before the illness, I wonder if he was the same boy before or if the illness has changed him.

The thought makes me consider Justin, who also has grown since learning about Brian. As much as I have tried to teach him about

309

kindness and giving to others, we have never had an occasion for it to be tested or tried. But when called to step up, he did so selflessly and wholly. Even fought me when I tried to stand in his way.

Shame at my actions then brings me a moment of self-reflection now. I watch Celine, amazed by how far we have come. Once my perceived enemy, Celine is now someone I dare to call my friend. And in that shift, that change, lies the evolution of my soul.

Past Brian and Justin, I have also changed. My compass, once always directed to winning, now considers multiple people and their feelings. I no longer stand on a mountain alone but instead am surrounded by people who matter. Brian's illness and revealing the truth have together given me a freedom and connection I have never considered valuable before. I spent my life alone and believed it better that way. Justin has shown me it is better with more.

After the race, I text Eric, asking if I can stop by. He responds right away, letting me know he will meet me at the apartment. We have not seen one another since my declaration of love, nor have we spoken. I consider what I will say and what Eric's reaction will be. But I know that no amount of preparation can guarantee the result. If nothing else, the last few months have taught me that.

On arrival, Eric immediately opens the door. Though his demeanor is calm and neutral, I sense his wariness. "Do you want anything to drink?"

"You spoke to Justin." I draw on the familiarity between us from all the years together to overcome the awkwardness from our last conversation. Multiple times I have picked up the phone to call him but at the last minute decided against it. Part of me was embarrassed and the other part angry, albeit mostly at myself. "What you said—thank you."

Eric shrugs. "It was the truth." He sighs, clearly feeling similarly uncomfortable. I hate what my admission has created. But I know that without it, I would have continued to wonder and wait. No matter what, I warrant better than that. "You deserve that job."

"I'm going to take it," I share. Pride and excitement cross his face. I pause at his reaction. Like a trailer of a movie, snippets of all the conversations over the years play in my mind. His unconditional support of my career, his constant encouragement, his never-ending belief in me and my talent. At some point I came to rely on it and even became inspired by it. "Justin said he'd stay with you when I am in California."

"Yeah?" Eric drops his head and swallows. I see how much the estrangement with his son has affected him. For all the heartache I have endured, his has been equal. "That would be great."

"He's coming home." I fight the urge to reach out and squeeze his hand in both gratitude and apology. "For you to have said what you did to Justin after I admitted what happened that night . . ."

"Can I say something?" Eric interrupts, apologizing first for doing so. On my agreement, he says, "You're incredible."

"What?" It's the last thing I was expecting to hear.

"In the financial world, everyone knows how brilliant you are." He glances at a picture of Justin, now sitting next to one of Brian. "All the years before that night, I always admired your intelligence and ambition. The night we came together, I remember how inspired I was by you."

I look away, unsure how to accept what he's saying.

"When you told me you were pregnant, my first thought was that I was trapped. My life as I'd planned it was over. My marriage to Celine, my focus on my work. But I was an idiot because you didn't need me. You raised Justin. You provided for Justin. You were there for our son in every way that counts. I was just trying to keep up." He scoffs. "Maybe it was an ego hit or I needed to prove something to myself, but you made it so that I was nothing more than the cherry on top."

I smile as his words settle inside me. "You don't have to say this."

"Yes, I do." Eric shakes his head. "Felicity, you deserve this job. I know how much you sacrificed to raise Justin. I never had to do the same. You never asked me to do the same." He reaches for my hand, shocking me. "I know you think you may have feelings for me, but can I say one thing? I call bullshit."

"Excuse me?" I say, my spine straightening.

Eric laughs. "You're a fighter. Always have been. You don't need anyone. You win all by yourself. And it's incredible to watch." He squeezes my hand. "And that's why our son is who he is. And he needed to remember that."

Shocked, I take a minute as warmth and love flow through me. I need time to process his words, to replace my reasons with his. If I miscalculated my feelings for him, then did he become my rationalization, my safe place, to convince myself out of the truth of who I really am—someone who is already complete?

"Eric, I can't thank you enough for what you just said. For reminding me of why we became such good *friends* and co-parents." I try to tell him with my words that I understand what he has said and accept it. And that the relationship we have is the one I want to hold on to.

"Brian is in remission." Eric says the words with awe and relief. "I can't thank you enough."

In one full sweep, everything wrong has been righted. I have my son back, and now my friend. I have a job that I am more excited about than I realize. I look to the heavens and give a silent thank-you. After everything I have done, I cannot believe that somehow I have been graced with so much happiness. But I know that never again will I choose any other way or be someone else. The people who love me, who count on me, deserve better. I deserve to be better. And Celine deserves me to be better.

I meant what I said to Celine—I have been in their marriage enough. Now it's time for me to live my life, as it was meant to be lived, and to leave them to their lives. And most importantly, I need to be the mother Justin admires, the example for him to follow. He deserves a role model he can be proud of. I need to take this job not despite him, but for him. So that he has his mom back, and I can start the journey of finding myself.

CHAPTER FORTY-TWO

CELINE

I wake up next to Austin, our arms wrapped around each other. Today is the day he leaves for home. I have dreaded it every day since he told me, missing him before he has even left.

"Is this goodbye?" I ask softly.

"No," he says, but I hear the question in his voice. He's as unsure about the future as I am. We turn toward each other. He slips a loose strand of my hair behind my ear. I warm at his touch. In a short amount of time, I have already become used to it, yearn for it, for him. "I don't want to lose you or us. I want to see what we can be, if you want the same thing."

"Time," I tell him. It's the most precious thing I have in my life, the one thing that I need. Time for Brian to heal. Time for Austin and I to find our way. Time for me to find myself. "We have time to discover what we can be." Unlike the last time he left, this time we will stay in touch. Allow the connection between us to grow and flourish. "To find our way to forever."

He pulls me in closer and kisses me. I open up to him, offering him my heart. And my future. Because this time there's no knight in shining armor or damsel in distress. Instead, I stand before him a woman who knows herself and what she wants. In choosing us, I am choosing myself. I am no longer the girl or woman waiting to be loved, but instead know the value of my love and of the love he's offering to me.

"I love you," he whispers against my lips. "I always have."

He wipes the lone tear that slips from my eye onto my cheek. I cover his hand with mine, kissing his palm before resting my head on his chest. Unlike before, these tears are from happiness. Because just when I was sure I would never see light again after the darkness, the shadows have passed and the sun is finally shining.

"I love you," I return. The future is ours to have, and forever feels like a gift from the fates. One that I'll cherish and never again take for granted. "I always will."

CHAPTER
FORTY-THREE

CELINE

I check in on Brian as he sleeps. Though over a month has passed since his remission, his body is still regaining energy and healing. But as I watch him, his breaths even, I send words of gratitude to the universe for his health, for giving me my son back. I head down to the kitchen, where I run into Eric returning home from work.

Reminiscent of a lifetime ago, his jacket hangs off one hand while his computer bag hangs off his shoulder. That night was before the cancer, before learning about the betrayal, before my life fell apart and then was put back together again.

Since Brian's return home, we have been living together, Eric in the guest room, and me in the main bedroom. It has given Brian the stability he needs.

"Do you have a minute to talk?" Eric asks. I pour us both a cup of tea, then join him at the table. "Thank you for everything." He pauses, then continues: "For Justin, for Brian, for us."

After Felicity took the job, we fixed up the basement for Justin to have his own space to stay with us when needed. It has given the boys the time they need to be brothers. Justin was thrilled when we ran the idea by him and Felicity. Later, I approached her privately.

"I'm not trying to take your place in Justin's life," I started, trying to reassure her. "I'm simply trying to thank you, to be there for your son as you were there for mine."

We hugged, two women, two mothers, two friends who had become family. After she moved to California, our days became focused on being there for Brian and Justin however they needed.

"Justin is applying to colleges in the area so the boys can be together," Eric shares.

I see his anguish, his fear, at the story that could have gone so differently. "They have time," I tell him. "To be brothers."

"I just wish I'd done things differently."

"I know." I clasp my hand in his, offering him comfort. "But because of you, Justin, and Felicity, Brian is here with us. And the boys have each other."

"What I did to you . . . ," he starts.

"Your son saved mine," I tell him. "That's all that matters."

"I never wanted to lose you," Eric says softly. "I know it doesn't excuse what I did, but I did love you."

Thoughts of Austin pervade my mind. A love borne from friendship and memories. Since he left, we speak on the phone daily and have plans to see each other regularly. Our need and our love for one another seem to grow every day as our plan to be together permanently in the future only strengthens.

My love for Austin doesn't take away my love for Eric or the years we have spent together. If anything, it's given me an understanding that love is defined not by people but by the connection between them. And that there's no right or wrong love, only the meaning our hearts give it.

"And I loved you." He flinches at the past tense. It's not my intention to hurt him, but I cannot lie to protect him. There has been enough of that to last a few lifetimes. "So much." I lean forward, a strength I never imagined having now fully a part of me. I wonder if it's Brian's illness or the betrayal or a combination of both, but I can no longer be the woman I was. Nor do I want to be. "I needed you. To make me believe I was safe. To give Brian the family I never had. To convince myself I was worthy of love from someone like you."

"Celine . . ."

"I asked you last time why you did what you did. Now, I understand. Because I never drew a line, and neither did you." I glance around our home, and my gut tightens as I finally face the truth. "What you did, whether you realize it or not, wasn't for Brian or Justin. It wasn't to keep our marriage or to have an affair with another woman. It was because both of us allowed you to be that person." I shake my head. "I have to accept the responsibility for the roles we both played."

"I'm sorry," Eric says, anguished.

"Brian has to know that he was born out of real love. And that even though we're not together, I'll always be grateful for the time that I had with his dad. Because the parts of you I knew? I was completely and totally in love with."

"Thank you for this partnership, this friendship," Eric says softly.

I think about my conversation with my mom, about Eric with Justin and Brian. How much Eric has fought for both of his children. It's reminded me of everything my own father never did for me. Though our marriage is over, friendship has become the bedrock of our relationship. It's the friendship we failed to find during our marriage. With it, I have learned that though life may not always go as planned, there's a way through the darkness to find the light.

"I'm sorry for causing you so much sadness," Eric murmurs. "I hope you find your happiness. No one deserves it more."

Mom had to fight her own fear to be there for me. Felicity accepted the job, choosing to be the woman her son needed her to be—even if it meant leaving him. Eric has chosen Justin and Brian. Now, my son must come first. Through his illness, I have learned that the sadness, the points in my life that I was sure were impossible to overcome, instead have made me find the strength I never believed I had in myself.

I am still learning about myself, my family, and my place in the world. Though the journey may take some soul-searching, tears, and losing the parts of myself that have caused me pain, I am grateful to be on it. With time, I hope I learn how to love the girl I was and the woman I am, to heal my heart and allow the love of others in. To find my happiness—with life, with Austin, with the person I am now and the woman I continue to grow into.

"I will," I promise him and myself at the same time.

As I head toward the stairs, I feel Eric's eyes on me, but I don't look back. With a renewed sense of purpose and energy, I move forward. The future and what I decide to make of it is waiting for me.

ACKNOWLEDGMENTS

Danielle Marshall: Thank you so very much for your partnership and for always supporting and believing in the stories. I am extraordinarily fortunate for your guidance and to be working with you. You have made every step of the publishing journey seamless, joyful, and empowering. Your mastery and vision are a testament to both you as a person and your exceptional leadership. Thank you.

Jen Bentham: Thank you so much for all your help in making the manuscript shine. I sincerely appreciate it.

Lake Union Team: Thank you so much for all your support for this novel and over the years. It is such an honor to work with your team. I will always be extremely grateful to every one of you for the standards you have set and for your partnership.

Alex Levenberg: Thank you so much for all your help over the years with translations, et cetera. It has been a true joy to partner with you, and I cannot emphasize enough what a pleasure it is to work with you and your team. You are truly the best of the best. My deepest gratitude, always.

Benee Knauer: My dearest friend—I have accepted I will never find the words to truly thank you for the years of friendship, support, and partnership. Your vision and belief paved my path. Your ideas and thoughts are fundamental to the success of every story. You are an inspiration to any writer fortunate enough to work with you. I am forever grateful. I love you as my friend and family.

Naze and Ramin: The dinners, the laughter, the years of togetherness, the children growing up together, the trust and honesty—we so deeply value you. You have made our lives better. Thank you for being not only the truest friends we could ask for but for also becoming part of our family. We love you.

Tiffany Yates Martin: You make every word better, every novel more captivating. Your brilliance and intuitive understanding of the characters and story allow them to shine. Thank you for all the years of working together, the friendship, and your extraordinary patience and understanding. I am a better writer and storyteller because of you.

Dr. Lynn Conners: Thank you so much for all your help. I sincerely appreciate it!

Tanya Farrell and the Wunderkind team: Thank you for all you do to get the stories out to the world. It has been such a true pleasure to partner with you and your team, and I so look forward to many more years of working together.

Readers: Thank you from the bottom of my heart for reading the stories. I am both humbled and honored by your support. For every reader who has shared their story and reached out via email, through social media, or at book clubs, it means so very much. I am grateful for each and every one of you.

Jaime Weatherby: I love working with you. When we started working together, both of us were just beginning our careers. The journey together has been so much fun. I so look forward to continuing to work together.

Kendra Harpster: It was such an absolute pleasure working with you. Your professionalism, kindness, and expertise taught me so much, and I was so grateful for having the opportunity to work with you. And I so value the friendship that formed from that time. Thank you.

Bill S. and Jena R.: Thank you so much for all your help in making the manuscript shine. I really appreciate your time and energy in making sure everything came together.

AS, MZ, BR, and VJ: You were lost too soon. Your lives were still ahead of you. The world is darker without your smiles, your love, your light. Though you are no longer here, we hold onto the memories, knowing your beautiful and bright spirits will forever live on.

BOOK CLUB QUESTIONS

1. Which characters did you relate to the most? Which one did you like the most?
2. Which character's actions influenced the plot or changed the direction of the story?
3. What was Felicity's primary motivation, and how did it change over the course of the story? What about Celine's? And Eric's?
4. Was Eric the primary antagonist? If not, who or what was it? Felicity? The cancer?
5. How was Justin both a protagonist and an antagonist?
6. How was the ending of the book aligned with the character's journey? Should Eric and Felicity have ended up together? What about Celine and Eric?
7. What was the book's biggest plot twist?
8. How did Felicity's story arc take her from antagonist to protagonist? Could you understand her need to protect Justin initially and then offer him unconditional support later to help Brian?
9. How did the author effectively build tension and suspense throughout the story?
10. What do you believe happened to Celine and Austin? Did they have their happily ever after?
11. How do you believe the horse farm affected Celine's

journey? Did it help or hurt her as she was fighting for Brian? What about with Eric?

12. How did Celine and Austin's childhood friendship affect their relationship? Did their time together help her heal from Eric?

13. What did you think about Celine and Justin's relationship? Celine admitted that in any other circumstance she would have hated Justin for what he represented. How much of a loss would that have been for both of them not to have the connection and friendship they formed?

14. Both Felicity and Celine took on mother-type roles to each other's sons—Justin and Brian. How did this make them better as women and mothers? How did Justin and Brian benefit from having them in their lives?

15. How did Justin and Brian's relationship evolve over the story? Do you believe they will ever feel hurt and anger at having been kept apart? Or did the situation feel resolved?

16. The author's previous two novels were drawn from her own life. She has spoken about the losses in her own life that inspired this novel. How do you believe it influenced her writing and the novel's storyline?

17. How did this novel compare to the author's other two novels? What is similar in all her novels?

18. The author focuses on women's struggles and the journey they take to find their strength, courage, and resolution. What were Celine's and Felicity's journeys individually and together?

19. What moment or scene in the book was your favorite? Which moment do you believe changed the trajectory of Celine and Felicity individually? What moment changed their relationship with one another?

20. What was the main message or theme of the book?

21. Did the title of the book resonate after you finished reading it?
22. How did cancer change Brian? How did Brian's cancer journey change Justin?
23. What surprised you the most about the book?
24. How thought provoking did you find the book? How did the book make you feel? Did you cry? Laugh?
25. Does this story relate to your life or someone you know? Has cancer changed your life?
26. Do you have a favorite quote from the book? What was the most challenging part of the book to read?
27. Should this book be adapted into a movie? Who would you cast in the leading roles?
28. Does what Eric did make sense? How could he have done it differently? Was he a good father to both Justin and Brian?
29. Would Celine and Eric have ended up as friends if not for Brian's diagnosis? Did Eric love Celine?
30. If you could ask the author one question about this book, what would it be?
31. What language, imagery, metaphors, et cetera did the author use in telling the story? How did this affect you as a reader?
32. What were the main themes of the story? How did the story make you feel? Did it teach you anything? Did it challenge your views or thoughts?
33. Which character resonated with you the most? Which character was the most complex? Least favorite?
34. What do you think happens to Eric after the story ends? What about Felicity?
35. What was the main conflict in the story? How was it resolved?
36. How were Elena's and Celine's stories similar? How

did they react differently to their individual husband's betrayals?

37. How were Felicity and Celine mirror images of each other? How did their similar stories affect their relationship? Both were hurt by their fathers. How did it change the way they reacted to the situation?

38. Eric admits that Celine's story with her father changed the way he reacted to Justin and the situation. Did his explanation change how you viewed him and what he did?

ABOUT THE AUTHOR

Sejal Badani is the Amazon Charts, *USA Today*, *Washington Post*, and *Wall Street Journal* bestselling author of *The Storyteller's Secret* and *Trail of Broken Wings*. She is also a Goodreads Best Fiction award and ABC/Disney Writing Fellowship finalist whose work has been published in over fifteen languages.